Chantelle Shaw lives on the Kent coast and thinks up her stories while walking on the beach. She has been married for over thirty years and has six children. Her love affair with reading and writing Mills & Boon stories began as a teenager, and her first book was published in 2006. She likes strong-willed, slightly unusual characters. Chantelle also loves gardening, walking and wine!

With two university degrees and a variety of false career starts under her belt, **Michelle Conder** decided to satisfy her lifelong desire to write and finally found her dream job. She currently lives in Melbourne, Australia, with one super-indulgent husband, three self-indulgent but exquisite children, a menagerie of over-indulged pets, and the intention of doing some form of exercise daily. She loves to hear from her readers at michelleconder.com.

D0806384

REUNITED BY A SHOCK PREGNANCY

CHANTELLE SHAW

THE BILLIONAIRE'S VIRGIN TEMPTATION

MICHELLE CONDER

MILLS & BOON

First Published in Great Britain 2019
by Mills & Boon, an imprint of HarperCollins*Publishers*
1 London Bridge Street, London, SE1 9GF

Reunited by a Shock Pregnancy © 2019 by Chantelle Shaw

The Billionaire's Virgin Temptation © 2019 by Michelle Conder

ISBN: 978-0-263-27338-0

MIX
Paper from
responsible sources
FSC™ C007454

This book is produced from independently certified FSC™ paper
to ensure responsible forest management.
For more information visit www.harpercollins.co.uk/green.

Printed and bound in Spain
by CPI, Barcelona

REUNITED
BY A SHOCK
PREGNANCY

CHANTELLE SHAW

For my girls, Rosie and Lucy.

So proud of the strong, independent women
you have become. xxx

CHAPTER ONE

SHE SHOULDN'T BE HERE! Not at her ex-husband's wedding.

Sienna Fisher glanced frantically around the packed church, wondering if she could escape without anyone noticing.

There was not a chance, she decided, her heart sinking. She was wedged into a pew filled with guests, and sitting next to her was the little girl she had found crying outside in the graveyard. Sienna's maternal instincts had been aroused by the child's distress and she'd taken hold of her hand and led her into the church via the vestry to find her grateful mother, who was sitting on the other side of her daughter.

The organist started playing and as the rousing notes of Handel's *Arrival of the Queen of Sheba* soared to the rafters, a ripple of interest ran through the congregation. Every head turned towards the main door to catch a first glimpse of the bride. Only Sienna stared straight ahead at the broad shoulders of Domenico De Conti, the man she had married in this very church ten years ago.

Standing with Nico was his younger brother, Daniele. Both men were tall but Nico had the advantage of a good three inches over Danny. Despite a five-year age-gap the brothers had always been close, and it was no surprise to Sienna that Nico had chosen Danny to be his best man again—just as he had done for *their* wedding.

Her breath caught in her throat when Nico turned his head. She assumed he would look towards his bride but instead his gaze was focused directly on *her*, as if some sixth sense had alerted him to her presence. From across the nave, she sensed his shock. Evidently her wide-brimmed hat did not conceal her face as well as she had hoped it would, but she hadn't planned to hang around long enough for Nico to notice her. She'd just wanted a glimpse of the man she had once been madly in love with before he had betrayed her and broken her heart.

Sienna hadn't intended to enter the church, and, earlier, she had hidden behind a tombstone when she'd seen Nico and Danny arrive. Nico must still have a passion for fast cars and had driven himself to his wedding in a sleek silver sports car. She'd watched the two men chat to the vicar for a few minutes before they had walked into the church, and she'd been about to leave when she was alerted to the sound of a child sobbing.

It was purely by accident that she was part of the congregation. Her heart fluttered in panic. She was too far away from Nico to make out the colour of his eyes that burned into her like laser beams, but she knew they were the bright blue of the sky above the moors on a cloudless summer's day. His eyes and incredible bone structure were the only features he had inherited from his English mother, but for the rest: his almost black hair that was swept back from his brow, the dark stubble shading his jaw and his olive-gold skin denoted his Italian heritage.

Ten years ago Nico had been a boyishly handsome bridegroom. Now he was in his mid-thirties, his features had honed and hardened to chiselled perfection. He was sinfully gorgeous, with a latent strength and power in his whipcord body that his elegant grey morning suit could not disguise.

Sienna snatched her gaze from Nico's, shaken by the effect he had on her after all this time. They had been divorced for eight years and she had come to the church today to prove to herself that she was over him. Her heart thudded as she waited for him to denounce her. Surely he would stop the wedding and instruct an usher to escort her from the building.

She felt her cheeks grow warm at the prospect of being humiliated in front of the population of the Yorkshire village where she had grown up. Although she hadn't recognised many locals in Much Matcham's pretty church of St Augustine's. She supposed that most of the guests at the high-society wedding were from London, or Verona where Nico's hotel business, De Conti Leisure, was based.

Her eyes were drawn involuntarily back to his dangerously attractive face and a sizzle of heat seared her body, a hunger that only Nico had ever stirred in her. Even more confusing was the fierce possessiveness that swept through her. He was *hers*, cried a voice inside her. But in a few minutes he would promise himself to another woman. Tears, hot and unexpected, stung her eyes when he finally turned his head away and looked to the front of the church while he waited for his bride.

Sienna's hands shook as she pretended to study the order of service sheet that an usher had given her. 'We're running a little late,' the usher had told her, interrupting her attempt to explain that she wasn't actually a wedding guest. 'Are you a friend of the bride or groom?'

'Groom, I suppose, but...'

'Sit here, please.' The usher had practically pushed her into a pew and now she was trapped and about to witness the marriage of her ex-husband to the vision of ethereal loveliness, wearing an exquisite wedding gown, who had joined Nico in front of the altar.

Except that it wasn't Nico. It was his brother standing next to the bride.

'In the presence of God, Father, Son and Holy Spirit, we have come together to witness the marriage of Daniele to Victoria,' the vicar intoned.

It was Danny's wedding! A riot of emotions stormed through Sienna. Her thoughts flew back to the previous weekend when she had visited her grandmother at the nursing home in York where ninety-year-old Rose Fisher had moved to eighteen months ago.

'Much Matcham's local newspaper is delivered to me every week and I was surprised to read that your husband is getting married again,' Grandma Rose had commented over tea and scones.

Sienna's stomach had swooped and she'd set her cup back on its saucer clumsily so that the delicate china rattled. 'There's no reason why my *ex*-husband shouldn't remarry,' she'd said coolly. But nothing fooled her grandmother and Rose had given her a sharp look. 'I imagine he needs a wife to help him run Sethbury Hall, and...give him an heir.' Pain had lanced through Sienna. Her inability to have a child was something she tried not to think about, just as she deliberately blocked out thoughts of the baby she had lost years ago.

'Who is Nico marrying?' She'd striven to sound un-interested as she'd taken the newspaper from Grandma Rose and skimmed down the births, deaths and mar-riages column to read the announcement of the wed-ding of Miss Victoria Harington and Mr Domenico De Conti, which would take place on the tenth of June at St Augustine's church in Much Matcham. There had not been a picture of the couple, and now, as Sienna watched *Danny* turn his head and smile at his bride, she could only suppose that the paper had muddled the De Conti brothers' names.

The rest of the wedding ceremony passed in a blur until the vicar finally pronounced that Daniele and Victoria were husband and wife. As the couple walked back down the aisle and the guests spilled from the pews to follow them out of the church, Sienna edged towards the vestry, hoping to slip away unnoticed.

'Sienna? What are *you* doing here?'

She had almost made it to the vestry door when an achingly familiar voice made her freeze and simulta-neously sent molten heat flooding through her veins. Nico's husky accent had always made her weak at the knees. There was nothing she could do but try to bra-zen it out, and she squared her shoulders before she swung round to face him.

'Hello, Nico.' Was that breathless, sexy voice hers? Sienna cursed silently, flushing when she saw mock-ery in his piercing blue eyes. He skimmed his gaze over her in a proprietorial manner that was totally in-appropriate considering their history. She felt a sharp, almost painful tingle in her nipples, and did not need to glance down to know that the betraying hard peaks were visible beneath her yellow silk dress.

She had deliberately worn a summery outfit: a white hat decorated with yellow flowers, champagne-coloured stilettos and matching handbag so that people would assume she was one of the wedding guests milling around outside the church before the ceremony. The predatory gleam in Nico's eyes made her acutely conscious of how the close-fitting dress clung to her breasts and hips and the silky material felt sensuous against her skin.

Up close he was even more devastating. A shaft of sunlight filtering in through one of the high windows danced in his night-dark hair and emphasised the hard angles and planes of his face. He smelled divine. Sienna breathed in the spicy notes of his aftershave mixed with something else that was evocatively male and uniquely Nico. An unbidden memory filled her mind, of him sprawled on the tangled sheets after they had made love, sweat beading the dark hairs on his chest, his shaft already hardening again as he pulled her down on top of him.

In the early days of their marriage they hadn't been able to keep their hands off each other and their passion had been explosive. But that was before she had lost the baby, and then sex had been dictated by fertility charts as her desire to fall pregnant again had become an obsession that had driven a wedge between her and Nico.

She was an idiot to have come here today, Sienna thought bleakly. It would have been better if she had never seen him again. Kinder to her foolish heart that still yearned for the relationship they had once had, even though her sensible head knew it had been a romantic fantasy she had built up in her imagination. But she wasn't imagining the frank awareness in Nico's eyes. She was overwhelmed by his raw sexual magnetism and dismayed by her reaction to him.

'Sienna.' The impatience in his voice pulled her mind back to the present and her embarrassing situation. 'I didn't see your name on the guest list.' He frowned. 'I'm certain Danny would have told me that he had invited you to his wedding.'

'I…um…' She could feel her face burning. 'I saw in the local paper that Danny was getting married at St Augustine's. Churches are open to the public and anyone has the right to attend a wedding taking place in a church. I wanted to give Danny and his new bride my best wishes.'

Nico's eyes narrowed. 'It's odd that you knew it was my brother's wedding. The local paper mixed up our names when they printed the forthcoming marriage announcement.'

'My grandmother told me.' Sienna crossed her fingers behind her back as she made the white lie. 'Rose keeps in touch with your grandmother and when they spoke recently, Iris told her about Danny's wedding.'

She lifted her chin and forced herself to meet Nico's speculative gaze, hoping to project an image of cool composure she did not feel. Her insides were churning, her heart was racing and there was a dull ache low in her pelvis that made her press her thighs tightly together.

'So you didn't come because you hoped to see me?' he drawled.

'Of course not. What reason could I possibly have

for wanting to see you again?' She was defensive, mortified that he might guess the truth. 'Our disaster of a marriage was over a long time ago.'

'I wouldn't call it a disaster,' he murmured, taking her breath away with that mind-boggling statement. 'There were good times.' His voice lowered in a way that sent a shiver across Sienna's skin. 'Some very good times.'

'When we were in bed, you mean?' She had intended to sound sarcastic but the words emerged as a whisper. She licked her dry lips with the tip of her tongue. When had Nico moved closer so that his thigh was almost touching hers? 'A marriage needs more to sustain it than dynamite sex.'

His lips twitched and she hated that he found her amusing, but when he spoke there was no mockery in his voice, nor in the fierce gleam in his eyes. 'We were dynamite together, weren't we, *cara*?'

'Don't,' she said sharply, trying to ignore the leap her heart gave at his careless endearment. She stiffened when he lifted his hand and brushed his finger lightly down her cheek. The action was a blatant invasion of her personal space but she didn't pull away, couldn't. Her feet were glued to the floor and her gaze was trapped by his as she drowned in the cobalt-blue depths of his eyes. Everything faded and there were only the two of them standing in the church where they had once promised to love and honour each other, forsaking all others, for the rest of their lives.

Nico lowered his head so that his impossibly wicked mouth was inches from hers. 'You are even more beautiful than my memory serves me, Si-*enna*.' He rolled the syllables around his tongue, making her name sound like a caress. 'It makes me wonder why I let you go.'

The spell shattered and she jerked away from him so forcefully that her hip bone collided with the end of a pew. 'You were sleeping with your secretary.' Hurt and humiliation, those two poisonous serpents that had haunted her for years, coiled inside her. 'You didn't let me go, I chose to leave,' she snapped, her voice too loud, bouncing off the walls of the church.

'Oh, Nico, there you are,' came a softer voice. Looking past him, Sienna wished the floor would open up and swallow her when she saw Nico's grandmother manoeuvring her wheelchair along the aisle towards them. But if Iris Mandeville had heard her angry outburst she made no comment. 'Sienna, how delightful to see you.' The elderly woman greeted her warmly. 'How is your grandmother? I haven't spoken to Rose for months.'

Sienna flushed when Nico gave her a hard stare. Clearly he was wondering how she could have known it was Danny's wedding if Iris had not told Grandma Rose.

'I am unable to visit Rose so often now that she lives in York and I have to use this wretched contraption.' Iris tapped the arm of her wheelchair. 'Rheumatoid arthritis has left me rather immobile,' she answered Sienna's unspoken question before turning her attention to her grandson.

'Domenico, you are wanted for the photographs. I can't get my wheelchair down the church steps but there is disabled access through the vestry. Sienna, my dear, would you be so kind to help me out to the car? Hobbs is bringing it round to the side of the church.

Jacqueline was supposed to help me, but of course she wants to be included in the photographs.'

Sienna had noticed Nico and Danny's mother during the ceremony. Jacqueline Mandeville loved being the centre of attention and her extravagant hat festooned with ostrich feathers had made her impossible to miss. When Sienna had married Nico, her mother-in-law had worn a dramatic ivory-coloured outfit, which had out-shone her store-bought wedding dress. She had been so young and unsure of herself, she remembered ruefully. Her voluminous dress had hidden her baby bump, but everyone in the church, everyone in the village, had known that she was pregnant.

She jerked her mind from the past and forced a smile for Nico's grandmother. 'Yes, of course I'll push your wheelchair out to the car.'

Footsteps sounded on the stone floor behind her. 'Nico, I've been looking everywhere for you,' a voice said tersely. 'The photographer wants to take group pictures and Victoria is going into meltdown because you'd disappeared and one of the bridesmaids says she feels sick.' Daniele De Conti stopped dead and stared. '*Sienna?* Wow! You look amazing.'

'Hello, Danny,' she murmured, taken aback by the undisguised male interest in Nico's brother's eyes. He had only been married for five minutes! But she re-membered that he had always been an incorrigible flirt. Danny was a year older than her and when they were teenagers he'd asked her out a couple of times. But it had been nothing serious, and the minute she'd met Nico she'd only had eyes for him.

Against her will, her gaze was drawn to Nico, and her heart collided with her ribs when she recognised a glint of possessiveness in his eyes as well as something hotter, hungrier that sent a tremor through her. She was barely aware that Danny was speaking again.

'I must say you are the last person I expected to be here today, Sienna.'

'I just came to the church…' she began awkwardly, feeling herself blush. She tensed when Nico slid his arm around her waist.

'Sienna is here because I invited her,' he told his brother smoothly. 'I didn't reveal the name of my plus-one guest as there was a chance that Sienna wouldn't be free to travel to Yorkshire this weekend. But luckily for me she was able to come to the wedding.'

What the devil was he playing at? She was conscious that Danny and Iris were both looking at her curiously but her gaze was riveted on Nico, on his mouth as he lowered his head towards her.

He was going to kiss her! She read the message in his brilliant blue eyes and her heart did a somersault. Her common sense told her to step away from him, run, scream—maybe all three, but she had never been sensible around this man. She opened her mouth to tell Danny that she wasn't Nico's plus-one guest, no way.

'Actually that's not…' The rest of her words were smothered by Nico's mouth as he crushed her lips beneath his in a fierce kiss that made her head spin. His arm felt like a band of steel around her waist and there was blatant possession in the way he clamped his hand on her hip.

Her brain told her to pull away from him and demand to know what he was doing. But her body reacted instinctively to the heat emanating from him and the bold demands of his mouth on hers. The years fell away and she was eighteen again, a girl on the cusp of womanhood, standing on a windswept moor and overwhelmed by the wild passion that Nico stirred in her. A tremor ran through her as she opened her mouth beneath his and kissed him back. Her body recognised his touch and desire swept fierce and hot through her veins as he deepened the kiss and her lips clung to his.

And then, as suddenly and unexpectedly as it had begun, it was over. He lifted his head and she saw a hard glitter in his eyes that sent a ripple of unease through her when she reflected on how easily, how shamelessly she had capitulated to him. Would she never learn that he was dangerous to her peace of mind? Their break-up had almost destroyed her but eventually she had grown up, moved on and established a good life for herself. She could not let a kiss from a skilled seducer who knew how to press all her buttons turn her into the doormat she had been when she was Nico De Conti's teenage bride.

He withdrew his arm from her waist and she felt as if part of her had been severed. Get a grip, she ordered herself angrily. Nico had taken an outrageous liberty when he'd kissed her and she should slap his face. At the very least, she should ask him why he had lied to his brother and grandmother about inviting her to the wedding. She was about to challenge him but he swung round and started walking towards the main door of the church.

'Photographs,' he reminded a startled-looking Danny. 'Sienna, if you wouldn't mind helping Nonna to the car? I'll see you back at the hall for the reception.'

Like hell you will. She clenched her hands by her sides as she watched him stride away. His arrogance made her seethe, but out of respect for his grandmother she swallowed her furious retort.

'Domenico is so commanding, just like his grand-father was,' Iris murmured when Sienna pushed her wheelchair into the vestry and down the ramp that led out of the church. Fortunately the chauffeur was on hand to assist the elderly lady into the car, and Sienna's muttered uncomplimentary remark about her ex-husband's bossiness went unheard.

'I'm not coming to the reception,' she told Iris. 'I don't know why Nico said he had invited me to Danny's wedding. Perhaps his plus-one guest couldn't make it.' She disliked the idea that he had decided she could stand in for his current girlfriend, whoever that might be. Nico had a high sex drive and it was inconceivable that he did not have a woman in his life.

Thankfully Iris did not refer to that kiss, but Sienna unconsciously ran her tongue over her stinging lips. The taste of Nico was still in her mouth. 'I have to drive back to London this afternoon and spend the rest of the weekend preparing for an important business meeting on Monday,' she made the excuse as she stepped back from the car.

Iris nodded. 'Rose told me that your organic skin-care company is hugely successful and you have won awards for your products. She is very proud of you.'

Sienna felt a pang of guilt thinking that she should visit her grandmother more often. She tried to get up to Yorkshire once a month, but running her own business left her little leisure time. She frowned, trying to remember when she had last met up with her friends for a drink. And as for dating, it was over a year since she had accepted a dinner invitation from a man.

Why had she allowed her social life to dwindle to practically nothing? she asked herself. She was only just twenty-nine and she had a sudden sense that life was passing her by. She loved her career and the independence it gave her but she was aware that something was missing. Love, companionship, *sex*. Where had that thought come from? Her lack of a sex life had never bothered her before today, but when Nico had kissed her it had felt as if a floodgate had opened and need had throbbed between her legs.

She was jolted from her thoughts when she realised that Iris seemed to be struggling to breathe. The elderly lady clutched her chest.

'What's wrong? Are you feeling unwell?' Sienna asked urgently.

'I'm having an angina attack,' Iris gasped. 'I thought I had put my medication in my handbag. It's a pump spray that I use under my tongue. But it's not here.' She closed her handbag that she had been rifling through. 'I must have left it in my bedroom.'

'Should I call an ambulance?'

'There's no need. I'll be fine once I have my medication. Will you come in the car with me back to the house? You can run inside and find the pump spray.'

'I'll go and fetch Nico.'

'No,' Iris said sharply. 'I don't want to cause a fuss and spoil the wedding.'

There was no time to waste arguing and Sienna ran round to the other side of the car and jumped in. The journey through the village only took a few minutes. When the chauffeur turned onto the driveway of Sethbury Hall she felt a familiar sense of awe as she stared at the imposing manor house where she had once lived with Nico. She had always felt like an imposter. The daughter of the village publican who had married above her station, some of the villagers had whispered. Cinderella had found her prince, but the fairy tale had ended in a bitter divorce.

The car came to a halt and Iris said faintly, 'You remember where my room is, Sienna? The pump spray should be on my bedside table. Please hurry.'

CHAPTER TWO

Nico located his grandmother in the orangery but Sienna wasn't with her. He strolled across to the open glass doors and scanned the terrace where most of the guests had congregated, but there was no sign of a yellow dress.

His jaw tightened. Inexplicably he was disappointed that his ex-wife hadn't accompanied Iris to Sethbury Hall. Frankly it was something of a surprise that Sienna had disobeyed him. When they'd been married she had always been eager to please him, especially in bed. Sometimes her puppy-like devotion had irritated him but she had been very young; a teenage bride, sweetly shy and biddable.

He frowned, remembering her accusation on the day she had walked out of their marriage that he had taken her for granted. With hindsight perhaps he had, he thought uncomfortably. *Dio*, but he had been young himself, with a weight of duty and responsibility on his shoulders. Sienna had been another of his responsibilities. Pregnant with his child and terrified of her abusive father. Nico had done the only thing he could do and offered to marry her.

He cursed beneath his breath. The last thing he

wanted was a trip down memory lane. When he'd spotted Sienna in the church earlier he had thought at first that he must have imagined her. Standing in front of the altar with his brother had evoked memories of his own wedding ten years earlier, when Danny had been his best man.

Nico remembered the sense of panic he'd felt on his wedding day, of being trapped. He'd looked over his shoulder towards the door, wondering if he could make a run for it. But at that moment Sienna had walked into the church. She had looked exquisite in her bridal gown, with her long hair streaming down her back. She'd held a bouquet of cream roses over her stomach and looked as nervous as he felt.

He'd accepted that he couldn't abandon her and his baby, and as he'd watched her walk towards him, he had been impatient for their wedding day to be over so that he could take her to bed. Their passion was white-hot and when he was buried deep inside her he did not care that he was marrying her out of duty. She was his exclusively and she was carrying his child. At least that was what he had believed then.

Nico jerked his mind away from the past and declined the glass of sherry a waiter offered him. He could do with a drink but his preferred poison was oak-barrel-aged cognac. As he strode up the sweeping staircase to his private suite of rooms, he told himself that he could take a short break from his best-man duties. Danny and his elegant bride were mingling with their guests while canapés were served on the terrace.

Entering his sitting room, he went straight to the bar and poured himself a drink. The cognac was smooth and mellow with a pleasant heat at the back of his throat. He looked across the room, puzzled that his bedroom door was open. He was sure it had been shut when he'd left the suite earlier. His heart kicked in his chest when he saw a white hat decorated with yellow flowers on the bed.

'I'm intrigued, *cara*,' he murmured, strolling into the bedroom just as Sienna emerged from the en-suite bathroom. 'First you were at the church and now I find you in my bedroom. Not that I am complaining,' he assured her. Far from it. Lust as hot as molten lava rushed through his veins when she ran her fingers through her hair. Was the gesture a deliberate ploy to make him notice the glossy waves that had been hidden beneath her hat in the church?

Her hair was the same shade of dark red as a vintage burgundy wine and he knew the colour was entirely natural. When she was younger her hair had been waist-length, but now it fell to just past her shoulders with layers framing her face and drawing attention to her peaches-and-cream skin and wide grey eyes.

'Your bedroom?' Sienna frowned. 'I thought your grandparents occupied the master suite?'

'They did when my grandfather was alive. But my grandmother has become less mobile in the last few years and when she moved into the new annexe on the ground floor I had these rooms refurbished.'

'That would explain why I can't find her medicine. Iris gave me the impression that she still used the same rooms as she did when I lived at Sethbury Hall. I expect she was confused. She asked me to fetch her angina pump spray, but I couldn't find it on the bedside table and I've been looking for it in the bathroom cupboards.'

'I don't understand why Nonna asked you.'

'She was having an angina attack.' Impatience flashed in Sienna's eyes. 'Don't just stand there. Your grandmother looked in a bad way and she needs her medication. How do I get to the annexe?' She went to step past him and stiffened when he caught hold of her arm.

'I meant why did she send you to get her medicine rather than one of the household staff who know where her rooms are?' Nico's eyes narrowed. 'Iris seemed perfectly well when I saw her a few minutes ago. She does suffer from angina but she takes tablets to control it. As far as I am aware she hasn't had an attack since she was diagnosed with the condition and she carries a pump spray merely as a precaution.'

'Well, maybe she forgot to take her tablet and that's why she had an angina attack.' Sienna threw her hands in the air. 'Don't you believe me? Why would I make something like that up?'

'To give you an excuse to visit my bedroom?' Nico had no idea what was going on but when he flicked his gaze to the four-poster bed, his libido didn't give a damn *why* his incredibly sexy ex-wife was in his room.

She whirled away from him and he noted how her silky dress clung to the rounded curves of her pert derriere. Fire licked through his veins and burned even hotter when she faced him and put her hands on her hips, causing her dress to pull tight across her breasts. Despite her slender build, Sienna had always been full up top, and Nico was definitely a breast man.

'That's right.' Her sarcastic tone forced his gaze up to her face and he was fascinated by the gleam of temper in her eyes. The girl he'd married had been timid and amenable and would not have dreamed of disagreeing with him, let alone glare at him as if she was itching for a fight. 'I was desperate to be alone with you so I invented the story that your grandmother had sent me to find her medication.' Sienna gave him a withering look. 'Your ego must be enormous if you think I was so blown away when you kissed me in the church that I want you to do it again.'

His ego wasn't the only thing that was enormous, Nico silently derided himself, conscious that his arousal was uncomfortably hard beneath his suit trousers. As for that kiss. Of course it shouldn't have happened. But he had seen the lascivious look in his brother's eyes when Danny had stared at Sienna, and he'd been overwhelmed by a fierce possessiveness, a need to claim her in front of Danny. Especially Danny.

That wasn't the only reason he had kissed her though. There had been something deeply primitive about his compelling need to put his mouth on Sienna's. It had been the same the first time he'd met her ten years ago. He had taken one look at her and known that he had to have her. He'd kissed her within the hour and slept with her three days later.

He knew every gorgeous dip and curve of her body; the little mole on her inner thigh that he'd always kissed before spreading her legs wide so that he could flick his tongue over the tight nub of her femininity until she writhed and begged him to possess her. Not that he'd needed any persuasion. Sex with Sienna had been wilder and hotter than with any other woman—a theory Nico had put to the test many times since his divorce.

He'd told himself that it couldn't have been as good

as he remembered. But when he had kissed her in the church a little while ago, their chemistry had been combustible. The soft gasp she'd made as she'd parted her lips beneath his had decimated his self-control and for a few moments he had forgotten that they had an audience of his brother and grandmother.

Now though they were alone, and as he watched Sienna's tongue dart out and slide over her slightly swollen lower lip a carnal hunger tore through Nico. 'Of course you want me to kiss you again, *cara*,' he drawled. 'I can read the signs.' He lifted his hand to the front of her dress and traced the outline of one pointed nipple, wildfire coursing through him when she drew an audible breath. But she made no attempt to move away and her pupils had dilated so that her eyes were inky pools edged with silvery grey.

'This is crazy,' she whispered. 'I did not have an ulterior motive for coming to your room. I wasn't even aware that this is your room.' She lifted her chin and said in a firmer voice, 'I don't care what you think, Nico. I'm not the besotted teenage bride who was in awe of you. I've changed.'

'But this hasn't changed,' he said roughly, threading his fingers into her hair so that he could tug her even closer and angling her head. Her breasts rose and fell jerkily and her lips parted in readiness for him to claim her mouth. The sexual chemistry between them was tangible and his nostrils flared as he dragged oxygen into his lungs. But as he lowered his face to hers, she put her hand on his chest to stop him.

'What about your grandmother?' Sienna drew a shuddering breath, as if she was struggling for control as much as he was. 'She needs her angina medicine.'

'Like I said, I saw Iris just before I came upstairs. She was on her second glass of sherry and regaling the new vicar with lurid tales of her youth.' Nico exhaled heavily, aware of the dull throb of unfulfilled lust in his groin. 'But regrettably this will have to wait until later. We need to get down to the marquee in the garden for the wedding dinner, and I have various duties to perform as best man.'

He dropped his hands down to his sides but could not bring himself to move away from her. His senses were inflamed by her perfume and the sharp, sweet scent of desire—hers, his—was thick in the air.

She shook her head and walked over to the bed to pick up her hat. 'There won't be a "later", Nico. If I hadn't gone to the church we would never have met again.' She flashed him a cool smile, but something like sadness chased across her face and her grey eyes were as haunting and mysterious as the mist that sometimes came down over the moors. 'We have led separate lives for eight years. We're strangers, and I'm not going to sit through your brother's wedding reception and pretend that we are friends.'

Sienna disappeared through the door with a swirl of yellow silk, leaving Nico faintly stunned when he realised that she was leaving him—again.

A memory flashed into his mind of when he had watched her walk out of the gates of Sethbury Hall eight years ago. She had carried a small suitcase containing the few chain-store clothes that were all she'd owned when she had married him. He had found all the designer dresses that he'd bought her hanging in the wardrobe, and she had also left behind the jewellery he'd given her, including her wedding ring.

As he'd watched her slender figure march down the driveway, her back ramrod straight, he had told himself he was glad she was leaving. *Lying bitch.* Her accusation that he had been unfaithful was all the more galling because he knew the truth about her. She was the cheat, the one who had kept secrets. *Dio*, he had trusted her, but after what his brother had told him, Nico had vowed that he would never again believe a word Sienna said.

His jaw clenched. He had never revealed to Sienna that he knew she had slept with his brother first, before him. Danny had admitted it when Nico had confided two years after his wedding that the marriage was in trouble. When Sienna had suffered a late miscarriage she had been advised to wait a few months before trying to conceive again. Nico hadn't told Danny or anyone else that after he and Sienna had tried unsuccessfully for a year to have another baby, he had done a home test, which showed he had a low sperm count.

Danny's confession had eaten away at Nico, and the suspicion that Sienna had been pregnant with his brother's child when he'd married her had festered like something rank and rotten in his soul. Sienna's accusation that he was having an affair with his PA had been the final straw. Her hypocrisy had infuriated him and divorce had been a way out of a marriage based on lies. He had set her free so that she could meet someone else who would give her a child—which he was unable to do.

He pulled his mind away from the past when he heard the click of her heels on the marble stairs and pictured her in her sexy, yellow silk dress. Ten years ago she had been a pretty teenage bride with no idea of her potential to be a stunning beauty in the future. The grown-up Sienna had exceeded all his expectations, he brooded. She was a ravishing, sensual siren and ever since he had caught sight of her in the church, desire had pulsed hot and urgent in his blood.

The sensible thing to do would be to let her walk out of his life as he had done once before. But he had never been able to forget her, and seeing her again had evoked an unexpected sense of regret that he had lost her. At the very least, he was curious to know why she had turned up in Much Matcham having read in the paper that he was getting married. Her excuse that Iris had told her grandmother Rose it was Danny's wedding was patently another lie.

Immediately after the divorce he had hated her, but now he was merely indifferent to Sienna's wiles, Nico assured himself. He grimaced as the ache in his groin reminded him that his body was not as uninvolved as he'd like. But he wasn't a young man at the mercy of his hormones any more. He was older, hopefully wiser, and he had learned not to mistake lust for a deeper emotion. Undoubtedly he could handle his inconvenient attraction to his ex-wife.

'Nonna will be disappointed if you leave,' he called after her as he strode onto the landing and leaned over the banister rail. 'Especially as she clearly went to some lengths to make sure you came back to the house for the reception.'

Sienna paused on her way down the stairs and looked up at him. 'Emotional blackmail won't work with me. You allowed Iris to think there is something going on between us but you'll have to tell her the truth.'

'Oh, I'm all for the truth, *cara*,' he murmured, walking swiftly down the stairs to join her on the half-landing. 'And the truth is we both still feel the wildfire attraction that burned between us a decade ago.' He felt a tremor run through her and saw hunger in her eyes before her lashes swept down and concealed her thoughts. Triumph surged through Nico, threatening the self-control he had been so confident would not waver.

'I had only left school a month before we met. What chance did I stand?' she demanded in a bitter voice. 'You were six years older than me and already worldly and experienced. In contrast I was painfully innocent but you soon changed that, didn't you, Nico? You were used to having whatever you wanted and it was my misfortune that you decided you wanted me.'

Misfortune? He had married her, hadn't he? He gritted his teeth. 'I don't remember hearing you complain, *cara*. But I do remember the moans you made when I kissed your breasts. *Please*, Nico, take me now,' he mocked, his satisfaction mixed with a stab of shame when fiery colour winged along her high cheekbones and hurt flashed in her eyes.

'You always were an arrogant bastard.' She pushed her hair back over her shoulders and he inhaled the scent of vanilla. Her foot was poised over the lower stair. 'This is a pointless conversation. No good ever comes from digging up the past. Goodbye, Nico.'

'Stay.' The word burst from him, harsher than he'd intended, but then he hadn't intended to plead with her. She stared at him, looking as shocked as he felt. She was so beautiful. He could look at her for ever and never grow tired of her delicate features. That sexy mouth of hers was a little too wide and all the more perfect for it, and her eyes were the colour of storm clouds. 'Please,' he said roughly.

She swallowed and the convulsive movement of her throat betrayed emotions that he sensed she was desperate to hide. 'I...' She did that flippy thing with her hair again, running her fingers through the layers and making him want to touch the silken strands of rich burgundy. 'Why do you want me to stay for the reception?' she asked huskily.

He shrugged to hide the fact that he was asking himself the same question. 'You said you've changed in the years since we were divorced and so have I. We are not the people we were then, but the attraction we both feel is as strong as when we first met.'

Her tongue darted across her lips. 'I don't know what you want,' she said in a low tone.

What he wanted was to whisk her back to his bedroom so that they could spend the rest of the afternoon in bed. And if she carried on looking at him with eyes that had turned smoky and held a gleam of sensual promise, he wouldn't be responsible for his actions. 'I'd like to get to know the grown-up Sienna Fisher,' Nico told her, startled to discover it was the truth.

Sienna looked around the huge marquee, which was decorated with extravagant floral displays, and sighed when Nico's grandmother gave her a friendly wave from across the room.

'My angina pump spray was in my handbag all the time. I don't know how I missed it,' she'd explained when Sienna had asked before they sat down to dinner if she was feeling better. 'I'm glad you decided to stay for the reception after all. It's good to see you and Nico getting on so well,' Iris had added pointedly.

She must be mad to have agreed to stay, Sienna thought. If Iris told Grandma Rose that she had returned to Sethbury Hall as Nico's guest, she would have some explaining to do. Nico had said that four hundred guests had been invited to the wedding. There was no top table and everyone, including the bride and groom, had sat at individual tables when the five-course meal was served by an army of white-jacketed waiters.

The food had looked exquisite but she'd been so conscious of Nico sitting beside her that she had barely tasted what she was eating. Now that the meal was over and the toasts and speeches were finished, the band had started playing and people were already on the dance floor.

Nico was talking to one of his relatives sitting on the other side of him and Sienna studied him covertly from beneath her lashes while she sipped her champagne. It was unfair that he was so indecently sexy, she brooded. His mother had been regarded as one of the great beauties of her generation. Like his grandfather before him, Nico's patrician features were an indication of an aristocratic lineage that could be traced back centuries to when English knights and barons had forced King John to sign the Magna Carta.

Jacqueline Mandeville's marriage to a handsome Italian playboy Franco De Conti, whose family's enormous fortune had derived from their exclusive hotel chain, had produced an heir and a spare, Danny had once joked to Sienna. They had been at Sethbury Hall where Nico had organised a tennis tournament with a group of friends. Sienna had been startled by the bitterness in Danny's voice. She'd told herself she must have imagined that he was jealous of his older sibling. But now, as she looked across the table and saw Danny staring at Nico with an odd expression on his face, she remembered that day all those years ago.

Nico had beaten Danny in a tennis match and Danny had stormed off the court. Later, he'd laughed and told her it was just brotherly rivalry. 'Nico wins everything, including my girlfriend,' he'd said. It wasn't strictly true. She had gone out with Danny a couple of times, but when he had tried to kiss her she'd explained that she just wanted them to be friends. Nico had arrived at Sethbury soon after and she had fallen instantly in love with him.

Sienna's mind jolted back to the present when Danny leaned across the table. 'When did you get back with my brother? I'm surprised Nico didn't mention that he was seeing you again.'

It was on the tip of her tongue to explain that she hadn't had any contact with Nico since their divorce. But there had been faint suspicion in Danny's voice, and bizarrely she wanted to protect Nico from embarrassment so she said lightly, 'Oh, we bumped into each other in London recently and he invited me to the wedding. Nico knew that you and I had been friends, and I was pleased to have the chance to wish you and your new bride a happy marriage.'

'Come and dance with me for old times' sake.' Danny stood up and walked around the table.

Sienna hesitated, unable to explain to herself why she felt reluctant to take his hand. 'I expect you want to dance with your wife.'

'Victoria is dancing with her father.' Danny tugged her out of her chair and led her over to the dance floor. He kept hold of her hand and slid his other arm around her waist. 'We were good friends when we were younger, weren't we? Do you remember when a group of us hired a river boat for the day in York and you fell in?'

'You pushed me in.'

'Ah, but I jumped in and rescued you, didn't I?' Danny went on to recount other stories from their youth, and Sienna was soon laughing at the memories. She had got to know Danny when he had been a regular at her father's pub where she'd served behind the bar most evenings and weekends, saving up to go to university. Not that her father had paid her much for all the hours she'd worked, but at least while he was being obnoxious to her he had left her mother alone.

Danny De Conti and his public school friends had seemed glamorous and exciting compared to the local boys from the village.

'Danny's not bad looking, but his older brother is drop-dead gorgeous,' the other barmaid, Becky, had told Sienna. 'Domenico spends much of his time in Italy, but my mum is a cook up at the hall and she heard that he's coming home next week. By the way, Lady Mandeville is looking for a part-time cleaner and Mum says she'll put your name forward if you like.'

Which was how, ten years ago, Sienna had been mopping the kitchen floor at Sethbury Hall when Nico had walked in, his riding boots leaving footprints where she had just cleaned. *Mi dispiace,* he'd murmured with barely a glance at her. But then he'd stopped and turned to stare at her, the faint frown between his eyebrows not marring the masculine beauty of his face. 'Who are you?'

She had been struck dumb; dazzled by the handsome, bronzed god who had materialised in front of her and could not possibly be real. She'd blinked but he had still been there, tall and strong-looking, his exotic appearance emphasised by his golden skin and unexpected brilliant blue eyes. As she'd stared back at him, a slow smile had lifted the corners of his gorgeous mouth and her heart had raced.

'Perhaps you are not real and that's why you don't have a name,' he'd teased. 'But if you are real your feet must be wet.'

Confused, she'd glanced down and discovered that the mop was dripping water over her trainers. 'I'm Sienna,' she'd blurted out, mortified when he'd run his eyes over her faded jeans and tee shirt. All her clothes had been years old but she hadn't had money to buy new, fashionable stuff like the other girls she'd known at school. Her tee shirt had been too tight, and because it had been a hot day she hadn't bothered to wear a bra.

To her horror she had felt her nipples harden, but when she'd hurriedly crossed her arms in front of her she had seen a gleam in Nico's eyes that had sent a delicious shiver through her. It had been the first time in her life that she'd felt desire, and in that instant she had become aware of her femininity.

'My name is Domenico, but my friends call me Nico,' he'd told her.

'I know, sir.' She'd suddenly remembered her lowly position and his exalted one. One day he would inherit Sethbury Hall and the title of Viscount Mandeville when his grandfather died.

He had laughed. 'I very much hope you will call me Nico, Si-*enna*.' Even the way he'd said her name had been sexy. 'You can't have wet feet for the rest of the day. Take off your shoes and we'll sit in the garden while they dry. You can tell me why a girl as beautiful as you is working here.'

She had been seduced by Nico's easy charm and his self-assurance that even back then had sat lightly on his broad shoulders. He had kissed her for the first time that same afternoon while they were sitting in the shade of a lilac tree covered with heavenly scented purple spires. Later she had walked home on air and even her father's drunken bad temper couldn't burst her bubble. She'd been in love with a handsome prince who she'd been sure would make all her dreams come true.

Right now, Nico looked as dangerous as the wicked wolf beloved of so many fairy tales. Time shifted to the present and Sienna found herself looking into the glittering gaze of her ex-husband. He was moving purposefully across the dance floor towards her, accompanied by the new Mrs De Conti.

'Let's swap. I don't want to be accused of monopolising your delightful bride,' he said to Danny, skilfully executing the change of partners before Sienna had time to object.

He swept her across the dance floor so fast that her head spun and her feet barely touched the floor. When she tried to ease away from him, he clamped his arm around her waist and pulled her towards him so that her breasts were crushed against his chest.

'What are you doing?' she muttered, struggling to speak with her face pressed against his shirt front. She could see the shadow of his dark chest hairs beneath the fine white silk. The heat of his body was melting her insides.

'I could ask you the same question,' he said in a terse voice, and when she glanced up at his face she realised that he was furious. 'Did you come to Danny's wedding to cause trouble?'

She was mystified. 'What do you mean by trouble? What have I done?'

'Did you give any thought to Danny's new bride while you were flirting with him in front of the wedding guests?'

'I was not flirting…'

'You were all over him like a rash. *Dio*, you've got every male in the marquee panting over you. Why embarrass Victoria like that? Was it to prove that you can have any man you want, including my ass of a brother?'

Sienna sucked in a sharp breath, her temper rising to meet Nico's. 'You asked me to come to the reception,' she snapped. 'It's ridiculous to make me out as some sort of man-eater. No one here is interested in me.'

'I don't believe you are unaware of the effect you have on men.'

'I only have an effect on you.' The words spilled from her mouth before she realised what she had said.

Nico tensed and stared at her, and the hunger in his eyes both excited and appalled her. He was her ex-husband and whatever there had been between them had died a long time ago, she reminded herself. So why did he make her feel dizzy and disconnected from reality?

She was barely aware of the other people on the dance floor. There was just Nico filling her vision and swamping her senses. He was even more dangerously handsome and charismatic than her memory of him but she was determined not to fall under his spell again.

CHAPTER THREE

SIENNA ATTEMPTED TO wrench herself out of Nico's arms and glared at him when he tightened his hold on her waist. 'I don't want to dance with you,' she told him, her fury mixed with panic that she could not control her response to him. She was tempted to dig one of her stiletto heels into his foot. 'You can't make me.'

'Do you want to put that to the test?' He laughed softly at her fulminating look. 'You did not have such a fiery temper when you were my wife.'

'At eighteen I was too in awe of you to say boo to a goose. But I grew up and I'm no longer the girl who worshipped the ground you walked on.'

'You've certainly changed. You are more confident and assertive, and very sexy, *cara*.' The unholy gleam in his eyes was part teasing and part male admiration that sent another sizzle of heat through Sienna. Nico dropped his hands from her waist and perversely she wished he was still holding her.

They had reached the door of the marquee, and when she followed him outside she took a deep breath to steady her racing pulse. In midsummer the days were long, and although it was past nine o'clock, darkness was only just falling, turning the sky a soft purple hue.

The air was warm and sultry, filled with the mingled scents of roses and lavender that grew in wide beds in the garden. In the distance there was an ominous rumble of thunder.

'I should go.' As she spoke, Sienna checked her watch. She would have to walk back to the village where she had left her car, and it would be completely dark when she drove across the moors to pick up the main road that led to the motorway.

'Come up to the house for a drink.' Nico's voice was casual, but when she glanced at him, something about his intent expression made her heart miss a beat.

'I can't,' she said quickly before she gave in to the temptation to spend another hour with him. It was unlikely she would ever see him again after tonight and she resented the little pang her heart gave. She was *so* over him, she reminded herself sternly. 'I had a glass of champagne when we toasted the bride and groom and I'll be over the limit to drive if I have any more alcohol. Besides, it's a good five-hour trip back to London.'

He frowned. 'You can't make that long journey tonight. Why didn't you book a hotel room?'

She shrugged, not wanting to admit that she'd made a spur-of-the-moment decision that morning to drive to Much Matcham because she'd mistakenly believed that he was getting married and she had been curious about his choice of bride. 'No rooms were available at The George, or at any of the local B & Bs. I suppose they were all booked by the wedding guests. If I'm tired on the way home, I'll stop at a motorway services hotel.'

'You can spend the night here at Sethbury Hall.' Nico gave her a speculative look when she stared at him. 'Why not?'

'I can think of several reasons why it would be a terrible idea for me to spend the night with you.'

'As a matter of fact I was going to suggest that you sleep in one of the guest rooms,' he drawled. The amusement in his voice caused a hot stain of embarrassment to flare on Sienna's cheeks and she was furious with herself for jumping to the wrong conclusion. 'To satisfy my curiosity, why would it be a terrible idea for us to sleep together? We are attracted to each other and we're both consenting adults.'

'You've got to be kidding.' She shook her head and tried to dismiss the erotic images in her mind of Nico making love to her on his huge four-poster bed.

The gleam in his eyes made her wonder if he could read her thoughts. 'What are you afraid of?' he asked softly.

That you will break my heart for a second time.

'I'm not afraid of anything,' she snapped. 'I simply think it's a bad idea.' She hated that he tied her in knots and without another word she swung round and started to walk along the gravel path that wound around the side of the house. But she had only taken a few steps when a thunderclap shattered the still air. The noise was as loud as an explosion and Sienna jumped when a bolt of lightning zigzagged like a white scar through the sky that had turned black as the storm clouds mustered. And then the rain fell; big, hard raindrops that stung her bare shoulders and arms.

In seconds it was a deluge. Nico grabbed her hand. 'Come on,' he shouted above the crash of thunder. Half-blinded by the torrential rain, she clung to his hand as they raced up the stone steps and across the terrace. Nico opened the French doors and pulled her behind

him into the drawing room. Sienna barely noticed her
surroundings. She was soaked to the skin and her dress
clung to her body. Following Nico's gaze, she glanced
down and saw that her nipples were jutting provoca-
tively through the wet silk.

He had closed the glass doors and the noise of the
thunderstorm outside was muted. But inside the room
a different storm raged. The sexual tension sparked
between them and Sienna's skin prickled; every one
of her nerve-endings acutely aware of him.

Nico took off his jacket and threw it carelessly over
the back of a chair. He shoved a hand through his wet
hair and prowled across the room towards her, as predatory as a sleek and very dangerous jungle cat. He stood
in front of her, so close that the flames of desire in his
eyes scorched her and she could not repress the shiver
of anticipation that ran through her.

'Are you cold?' His eyes were fixed on her breasts
and Sienna lost the battle with herself.

'I'm burning up,' she admitted in a husky voice she
did not recognise as her own. Maybe she was crazy.
All right, she was definitely crazy, but she could not
make herself step away from Nico. She had wanted
him from the moment she'd seen him in the church
today. But she was no longer a shy eighteen-year-old,
she was a confident woman who knew her own mind
and was in every way his equal.

Although Sienna was wearing four-inch heels Nico
towered over her. She watched his head descend and
impatience swept through her. Pushing herself up onto
her toes, she grabbed hold of his tie and pulled his
mouth down onto hers. Just like when they had been
in the church, the kiss exploded between them as their

mouths fused together. He wrapped one arm around her waist and threaded the fingers of his other hand through her hair, cupping her nape and tugging her head back to allow him to plunder her lips with the mastery that was an integral part of Nico De Conti.

Sienna couldn't resist him. She had never been able to, she acknowledged. He was a sorcerer and when she was in his arms she was enchanted by his sensual magic. His kiss stole her sanity as he increased the pressure of his lips on hers and pushed his tongue into her mouth to explore her with mind-blowing eroticism.

She had missed him so much. Memories she'd tried to suppress for years burst into her mind like fireworks, silver and gold, shimmering and incandescent. The past merged with the present as she pictured them naked, their limbs entwined, his hands sliding over her body just as they were doing now. He eased away from her a fraction so that he could spread his fingers over her breasts and caress them through the silk of her dress. The warmth of his palms was intoxicating but it wasn't enough, not nearly enough.

His jacket had taken the brunt of the rain when they had been caught in the storm, but his shirt front was damp beneath Sienna's hands as she ran them over his chest. She could feel the heat of his body through the fine material and she tugged at the buttons, eager to touch his bare skin. Pulling his shirt tails from the waistband of his trousers, she gave a soft sigh as she spread the edges of the shirt wide and skimmed her fingertips over his bronzed, satin skin overlaid with whorls of silky black hair.

His hands were busy too, sliding up to tug the straps of her dress down her arms. 'There's a zip,' she muttered against his mouth when he broke the kiss so that they could both snatch a breath. He gave a grunt and claimed her lips again, hot and hungry, seeking a response she had no thought to deny him.

She lifted her hands to his shoulders and felt him slide her zip down the length of her spine. He peeled her dress from her breasts and made a rough sound in his throat when he discovered that she was braless. He dragged his thumb pads over her taut nipples, making her gasp and shudder as sensation arced down her body to meet the ache between her legs.

'You are exquisite,' Nico said hoarsely, a hard glitter in his eyes as he stared at her firm breasts, each adorned with a dusky pink nipple standing erect. *'Perfetto.'* Dull colour streaked along his sharp cheekbones and his features hardened, giving him a feral appearance that sent another shiver through Sienna.

'Let me warm you.' His voice was like rough velvet. 'Hold on tight, *cara*.' He scooped her off her feet, one arm around her waist and the other beneath her knees. She wound her arms around his neck and pressed her face against his throat, her tongue darting out to lick the faint saltiness of his skin. He tasted divine and, driven by an elemental need that only this man had ever evoked in her, she gently bit his neck.

'Dio,' he growled, his arms flexing around her as he strode out of the drawing room and across the hall. 'Wait until we are upstairs and then you can bite me all you like. But be warned that I bite back.'

He carried her up the sweeping staircase as if she weighed nothing. On the landing, he paused and sought her gaze with his bright blue eyes that burned down to her soul. 'My bedroom is along the corridor on the

right, and to the left are the guest rooms. Your choice.'
His tone was as blank as the expression on his far too
handsome face.

For a moment Sienna wished he had made the decision for her and simply carried her to his room. That
way she could absolve herself of the guilt that she was
shamefully weak where he was concerned. But she
wasn't the overawed girl who had married him, she reminded herself. Since their divorce she had taken control of her life and she was entirely capable of making
her own decisions. She wanted everything that Nico
could give her. For this one night only. A chance to
come to terms with the past so that she could evict him
from her mind and her heart once and for all.

'Right,' she said huskily, ignoring the voice in her
head advising her to run as far and as fast from him as
she could. He did not ask again, he simply turned and
strode down the corridor, shouldered the door into his
private suite and carried her through to his bedroom.
Closing the door, he set her down on her feet and pulled
her into his arms, his mouth seeking and finding hers
in a kiss that was hotter and more urgent than anything
that had gone before.

The top of her dress was bunched around her waist.
Nico tugged the rain-soaked silk over her hips and the
dress slithered to the floor, leaving her in just a pair
of tiny knickers that were wet from her arousal. His
hands were everywhere on her body, sliding down her
back and shaping the curves of her bottom before he
pushed one hand between her legs and cupped her sex
through her damp panties.

She arched her hips towards him and he muttered
something in Italian as he shoved her up against the

door, his mouth still fused with hers. He kissed her until she was dizzy with desire, until nothing existed but Nico's lips on her lips, her throat and then, *at last*, on her breasts as he sucked on one hard nipple and then the other.

Sienna gave a guttural cry; need pulsing through her as Nico tormented the sensitive peaks with his tongue. She skimmed her hands over his chest and flat abdomen, following the arrowing of dark hair that disappeared beneath his waistband. Hesitating for a second, she moved her hand lower and traced the hard outline of his erection straining beneath his trousers. His breath rasped in his throat, and when she lifted her eyes to his, the burning heat of his gaze added fuel to the fire inside her.

She fumbled with his zip, her knuckles scraping across his burgeoning arousal. Nico swore and pushed her hand away, yanking the zip down so that he could free himself from the constraint of his trousers and silk boxers.

Dear Lord, he was huge. Not that she had any personal experience of other men to compare him with, Sienna acknowledged. There had only ever been Nico. And it had been so long since she had felt him inside her. Molten heat pooled low in her pelvis at the thought of what she wanted him to do.

'I need you now.' She didn't realise she had spoken aloud until he made a choked sound, halfway between a laugh and a groan.

'It's the same for me, *cara*. I can't wait.' He slid his hand down her body, pushed aside the scrap of lace between her legs and eased a finger into her wet heat. She almost went up in flames. The sensation of him swirling his finger inside her and gently stretching her, before he pushed a second digit into her opening, made her gasp and tense as the first ripples of an orgasm threatened to shatter the remnants of her control.

But she wanted more, and when she felt Nico's rock-hard erection press between her thighs, her insides turned to liquid. He tugged her knickers down and she stepped out of them. 'Wrap your legs around me,' he muttered, his hands cupping her bottom cheeks as he lifted her off her feet. Sienna obeyed him mindlessly, compelled by a primal urge to take him inside her and let him possess her utterly.

She hooked her legs around his hips and somehow managed to kick off her shoes. And then he simply drove into her with a powerful thrust that made her gasp as she discovered just how hard he was, how thick, filling her inch by mind-blowing inch.

'*Dio*, you're so tight,' he said unsteadily. 'Am I hurting you? Do you want me to stop?'

'No…and no,' she whispered. It was difficult to speak past the lump in her throat. She was unprepared for the emotions that stormed through her. She felt as if she had come home. 'I just need a moment.'

She felt him start to withdraw and tightened her legs around his waist while she dug her fingers into his shoulders, pressing her breasts against his chest. His chest hair felt abrasive rubbing across her sensitive nipples, creating a delicious friction that evoked a coiling sensation low in her pelvis. 'Don't stop,' she said fiercely.

He must have sensed her urgency and the ragged groan he gave told her he shared it. Gripping her bottom cheeks tighter, he pushed her up against the door and thrust deep into her, withdrew a little way and repeated the action over and over. It was wild and frantic as he ground his hips against hers, the harsh sound of his breaths mingling with her gasps and moans. She wondered if her spine would be bruised from where Nico was holding her up against the solid wooden door, but right now there was just pleasure building inside her, intensifying with each devastating thrust as he took her higher.

His mouth captured hers again in a sensual and unexpectedly tender kiss that was nearly her undoing. 'Nico…' She gasped his name, too overwhelmed to care about the pleading note in her voice.

'I know, *cara*.' He quickened his pace and drove into her faster, harder, taking her to the edge of heaven. It was too much. He had always been too much. 'Angel, I'm going to…' His voice rasped against her throat. And then he slipped his hand between their joined bodies and flicked his thumb over the ultra-sensitive tip of her clitoris. The pleasure was so intense that Sienna shattered. She dug her fingers into his shoulders to anchor herself to him as her orgasm sent her into free fall.

Nico thrust deep, tensed and let out a savage groan as he exploded inside her, his big body shuddering with the force of his release. In the aftermath, as their breathing gradually slowed, a sweet lassitude swept over Sienna and once again she felt a sense of homecoming. This was where she belonged, whispered a little voice in her head, and her heart agreed.

What the hell had just happened? As Nico withdrew from Sienna he felt a sense of regret—not that he'd had sex with her but that it was over. He liked being buried deep inside her—although *liked* was an understatement. He'd just had the most amazing sexual experience of his life and astonishingly he was already hardening again. He enjoyed sex as much as any other red-blooded male. Women offered a pleasurable diversion and a release from tension—he was a self-confessed workaholic. But his affairs were always on his terms. Only Sienna made him mindless with desire. No other woman had ever made him lose control, and now that his hunger had been appeased—even if only temporarily—he felt a stirring of unease that she'd had such a devastating effect on him.

He was appalled by his lack of finesse. *Dio*, he hadn't even made it as far as the bed with her, he derided himself. He'd taken her up against the door with no consideration for her comfort or enjoyment. Although she *had* enjoyed it. Her moans of pleasure were still in his ears and his shoulders were stinging where she had dug her fingernails into his skin when she'd climaxed moments before his own incredible orgasm.

She lifted her face from the crook of his neck, her grey eyes still smoky with desire. But then she became aware of her surroundings, of what had just happened, and her expression turned wary. Nico's jaw tightened and he dismissed an odd sense of loss as he set her back down on her feet.

'I didn't take precautions,' he said roughly. Although he had reason to believe that he was infertile, it made sense not to take risks when he had sex. The fact that it hadn't even entered his mind to wear a condom when he'd thrust his way into Sienna's molten heat was further proof of his worrying lack of self-control with her.

'Precautions?' Her frown cleared and she gave him

a wry glance. 'An unplanned pregnancy is not likely to be an issue for us, is it, Nico?'

The truth of her statement sent a lightning bolt of anger through him as it seemed to confirm his suspicion that she had known the child she'd been carrying when he'd married her had not been his.

'Pregnancy is not the only possible result of having unprotected sex,' he reminded her coolly. 'I am not usually so irresponsible.'

'Same here,' she mumbled, bending down to pick up her dress from the floor.

Nico had the feeling she wanted to avoid his gaze, as if she was embarrassed by what had happened.

'I don't normally behave like a tramp and leap into bed with a man at the first opportunity.' She was twisting her dress between her fingers, mangling the already crumpled silk. 'I don't know what came over me.'

He knew it was ridiculous to feel pleased by her admission that she did not make a habit of having casual sex. But she was in her late twenties and presumably she'd had other relationships in the past eight years. The fierce possessiveness that swept through him was inexplicable. After the divorce he had filed away their brief marriage as a mistake and moved on with his life. But he'd just proved that he was not completely over Sienna as he'd assumed.

'I must go.' She shook out her dress and grimaced at the sight of the badly creased silk. Her handbag was on the floor where she had dropped it. She frowned as she took out her phone. 'The battery has died. Would you mind calling a taxi for me? It will take ten minutes to walk to the village where I left my car, and I'll get soaked.'

The rumbles of thunder had quietened as the storm moved away but the rain was still hammering against the windows. It was completely dark now and Nico touched the remote-control panel on the wall to turn on the bedside lamps. Sienna blinked and he was intrigued by the soft colour that swept over her cheeks. She looked younger and vulnerable, stripped of her air of sophistication, and he felt a tug on his insides, possessiveness mixed with a fundamental urge to protect her.

'You used to like walking on the moors in the rain,' he murmured, brushing a few strands of hair back from her face. 'The first time we made love was on the moors in a thunderstorm. Do you remember?'

Her flush deepened but she ignored the question. 'I haven't got a change of clothes with me and I don't relish the thought of driving back to London in my dress that will be even wetter if I have to go outside in the rain.'

Seriously, did she expect him to send her on her way after he'd had his pleasure with her as if she were a hooker he'd picked up in a seedy bar? The idea that she had such a low opinion of him made him feel uncomfortable. He hadn't forced her to come to his room, he reminded himself. It had been her choice. And whether or not it was sensible, he wasn't ready to let her go yet.

He slid his hand beneath the heavy silk of her hair and curved his fingers around her nape. *'Idiota,'* he said gently. 'You'll stay here with me tonight.'

She bit her lip, drawing his attention to her mouth that was reddened and slightly swollen from where he had kissed her and where he was impatient to kiss her again. 'Nico, I can't.'

He heard determination in her voice but her eyes were as soft as woodsmoke, and a tremor ran through her when he tugged her dress out of her hands and drew circles around one dusky pink aureole with his finger-tip. 'Tell me you don't want this and I will drive you to the village so that you can collect your car,' he told her, dipping his head so that his words grazed her lips.

She made a muffled sound somewhere between a sigh and groan, but she did not protest when he swept her up into his arms and carried her over to the bed. His heart thundered with triumph at her capitulation and anticipation that very soon he would slake his de-sire for her again. Maybe he was this hungry because he hadn't had sex for a couple of months after he'd ended an affair that had run its course. Celibacy was not a natural state for him, Nico acknowledged wryly.

He pulled back the bedspread and laid Sienna down on the pure silk sheets before he quickly stripped off his clothes and stretched out beside her. Emotions he refused to examine, much less define, swirled inside him as he spread her burgundy hair across the snowy white pillows.

When she was younger, Sienna had been so slen-der that she'd looked as breakable as spun glass. In the intervening years her figure had softened to a sym-phony of sexy curves that Nico was eager to explore. He could not bring himself to regret that he had made love to her. But once wasn't enough.

The night was long, and he planned to have her in as many varied ways as his imagination could conjure, taking them both to the absolute extremes of sexual satisfaction. And he fully expected that by the morn-ing his desire for his little liar of an ex-wife would be sated once and for all.

CHAPTER FOUR

FROM THE TRAIN CARRIAGE, Sienna watched the picturesque Yorkshire countryside flash past the window. Her phone pinged to announce she had a new text message and her heart lurched when a number she did not recognise flashed onto the screen.

Maybe it was from Nico? She'd heard nothing from him for the past month and had almost given up hope that he would get in touch. She had even stopped checking her texts and emails quite so obsessively. Although to be fair she hadn't left him her number when she'd sneaked out of Sethbury Hall at first light on the morning after she'd spent the night with him. He had fallen asleep after he'd made love to her for a fourth time, leaving her body quivering and her mind in turmoil. Her grand plan to have sex with him to get him out of her system had backfired, and she'd feared that she was hopelessly addicted to him.

When faced with danger, most species, including humans, went into fight-or-flight mode. Sienna had chosen to flee. She'd waited until Nico's breathing had slowed before she'd eased out from beneath his arm that he'd draped across her waist as if he wanted to anchor her to him. It was that kind of dangerous wishful thinking that had spurred her to scramble into her horribly creased dress and gather up her shoes and handbag. She couldn't find her knickers and had given up looking for them when Nico stirred.

Pausing in the doorway, she had looked back at him sprawled on the bed, one arm across his face, the sheet over his thighs and just covering his manhood that unbelievably had still been semi-aroused. She'd remembered when they were married she had often lain awake at night and watched him sleeping, hardly able to believe that he was hers.

The truth was he never had been hers. She understood that now. But at eighteen she had been so in love with him that she'd ignored the rumours flying around the village that Nico had only married her because she had been pregnant and he'd been under pressure from his grandfather to claim the future heir to the Sethbury estate.

In the end there had not been a child. She had suffered a miscarriage in the fifth month of her pregnancy and their tiny son had been stillborn. Luigi's grave was marked by a simple headstone in St Augustine's churchyard. Sienna swallowed the lump that had formed in her throat. She had been heartbroken, and even though many years had passed, the grief she'd felt for her baby, who had been so perfect that he had looked like a little doll, still felt like a knife in her heart.

She read the text message on her phone.

Have fitted a new brake cable on your car. Vehicle is ready for you to collect.

The message was from the garage where she had taken her car for a routine service. Swallowing her disappointment, she quickly checked for any new emails in her inbox but there was nothing from Nico. If he had wanted to contact her, he could have searched for her website on the Internet. When they had chatted over dinner at his brother's wedding reception, she had told him that she co-owned an organic skincare business called Fresh Faced.

The fact that she hadn't heard from him since he had taken her apart in his bed was proof, if she'd needed it, that she was a fool. There had always been a white-hot chemistry between them but she couldn't accuse Nico of taking advantage of her or making false promises. They'd had amazing sex but that was all it had been. It was time she stopped fantasising that there had been a special connection when they'd made love and put the night with Nico out of her mind, as he had clearly done.

It was a ten-minute walk from York train station to the care home where Grandma Rose lived semi-independently in a private suite of rooms. On the way, Sienna collected the birthday cake she had ordered from a bakery and stopped at a florist's to buy a bunch of flowers. At Heath Lodge she gave her name at Reception before taking the lift up to the fourth floor. Juggling her overnight bag, the flowers and the boxed cake, she turned the door handle and entered her grandmother's rooms.

'Hi, Nanna, it's me.' She walked into the sitting room and came to an abrupt halt when she saw Nico standing by the window. Her first instinct was to bolt and only her stubborn pride stopped her from running out of the door. From across the room she felt the searing intensity of his gaze burn through her cotton sundress. At least this time she was wearing a bra, she thought.

She belatedly noticed his grandmother Iris was sitting in an armchair next to Grandma Rose. 'Oh, you're having a birthday party! Lucky I brought a cake.' Sienna cringed at the sound of her overly bright voice. She forced her feet to walk further into the room but she tripped on the edge of the rug and the cake box slipped out of her hand. With lightning reactions, Nico sprang forwards and caught it before it hit the floor.

'I hope you don't mind us being here for Rose's birthday celebration,' he murmured.

'Of course not. The more the merrier.' She smiled gaily at Iris and prayed that her thundering heart wasn't audible to Nico and their respective grandmothers.

'I managed to persuade Nico to stop working for the afternoon so that he could bring me to visit Rose,' Iris explained.

So he hadn't engineered the visit because he'd hoped to see her, Sienna registered, annoyed with herself for feeling disappointed. Of course Nico hadn't thought about her constantly for the past weeks as she had thought about him. She wished he would move away from her. The spicy scent of his aftershave made her head spin. It didn't help that he looked utterly gorgeous in black jeans and a cream polo shirt, open at the neck to reveal a vee of tanned skin and a sprinkling of black chest hair.

'I'd better put your flowers in water,' she told Rose. Her eyes were drawn to the exquisite bouquet of roses, lilies and exotic orchids in a vase on the table. The stunning floral display made her bunch of yellow chrysanthemums seem very ordinary.

'Aren't they lovely? Nico bought them for me,' her grandmother said, following her gaze. 'It was very kind of you, Nico.' Rose gave him a fond smile. 'You already do so much for me. I wouldn't have been able to move into Heath Lodge without your help.'

Frowning, Sienna spun around from Saint Nico and headed into the little kitchen, saying, 'I'll make tea.'

'I'll help.' He followed her, and while she filled the kettle he leaned against the kitchen unit, his tall frame dominating the small space.

Waiting for the kettle to boil, Sienna muttered, 'What did my grandmother mean?'

He hesitated for a moment. 'I pay the fees so that Rose can live at Heath Lodge.'

'What?' She could not hide her shock. 'Why? Nanna sold her cottage before she moved here and I assumed she uses the proceeds to pay the care home's monthly fees.'

'A few years ago Rose took out a loan and put her cottage up as collateral. She gave the money to her father to try to prop up his pub business, but the pub failed, and Clive never repaid her.'

Sienna grimaced. 'That sounds like my father. The last I heard of him, he had moved to Ireland and was working in a friend's bar, probably drinking all the profits. I'm glad Mum finally found the courage to leave him.' She poured boiling water into the teapot and tried not to react when Nico passed her the milk and his fingers brushed against hers, sending a jolt of electricity up her arm. 'Why are you involved? Rose isn't your responsibility. If I had known about her money problems I'd have covered the care home's fees.'

'She didn't want to trouble you while you were establishing your business. When I heard about your grandmother's financial situation I was happy to help.' Nico's eyes narrowed. 'Why does my helping Rose bother you?'

'You shouldn't have to. It's not as if she is your relative.'

'My grandmother has been friends with your grandmother for many years and when you became my wife, our families had a closer connection. If you had accepted a divorce settlement from me, your financial situation would have been easier.' He frowned. 'Why did you return the cheque my solicitor sent you?'

'I didn't want anything from you. If I'd accepted the cheque it would have added weight to the rumours in the village that I had married you for your money.' Sienna loaded a tray with cups and saucers and set the sugar bowl down with a clatter. 'There were even whispers that I'd deliberately got pregnant so you would have to marry me.'

'Did you?'

She stared at him, wondering if she had heard him correctly. He stared back at her, his blue eyes coolly assessing and causing a little shiver to run down her spine. 'Of course I didn't. My pregnancy was an accident. A one-off miracle, as it turned out,' she said huskily, remembering her heartache after the miscarriage when she'd failed to conceive again. 'You didn't wear a condom the first time we made love up on the moors,' she reminded him. A decade later, the memory of their wild passion when he'd tumbled her down in the heather and they had frantically ripped each other's clothes off still heated her blood.

Nico gave her a warning look and she bit her lip,

aware that Rose and Iris were within earshot. Lowering her voice, she said curtly, 'I can't believe we are having this discussion now. If you'd thought I had trapped you, why didn't you say so ten years ago? But the gossip in Much Matcham was partly right. The only reason you married me was because I was expecting your child, but when I failed to give you an heir there was no reason to continue with the marriage that you hadn't wanted. That's the truth, isn't it, Nico?'

Sienna sounded so convincing that Nico almost believed her. Almost. But he knew what a clever liar she was. He'd had no reason to think the baby she had been expecting wasn't his. She had told him she was a virgin before they'd made love for the first time, and he'd been surprised and delighted by her fiery passion that matched his own. He'd never suspected that she had slept with his brother just a week earlier.

'Why didn't you say that she was playing us both along?' he'd asked, when he'd confided his marriage problems to his brother and Danny had admitted that he and Sienna had got together before Nico had arrived in Much Matcham that summer ten years ago.

'I had gone to Monte Carlo the day before you turned up at Sethbury Hall,' his brother had reminded him. 'By the time I came home you had announced your engagement to Sienna, and everyone knew she was expecting your baby. There didn't seem any point in mentioning that I'd had a fling with her. I figured that if she had wanted you to know she would have told you herself.'

Instead Sienna had fooled him into believing that he was the father of her unborn child, Nico thought darkly. He had been twenty-four and the idea of fatherhood had been terrifying. Another responsibility to add to his list. He was the oldest son and heir to his English and Italian family's fortunes and he'd grown up knowing that one day he would be in charge of Sethbury Hall and estate, as well as the hotel business De Conti Leisure. The weight of expectation on him was huge. When he had looked at the grainy scan image of his baby son he'd felt overwhelmed rather than excited.

His father's unexpected death a mere three months after Nico had learned that he was going to be a father himself had been a terrible shock. But more shocking still had been the discovery that Franco De Conti had fathered several illegitimate children while he had been married to Nico's mother.

Memories that Nico had suppressed for years forced their way into his mind. In the months after his father's death he had been under intense emotional strain when he'd flown to California on a business trip. But within hours of his plane landing, he'd received a phone call from the hospital in York where Sienna had been taken by ambulance after she'd started to bleed heavily. It had been Nico's grandmother who had broken the news that his baby son had been stillborn.

Numb with shock, he'd immediately flown back to England. Sienna had been utterly distraught, but Nico felt frozen inside, and even when he'd been taken by a nurse to see his lifeless baby there had been a sense of unreality. He had not held his child, but when he'd walked out of the room Nico had heard the ragged sound of his own breathing. He'd felt like he had run a marathon and his heart was about to burst out of his chest. Somehow he'd got himself together, knowing that he must support Sienna. But her grief had made him feel helpless, just as he'd felt helpless when he was a young boy and his mother had sobbed because of his father's infidelity.

They had named the baby Luigi, and held a funeral for him a week later. But once again it had felt unreal standing in the graveyard of St Augustine's church. Nico's throat had felt raw as if he'd swallowed broken glass when he held a weeping Sienna in his arms, but he hadn't cried. He couldn't. Tears and uncontrolled emotions terrified him. Nico's way of dealing with his emotions was to ignore them, but Sienna had accused him of being distant and uncaring. Then, when she'd failed to fall pregnant again and had become obsessed with ovulation charts and tips to improve fertility, he'd believed that she only wanted sex with him in order to conceive another child.

One thing he found puzzling was why Sienna had refused the generous divorce settlement he had instructed his lawyer to offer her. Although their marriage had been over he had still felt responsible for her. He'd supposed she had named him as the father of her child rather than Danny because he'd been in line to inherit the title of Viscount Mandeville. Perhaps Sienna had fancied herself as a viscountess. But in that case why had she walked away from their marriage with nothing?

Since the divorce Nico had pushed the question to the back of his mind. But a few moments ago Sienna had sounded hurt by the rumours that had abounded in Much Matcham at the time of their wedding that she had gone to extreme lengths to secure herself a rich husband.

Even more puzzling and infuriating was that for the

past month Nico had been unable to forget the night they had spent together. The sex had blown him away. *Dio*, she was hot. He had woken the next morning to the pleasurable ache of over-used muscles, and he had been hard again, his body clenching with anticipation of a leisurely morning ride with his very sexy ex.

Maybe it had been so good because their bodies had recognised each other's, and had known how to give and receive the most intense satisfaction. He had realised that one night with Sienna was not going to be enough. An affair was the obvious answer but she would have to understand that there were rules and boundaries. Commitment was not something he sought or could offer.

He had rolled over in the four-poster bed, impatient to pull her beneath him. But there had been an empty space on the mattress and a faint indentation on the pillow where her head had lain. The en-suite bathroom had been empty, and when he had walked back into the bedroom he'd discovered that her clothes had gone, except for a pair of lace knickers that he found on the floor when he picked up his shirt. Sienna, it seemed, had her own rules, and Nico had assured himself that he was relieved to avoid a tedious conversation about expectations that, in his experience, most women harboured.

Jerking his mind from his tangled thoughts, he followed her into the sitting room. She had placed the tea tray on a low table and was sitting on the sofa facing the two elderly ladies who occupied the armchairs. Nico lowered his tall frame onto the only vacant seat next to Sienna on the small sofa and felt her tense when his thigh inadvertently brushed against hers. The knowledge that he unsettled her was a salve to his wounded pride when he had woken after the most incredible night of his life and discovered that she had walked away from him *again*.

Sienna busied herself by pouring the tea. 'Did you enjoy Danny's wedding?' Iris asked her. 'I looked for you in the marquee after dinner, but I couldn't see you.'

'I had to leave the reception early to drive back to London.' A pink stain swept along Sienna's cheekbones and Nico was amused when she avoided his gaze.

'Actually I have something of yours that you left behind.' He slipped his hand into the pocket of his jacket, which was hanging over the arm of the sofa, and handed her a little cardboard box tied with ribbon. When she stared at it warily, he murmured, 'It's wedding cake. Every guest was given a slice. What were you expecting, *cara*?'

Her blush deepened and he knew she had feared that he had been about to return her underwear that she had left in his bedroom. It would certainly have added fuel to their grandmothers' curiosity. The memory of how he had ripped Sienna's panties off and made love to her, hard and fast, up against the bedroom door sent desire corkscrewing through him.

It was no use fighting his desire for Sienna. He must have her again, Nico decided. She had got under his skin and he wanted to ruffle her composure. She was so cool sitting there with a faint smile playing on her lips as if she was aware that he was painfully hard beneath his jeans. So she found it amusing that she tied him in knots, did she? But he could play games too. He shifted in his seat to try to alleviate the throb of his erection and stretched his arm along the back of the sofa, bringing his body into closer contact with hers.

The pulse beating frantically at the base of her throat betrayed her awareness of him and he fought an urge to press his lips to the fragile line of her collarbone. He was desperate to be alone with her, but he reminded himself that Sienna had come to Yorkshire to visit her grandmother and he would have to be patient.

Iris spoke again. 'I remember you said at the wedding that you needed to prepare for an important business meeting, Sienna. Was the meeting successful?'

Suppressing a sigh of relief, Sienna seized on the safe topic of work, hoping it would distract her from Nico's brooding presence beside her. She wished he would move his arm from the back of the sofa. The scent of his aftershave teased her senses. He was too big, too close, too overwhelming. He made her feel like a silly teenager again with a massive crush on him.

'Yes, I persuaded the managing director of a chain of beauty salons to stock my range of organic skincare products,' she told Nico's grandmother. She was proud of her business that she'd built into a thriving company from the early days when she'd come up with the idea of Fresh Faced and developed a few products, which she'd sold online.

'I was telling Iris how you use a special ingredient that comes from an African fruit in your skin creams,' Grandma Rose said.

'Marula oil is the base of most of the products we make at Fresh Faced. The Marula trees grow mainly in southern Africa and the yellow fruits they produce are about the size of a peach,' Sienna explained. 'The fruits have a large nut inside, and it is from the nut that the Marula oil is extracted.'

'I assume you import the oil into the UK, and then do you have a laboratory or workshop where your products are manufactured?' Nico asked.

'The workshop is in London—at Camden Lock by the Regent's Canal. I employ a small team of three people, and all the products are handmade using fresh, organic ingredients. The Marula oil we use is sourced from Tutjo. It's a small African state bordering Namibia and South Africa,' Sienna said when Iris looked puzzled.

'At Fresh Faced we work with a women's cooperative in Tutjo and abide by the Fairtrade standards. The women harvest the Marula fruit and using basic tools they remove the nut, crack it open and collect the kernels, which are then cold-pressed to produce Marula oil. There is no mass production, it's all done by the village women, and Fresh Faced donates twenty-five per cent of the company's profits to the cooperatives to support health and education for women and children in Tutjo.'

Iris shook her head. 'What a fascinating job you have, Sienna. I must admit that I have never heard of Marula fruit, or, for that matter, Tutjo. Have you visited there?'

'Several times, and I'm planning to go again later this year.'

Nico frowned. 'The King of Tutjo has ruled for decades, but I've heard reports of increased unrest in the country and a while ago there was a threat of a military coup.'

'I believe things have settled down now. My partner,

Brent, lives in South Africa and he follows the political situation in Tutjo closely. It's a poor country but the cooperatives offer women a chance to earn an income, which many of them use to pay for their children to be educated. I'm proud that Fresh Faced helps women to be independent. It's something I feel very strongly about.'

The conversation moved on to other subjects but Sienna continued to be fiercely aware of Nico. A few times she glanced at him and caught him looking at her intently as if he was trying to fathom her out. She was almost relieved when she noticed Rose's eyelids droop. Her grandmother was ninety-one and tired easily, although her mind was as sharp as ever.

'Nanna, I'm going to go and check into my hotel. I'll come back tomorrow and we'll go out somewhere for lunch.'

'Come and have lunch at Sethbury Hall,' Iris invited. 'I'll send Hobbs in the Bentley to collect both of you.'

'Oh, that's very kind of you, but we couldn't impose.' Sienna sent Nico a silent appeal for help. She was sure he did not want to extend the awkward afternoon over to the following day any more than she did.

'That's an excellent idea.' He ignored her frown and smiled at her grandmother. 'I expect you would like to see Much Matcham again, Rose. Shall we say lunch at one o'clock?'

The invitation did not mean that Nico wanted to see *her* again, Sienna told herself firmly after she had kissed her grandmother goodbye. Nico followed her into the lift, pushing his grandmother in her wheelchair. When they exited the care home a silver Bentley pulled up alongside them. 'Nico arranged for Hobbs to drive me home because he has some business in York,' Iris explained.

The chauffeur helped the elderly lady into the car and after it had driven away Sienna hooked the strap of her holdall over her shoulder. 'I guess I'll see you tomorrow,' she muttered, wondering what kind of business Nico planned to do. Perhaps he had a mistress in York and would spend the night with her. Jealousy jabbed like a sharp knife in her stomach.

Nico had donned a pair of designer sunglasses and he looked very Italian and sexier than ever. Years ago she had been infatuated with him but at eighteen she'd had no experience of the world, Sienna reminded herself. Now she understood that he belonged to an exclusive breed of powerful men who lived life by their own rules. Rich, handsome and charismatic, Nico could have any woman he wanted, but he refused to be owned and any woman who tried would end up with a broken heart as she had done.

'My car is parked over there.' He nodded to a silver sports car. 'I'll give you a lift to your hotel. Where are you staying?'

'The Arlington. It's only a five-minute walk from here. I always stay there when I visit Rose.'

He fell into step beside her as she walked along the street and lifted her bag from her shoulder before she could argue. 'I didn't want to say too much in front of your grandmother but you should think seriously about visiting Tutjo. The Foreign Office's advice is to only travel to that region of Africa if it is absolutely essential.'

'The advice was recently updated and currently the travel risk to Tutjo is low.'

'Even so, it would be better if you postponed your trip.'

She stopped walking and swung round to face him. 'I'm not your responsibility, Nico. If we hadn't met at Danny's wedding you wouldn't know anything about my travel plans.'

His eyes glittered. 'But we did meet and we ended up in bed. I haven't been able to forget that amazing night, *cara*, and I suspect the same is true for you.'

'You are so arrogant…' she began, her voice faltering when he lifted his hand and brushed his thumb pad lightly over her cheek.

'The dark circles beneath your eyes suggest that you haven't been sleeping well recently.'

'And naturally you assume that I've stayed awake every night thinking about you,' she said tartly. 'Maybe my restless nights were for another reason.'

His gaze cooled to the chilly blue of an Arctic sky. 'Were you thinking of your lover in South Africa? This Brent guy who you said is your partner,' he growled when she looked puzzled.

'Brent is my brother-in-law. He's Allie's husband and my business partner.' Sienna ran her fingers through her hair, pushing the long layered style back from her face. She wondered why Nico suddenly looked tense. 'After the divorce I went to stay with my sister and her husband at their home in South Africa. Brent is an environmental scientist and was already working with women's cooperatives in Tutjo. Allie had become interested in natural skincare lotions after she developed very bad eczema and she is allergic to most of the synthetic chemicals found in beauty products.

'I'd graduated with a degree in business and marketing before I left England, and I went on to qualify in organic skincare formulation. My sister has taken a step back from the business since she has become a mother.'

Sienna could not hide the tremor in her voice. She adored her two little nephews, but when she'd held them soon after they were born, her arms had ached to cradle her own child. 'Two years ago I moved back to the UK to establish a base for Fresh Faced in Europe.'

They had reached her hotel and she held out her hand to take her bag from Nico, but he kept hold of it and opened the door so that she could precede him into the lobby. 'What's it like here?' he said, casting a curious look around the smart, boutique hotel.

'It's not bad. It was originally a private Victorian house with rooms in the attic where the scullery maids slept. The hotel offers small, single rooms at a cheap rate—small being the key word,' she said ruefully. 'But I only need a bed to sleep in when I come to York to visit Grandma Rose.'

An unbidden memory popped into her mind of Nico's huge four-poster bed at Sethbury Hall. They had barely slept at all the night she had spent with him. His gaze sharpened on her flushed face and he seemed to have the ability to read her thoughts. 'Why did you leave without waking me?' he asked abruptly.

She shrugged. 'I didn't want a post-mortem any more than I imagine you did. What happened was crazy but it was just sexual chemistry.' That was what she had repeatedly told herself for the past month. 'It seemed like a good idea to forget it ever happened.'

'But you haven't succeeded in forgetting the night we spent together.'

'Yes, I have,' she snapped, riled by his superior tone.

'Just as you obviously haven't given me another thought.' His failure to phone her even just once to check that she had got back to London safely had hurt, dammit.

'If that was the case I wouldn't have cut short a business trip to Brussels so that I could bring Iris to have tea with your grandmother, when I heard that you would be visiting Rose this weekend,' he said drily.

Did he mean it? She did not know how to respond, and luckily the receptionist at the desk became free after she had finished dealing with another guest. Sienna completed the check-in procedure and when she looked round she discovered that Nico had gone. He had left her holdall on the floor by her feet. There was just lunch tomorrow to get through and then she would never have to see him again, she consoled herself as she walked over to the lift. The budget-rate rooms were on the fifth floor and she did not intend to take the stairs.

'Miss Fisher.' Sienna turned her head and saw the receptionist hurrying towards her. 'I'm so sorry, I allocated you the wrong room. You will be staying in the Executive Suite on the first floor.'

'I think there must be a mistake,' Sienna began.

The receptionist looked flustered. 'Um…it's a free upgrade to thank you for being a loyal guest.'

Bemused, Sienna allowed the porter who had appeared at her side to carry her holdall and when the lift stopped at the first floor she followed him along the corridor. He opened a door and ushered her into the suite. 'If you require anything, please dial two on the phone for room service.'

The upgraded room was bound to be a mistake, she thought as she looked around the charming open-plan

suite. Something as nice as this did not happen to her.
For years she'd survived on a shoestring until her skincare business had taken off, and although she now
earned a reasonable salary, she couldn't justify paying
for a luxurious suite.

Next to the bed there was an enormous, free-stand-
ing bath with views out of the window over the river.
The idea of a long soak to ease the tension in her neck
and shoulders was inviting. She turned on the taps and
added a liberal splash of rose-scented bubble bath from
the Fresh Faced range of travel-size toiletries that she
had brought with her. It seemed rather decadent to take
a bath in the afternoon, she thought guiltily as she undressed and piled her hair on top of her head, securing
it with a couple of pins. Usually she would be hard at
work—even at weekends.

Lying back in the foamy water, she wondered if she
could persuade the hotel manager to stock some of her
company's products. Business was never far from Sienna's mind, and being financially independent was vital
to her. When she was growing up her father had been
a violent bully, but her mother had been trapped in the
marriage because she did not have any qualifications
or career prospects. Sienna had vowed never to allow
any man to have power over her, but her determination
to go to university had been another source of tension
between her and Nico, she remembered.

She had started studying for a business degree soon
after they had met. When she'd discovered that she was
pregnant and Nico asked her to marry him, she had
hoped to combine her studies with motherhood. But
fate had delivered a cruel blow and after the miscarriage she had focused on gaining her degree to take her

mind off the monthly disappointment when she failed to fall pregnant again.

With a sigh, Sienna sank deeper into the scented bubbles and let her mind drift back to the past. Nico had spent a lot of time in Italy after his father had died and he had taken over as CEO of De Conti Leisure. He'd asked her to go to Verona with him but she had wanted to remain in England to finish her degree. She had also wanted to stay close to her mother. Lynn Fisher had led a miserable life with her drunkard husband and had relied on Sienna after her older sister Allie had moved to South Africa.

Sienna had resented Nico's frequent trips to Italy and blamed his absences for her failure to conceive another baby. The truth was that they had married too young, she thought ruefully. Neither of them had been prepared to make compromises that might have given their relationship a chance.

A knock on the door of the suite pulled her mind back to the present and she jolted upright so that water sloshed over the sides of the bath when a voice called out, 'Room service.' She was startled when the door opened and hastily sank beneath the bubbles, aware that the bath was visible from the doorway.

'Go away. I didn't order anything.'

Her heart missed a beat when Nico strolled in, carrying a tray with a bottle of champagne and two glasses. The gleam of amusement in his eyes turned to something hotter and hungrier as he stared at her naked shoulders above the foam.

CHAPTER FIVE

IN AN INSTANT Sienna went from relaxed to fiercely aware of Nico and of her femininity. 'Did you arrange for my room to be upgraded?' she asked stiffly.

His mouth crooked in a sexy smile that stole her breath. 'I couldn't allow you stay in the attic where the scullery maids used to sleep.'

'It's no concern of yours where I sleep.' She could not take her eyes off him when he strolled across the room and put the tray of champagne down on a bedside table. Ten years ago she had been the modern equivalent of a scullery maid—a lowly cleaner at Sethbury Hall when Nico, the handsome heir to his family's ancestral home and a future viscount, had swept her off her feet. She had been desperately in love with him but he had not returned her love.

She opened her mouth to tell him to leave but the words stuck in her throat. There was a soft 'pop' of a cork as he opened the champagne. 'What shall we drink to?' he said when he had filled the two flutes and handed one of them to her. 'Old friendships, or new beginnings?'

'We were never friends, not really. On our wedding day we were virtually strangers.' Sienna took a sip of her champagne before she placed the glass on the windowsill. 'And this is not a new beginning.'

Nico's eyes burned into hers. 'What is it, then?'

It was madness, Sienna told herself. But her internal voice of caution was drowned out by the thunderous beat of her heart as she rested her hands on the edges of the roll-top bath and stood up. Water streamed down her body and the silken glide of it felt sensuous on her skin as each one of her nerve endings quivered with a need that was primitive and urgent. A woman calling to her man.

She removed the pins from her hair and tossed her head so that her hair swirled around her shoulders. 'It's just sex, isn't it, Nico.' It was a statement rather than a question. She was no longer a teenager with a head full of dreams. She understood that the emotion blazing in his blue eyes was lust, not love, and with that knowledge came power and freedom to do whatever she wanted to do.

What she wanted was Nico.

He had gone very still when she'd risen, naked and proud, from the bathwater. A nerve flickered in his cheek and he swallowed his champagne in a couple of gulps before placing the glass back on the tray.

'Right now, I don't give a damn what it is,' he growled. 'All I can think about is being inside you.' He ignored the towel she had draped over the towel stand and scooped her wet body into his arms, lowering his head to capture her mouth in a fierce kiss that was both a punishment and a promise.

It was even better than before, when they had spent the night together at Sethbury Hall after his brother's wedding. Maybe it was because she had given up trying to fight her desire for Nico and accepted that she was a lost cause, Sienna thought.

He kissed her again as he laid her on the bed, and when he straddled her, his knees on either side of her body, she stopped thinking altogether. She wanted to make love with him, although she was aware that love—that dangerously beguiling emotion—was not involved.

'I've made your shirt wet,' she murmured.

'You had better take it off, then.' His voice was very deep, and when he sat back on his haunches and stared down at her, the hard glitter in his eyes sent a shiver of excitement through her. Impatient to get her hands on his body, she gripped the hem of his polo shirt and pulled it up. He helped her tug it over his head and groaned when she skimmed her fingertips over his chest, traced the ridges of his impressive abdominal muscles and continued down to unbuckle the belt on his jeans. She did not hesitate or pretend to be coy. She wanted him inside her, *now*.

But Nico would not be rushed and took his time to explore every dip and curve on her body with his mouth. He kissed her throat and nuzzled the sensitive place behind her ear, returning between each caress to claim her lips with fierce passion and an underlying tenderness that tugged on her foolish heart. His foreplay was unhurried and exquisitely sensual. He played her body like a master musician and wrung husky moans of pleasure from her when at last, *at last* he kissed her breasts and sucked one nipple and then the other until both tips were hard and rosy red.

He stood up and stripped off the rest of his clothes before he stretched out beside her on the bed. Propping himself up on one elbow, he traced a lazy path with his finger down her body, paused to explore the indent of her navel before moving lower to the neat triangle of curls at the junction of her thighs. 'You are so beautiful.' His voice was soft, but when he slipped his hand between her legs and discovered the slick heat of her arousal, he smiled and murmured, 'You *are* eager, *cara.*'

His satisfied tone sent a little chill through Sienna. Nico was used to women falling at his feet—or rather into his bed—and although his eyes blazed with desire, something about his cool smile warned her to guard herself against his charisma.

She slid her hand down to clasp his powerful erection. 'So are you.' His breath hissed between his teeth when she tightened her fingers around his shaft. Taking advantage of his preoccupation, she moved suddenly and reversed their positions so that he was flat on his back and she was on top of him. She saw a flicker of surprise in his eyes and sensed that he was uncomfortable with the idea of relinquishing control.

'Kiss me,' he ordered, regarding her from between his half-closed eyelids. His head was thrown back against the pillows and he reminded her of an indolent sultan choosing a favourite concubine to pleasure him.

Once she would have covered him in kisses and been desperate to please him. She had been needy and immature, but thank goodness she had grown up, Sienna thought. At eighteen she had been too young and unsure of herself to get married. She had put Nico on a pedestal but he had his faults just as everyone did, and like most powerful men he was determined to take charge of every situation.

'Oh, I'll kiss you,' she murmured. But she evaded his hand when he tried to catch hold of a lock of her hair to pull her mouth down to his. She wriggled down his body, making him groan when she rubbed the tips of her breasts over his chest. He swore as she moved lower still and he realised what she intended to do.

'Not this time, *cara*. I'm too close to the edge,' he said harshly. She ignored him and ran her tongue along the length of his erection before she took the swollen tip into her mouth. He inhaled sharply. 'Witch.' He tried to roll her beneath him but she laughed and pushed him back against the pillows.

'You asked me to kiss you but you didn't specify where,' she teased him. 'You need to learn to let go of your iron self-control, Nico.'

'Are you going to teach me how?' he asked drily, but he could not disguise the thickness in his voice or the fierce glitter in his eyes.

'Why don't we find out?' she murmured before she put her mouth on him.

Sienna felt a shudder run through his big, taut body, and realised that she was shaking too. It seemed ridiculous that at the age of twenty-nine she had never done this before. During their marriage Nico had always taken the lead and ensured that sex was wonderfully fulfilling for her. He had built her up and taken her apart until she'd sobbed his name in the shattering ecstasy of every orgasm he gave her. Only when she'd been utterly wrung out had he taken his own pleasure, but his self-control had never cracked.

Once she had been a slave to her need for him, she thought ruefully. But now the harsh sound he made when she flicked her tongue across the tip of his manhood filled her with a heady sense of self-confidence. She would play the dominant role and bring Nico to his knees.

Shaking her hair back over her shoulders, she caressed his steel-hard length with her hands and mouth, ignoring his savage commands to stop what she was doing before it was too late.

Sienna hadn't expected that pleasuring him would be such a turn-on, and she concentrated on her task, encouraged by the laboured sound of his breathing. He stretched his arms out on either side of him and curled his fingers into the sheet as if to anchor himself to the bed. It gave her a thrill to know that this enigmatic man was at her mercy.

'*Tesoro.*' His voice was low and strained. He sank his fingers into her hair but did not attempt to pull her away from him. She continued to use her mouth on him and felt him start to shake. The explosion as he came was spectacular. He gave a shout that sounded as though it had been torn from his throat. Every muscle on his body tensed and he let out a groan that resonated deep inside Sienna's chest.

She lifted her head and silently told herself not to be stupid when she felt heat spread across her cheeks as she met Nico's gaze. She wished she knew what he was thinking but his handsome face gave nothing away.

'Why do I have the idea that you were proving a point?' he murmured.

Feeling oddly vulnerable, she inched across to the edge of the bed, but before she could stand up he snaked an arm around her waist. 'You're not thinking of running out on me again, are you, *piccola*?'

His voice was like rough velvet and she steeled herself against the lure of his husky endearment. In the early days of their marriage Nico had often called her 'little one'. She had been so happy then; married to the man she adored and expecting his baby. But she had been heartbroken when she'd miscarried their son and, engulfed in grief, she had sensed a distance between her and Nico, which had seemed to prove that the rumours in Much Matcham had been right and he had only married her because she had been pregnant.

Sienna closed the door on painful memories of the past. 'I want some champagne.' She had left her drink on the windowsill. Nico picked up his glass from the bedside table and handed it to her. She took a few sips before she returned the glass to him and gasped when he poured the remainder of the champagne over her breasts.

The cold liquid had a predictable effect on her nipples and she did not need to glance down to know that they were as hard as pebbles. She felt a sharp tug of anticipation shoot down to her pelvis when he closed his mouth around one taut peak and sucked hard. Before she could blink, she found herself flat on her back. Nico pinned her wrists above her head with one of his hands and with his other he pushed her legs apart and stroked his fingers over her opening.

'You didn't think I would allow you to escape retribution, did you, *cara*?' he drawled. The gleam of amusement in his eyes darkened to desire as he settled himself between her thighs, bent his head and licked his way into her.

Nico had planned to take Sienna to dinner, but it was late in the evening when he reluctantly lifted himself off her after they had made love for a third, or maybe fourth time—he'd lost count. He called room service and ordered a meal to be sent up to the suite, and then he refilled the bath and joined her in the foamy water while they finished off the bottle of champagne.

'Why didn't you call me after Danny's wedding?' she asked him later, while they ate parmesan risotto with roasted shrimps.

Nico studied her across the table. She had pulled on a white towelling robe when she'd stepped out of the bath and he missed the sight of her naked body as much as he missed the feel of her soft limbs spread beneath him. She was so beautiful. When she ran a hand carelessly through her burgundy silk hair, he felt hunger gnaw in the pit of his stomach that food could not assuage.

Dio, when she'd pleasured him with her mouth he'd thought he had died and gone to heaven. He couldn't remember the last time he had lost control like that. Maybe never. He shoved away the idea that sex with his ex-wife had been more intense than it had with any of the women he'd slept with since their divorce. His relationships were always brief, sex-without-strings affairs, and he made it clear from the outset that commitment was not on the cards.

There had not been accusation in Sienna's voice, merely a mild curiosity. She was different from the girl he had married a decade ago, but how different?

He shrugged. 'I didn't want you to fall in love with me, or hope that I might fall in love with you.'

She stared at him and then said drily, 'It's lucky you arranged for my room to be upgraded to the biggest suite in the hotel. Your swollen head wouldn't fit into anywhere smaller.'

So—no pout, or tantrum, or eyes filling with tears. Nico's lips twitched at her comment and he slowly relaxed. He hated tears especially. His earliest boyhood memories were of his mother crying. 'Your father doesn't love me,' she had told him when he'd climbed onto her bed and patted her heaving shoulders, trying to comfort her. 'How can Franco treat me like this? My life is not worth living now he has broken my heart,' Jacqueline had sobbed. 'And all for a cheap little tart half his age.'

Worse than the crying had been the drug overdoses, Nico thought grimly. He had been older by then. Only eleven or twelve, but old enough to understand that his mother had attempted to take her own life by swallowing a handful of sleeping pills. The first incident had happened after his parents had officially separated and his father moved to Paris to live with his French mistress. The next time his mother had tried to kill herself had been the day after Franco De Conti had married an American actress.

Nico remembered his grandparents' distress when their only daughter had been in intensive care. He had dreaded that his mother might die, but he'd had to be strong for Danny, and he'd hidden his emotions—a trait that he had carried into adulthood. He was the oldest, and it had been his responsibility to protect his younger brother from the drama and acrimony of their parents' hellish marriage.

'Why do you make Mama unhappy?' Nico had once asked his father.

Franco had given an eloquent shrug of his shoulders. Women did not understand that it was unnatural for a man to remain faithful to one woman, he had advised his teenage son. Nico would learn that women had impossible expectations.

His father had been right. By the time Nico had developed from a boy to a young man, he'd discovered that women were fascinated with him and he had not had to try very hard to persuade them to fall into his bed. Unfortunately many of them had also fallen in love with him and expected him to return their feelings. When he had met Sienna ten years ago, their sexual chemistry had blazed out of control before he'd had a chance to establish the rules of their relationship. Her pregnancy had catapulted him into a marriage he had not been ready for.

Sienna had said that they were strangers on their wedding day and in many ways it was true, he acknowledged. They had both kept secrets, but Nico had been aware that she was in love with him and he had been afraid that he would hurt her as his father had so often hurt his mother.

'There's no need to get worked up, Nico.' Sienna's voice pulled him back to the present. 'You are the last man on the planet I'd fall in love with.'

The amusement in her tone rankled. Naturally he was relieved by her assurance, but 'worked up'? Had she been making a subtle reference to the way he'd lost control so spectacularly when she had given him a blow job?

Nico's jaw tightened. Inexplicably he was tempted to ask her why she was so certain she wouldn't fall for him. He hadn't been *that* bad a husband. When Sienna had been his wife, he had bought her beautiful clothes

and jewellery and she had lived in luxurious surroundings at Sethbury Hall.

'Would you like coffee?' he asked when they had
both finished eating. She nodded and he carried the
tray containing a cafetière over to the low table in front
of the sofa. Sienna joined him, curling up on the sofa
and tucking her feet beneath her. Nico poured the coffee and handed her a cup.

'I shouldn't have caffeine this late. I'll be awake all
night,' she said ruefully.

'That's the idea, *cara*,' he drawled. 'Why do you
think the Italians invented coffee?'

She laughed, and the husky sound fanned the flames
of Nico's desire once more. 'You were on my mind a
lot over the past month,' he admitted. If he was honest he had expected her to contact him. She knew the
phone number for Sethbury Hall, and he had told his
housekeeper to give Sienna Fisher his mobile number
if she called. But she hadn't. 'Did you think about me?'

She shrugged. 'I've been very busy lately.'

Her cool tone irked him, but the soft colour that
touched her cheekbones was an indication that her answer hadn't been completely honest. He stretched out
his hand and idly wound a lock of her hair around his
finger. 'You were busy at work?'

'Mmm.'

Why was she avoiding his gaze? Did she have a
lover in London who kept her busy? Nico stiffened as
the unwelcome thought slid into his mind. It was obvious from the way she became a wildcat when they
made love that she was sexually experienced. *Dio*,
maybe she had gifted the same pleasure she'd given
him with her mouth and wicked tongue to a boyfriend.

Acid burned a corrosive path down to the pit of his stomach. Indigestion, he told himself. It was certainly not jealousy.

'After we divorced I thought you might have remarried and had a family.' He kept his tone casual.

She gave another laugh but this time it sounded brittle and faintly bitter. 'I'm sure you've heard the saying once bitten, twice shy. I've seen enough bad marriages, including my parents' travesty of a marriage, to put me off wanting to go down that road again. As for having a family of my own, I've had to come to terms with my inability to have a child.'

The slight unsteadiness of her voice suggested to Nico that she wasn't being entirely truthful. He frowned. 'You sound as though you blame yourself because we couldn't have a baby. But you shouldn't,' he said shortly.

'We split up before we were due to start tests to investigate why I couldn't conceive, but I think it could be a genetic problem. Grandma Rose told me that after she had my dad, she hoped to have more children, but she couldn't fall pregnant again.'

Surely Sienna must have realised that the problems they had experienced were nothing to do with her, Nico brooded. It did not take a science degree to work out that she had fallen pregnant by his brother but she hadn't conceived a child with him even though they had tried for a year. He forced himself to concentrate when she spoke again.

'I guess you could say that my business is my baby substitute,' she said wryly. 'Fresh Faced was my idea, and it's been a hard slog to break into the skincare market, which is already crowded. But I believe absolutely in the ethos of the company and what we are trying to achieve. Working with the women's cooperatives in Tutjo to develop wonderful products that are kind to humans and the environment has taken over my life for the past few years. The only downside is that I haven't had much time for relationships.'

'But you have had other lovers?' Of course she had, Nico told himself. Sienna was a beautiful and highly sensual woman. He shouldn't give a damn that she must have shared her exquisite body with other men. He *didn't* give a damn. 'Out of interest, how many?' he heard himself ask.

She gave him a cool smile but he felt tension in the fine bones of her shoulders when he moved his hand up to cup her nape. 'Not as many as you, I'm sure,' she said lightly. 'Why do you care, Nico?'

'I don't,' he lied. 'I merely wanted to make sure that I'm not stepping on another man's toes.' At her frown, he elaborated. 'You might have a boyfriend in London.'

'I don't.' Her gaze turned stormy. 'If I did I wouldn't have slept with you. But now that you have mentioned the subject, are you currently having sex with anyone?'

'Not currently,' he murmured, his hands untying the belt of her robe. He watched her grey eyes darken, the pupils dilating when he bared her breasts and rubbed his thumb pads over her nipples, making them swell and harden. 'Ask me again in twenty seconds from now and I can guarantee my answer will be different,' he whispered against her mouth. She made a muffled sound that might have been a protest, but her lips parted beneath his and Nico's heart slammed into his ribs as the magic started all over again.

A long time later, after Sienna had fallen asleep

and Nico lay beside her while his heart rate gradually returned to normal, he acknowledged that having sex with her again had not satisfied his hunger for her. She was like a narcotic in his blood and he needed her.

The thought made him frown. Of course he wasn't addicted to Sienna. He did not need any woman, and certainly not his traitorous ex-wife. But there was no reason why he shouldn't enjoy her mind-blowing sensuality for a few more nights, until what was new and exciting became familiar and mundane, as his affairs invariably did. And then he would have no problem walking away from Sienna, he assured himself.

Lunch at Sethbury Hall the next day turned out not to be the ordeal that Sienna had dreaded. By tacit consent she and Nico made no reference to the fact that they had spent the previous night together. She certainly didn't want Rose or Iris to think that a reunion between them was likely. Which of course it wasn't, she reminded herself. At the most, she and Nico would have an affair that they both knew from the start would end. He was gorgeous, but she would not be foolish enough to fall in love with him again.

Although she'd had to remind herself to guard her heart against him when he had woken her in the morning with a kiss that had quickly become a ravishment of her senses. He had made love to her with such passion, coupled with an aching tenderness that could have tricked her into believing that he had missed her as much as she had missed him for the last eight years.

They did not get up until late morning, and he gave her another lingering kiss before he finally departed from the hotel suite. Sienna raced into the shower before donning a green silk wrap dress that comple-mented the dark red of her hair.

'You look as bright as a button,' her grandmother commented when they were travelling in the chauf-feur-driven Bentley that had come to collect them from York. 'Did you sleep well?'

Luckily they arrived at Sethbury Hall and Sienna mumbled a reply, trying to hide the blush that she could feel spreading across her face when Nico came down the front steps to meet them. He was wearing close-fitting black trousers and a black shirt with the sleeves rolled up to his elbows. The gold watch glint-ing on his wrist nestled among the black hairs that covered his tanned forearms. Sienna immediately vi-sualised the whorls of black hair that grew thickly on his chest.

'Rose, welcome to Sethbury Hall,' he greeted her grandmother, before he turned his attention to her. 'It's good to see you again, Sienna.' He captured her hand and lifted it up to his mouth, brushing his lips over her knuckles and sending a sizzle of electricity down to her toes. 'You look lovely. I trust you slept well.'

'Everyone is obsessed with how I slept,' she said lightly. Inside, she was furious with herself for blush-ing again.

'I admit I'm obsessed with you,' Nico murmured in a soft voice. Sienna hoped her grandmother did not no-tice her scarlet cheeks when she took Rose's arm and helped her climb the steps up to the house.

During lunch she focused her attention on the two elderly ladies. She had become fond of Iris when she had lived at Sethbury Hall as Nico's wife and she adored her grandmother, whose husband and son had both been heavy drinkers. Despite the many difficulties in her life, Grandma Rose was one of the most resilient women Sienna had ever met.

'What time is your train?' Nico asked later when he found her outside on the terrace. Despite her best efforts to appear composed during lunch, Sienna had been agonisingly aware of him sitting next to her, and she had barely eaten anything, which had prompted her grandmother to ask if she was feeling unwell. In fact she had felt nauseous for the last couple of days, but she had put it down to the current heatwave in what was being called one of England's hottest summers.

'I don't have a return ticket,' she told him. 'I'd planned to catch a flight from Leeds airport to France later today and spend tomorrow researching possible sites for a new workshop for Fresh Faced in Paris, before a business meeting on Monday morning. But the meeting has been cancelled so I'll postpone my research and aim to catch the four o'clock train back to London.'

She glanced at him and flushed when her gaze crashed into his. Memories of their wild passion the previous night flooded her mind, and the gleam in his eyes warned her that he could read her thoughts. She cleared her throat. 'It was nice to meet you this weekend.'

His brows lifted. 'Nice? I am mortified, *cara*.'

Oh, hell. The way his mouth crooked at the corners when he smiled made her melt. 'Stop fishing for compliments,' she told him, drowning in the deep blue pools of his eyes. He was utterly irresistible, she thought with a flash of despair.

'Come to Italy with me.'

She stared at him, her heart thudding painfully hard. 'Why?'

'I'm hosting a cocktail party at the villa at Lake Garda this evening for my senior executive team. The party will only be for a few hours,' he murmured, moving closer and winding a lock of her hair around his finger. 'The truth, *cara*, is that I will spend every minute of those hours trying to curb my impatience to take you to bed.'

His face was so close to hers that she felt his warm breath brush across her lips. The scent of his aftershave tantalised Sienna's senses and the undisguised hunger in his eyes sent a shudder of longing through her. She lifted her hand to his chest, wishing she could rip off his shirt and touch his satiny skin beneath it. She would be crazy to agree to go to Italy with him.

'I don't have anything with me to wear to a party,' she said distractedly, willing him to lower his mouth a few more centimetres so that he could kiss her.

'Tell me your dress size and I'll arrange for an evening gown to be delivered to the villa.' Nico's voice deepened to a sexy drawl that sent a wave of anticipation across Sienna's skin. 'You won't need any other clothes because, aside from the party, I plan for you to be naked for the rest of the weekend.'

Of course she was going to refuse to go with him. 'I can only stay for one night,' Sienna heard herself say.

His wicked grin dismantled the last of her defences. 'In that case we had better make it a night to remember. I hope you don't expect to get any sleep.' Nico dipped his head and crushed her lips beneath his, kissing her with a devastating sensuality that left her trembling.

She gave a moan of disappointment when he set her away from him.

'Rose and Iris are sitting in the orangery and might see us. We don't want them to think we are having a romance,' he said coolly.

His words were a reminder that she should not have any illusions about why he had invited her to his home in Italy, Sienna acknowledged. The sexual chemistry between them was explosive, but it would burn out and she was confident that she would walk away from him with her heart intact.

CHAPTER SIX

THEY FLEW TO Italy on Nico's private jet and a chauffeured limousine was waiting at the airport to take them to the villa. Sienna remembered that when she had been Nico's wife she'd never grown used to her new, luxurious lifestyle.

Her lack of self-assurance had meant that she did not fit in with his wealthy social circle, and she'd been conscious of the rumours that she had married him for his money. Nothing could have been further from the truth. He had been her first love—her only love so far, she admitted wryly. As a teenager, she had been infatuated with him, and, caught up in the intensity of her own emotions, she had naively assumed that he felt the same way about her.

With a soft sigh, she turned her head and looked at Villa Lionard as it came into view. The De Conti's magnificent mansion, which Nico had inherited when his father died, stood on a peninsula on the shores of Lake Garda. The house was set in exquisitely landscaped grounds with uninterrupted views over the lake to the mountains beyond.

It was early evening and the sun was just lowering in the sky, bathing the lake in a golden light and dancing across the villa's large swimming pool. The mingled scents of lemon and olive groves that grew on either side of the driveway drifted in through the car's open windows. Nico was sitting beside Sienna and she felt him relax when the car stopped in front of the house. He had once told her that he regarded Villa Lionard as his true home. But although she could appreciate the beauty of the villa she had never felt that she belonged here, and she was beginning to question whether it had been a good idea to come back to the house that held painful memories for her.

They had spent their last Christmas together at the villa. It had been bitterly cold and the snow-covered mountains surrounding the lake had looked beautiful, but Sienna had barely noticed the scenery. She'd been desperately unhappy and her failure to fall pregnant again had put a strain on their marriage. A distance had grown between her and Nico, and he had seemed to withdraw from her even more after he'd visited his brother Danny in London, although he had denied that anything was wrong when she'd asked him.

She had hoped they could resolve their issues while they were in Italy, but, with the exception of Christmas Day, Nico had gone to his office in Verona every day and had often spent the night at his apartment in the city instead of driving back to the villa. He'd made the excuse of not wanting to drive in the snow, but she had been torn apart by jealousy, convinced that he was having an affair with his glamorous personal assistant, Rafaela Ferrante.

There was no point dredging up the past, Sienna told herself when Nico ushered her into the villa. She was a different person from the girl with a head full of dreams she had been years ago. He drew her into his arms and kissed her with a thoroughness that stirred the embers of her desire to fierce flames and drove every other thought from her mind except for her longing for him to take her to bed.

'I have a couple of calls to make,' he said when he finally stepped away from her, breathing hard. 'The maid will show you the dresses I ordered from a designer in Verona. I wasn't sure what style you would like, but my personal favourite is the black velvet.'

Nico had good taste, Sienna decided later, when she'd followed the maid into the dressing room of the master suite where a selection of dresses was hanging on a rail. The black velvet gown emphasised her narrow waist and the daringly low-cut neckline framed the creamy upper slopes of her breasts. Her pulse quickened as she wondered how he would react when he discovered that she was wearing the sheer stockings that had been left for her together with exquisite black lace underwear. A pair of high-heeled silver sandals gave her an extra four inches of height, and a silver clutch bag was the perfect accessory.

She had caught her hair up in a loose chignon and was wearing more make-up than usual. The dress was sexy yet sophisticated; the kind of dress a rich man's mistress would wear. Was that why Nico had picked it for her? She smoothed her hand over the curve of her hip, enjoying the feel of the sensuous material beneath her fingertips as she imagined Nico doing the same thing. She felt wickedly decadent. He wanted a mistress and she was happy to fulfil the role without hope or expectation that their relationship would develop outside the bedroom, she assured herself.

The hairs on the back of her neck prickled and she turned her head to see Nico enter the suite. He looked mouth-watering in a black tuxedo and snowy white shirt that contrasted with his olive-gold skin. When he strode into the dressing room he stopped abruptly and his blue eyes blazed with a sultry heat that caused Sienna's heart to skip a beat.

'You look incredible.' He slipped an arm around her waist and dipped his head to claim her mouth in a hungry kiss. Something feral tightened his features when she responded to him with an eagerness she did not try to hide. 'Have pity on me, *cara mia*,' he said thickly. 'I'm going to spend the evening fantasising about taking your dress off.'

The party was in the villa's huge reception room. Nico introduced Sienna to the other guests and she was pleased by how much Italian she recalled from the lessons she had taken during her marriage. They had planned to bring up their baby to be bilingual, and she felt a familiar ache in her heart as she thought of her tiny son who had never lived.

'*Buonasera*, Sienna. I did not know that you would be here tonight.'

Sienna turned away from the window where she had been watching the moon glinting on the lake and her heart gave a jolt as she met the cool stare of Rafaela Ferrante. The Italian woman looked elegant in a white halter-neck dress, with her black hair falling in glossy waves around her shoulders.

'Rafaela. I wasn't expecting to see you, either. Are you still Nico's personal assistant?'

'Yes, but not for much longer.' Rafaela smiled. 'Nico has known for a long time what I want, and now at last my hopes are about to come true. I must go and speak with him. Excuse me, *per favore*.'

Sienna stared after Nico's PA, shaken by the realisation that Rafaela had played an important role in his life for the past eight years. She watched Nico greet Rafaela with a kiss on each cheek. It was a common continental greeting, but the intimacy evident between them evoked an acid burn in the pit of Sienna's stomach when the pair moved away to a quiet corner of the room, their dark heads close together while they were deep in conversation.

She was still wondering what Rafaela had meant when Nico returned to her a while later. 'Why are you frowning, *cara*?' he murmured as he swept her into his arms and onto the dance floor. She caught her breath when he pulled her close to him, helping to allay her old insecurities about his relationship with his beautiful secretary.

'I was wondering when the party will finish,' she said, skimming her hand over his shirt front and dragging her nails across one hard male nipple.

He swore and dropped his hand from her waist to the base of her spine, bringing her pelvis into sizzling contact with his. 'Soon, if there is a god,' he growled. 'See what you do to me, *bellissima*.'

'I can feel what I do to you,' she teased, moving her hips sinuously against him. She had never thought of herself as a seductress before, but Nico made her feel wild and free and very sexy.

'You know I will have to punish you later,' he warned, the gleam in his eyes sending a thrill of anticipation through her. He kept to his word when the last guests departed and he scooped her into his arms and carried her up to his bedroom. He set her down on her feet and unhooked her arms from around his neck. 'I am going to undress you,' he told her, his gravelly voice scraping across her nerve-endings, 'but you are not allowed to touch me until I say so.'

She pouted at him but could not restrain a shiver of excitement when he stood behind her and ran the zip of her dress down her spine. He tugged the bodice down to her waist and slid his arms around her, cupping her bare breasts in his palms and rubbing her taut nipples between his fingers until she whimpered with pleasure. Sienna leaned back against his chest, watching their twin reflections in the mirror as Nico pressed his mouth to her white throat, trailed his lips up to her earlobe and then moved down to feather kisses along her collarbone.

'You are so goddamned beautiful,' he said in a harsh voice, as if he was struggling for control. In the mirror she saw his skin tighten over his sharp cheekbones. He reminded her of a wolf, dark and dangerous, and he had very sharp teeth, she discovered, catching her breath when he bit her neck.

He stripped the velvet dress from her body and tugged her lacy thong down her legs. But he left her stockings on when he pushed her down on the bed and put his mouth between her thighs to bestow an intimate caress with his wickedly inventive tongue that brought her to a shattering orgasm.

'You can touch me now,' he said, laughing at her eagerness as she tore at his shirt, sending buttons flying in her feverish haste to get her hands on his bare skin. She dealt with his trousers and boxers with the same urgency before she pushed him down on the mattress and straddled him. A grin lit his handsome face and made him even more gorgeous. 'You're amazing, *gattina*. Just watch what you are doing with your sharp, kitten claws.'

In a swift movement he reversed their positions and knelt over her, nudging her legs apart with his knee before he entered her with a deep thrust that drove the breath from her body. He made love to her again and again until they were both finally sated, and Sienna fell asleep with Nico's arms around her.

He was still holding her when she woke first the next morning. She lay quite still and studied him. While he slept his chiselled features were softer and reminded her poignantly of the boyishly handsome Nico she had married. A decade on, his face was all hard angles and planes, and his body was a powerhouse of taut muscles. She wondered how many lovers he'd had since they had divorced. Whatever the tally, it was a hundred per cent more than she'd had, but she certainly would not admit that to him.

With a soft sigh she started to ease away from him, but his arms tightened around her, and her heart missed a beat when she lifted her eyes to his face and found him watching her from beneath his thick black lashes. He gave her a lazy smile. 'Why the sigh, *cara*?'

'I'm hungry.' It was partly the truth, she acknowledged when her stomach growled. Thankfully the nauseous feeling she'd had for the past few mornings had gone and she put it down to a mild stomach upset.

'I may be able to do something about that,' Nico drawled, throwing back the sheet to reveal his erection. He took her again with such mind-blowing sensuality that she wondered how she could possibly bring herself to leave him and go home. But she was due to leave in a few hours. Nico had arranged for her to be flown back to London on his private jet later in the afternoon and so far he hadn't mentioned a date in the future when they might meet again.

From the en-suite bathroom she heard the shower running, and molten warmth pooled between her legs as she pictured him standing beneath the spray, the water streaming over his muscular body. She was turning into a sex maniac, Sienna thought ruefully. More worrying was her emotional response to him. She would be a fool to fall in love with him, but when had love ever been sensible?

Her phone rang and, half asleep, she stretched out her hand to pick it up from the bedside table. But it was Nico's phone that was ringing and she realised they had the same ringtone as she stared at Rafaela's name on the screen before the phone went silent. Wide awake now, she rolled onto her back and frowned at the ceiling.

Why was Rafaela calling Nico so early? Could a work-related issue be so urgent that his PA needed to disturb him on a Sunday morning? She remembered Rafaela's curious statement at the party that her hopes were about to come true, and how Nico had spent ages talking to her. It was often said that the relationship between a boss and his personal assistant was as close as that between a husband and wife. That had been true in her own marriage, Sienna thought bleakly.

'You had a missed call,' she told Nico when he strolled out of the en-suite bathroom. He was wearing a towel tied around his hips and droplets of water glistened in his chest hair. He leaned over the bed and dropped a light kiss on her mouth. Before he could move away, she stroked her hand over his taut abdomen and slid her fingers beneath the edge of the towel. A part of her hated herself for wanting to keep his attention on her rather than on his phone.

'You are insatiable, *cara*,' he teased. He picked up his phone, glanced at the screen and straightened up. 'The household staff have Sundays off, so I'll go and make some coffee.'

When he walked out of the bedroom, Sienna heard his voice, low and intimate, as he headed along the corridor towards the stairs. Knowing that he was talking to Rafaela evoked a sharp stab of jealousy in her heart. She felt marginally better after she'd showered and dressed in her jeans and a silky top. Before she went to find Nico she carried her overnight case downstairs to the hall.

He was still talking on his phone and she hovered uncertainly in the kitchen doorway. He glanced over at her and murmured something in Italian into his phone that she did not catch before he ended the call.

'You didn't have to get up yet,' he said as he poured her a cup of coffee from the jug. 'We have a few hours until you fly back to London and it would be a shame to waste them.'

'Would it?' she said stiffly. 'I mistook your phone for mine and saw that it was Rafaela who called you. Perhaps you have other plans.' The minute she uttered the words she realised how childish she sounded, but it was too late to retract them.

Nico's eyes narrowed. 'Are you sulking because I spoke to my personal assistant?'

'I'm not sulking.' His arrogant tone made her temper

simmer. She lifted her cup to her lips, but the strong aroma of coffee exacerbated the nauseous feeling that had swept over her when she'd got out of bed. Jealousy had unpleasant side-effects, she thought grimly. 'I admit I was surprised that your secretary phoned you at the weekend. Maybe I should have expected that you still have a close relationship with Rafaela. But you assured me that you aren't involved with anyone else.'

'So do you think I lied?' Nico's voice was cool. 'What exactly are you implying? Stop skirting around whatever it is that's bothering you and spit it out.'

She gritted her teeth. 'All right, I will. Do you have a personal relationship with Rafaela?'

His eyes narrowed on her flushed face. 'Is that really what you think? That after spending the night making love to you I raced out of bed to talk in secret to my mistress?' Nico gave her a scathing look. 'I thought you had grown up, Sienna, but clearly I was wrong. Your illogical suspicions were part of the reason we divorced.'

'It wasn't illogical to believe that you and Rafaela were lovers when I found her in your arms eight years ago,' she snapped.

She remembered how she had gone to the apartment in Verona, hoping to make up with him after their latest row. She hadn't told him she was coming and had used her key to let herself in. But when she'd walked into the lounge she had found Nico sitting on the sofa with his beautiful assistant. His arm had been around Rafaela's shoulders, and they had been deep in conversation. At her cry of distress they had sprung apart, looking guilty.

She stared at Nico across the kitchen counter. 'It would be ironic if you had been having an affair with

Rafaela for the past eight years. Many marriages don't last that long. Ours certainly didn't.'

'But Rafaela's marriage is still going strong, and she and her husband recently celebrated their tenth wedding anniversary.'

Shocked, Sienna stared at him. 'Rafaela is married?'

Nico nodded. 'Soon after their marriage her husband had a car accident, which left him partially paralysed. Rafaela was distraught when Claudio wanted to divorce her so that she could meet someone else. She confided in me because she couldn't talk to her family. Fortunately she managed to convince Claudio that he is the love of her life. Last night she told me that their application to adopt a baby boy has been accepted, and she intends to give up work and devote herself to being a mother. Her call this morning was to update me with the news that she and Claudio will take their new son home next week.'

'Why didn't you tell me about Rafaela's problems when we had problems with our own marriage?' Sienna bit her lip. 'You knew I suspected that you were involved with her but you didn't deny there was anything going on between you.'

'I shouldn't have had to deny it,' he said harshly. 'You should have trusted me. I had never given you reason to doubt my commitment to our marriage.'

'A marriage you didn't want.' Her voice shook with the emotions she could no longer contain. 'I loved you, but you married me out of duty because I was pregnant, didn't you, Nico?'

He shrugged. 'Perhaps.'

His reply felt like a knife in her heart, and with a flash of insight Sienna understood that his relationship with his PA had not been the real issue with their marriage. She had convinced herself that Nico was having an affair with Rafaela rather than acknowledge that his coolness and the way he kept an emotional distance from her were because he did not love her and he felt trapped in their marriage that he hadn't wanted. With painful honesty she realised that she had been kidding herself to think that she could have a sex-without-strings affair with him. It wasn't enough for her. But Nico had made it clear that he would not offer more, certainly not his heart.

He drained his coffee and set his cup down on the counter so hard that she was surprised the china didn't smash. 'I'll go and put some clothes on, and then we'll have some breakfast. Perhaps your mood will improve after you've eaten,' he said sardonically.

Sienna's stomach churned at the mere thought of food. Worse was the shameful throb of desire between her legs when his half-naked body brushed against her as he walked past. No, she corrected herself. *Worse* was the temptation she felt to follow him upstairs to the bedroom and make love with him again. He was like a drug in her system but the longer she stayed with him, the harder it would be to break her addiction. A clean break was necessary.

She waited in the kitchen until she heard the slam of the bedroom door upstairs, and then she grabbed her holdall from the hall and raced out of the villa, searching on her phone for the number of a local taxi company. As she hurried down the driveway towards the main gates she promised herself that this time she was leaving Nico for good.

CHAPTER SEVEN

Nico slammed his fists into the punchbag; right fist, left fist, again and again until his arms and shoulders ached. Finally he pulled off his boxing gloves and threw them onto the floor of Villa Lionard's well-equipped gym. His jaw clenched. It seemed that not even hard physical exercise could prevent his thoughts from turning to Sienna after she had walked out on him *again*. The third time she had done so.

It was two months since they had argued and he'd watched her from the bedroom window climbing into a taxi. He had told himself that he was well rid of her. It had been a mistake to get involved with her again and he'd vowed to forget about her. But she was on his mind constantly. He had pulled her number up on his phone countless times but his pride had stopped him from calling her.

He assured himself that what he missed was the amazing sex. But the thought niggled that if it was only physical satisfaction he wanted he could find a release for his urges easily enough. He'd never had a problem attracting women. The problem was that the only woman he wanted had an annoying habit of leaving him.

He told himself that he didn't give a damn. But deep down he felt a gut-wrenching ache of rejection; the same feeling he'd had when he was a boy and his mother had tried to take her own life. There must be something wrong with him that his mother would have preferred death to staying alive to care for her sons, he'd reasoned. That was why he had always looked after Danny and tried to be a parent to him, after their own parents had, in one way or another, abandoned their children.

Cursing beneath his breath, Nico shoved his emotions back into the box where he had locked them away since he was twelve years old. His life functioned perfectly well without messy feelings and without his ex-wife, he assured himself.

His phone rang, and his expression softened when he saw the name of the caller. '*Buongiorno*, Nonna. What's the weather like in Yorkshire?'

'Domenico, have you seen the news reports?' Iris sounded anxious. 'There has been a coup in Tutjo and the King has been deposed. Civil war has broken out and the situation there looks terrible. I've just had Rose Fisher on the phone. She is desperately worried because Sienna flew to Tutjo a few days ago.'

Nico frowned. 'I told Sienna not to travel to that area of Africa. Trouble has been brewing on and off in Tutjo for months.'

'I don't think Sienna would react well to being told what to do, or not do,' his grandmother said thoughtfully. 'I admire her independent spirit.'

'Let's hope it hasn't got her into serious trouble,' Nico muttered, using the remote to switch the TV onto the news channel. The pictures of the escalating violence in Tutjo were horrifying. Sienna wasn't his responsibility, he reminded himself. But the lump of fear that dropped like a lead weight into the pit of his stomach mocked his belief that she meant nothing to him.

Sienna fanned her hot face with her hand. The tiny room where she was confined did not have air conditioning and the window was locked the same as the door. The heat was stifling. When the men who had brought her here at gunpoint came back, perhaps they would bring her some water.

Fear gripped her when she looked out of the window at the main street of Assana, the capital city of the small African state of Tutjo. Burning tyres, shattered glass from shop windows, burnt-out trucks and gangs of men carrying guns were signs of a violent uprising by rebels opposed to the King. The coup had started two days after she had arrived in Tutjo. There had been no warning on the UK government's Foreign Office website that it was unsafe to travel to the region, and her brother-in-law in nearby South Africa had assured her that the recent tensions in Tutjo had calmed down.

She hugged her arms around her, trying to quell her panic as she wondered what would happen to her now that Tutjo was a lawless state. Yesterday she should have gone to meet the women from the cooperative that supplied her with Marula oil, and she hoped that they were all safe.

The door suddenly opened and Sienna spun round and stared at the armed man who entered the room. He pointed his gun at her, and her heart thudded with fear when he spoke in a heavy accent. 'You, come.'

Maybe the rebels were going to let her go free, she

told herself as she walked along a corridor. But if that was so, why was she being threatened with a rifle in her back? When she had been seized from her hotel, one of her captors who spoke a little English had told her that they suspected she was a foreign journalist working for the deposed King.

'In here.' The gunman opened a door and pushed her into a room. There were four or five men gathered around a desk, but Sienna's gaze flew to the man standing apart from the others.

'Nico!'

He strode towards her and caught her as she hurtled into his arms. 'Are you all right?' He slid a hand under her chin and tipped her face up to his, swearing softly when he saw tears in her eyes. 'If the men have harmed you in any way…'

'I'm fine,' she reassured him. She sagged against his whipcord body, feeling weak with relief and shock at seeing him again. The evocative scent of his aftershave was like a homecoming. She was conscious that her cotton trousers and shirt were crumpled, and strands of hair had escaped her ponytail and were sticking to her hot face. Nico wore faded jeans that hugged his lean hips and a denim shirt with the sleeves rolled up to his elbows. The dark stubble on his jaw was an indication that he hadn't shaved for a couple of days and he looked sexier than ever. 'How did you know where I was?' Sienna asked him shakily.

'Your brother-in-law knew which hotel you were staying at. Most of the staff who worked there had gone, but I found someone who had seen you being taken away by the gunmen, and I discovered that this office block is the rebels' headquarters.'

'I'm so worried about the women who work for the cooperatives and their families.'

An odd expression crossed his face. 'You are something else, *cara*. Captured by gunmen but your concern is for others rather than yourself.' He smoothed her hair off her face, but the man who had brought Sienna to the room grabbed hold of her arm and pulled her away from Nico.

'If you want your woman you must pay for her.'

'What did he mean?' she whispered when Nico threw the bag he was holding down on the desk.

'I've been trying to negotiate your release.'

Her fear turned to anger as she looked around at the men who were all brandishing weapons even though they knew that she was unarmed. They were pathetic bullies. 'Have the rebels demanded money? How much do they want?'

'One million US dollars,' Nico told her in a low tone, his eyes on the gunmen.

'That's outrageous…' The rest of her angry words were muffled beneath Nico's lips as his head swooped down and he captured her mouth in a hard kiss. 'What are you doing?' she muttered when he allowed her to draw a breath.

'Saving your life and probably mine. These guys aren't carrying toy guns.' His eyes glittered with a warning and she felt guilty thinking that he had risked his life by coming to Tutjo to rescue her. The situation was highly dangerous and the best thing she could do was allow Nico to deal with the rebels.

He spoke with the man who seemed to be the leader of the gunmen, but the voices washed over Sienna as she fought another bout of dizziness that had plagued her even before she had come to Africa. She had mentioned that she'd been experiencing dizzy spells to a nurse friend who had suggested that she could be anaemic. When she got home—*if* she got home—she would make an appointment with her GP and ask for a blood test.

Nico handed the backpack over to one of the men who proceeded to take out wads of dollar bills and count them. Finally the man seemed satisfied and threw Sienna's passport down on the desk.

'They're letting us go,' Nico murmured in her ear. She swayed on her feet and was grateful for the arm he clamped around her waist as he strode out of the room with her. 'Keep on walking. There's a truck waiting outside for us.'

The journey through rebel-held Tutjo to neighbouring South Africa was tense, and Sienna only relaxed when they were aboard Nico's jet and it took off from the runway. She hadn't slept since her capture, and she did not argue when Nico showed her to the bedroom on the plane and suggested she get some rest. She was asleep as soon as her head was on the pillow and barely stirred when the jet landed and she was carried to a car.

'Are we in London?' she asked when she opened her eyes and looked out at dark, unfamiliar streets.

'Italy. We'll arrive at Villa Lionard in a few minutes,' Nico told her.

'I thought you were taking me back to my flat.' She flushed when she realised that she had been sleeping with her head on his shoulder, and quickly sat upright.

His eyes gleamed in the dark car. 'We have unfinished business from the last time you were at the villa.'

Sienna bit her lip, remembering her stupid accusation that he was having an affair with his secretary. 'I'm sorry I suggested that you were sleeping with Rafaela,' she muttered.

The car came to a halt and Nico sprang out and scooped her off the back seat into his arms. 'The only woman I want to sleep with is you, *mia bellezza*.' He looked down at her, and his wolfish expression was accentuated by his grin that revealed his white teeth.

She had promised herself that she wouldn't do this again. But how could she resist him, she thought despairingly, when his arms were like bands of steel around her and he was holding her against the solid wall of his chest, against his heart? She felt safe, which was crazy, because Nico—or rather her reaction to him—was a danger she knew she should avoid at all cost. Yet he had rescued her from the rebels in Tutjo and in all likelihood he'd saved her life.

He carried her upstairs and into the master bedroom, setting her on her feet in the en-suite bathroom. His fingers deftly unfastened the buttons on her shirt and she caught her breath when his knuckles brushed against the side of her breast as he removed her bra.

'I can take a shower on my own. I'm not a child.'

'I have yet to be convinced of that,' he told her sardonically. 'You disobeyed me after I warned you against going to Tutjo.'

'Disobeyed?' she choked. 'You are so arrogant, Nico. I don't have to obey you. You don't own me.'

'As a matter of fact, I do.' He tugged her trousers down her legs, followed by her panties and lifted her into the shower cubicle before he turned on the spray. 'I paid one million dollars for you.'

The water from the shower cascaded over her face and hair, washing away the grime and fear of the past days and making her skin tingle. Excitement heated her blood as she watched him strip off his clothes before he stepped into the cubicle with her. She lifted her hands to his chest, but instead of pushing him away as her brain told her to do, she ran her fingers through the dark hair that arrowed down his torso. She'd missed him. *Missed* him so badly. 'Do you expect me to have sex with you to repay the debt I owe you? I thought you were a gentleman.'

Nico laughed. 'I'm afraid I am not, *cara*.' He splayed his hands over her breasts, bringing her nipples to stinging life when he rolled them between his fingers. 'How many nights in my bed do you think it will take to work off a million dollars?' He captured her chin and tilted her face up to his. The amusement in his eyes was replaced with an emotion Sienna could not define but which made her heart lurch. 'I thought I'd lost you,' he said roughly before he brought his mouth down on hers and kissed her with an urgency that simply destroyed her.

She parted her lips to the fierce demands of his and kissed him back with mounting passion, wild and hot, her hands moving over his body, exploring the hard ridges of his abdominal muscles, sliding round to his back and down to his taut buttocks. He felt divine: satin skin, hair-roughened thighs and his shaft was steel encased in velvet as he hardened to her touch.

He muttered her name, and then his mouth was on her breast, his lips closing around the nipple, and sucking hard until the pleasure was too intense and she cried out. Her fingers gripped his hair as he moved across to her other breast and wrought havoc with his tongue, while he slipped his hand between her legs and found the slick heat of her arousal with one probing finger and then two.

'Wrap your legs around me,' he growled as he lifted her, cupping her bottom cheeks and settling her against him so that his erection was there at her opening. And then he simply drove his hard length into her, taking her breath away with the mastery of his possession. She gloried in his fierce desire for her, in his harsh groans as she welcomed each bold thrust, tilting her hips so that he could go deeper.

Nico paused for a moment and rested his forehead against hers, his chest heaving. 'I'm going to come,' he said harshly. 'You always make me lose control.' He sounded almost angry, but Sienna could only concentrate on the coiling sensation inside her that was pulling tighter and tighter. She was lost to this man, only this man. He began to move again, his hands gripping her hips, his eyes closed as he pumped in and out, faster and faster, taking them both higher until she screamed his name and tumbled into the mindless, indescribable pleasure of her orgasm.

He tensed, and she sensed he was trying to hold back the tide. His eyes glittered beneath the sweep of his thick black lashes. *'Tesoro mio,'* he muttered, before he drove into her one more time, his face pressed against her throat so that when he exploded inside her she felt his triumphant shout ricochet through her.

A long time later, after he had taken her to bed and made love to her with an inventiveness that had her on her knees, her face buried in the pillows while he positioned himself behind her, Sienna hovered on the edge of sleep and remembered that the English translation of *tesoro mio* was *my treasure*. Dared she hope that he meant it?

Dio! What a night! Nico stretched luxuriously. The pale light of early morning filtered through the blinds, and he rolled onto his side, propping himself up on his elbow so that he could study Sienna, still asleep beside him. Her dark red hair streamed like ribbons of silk over the pillows and her eyelashes made crescents on her cheeks.

His beautiful English rose. Something moved inside him, a possessiveness he wanted to reject. Frowning, he shifted onto his back and stared up at the ceiling. The chemistry between them had always been off the scale but he knew better than to look for a deeper meaning that might explain why he had slept with one arm clamped across her waist to prevent her from leaving him in the middle of the night.

'Thank you for rescuing me from the rebels.'

He turned his head and looked into her smoke-soft grey eyes. The hint of vulnerability on her lovely face got to him more than he was comfortable with. 'It was my pleasure,' he murmured, feeling his heart kick in his chest when he drew her unresisting body towards him. He had taken his pleasure with her several times last night and he was as hard as a spike again. Stranger to understand was the sense of completeness he felt every time he had sex with Sienna. What he felt for her *was* only physical attraction, he assured himself. But he wasn't ready to let her go—yet.

Her mouth opened like the petals of a flower when

he kissed her, but she pushed against his shoulder as he moved over her. 'I need to go to the bathroom first.'

Reluctantly he released her so that she could swing her legs over the side of the bed. But when she stood up, the colour drained from her face and she gave a low cry. Nico realised that she was about to faint, and he threw himself across the bed, just managing to catch her as her legs crumpled beneath her.

'It was probably a reaction to the stress I was under in Tutjo,' she argued a few minutes later, after he had put her back into bed. 'There was no need for you to call a doctor.'

'Nevertheless *il dottore*—Dr Belucci—will be here soon to check you over. He is an old family friend and lives not far from the villa.' He kissed away her pout. 'Don't sulk, *cara*. Perhaps there is a simple reason why you fainted but I want to be sure.'

Stefano Belucci had been a physician to the De Conti family since before Nico was born. When the maid ushered the doctor into the bedroom, Nico glanced at Sienna. 'Do you want me to leave the room, *cara*?'

She shrugged. 'Stay if you want to.'

Sienna answered all the doctor's questions about her general health. 'There's nothing wrong with me,' she insisted.

'I will take some blood and urine samples, Signorina Fisher. There are a number of reasons which could explain the dizziness that you say you have experienced recently.'

Nico moved over to the window while Dr Belucci performed various tasks, and then Sienna went into the bathroom and returned soon after and handed the doctor a small container. She was still pale, and her air

of fragility made Nico feel guilty that he had been too
demanding last night. Her passion had matched his,
he reminded himself, but inexplicably he felt a need
to protect her.

'When will you have the results of the blood tests?'
he asked the doctor.

'In a day or two. But I am confident that I know
the cause of Signorina Fisher's symptoms.' Dr Belucci
looked from Nico to Sienna, and smiled. '*Congratu-
lazioni!* You are pregnant.'

CHAPTER EIGHT

How was he in this situation again? Toxic anger surged through Nico's veins. The realisation that Sienna must be laughing at him made him want to punch the wall of the study where he had come after the doctor had made his astonishing announcement.

She was pregnant! His lying, cheating ex-wife had played him for a fool once again. And the worst of it was she was so goddamned clever that he had almost been taken in by her shocked expression. He had almost been convinced that she hadn't planned this all along.

'I can't believe it,' she'd whispered, and the stunned look in her wide, grey eyes had been a touching performance worthy of a standing ovation. Nico had walked out of the room then, and ignored her when she'd called after him, but her soft voice had cut like a jagged knife blade through his soul. She was pregnant but it wasn't his child.

He welcomed his fury that burned as hot as the fires of hell in his gut. It released him from the spell she had cast on him when he'd glanced over his shoulder in the church at Danny's wedding and seen a vision of loveliness in a yellow dress. But now he felt nothing but contempt for her.

'Nico.'

He tensed and jerked his head round to see her standing in the doorway. If anything she looked even paler than she had when she'd fainted, and the slight tremble of her lips before she pressed them firmly together should not have tugged on his heart. It didn't, he told himself.

'The news is incredible, isn't it?' she murmured as she walked into the study and closed the door. 'I'm still in shock. But Dr Belucci is one hundred per cent certain that I am going to have a baby.'

'I'm not sure what you want me to say,' he bit out. 'Do you want me to offer you my congratulations? Out of curiosity, is the father someone you were involved with before you slept with me on a number of occasions, or did you meet your lover after you stormed out of the villa two months ago?'

'You don't understand.' The stricken look on her face was a masterpiece of acting, he thought sardonically. 'I am expecting your baby, Nico. The pregnancy test showed that I am approximately fourteen weeks pregnant which means that I must have conceived in June. We made love after Danny's wedding,' she reminded him, and then he understood.

'I wondered why you had turned up at the church. And then there was the story you spun about Iris having an angina attack, which was patently an excuse for you to visit my bedroom. You were keen to have sex with me that night so that you could name me as the father of the child you were already carrying. Very clever, *cara*,' he said mockingly. 'But I am not so stupid as to fall for the same trick twice.'

Sienna made a soft sound of distress, and Nico tore

his eyes from her, fighting an inexplicable urge to take her in his arms. Her lush body with those firm, round breasts acted like a siren's song and he despised himself because, even now, knowing what she was, he still ached to touch her.

'What do you mean? I've never tried to trick you.' Her voice was a thread of sound but she lifted her chin and said in a firmer tone, 'This baby is most definitely yours because you are the only man I've ever had sex with.' She bit her lip when he gave a snort of derision. 'It's the truth. Why would I pretend that you are the father of my child?'

'For the same reason that you fooled me into believing I was responsible for your first pregnancy. I am very wealthy.' He shrugged. 'And perhaps you fancy yourself as a viscountess. You really are a very good actress. I could almost be taken in by you. But the baby you are carrying cannot be mine because I am infertile.'

'But…you can't be.' She swayed on her feet, and the memory of how he had caught her just before she'd collapsed onto the bedroom floor when she'd fainted earlier caused Nico to swear.

'Sit down,' he said roughly. He steered her over to the sofa, his jaw clenching when she leaned her head back against the cushions. How dared she look so vulnerable when he knew it was an act?

'Why do you think you are infertile?' Sienna sounded as weary as Nico felt. He was tired of lies, tired of wishing for something that he did not fully understand and had decided a long time ago that he did not want. At a young age, his parents' volatile marriage had taught him that emotions and relationships were a combination doomed to failure.

'I did a test which showed that I have a low sperm count,' he said curtly. 'We had been trying for a year to have another baby and it seemed odd that you didn't conceive, especially considering that you had fallen pregnant the first time we'd slept together.' He exhaled heavily. 'You were obsessed with ovulation charts and sex had become a means to an end. It seemed as though you only wanted to make love if there was a chance you would get pregnant. Every month when I found you crying, I felt a failure.'

'I felt a failure too,' she said quietly. 'I had miscarried your heir and I couldn't give you another child.'

'But Luigi wasn't mine.' Nico ignored her gasp, reminding himself again that Sienna was a clever actress. Maybe everything she did was an act, and her husky moans when he'd held back from taking his own pleasure so that he could give her multiple orgasms had been as fake as her claim that he was her only lover. 'I know that you slept with my brother before we became lovers ten years ago.'

She blinked. 'With *Danny*?'

'I only have one brother,' he drawled.

Colour flared on her white face. 'I didn't sleep with him or anyone else. I *was* a virgin when I made love with you.' She pushed her hair back from her face. 'Where did you get the crazy idea that I had slept with Danny?'

'He admitted that you'd had sex with him only a few days before I arrived at Sethbury Hall,' Nico said abruptly. 'When we met, you immediately dropped

Danny and turned your interest on me, I assume because you knew I would inherit the estate and peerage.'

'It's not true. I went on a couple of dates with Danny before you came to Much Matcham. I suppose I knew that he wanted to take our relationship a step further. I liked him as a friend but I wasn't in love with him and nothing happened between us.'

Nico's jaw clenched. 'Danny is my kid brother and I've looked out for him since he was a toddler. He and I have always been close. Best friends as well as brothers.'

'Danny was jealous of you. He said that you were the heir and he was the spare. I was never his,' Sienna said in a fierce voice that added fuel to Nico's fury because she was such a damned good liar.

'I don't believe my brother would lie to me. I suppose it's possible that you did not know which of us— Danny or me—was the father of your child, but you were in love with me and so you let me think it was my baby, knowing that I would be duty-bound to marry the mother of my heir,' he told her brutally.

Sienna hunched forwards and covered her face with her hands. 'Luigi was yours,' she whispered. She lowered her hands and stared at him. 'Maybe the result of the fertility test was wrong. It must have been, because I am expecting your baby now. But if you believed you were infertile when we tried to have a child why didn't you tell me? I thought it was my fault.'

Guilt stirred uncomfortably inside Nico. He hadn't mentioned the sperm test and its devastating result because he'd been embarrassed. It had felt like a slur on his masculinity, especially when he'd realised that his brother must have been responsible for Sienna's first pregnancy. 'We got divorced and I assumed you would meet someone else and have a child,' he said gruffly.

He looked away from her hurt expression, infuriated by the dull ache that had lodged beneath his breastbone. This was why he avoided emotions, he thought grimly. Sienna was a treacherous bitch and he had every right to evict her from his life without feeling as if he was the monster in a ridiculous melodrama.

He leaned his hip against the desk and folded his arms across his chest, his mouth twisting into a contemptuous smile when he saw the shimmer of tears in her eyes. 'So you see, Sienna, why I am certain that your pregnancy is not my concern. And why I want you to get out of my house and stay out of my life. I never want to set eyes on you for as long as I live,' he finished savagely.

'Don't worry, Nico. You will never see me again or meet your baby.' Sienna stood up and walked over to the door. Her eyes ached with the effort of holding back her tears, but she was determined not to let him see her cry. He had humiliated her enough and hurt her so badly with his vile accusations that she could never forgive him.

She did not have the energy to try to defend herself, and what was the point? Nico believed the lie his brother had told him and he refused to believe that he was the father of her baby. She was still struggling to absorb the news of her pregnancy. She hadn't noticed any signs, although she realised now it would explain her bouts of nausea and other odd symptoms. Her periods were sometimes light or irregular, and her mind had been on other things recently—mostly on Nico—so that she hadn't noticed her cycle was very late.

Nico's stunned expression when the doctor had made his announcement had reflected her own shocked disbelief, but when he'd walked out of the bedroom without saying anything, or even looking at her, she'd guessed he didn't share her joy. Maybe he just needed time to get used to the idea, she'd told herself as she'd quickly pulled on some clothes and gone after him. He might be angry at first but he would calm down and realise how lucky they were to finally be expecting a child together. The contempt in his voice when he'd told her to get out of his life had shattered her fragile hope that he would want her and his baby.

She resisted the urge to glance back at him as she walked out of the study. In the hall she found the chauffeur was waiting by the front door. He was holding the backpack that she'd brought with her from Tutjo. Head held high, she followed the chauffeur out of the villa, and when he opened the car door she climbed inside. She had no idea if Nico watched them drive away and told herself she didn't care. It was over.

His private jet landed in London a few hours later. She supposed she should be grateful that he had arranged for her to be flown home, instead of having to catch a commercial flight. A taxi delivered her to her flat in Camden and she went straight to her bedroom. Unable to hold back the storm of emotions that had been building since Nico had evicted her from his life, she threw herself down on the bed and cried until she could cry no more.

'It's just you and me, baby,' she whispered. Resting her hand on her stomach, she felt a faint but discernible swell—not a sign that she needed to hit the gym and tone up her stomach muscles as she'd thought, but evidence of a new life developing inside her. Through her misery came a gleam of light and a faint smile tugged at her lips. She sat up and wiped away her tears. Tomorrow she would make an appointment with her GP, and she knew from friends who'd had children that in the next couple of weeks she would be offered an ultrasound scan.

The pregnancy test that the doctor in Italy had carried out suggested that she was already past the crucial first three months. But her first pregnancy had ended at twenty-two weeks and she was scared to look too far into the future. All she could do was hope for the best. And she needed to look after herself, starting with eating properly, Sienna decided as she slid off the bed and went to the kitchen to cook herself some dinner. Nico had made it clear he did not want to be involved with the baby but they would manage just fine without him.

Nico emerged from a private clinic in Harley Street and climbed into the limousine that was parked beside the pavement. After instructing his driver to take him to an address in Maida Vale he leaned his head against the back of the seat and tried to make sense of the results he'd received, following tests he'd undergone to check his fertility.

'Everything is absolutely normal,' the specialist at the clinic had told him. 'It's possible that the test you did previously was flawed. Home fertility tests have improved in recent years, but the ones available in the past were unreliable and did not always give an accurate result.'

It was too late now to wish that he had discussed his concerns with a doctor and been tested properly years ago, Nico thought heavily. He had been much younger then, and a mix of immaturity and hurt pride had made him jump to the conclusion that Sienna had conceived his brother's baby after Danny had said that they had been lovers.

Although Nico had now discovered that it was perfectly feasible for him to be able to father a child, it did not automatically mean that he was responsible for Sienna's current pregnancy, he reminded himself. But her insistence that the result of the fertility test from years ago must have been wrong had led to his decision to be re-tested. He'd assumed that the latest result would confirm he was infertile and prove once and for all that Sienna was a liar. But that hadn't happened, and for the first time in his life Nico felt uncertain how to proceed.

She had looked so shocked when he'd accused her of sleeping with his brother. In the heat of his temper he'd believed she was a clever actress. But her denial had been so fierce, *so convincing*, that he'd started to wonder if she had told him the truth—which would mean that his brother had lied to him.

Nico raked his hand through his hair. He would trust Danny with his life. But the memory of Sienna's unhappy face haunted him. He knew he had been unnecessarily cruel when he'd sent her away. What if he had been wrong about her and the child was his? His jaw clenched as he remembered her parting words to him. 'You will never...meet your baby.'

Dio! He needed to have a conversation with his brother urgently.

Danny's penthouse flat was close to De Conti Leisure's London head office. Nico had created the role of Assistant to the Director of PR for his brother, but the reality was that Danny only worked when it suited him and he enjoyed a busy social life funded by the generous trust fund Nico had established for him. Sometimes the traitorous thought had crossed Nico's mind that his brother was as selfish as their mother. But Danny had been just a kid when their parents had divorced and Nico had always tried to shield him from life's upsets.

'What brings you to London?' Danny asked when he invited Nico into the penthouse and offered him a beer. 'Are you meeting Sienna? I admit I was surprised when Nonna told me that you'd invited your ex-wife to Sethbury Hall for lunch. I didn't think it was your style to resurrect an old relationship.'

'Would it bother you if I was seeing Sienna again?'

'Of course not. Why should it?' Danny suddenly seemed keen to avoid Nico's gaze.

'She denies that the two of you slept together ten years ago. So what is the truth?'

'For God's sake, why does it matter now?'

'It doesn't matter. I was merely curious,' Nico said in a deliberately bland voice.

'Oh, well.' Danny gave a shrug. 'I admit that I wasn't entirely truthful when I told you I'd slept with Sienna.'

Nico felt his stomach hit the floor. Hard on the heels of his shock at his brother's betrayal came the realisation that he had been terribly wrong about Sienna. *Madre di Dio!* She hadn't lied to him and it was possible, probable, he amended, remembering how she had insisted that he was the only man she'd had sex with—*in eight years*—that she was expecting his baby.

'Why did you lie to me?' he asked Danny in a low voice, trying to control his anger, trying even now to protect his brother, he thought bitterly. He felt gutted by Danny's deceit, which had cost him his marriage. But the unpalatable truth was that he couldn't blame anyone but himself, Nico acknowledged. His lack of trust had come between him and Sienna eight years ago and driven a wedge between them now.

'I knew you would hate the idea that I'd had Sienna first,' Danny muttered. 'You had everything, Nico. You were the heir and I was the afterthought. I really liked Sienna but the minute you showed up I might as well not have existed. You never cared that girls always fell in love with you. But it was different with Sienna. You were in love with her.'

Nico said nothing. He finished his beer and crushed the can in his fist. After a moment, Danny continued bitterly, 'I realised that Sienna was your weakness. I know it was a stupid thing to do, but when I told you that she'd been with me first it felt good knowing that you were envious of me for once. You had the money and the title and the power, but I'd had your girl. Except that really I hadn't. Sienna was madly in love with you. Surely you asked her for the truth while you were married to her? She would have denied sleeping with me.'

'I trusted you,' Nico said grittily. 'You are my kid brother and I thought there was a bond between us. I believed you.' The sense of betrayal he felt evoked a burning sensation behind his eyelids and he pinched the bridge of his nose while he attempted to marshal his thoughts. In his mind he pictured Sienna with tears in her eyes when he'd told her to stay out of his life.

What the hell had he done?

He'd heard nothing from her in the past three weeks. Surely if the child she was carrying was his, he would have received some sort of communication from her lawyers by now? But there had been nothing, no paternity claim—which might be because Sienna had slept with another man earlier in the summer and knew that she was pregnant with her lover's baby.

He had to know the truth. And if she *was* expecting his baby he *would* claim his heir. No way would he be as irresponsible as his father, he vowed grimly. Franco De Conti had fathered several illegitimate children and cut them out of his life. Nico had inherited his grandfather Rupert Mandeville's strong sense of duty, and, although he had loved his father, he had lost respect for him.

Sienna's business operated from a workshop beside the Regent's Canal in Camden. The door was unlocked, and when Nico walked in he found the desk in the small reception area was unmanned. It was early evening and he guessed that most of the staff had gone home. But when he pushed open the door into the workshop, he saw three people standing at a counter where there was an array of bottles and jars. At another time he would have been interested in the Victorian building with its redbrick walls, vaulted ceiling and exposed wooden beams. But his eyes were riveted on Sienna and he felt a painful sensation in his chest as though his heart had been squeezed in a vice.

She was so beautiful. He had committed every one of her features to his memory but he had forgotten the impact she always had on him, the way his breath felt as if it were trapped in his lungs when he stared at her lovely face. He skimmed his eyes over her, searching for signs of her pregnancy. But she looked slim in close-fitting black trousers tucked into knee-high black boots, and a loose white jumper that slipped down to reveal one bare shoulder.

Nico froze as it occurred to him that there might not be a baby. Sienna had suffered a miscarriage in her first pregnancy. *Dio!* He was only just coming to terms with the idea that she had conceived his child and he couldn't grasp that she might have lost it.

For a heartbeat Sienna could not hide her shock when her gaze met his, but she quickly schooled her expression to one of utter indifference that made Nico grind his teeth, even though he accepted that he deserved for her to look at him as if he were something unpleasant she had trodden in.

The two women with Sienna looked up as he walked across the workshop but they carried on packing jars of what he guessed was skin cream into boxes. Sienna glared at him fiercely as if she hoped he would get the message that he was unwelcome. But Nico wasn't going anywhere until he had an answer to the question that was eating away at him.

She glanced at her watch and spoke to the women. 'Carley and Liz, you can go now and I'll finish up here. Thanks for staying late. The courier will collect the order first thing in the morning.'

When the women had left the workshop she looked directly at Nico. He noted how her breasts rose quickly as she took a deep breath, and the idea that she was nervous gave another squeeze on his heart.

'I have no idea why you are here and I want you to leave,' she said coldly.

'We need to talk.'

'Really?' Her voice dripped with sarcasm. 'I can't say I feel the need to talk to you, Nico. The last time we met I distinctly remember you saying that you never wanted to see me again.'

She had not mentioned the baby. He stared at her, noting the faint purple smudges beneath her eyes, which suggested that her sleep had been as disturbed as his. 'Should you be working this late in the evening in your condition?' he growled.

'As if you care.' Her bitterness hit Nico like a punch in his gut and his jaw clenched when she continued in a hard voice that he had never heard her use before. 'You made your feelings for me and your child absolutely clear.'

So there was still a child. Relief and a host of other emotions he did not care to define roughened his voice when he said, 'I know now that Danny lied. When I confronted him he admitted he'd made up the story that you and he had been lovers. You were right, he was jealous and wanted to hurt me.' It scraped a raw place inside Nico to know that his brother had resented him.

'It took you three weeks to get around to asking your brother for the truth. I'm surprised you bothered at all.' She gave him a scathing look that would have felled other men less determined than Nico. He was taken aback by Sienna's fury. Perhaps he should have expected her anger but the teenager he'd married ten years ago had been sweetly anxious to please him. He had assumed he would be able to win her round easily, he acknowledged ruefully. Clearly that was not going to happen.

The woman watching him suspiciously was a lioness protecting her cub. She moved her hand over her stomach and the instinctive gesture of maternal devotion for her unborn baby crucified him when he remembered how he had rejected her and his child. Both his children, he was reminded when she spoke.

'How could you have believed that Luigi wasn't your son? The poor little boy was denied a life and denied his father's love. I will never forgive you for that.'

Nico doubted he would ever forgive himself. He had never told anyone that after they had lost Luigi he had often visited his son's grave at night, and alone in the darkness he had given in to the grief that was a permanent ache in his heart. Nico had been filled with regret that he hadn't been more enthusiastic when Sienna had announced she was pregnant. He'd been unprepared for fatherhood, but over time he'd begun to feel excited and it had been a savage blow when the baby had been stillborn. Later, when he'd believed that Luigi had not been his child, he'd stopped visiting the churchyard.

But right now was not the time to tell Sienna how much he regretted his past mistakes. He needed to convince her that he was here to put right the mistake he'd made when he had sent her away from Villa Lionard.

'I know Luigi was mine and I am prepared to believe that I am the father of the baby you are expecting.'

'How good of you,' she said scornfully. 'Although prepared to believe suggests you would want it confirmed by a paternity test.' She gave a hollow laugh as if she'd guessed that he had considered asking for a DNA test to be certain. But that had been before he'd seen her again and realised that, among other complicated things, he trusted her completely.

'Here's some news, Nico. I don't care whether you

think this baby is yours or not. You will never have any involvement in his life.'

'His?' he said roughly, struggling to control the emotions that swept like a raging river through him. 'You are expecting my son?'

She tensed when he strode around the counter and halted in front of her. 'Yes, I'm having a boy,' she muttered. 'But you told me you are infertile, so he can't be your son. I must have fallen pregnant by one of my legions of lovers.' This time her sarcasm did not quite mask the quiver of hurt in her voice.

'You said I was the only man you have ever made love with. But even if you'd had hundreds of other lovers it wouldn't matter. I believe this baby is mine.'

'I still don't give a damn.' She tried to step past him, but Nico moved closer so that she was trapped by the counter behind her and him in front of her.

'I had more tests at a fertility clinic, and today I learned that my sperm count is normal and I am not infertile. The test I did years ago gave an inaccurate result.'

She shook her head. 'So on the strength of one unreliable test result and a lie your brother told you, you were judge and jury and found me guilty of a crime I didn't even know I was supposed to have committed.' Sienna ran her hand over her eyes, but when Nico touched her arm—wanting, needing to make a connection with her—she shrugged him off. 'You told me to get out of your life and I have done what you asked. I don't know why you have come here. I don't want to know. At the risk of repeating myself, *I don't care.*'

Nico was fascinated by the temper that made her eyes flash as fiery bright as the lightning that had lit the dark sky during the electrical storm on the night of Danny's wedding. The night their child had been conceived, he now knew. He also knew that there was only one course of action open to him, to them.

He stepped closer to her and captured her chin between his fingers, tilting her face up to his. 'I've come to marry you, of course.'

CHAPTER NINE

SIENNA LAUGHED AND LAUGHED. Even when Nico did not join in she laughed, because surely his statement had been a joke—a crass and tasteless joke, but a joke nevertheless.

'I'm glad you are not averse to the idea,' he drawled when she wiped away her tears of amusement—it was definitely amusement she felt. They were not tears of heartbreak, she assured herself.

'Not averse?' She jerked her chin out of his lean fingers. 'Nico, there is no way I will marry you. Never again. Not in this lifetime.'

He smiled, and God forgive her but she could not prevent herself from staring at his mouth that could be sensual or cruel but right at this moment was pure temptation. 'Why not?' he said mildly.

'Seriously, you need to ask? Why would I be idiotic enough to repeat the mistake we made ten years ago? Why would you? I'm not eighteen and scared of my father's temper, and you are not under pressure from your grandfather to do your duty and legitimise your child. You told me that you never wanted to set eyes on me again and I share that sentiment.'

Her tenuous control on her emotions shattered and

she clenched her hands by her sides to stop herself from lashing out at him. 'Go away, Nico. Go to hell for all I care. Just keep away from me and my baby.'

'He is my son too, *cara*.'

'Don't.' She hated the way her insides melted and reminded herself that she hated *him*. But that huskily spoken *cara* had tugged on her traitorous heart.

'I know I screwed up in Italy, but I need to make my position clear. Maybe you hate me right now,' he murmured with an arrogance that made her grind her teeth. Nico would find it impossible to believe that any woman could hate him. The fact that she didn't hate him made Sienna furious with herself. He had treated her appallingly and she would not be taken in by his easy charm ever again. It had been the problem in the past. She had made it too easy for him. He hadn't had to try to win her. She'd rolled over like an eager puppy, she thought grimly.

But the indisputable fact was that she was expecting Nico's baby. 'If you think I'll agree to a DNA test while I'm pregnant, you can take a running jump,' she said sharply. 'A prenatal paternity test is an invasive procedure, and I refuse to do anything that could put the baby at risk. And anyway, there can only be one outcome. You are the father and if you are serious about wanting to have a role in your son's life I won't object. But this isn't the Dark Ages and it's ridiculous to suggest that we have to get married, especially when we tried it once before and it was a disaster.'

'So what is your suggestion?' Nico demanded.

The hard gleam in his eyes warned Sienna that he was angry. That made two of them, she thought. But her shock at seeing him again when she'd truly believed that she never would was having an effect on her. The fight drained out of her, and it didn't help that she was exhausted after a long day at work. She had been awake for a couple of hours before her alarm had gone off at six that morning, worrying about how she was going to manage to run her business and look after a baby. Especially with the Tutjo coup threatening her Marula oil supplier—she hoped the women and families at the cooperative were okay. It was also, she realised when she glanced at her watch, well past dinner time. She had an appetite like a horse at the moment and her stomach was reminding her that it was empty.

'I'm going home.' She pushed past him and headed towards the door. 'I suggest you go back to Italy. I'll contact you after the baby is born and you can decide then how involved you want to be.'

His rigid jaw warned her that he did not appreciate being spoken to like that. Nico always wanted to be in control. After a moment he said tersely, 'I'll take you home. My car is outside.'

'I prefer to walk. My flat's not far away.' But when she preceded him outside and locked the workshop, it was raining hard. Autumn had brought an end to the summer heatwave and the nights were drawing in. Nico's chauffeur opened the car door and Sienna decided there was no point getting soaked for the sake of her pride. 'If you go along the high street for about a mile, I live in a flat above the kebab shop,' she explained.

Nico slid into the car beside her and gave her a simmering look. 'The future Viscount Mandeville will not spend his formative years living above a kebab shop,' he said brusquely. He leaned forwards and murmured something to the driver, and seconds later the privacy screen slid up. Sienna shifted along the seat away from him but the evocative scent of his aftershave stirred memories of being in his arms, her face pressed against his neck while he used his hands and mouth to bring her body to the pinnacle of pleasure over and over again. She hated that she was so aware of him, hated her weakness and the stupid little flicker of hope inside her that maybe he didn't despise her now he knew she hadn't lied.

The smooth motion of the car made her feel sleepy, but when they stopped at a red light she peered out of the window at the neon-lit streets. There were no traffic lights on the route to her flat. 'This isn't the way to where I live.'

'I've arranged for us to have dinner at my hotel,' Nico said coolly. 'I would like to have a proper, adult conversation with you about the future when we become parents to our child, who is the innocent one in all of this,' he added before she could argue.

Damn him for being right, Sienna thought heavily. Of course she wanted to do the best for her baby, and that meant she must put aside her resentment of Nico and at least try to establish a cordial relationship with him. 'I'm not dressed for dinner at a five-star hotel,' she muttered when the car stopped outside the hotel's grand entrance.

'You look fine.' Nico captured her hand in his, as if he expected her to run away. The glint in his blue eyes when he stared down at her made her heart pound. 'You look beautiful, always, Sienna,' he murmured.

Don't fall under his spell, she told herself as he escorted her into the hotel. If she hadn't been so famished she would have put up more resistance, but she felt light-headed—a sure sign that her blood sugars had dropped too low. 'Aren't we eating here?' she asked when Nico whisked her across the foyer and they passed the entrance to the hotel's restaurant.

'We'll have dinner in my suite so that we can be assured of privacy while we talk,' he said, ushering her into the lift.

'As long as talking is all you want to do?' She flushed when his brows rose, and instantly regretted her provocative comment that was a defence against the way he made her feel. She was fiercely aware of him but she did not know if he was still attracted to her. Although she was nearly four months pregnant her baby bump was barely showing. But she was conscious of other changes to her figure: her thickening waistline and fuller breasts. It didn't help that Nico was so incredibly handsome, she thought ruefully. The woman at the reception desk had practically drooled over him.

'I'm not planning to leap on you the minute we're alone,' he told her curtly, which should have reassured her but had the opposite effect.

The penthouse suite was ultra-modern—all moody colours on the walls and a lot of black glass and silver chrome. A table was set for two, and a butler served them dinner. Sienna remembered when Nico had come to her hotel room in York and they had made love throughout the night. They had been so hungry for each other. It seemed a lifetime ago when she had decided to enjoy a sex-without-strings affair with him. Now they were inextricably linked by the baby who was the result of their passion.

Her tension went up a notch when the butler left

them alone, but Nico seemed in no hurry to talk, allowing her time to focus on the delicious food. The *boeuf en croute* melted in her mouth and she gave a sigh of contentment when she'd finished her dinner.

He sipped his wine and topped up her glass of sparkling water. 'Are you keeping well?'

She nodded. 'I had a scan last week, which is when I found out that I'm expecting a boy. Apparently everything is fine and I'm having a textbook pregnancy so far.' She bit her lip, aware of how quickly the situation could change. The miscarriage years ago had happened without warning. She had been excited that she was over halfway through her pregnancy but a few hours later she had held her lifeless baby in her arms.

'I'm looking after myself and eating well,' she told Nico. 'I was lucky that I didn't really suffer from morning sickness. Although if I'd felt worse, perhaps I would have realised earlier that I was pregnant.' She fell silent, remembering his reaction to the news of her pregnancy. He had been so horrible and said such hurtful things that she doubted she would ever forget them, even if she managed to forgive him.

She pulled her mind back to the present and looked at him, wishing she could read the thoughts behind his inscrutable expression. The distance between them was far wider than the table where they were sitting opposite one another. She didn't know how to breach it, or if she even wanted to.

'I can only spend a few days in England and I want you to come back to Lake Garda with me,' he said abruptly. 'I will arrange for a top obstetrician in Italy to oversee your care for the rest of your pregnancy.' Nico's jaw tightened when she shook her head. 'I want to be able to support you while you are pregnant and after the baby is born, but it will be difficult if I am in Italy and you are here. It makes sense for us to get married as soon as possible.'

'How can there be any sense in a marriage that neither of us wants?' Sienna said, frustrated.

His face hardened, determination stamped on his patrician features. 'My son will be born legitimate.'

'You can't force me to marry you.'

'Have you forgotten that I paid the rebels in Tutjo one million dollars for you?'

She made a choked sound, a mixture of anger at his arrogance and a sense of helplessness at the realisation that Nico would fight dirty if he had to. Beneath his civilised veneer he came from a bloodline of barons and warrior knights that stretched back through centuries of some of Europe's most violent history. 'I'll repay the money somehow,' she said stiffly, 'even if I have to work twenty hours a day.'

'You won't be able to work at all when the baby is born. Or are you planning to leave him in an all-day nursery when he's a week old while you pursue your career?'

'*You* have a career. Why shouldn't I?' she shot back at him. 'My skincare company might not be a multi-million-pound business like De Conti Leisure, but I started Fresh Faced with a small bank loan and now it turns over a healthy annual profit.'

'The point I am making is that you would not need to work if you were my wife.'

She gave an exasperated sigh. 'You are missing the point. I want to work and be financially independent. My mother stayed with my father even though he was a drunkard and a bully because she was financially reliant on him. She didn't have a good education or means to a career. I was determined that I wouldn't be caught in the same trap, which is why I studied for a degree and started my own business.'

Nico frowned. 'I wasn't suggesting that you would have to give up running Fresh Faced. If you marry me, we can employ a nanny to help with the baby so that you can continue to work.'

Sienna's head ached and she massaged her brow with her fingertips. The truth was that she did not know how she was going to manage to juggle work and motherhood. She was haunted by memories of losing her first baby, and in this pregnancy she was scared to hope that she would end up with a healthy baby in a few months' time.

'Would you have asked me to marry you if I was expecting a girl?'

Nico's gaze did not waver from hers. 'Of course.'

'I wondered if you wanted the baby because it's a boy.'

'The sex of our child makes no difference to me.' He hesitated. 'But the fact that you are having a boy *is* relevant. At the beginning of the last century the fifth Viscount Mandeville made a covenant which stipulates that only a *legitimate* firstborn male can inherit the title and the Sethbury estate. The baby you are carrying can only be my heir if we are married. Would you deny our son his birthright, Sienna?'

'There isn't a baby yet.' She stared down at the tablecloth while she struggled to hold back her tears. She didn't know how she could bear it if she lost this baby too. A part of her was tempted to let Nico take over.

If she agreed to marry him he would sweep her into his wealthy, privileged lifestyle and she wouldn't have to worry about paying the rent for her one-bedroom flat that was not an ideal place to bring up a child. For Nico it would be a marriage of convenience for the child's sake, which was the reason he had married her ten years ago. But now, as then, it wasn't enough for Sienna.

She picked up the cup of jasmine tea that Nico had poured her instead of coffee at the end of the meal and carried her drink over to the low table in front of the sofa. With a sigh, she sat down and leaned back against the cushions. Tiredness swept over her in a great wave and her eyelids drooped. In a minute, she would ask him to take her home, she told herself.

Sienna surfaced from a deep sleep. Last night she had been exhausted and she'd slept better than she'd done for weeks, she realised, giving a lazy stretch. She didn't even remember arriving back at her flat or putting her pyjamas on. Her hand met something warm and solid that felt remarkably like a muscular, male body. She turned her head on the pillow and her heart clattered against her ribs when she stared into a pair of brilliant blue eyes. 'What are you doing in my bed…?' Her voice trailed away as she glanced around the room and discovered that she was in Nico's hotel room. In his bed.

'Buongiorno, cara,' he drawled.

She sat up and flushed when she discovered that she was wearing her bra and knickers. The bra was at least two sizes too small and her breasts spilled above the lacy cups. Quickly pulling the sheet up to cover her body, she said tautly, 'Did you undress me?'

'You fell asleep on the sofa after dinner and I didn't have the heart to wake you.'

'Oh, yes, you are all heart,' she snapped sarcastically, her cheeks burning hotter at the idea of him taking her clothes off. 'You should have woken me.' She stiffened when she tried to move her leg and discovered that it was trapped beneath Nico's hair-roughened thigh. Another shocking thought, worse than finding herself in bed with him, came into her mind. 'Did we…?'

The amusement disappeared from his eyes and he swore. 'No, we didn't make love. Is that the opinion you have of me, that I would have sex with you without your knowledge or consent?'

Sienna told herself that she must have imagined he sounded hurt. He flung back the sheet and stood up, and she did not know whether to feel relieved or disappointed when she saw that he was wearing a pair of black silk boxer shorts. 'No, I don't think you would do that,' she mumbled.

He let out his breath slowly but the tension between them was still tangible as anger and mistrust was replaced by a simmering awareness. 'I resisted you when you cuddled up to me so sweetly during the night, and I even managed to resist the temptation to satisfy my desire when you stroked your hands over every part of my body, and I do mean *every* part,' he said mockingly.

'I did not.' Sienna gave a silent groan as she recalled her very erotic dream in which she had tormented Nico with her hands and mouth. In her dream she had circled her fingers around his hard shaft—but perhaps she hadn't dreamed it!

She was too embarrassed to look at him when he sat

down on the edge of the mattress. He slid his hand beneath her chin, tipping her face up so that she couldn't evade his gaze. A feral hunger sharpened his features and his eyes glittered when her tongue darted out to moisten her lips.

'Your subconscious knows what you want, even if you refuse to admit that you want me,' he said. 'There has always been this fire between us.'

'It's called lust,' she whispered.

'It doesn't matter what we label it. Whatever you think of me, the passion we have for each other is unique. I've never found anything to equal it, and neither have you or you would have had other lovers.'

'I dated a few other men.' She didn't want him to think she'd lived like a nun since their divorce, although it wasn't far from the truth, Sienna acknowledged.

'But you did not give your body to any of them because you are mine,' Nico growled. The possessiveness in his voice sent a tremor through her and she watched helplessly as his head descended. Where was her outraged denial? Where was her pride? taunted a voice inside her. Was she really going to lie there and let him kiss her?

And then he was doing just that and she made no attempt to stop him. His warm breath whispered over her lips and she expected him to claim her mouth with the same fierce possession that had been in his voice. But his kiss was as soft as gossamer. Gentle, almost reverent, healing the hurt that his damning accusations had wrought as he coaxed her lips apart.

She couldn't resist him, and in truth she did not want to. His skin felt like satin beneath her fingers when she put her hand on his shoulder and moved it up to his nape. She stroked his hair and then continued her exploration, discovering the sharp angles of his face and the rough stubble on his jaw. Her head fell back against the pillows and she opened her mouth beneath his as he deepened the kiss, sliding his lips over hers and tasting her with little sips that made her long for him to drink deep. But he was in control and when at last he lifted his mouth from hers she stared at him, unable to speak or think or move away from him, even though she knew she should do all three.

Warily she waited for him to mock her eager response to him. He knew now that she was hopelessly weak. As if he needed more power over her, she thought wryly.

'You mentioned an idea of establishing a new workshop for Fresh Faced, possibly in Paris,' he said. 'Have you found a suitable premises?'

Sienna remembered that she'd postponed a trip to Paris and gone to Italy with Nico for a party at Villa Lionard—a lifetime ago, it seemed. 'No, I've been busy with other things,' she said drily. 'The long-term plan is for me to set up another workshop in central Europe, and my assistant Carley will run the London workshop. But expanding the business will have to wait until after the baby is born.'

'Why not open a workshop in northern Italy? My office is in Verona and I want to bring our son up at Lake Garda. You can speak Italian and it would be the perfect solution.'

It was something to consider, Sienna conceded. She watched Nico put on his trousers before he crossed the room and took a shirt out of the wardrobe. Glancing around, she spied her clothes on a chair. When he disappeared into the en-suite bathroom, she jumped out of bed, intending to be dressed by the time he returned. She was halfway across the room when he walked back into the bedroom, and heat spread across her face when he stopped in his tracks.

'Don't stare at me,' she muttered self-consciously. 'My hips and bust are in competition to see which can expand faster.'

'You look gorgeous.' He came towards her, the undisguised hunger in his gaze causing molten warmth to pool between her thighs. 'Italian men appreciate a voluptuous female figure.' He grinned when her eyes flashed angrily. 'I am Italian, *cara*, and I love your curves. But you need a new bra.' He touched the red mark on her skin where the strap of her bra had cut in. 'Or better still, no bra,' he murmured, releasing the clasp before she realised his intention.

Freed from the restrictive garment, she took a deep breath and held it when Nico lightly circled one taut nipple with his finger. It felt so good. She wished he would tumble her down on the bed and kiss her breasts. Pregnancy had made her nipples ultra-sensitive.

But her pregnancy was the only reason he had come to look for her in London. The thought dropped into her brain, a cold, hard reality that Sienna could not ignore. Nico wanted his child and it was in his interest to keep her happy with sex. Furious with herself for allowing him to control her, she moved away from him and pulled on her jumper and trousers before zipping up her boots.

'I have somewhere in mind that could be an ideal premises for your new workshop,' Nico told her. 'I'll give you the rest of the week to hand over to your assistant who you said will manage Fresh Faced in London when you come to live at Villa Lionard.'

'I haven't agreed to live at the villa. I said I'll think about opening a workshop in Italy.' She bit her lip when she saw the determination on his face. 'Don't push it, Nico. After the way you treated me, you should be thankful that I am willing to consider the idea of sharing parenthood with you.'

'Would you put your pride before the best interests of our child?' he demanded. 'I can provide our son with two beautiful homes in England and Italy. If necessary, a court will have the final say on where he will grow up, and the decision will be made based on which of us can give our child the most stable and secure upbringing.'

Sienna opened her mouth but no words emerged. She felt sick as fear, shock and searing anger churned inside her. 'Are you saying that you will seek custody of the baby?'

'I hope it does not come to that,' Nico said coolly. 'But yes, I will do everything in my power to be a full-time father to my son and bring him up in Italy.'

'You really are a bastard,' she choked. She raced over to the door, desperate to get away from him before he saw the tears that blurred her vision. But before she could step into the corridor he caught hold of her arm and spun her round to face him.

'Think what you like of me. But no one will be able to call my son a bastard,' he said harshly. 'You *will* marry me, Sienna. I advise you not to keep me waiting too long.'

CHAPTER TEN

THE FLOWERS ARRIVED later that afternoon. Two dozen red roses, each a perfect bloom with velvety petals and a sensuous fragrance that permeated through the workshop, even though Sienna left the flowers in a vase on the reception desk out of her sight.

The card attached to the bouquet simply had Nico's name scrawled across it. She did not know if the roses were a peace offering or a calculated ploy to try to win her round. An angry silence had simmered between them in the car when his chauffeur had driven them from the hotel to her flat, en route to taking Nico to the airport. Nico had looked at the shop front on Camden High Street with the name Ali's Kebabs over the door and muttered something uncomplimentary beneath his breath.

The next day a bouquet of lilies was delivered to the workshop and the day after that it was freesias, gerberas and daisies tied with a pink ribbon.

'Well, I think it's romantic that Nico is so keen to be reconciled with you,' Carley said at the end of the week, when Sienna plonked the latest delivery of exquisitely scented white orchids into a bucket of water. They had run out of vases.

'He's only keen to have his own way,' Sienna muttered. 'Nico doesn't like to take no for an answer.'

'How well you know me, *cara*.' A familiar, oh, so sexy voice came from the doorway. She spun round and stared at Nico as he strolled into the workshop. He was wearing faded jeans and a grey sweater topped by a tan leather jacket that looked butter-soft. Raindrops clung to his dark hair and he lifted a hand to push it off his brow. Sienna was aware that Carley's jaw had dropped. It wasn't fair that Nico was so gorgeous, she thought when she introduced him to her assistant and best friend.

'You had better come into my office,' she told him, furious with herself for the rush of hot jealousy she felt when he smiled at Carley. 'Are you in London on business or…um…pleasure?' She flushed when his eyes gleamed wickedly.

'It is always a pleasure to see you, Sienna,' he murmured. 'I have found premises for your new workshop and thought you would like to take a look at it.'

She frowned. 'In Italy, do you mean? When will I need to fly out?' During the last week she had come to the conclusion that establishing a branch of Fresh Faced in Italy made sense for the business and for her personally because it would allow her to combine work and motherhood. She was afraid that Nico had not made an idle threat when he'd said he would be prepared to fight for custody of their child. But if she found a place to live for her and the baby near to Villa Lionard, perhaps he would be content to visit whenever he wanted.

'The pilot is preparing my plane for the return flight to Verona, and my car is outside now to take us to the airport,' he said smoothly.

She bit her lip, angry that once again he thought he could simply take over her life. But it was Friday lunchtime, all the orders were up to date and for once she had the weekend free. There was no harm in going with him to see if the premises he had found could be turned into a workshop.

'I suppose Carley can take over here for the rest of the day,' she said reluctantly. 'But I'll have to go back to my flat and pack an overnight bag.'

'There's no need for you to bring anything. I've arranged for you to meet a personal shopper in Verona. It won't be long before you will need to wear maternity clothes,' he pointed out before she could argue.

Lake Garda in the autumn was astonishingly beautiful. The trees were a riot of red, gold and bronze, and the calm lake reflected the pink clouds in the sky above, stained by the sun as it slowly sank below the horizon.

Nico drove them from the airport in his scarlet Ferrari. When he turned the car onto the driveway of Villa Lionard, the knot of tension in Sienna's stomach tightened as she remembered how he had dismissed her from the house and his life a month ago. Now he believed the baby she was expecting was his but she wasn't foolish enough to think he had sent her flowers as a romantic gesture. He wanted his son and she was a necessary part of the equation—at least she was until she gave birth, and only then if the baby survived.

'When are you taking me to see the new workshop?' she asked as she climbed out of the car. 'Is it in Verona?'

'It's here, and you can see it now.' He smiled at her look of surprise and wrapped his hand around hers. Instead of ushering her inside the villa, he led her around to the courtyard at the rear of the house and over to what had, a century or so ago, been a farm outhouse. The building had been turned into garages where Nico kept his collection of sports cars. But when he opened the door there were no cars inside.

'Welcome to your new workshop,' he said. 'What do you think of it?'

'It's impressive,' Sienna said slowly. She walked around the big space, noting the long work counter in the centre of the room and more worktops next to the double sinks along one wall. There were plenty of cupboards and shelves, as well as two fridges for storing the perishable ingredients she used in her products. At the far end of the workshop double-height windows looked out over Lake Garda, and, although the light was fading as dusk fell, she could see big containers on the patio where she could grow herbs and plants such as lavender and chamomile for her products. The workshop was perfect, she acknowledged, but she couldn't help feeling that she was being manipulated by Nico.

'Builders have worked all week to reconfigure the garages into a workspace for you,' he said.

'Where will you keep all your cars?'

'I intend to sell most of them. Becoming a parent will require me to give up some of the things I enjoy, but it will be a small price to pay when I have my son.'

Sienna wondered what other things he planned to give up. Sex-without-strings affairs with beautiful women, perhaps? Or would he just be more discreet when he took lovers?

'You don't seem very thrilled. If there is anything else you need, tell me.' He walked towards her, his eyes narrowing on her tense face. 'I had the workshop created so that you can live at the villa and continue to run your business after the baby is born. You told me that you want to carry on working.'

'I do,' Sienna muttered.

'So what's the problem?' he demanded, sounding annoyed by her lack of enthusiasm. He made her feel like a stroppy child, she thought angrily.

'You're the problem, Nico.' She made a frustrated sound when his brows lifted. 'The workshop is wonderful, and I'm grateful.' She almost choked on the word. She didn't feel grateful, she felt infuriated by his determination to control every situation, to control her. 'But you didn't create the workshop as a nice gesture to make me happy. You did it so that I wouldn't be able to refuse to move to Villa Lionard.'

His brows drew together in a heavy scowl. 'Why don't you want to move here? We agreed that it is the best place for the baby to live.'

'*I* didn't agree to anything. *You* threatened to take my baby away.'

He swore. 'I am trying to find a solution that will allow us to both be parents to our child.'

'You always want your own way.' Her voice rose as she gave vent to her temper that had simmered since Nico had swept back into her life and clearly expected her to be grateful that he wanted his baby. 'You think that if you send me flowers and present me with a workshop I will fall in with your plans just as I did when I was your teenage bride. But I am not the girl who worshipped the ground you walked on.'

Sienna broke off to snatch a breath. Nico looked stunned that she had the temerity to tell him a few home truths, but she didn't care. It was time he realised that he couldn't push her around. 'When I married you I was so in love with you and I would have done anything to make you happy. But you didn't love me and you didn't trust me.'

'How could I have known that Danny lied to me?' Nico said curtly.

'You could have asked me for the truth. You *should* have asked me.'

'He is my brother...'

'I was your *wife*.' She felt angrier than she had ever been in her life, and Nico's shuttered expression made her angrier still. She never knew what he was thinking. He never let her in. 'You haven't even apologised for the terrible things you accused me of when we found out about this pregnancy.' She hated that she couldn't hide the hurt in her voice, the faint quiver that betrayed her.

'I regret that I said those things,' he said gruffly. 'I regret that I allowed my brother's jealousy ten years ago to come between us, twice.' His gaze burned into hers and she sensed that he was struggling to maintain his iron self-control.

'There is no us, Nico.' It was painful to say and it made her realise how much she had secretly hoped there could be when they had met again eight years after their divorce. 'There never was *us*. There was sexual attraction that would have burned out if I hadn't fallen pregnant. I would have suffered a broken heart for a few months and you would have married someone more suitable to be your viscountess than the village publican's daughter.'

'But it didn't burn out,' he said, his eyes blazing as

he walked towards her. 'Ten years after we first made love on a windswept moor, the chemistry between us is as combustible as it ever was.'

Sienna shook her head but he kept coming closer, backing her up against the work counter and stretching his arms out on either side of her so that she was caged in. Too late, she realised that she had unleashed the tiger, but she did not turn away when he lowered his head so that his warm breath grazed across her lips. Her heart clattered against her ribs when he tangled his fingers in her hair. Desire ran like quicksilver in her blood. 'Do you want me to do this?'

All she could do was whisper, 'Yes,' then he crushed her lips beneath his.

Relief swept through Nico when Sienna opened her mouth to the demands of his and responded to his kiss. The force of her anger had been like a wild storm. He'd thought he had lost her, and he was shocked by how much it bothered him. If she walked away from him, he knew it was what he deserved. He had let her down badly and she did not trust him, but somehow he would convince her that if she married him he would never give her a reason to doubt his commitment to their marriage or their child.

He fisted her hair and deepened the kiss, tangling his tongue with hers in an erotic dance that set his blood on fire. She wrenched her mouth free, her eyes glinting like silver flames. 'Sex doesn't solve anything,' she told him bitterly.

'Let's see, shall we?' He sought her lips again, but she evaded his mouth and sank her teeth into the side of his neck. 'Wildcat,' he growled, supremely turned on by her fierceness. 'So you want to play rough, do you? I hope you can take as good as you give.' He kissed his way up her throat before he bit her earlobe. She gasped and he smothered the sound with his mouth, kissing her with mounting hunger as she threaded her fingers into his hair and gave a hard tug.

'I hate what you do to me, the way you make me feel,' she muttered, anger and vulnerability darkening her eyes when they came up for air. 'I hate myself for responding to you like a sex addict when I don't even like you.'

'It's the same for me,' he told her, catching her hand and holding it over the burgeoning proof that he was very, very aroused. 'I only have to look at you and I'm desperate. But as well as desiring you, I like you, Sienna.' It was a truth he could not deny to himself or to her. 'I admire your independent spirit, your determination and your compassion, and I hope our son will grow up to have those qualities.'

Tears shimmered in her eyes. 'You say these things but I don't know if I can believe you.' Her voice cracked. 'I don't know how to handle you.'

He circled his hips against her hand where it was resting on his crotch and groaned when she explored the hard ridge of his erection through his trousers. 'You are handling me perfectly, *cara*.'

Her dress was a wrap-around style and he untied the belt and ran his hands greedily over her body when the dress fell open. Quickly dispensing with her bra, he cradled her heavy breasts in his hands.

'Your breasts are bigger.' He did not try to hide his satisfaction. Pregnancy had made her body softer and even more sensual. Nico was impatient to discover every inch of her new voluptuous shape, to taste her vanilla-scented skin. He bent his head and drew one taut nipple into his mouth, enjoying the husky moans she made as he sucked hard before transferring his mouth to her other nipple and feasting on the cherry-red peak.

She gave a startled gasp when he lifted her and sat her on the edge of the work counter. Her eyes were wide, the pupils dilated as he tugged her dress off. 'If I'd known you were wearing stockings I would have had my hands on you long before now,' he said rawly, running his fingers over the lacy bands at the top of her thighs. Her legs looked gorgeous in sheer black stockings and the sweet scent of her arousal surrounded him when he pushed the panel of her panties to one side and buried his face between her thighs.

'Nico.' Her moans grew louder as he ran the tip of his tongue over her opening and then pushed it into her moist heat. She tasted of cream and the heavenly musk of her femininity heightened his desire as he pushed her legs wider apart and teased the tight nub of her clitoris with his tongue.

She arched backwards, thrusting her hips towards him while she supported herself with her hands flat on the counter. 'Oh, God, Nico, I want you inside me.'

He wanted that too. He wanted her so badly that his hands shook as he opened his zip and freed his erection from his trousers. She was so beautiful. Nico felt drunk with desire as he studied her creamy skin and the flush of rose pink on her cheeks and breasts. Her burgundy hair gleamed like raw silk on her shoulders.

He pushed her down so that she was lying on her back on the counter and tugged her panties off before he climbed on top of her, shoving her legs apart with his thigh. 'You are so wet, *cara*,' he said hoarsely when he slid a finger inside her and then withdrew it and licked her sweetness from his skin.

She wrapped her legs around his back, her fingers attacking his shirt buttons before she ran her hands over his bare chest. 'Now,' she said fiercely. 'I want you *now*.'

Her boldness excited him, and knowing that he was the only man who had ever possessed her evoked an odd tightness in his chest. Eyes locked with hers, he pressed forwards so that the tip of his manhood pressed against her entrance, and then he slid in deep, every one of his muscles locked as he fought to control the raging fire that threatened to consume him.

'*Sei mio,*' he whispered, his mouth pressed to her throat. In a distant recess of his mind an alarm bell rang. Possessiveness was an unknown emotion to him. And yet when he thrust into her, faster, harder, and took them both to the edge before they fell into the abyss together, a voice inside him insisted, *Mine*.

A long time later, when his heart-rate had returned to something like normal, Nico lifted himself off her and refastened his trousers. He looked at Sienna and found her watching him from beneath the sweep of her lashes.

'I will never be able to make my skincare creams here without remembering that we used this work counter for a very different reason,' she said ruefully.

'But you will set up a branch of Fresh Faced at Villa Lionard.' He made it a statement rather than a question and she gave him a measured look but did not disagree. He lifted her down from the counter and helped her into her clothes before he took hold of her hand and led her outside and across the courtyard to the main house. 'You can move into the villa immediately. I'll show you to your room.'

At the top of the stairs he turned down a corridor and opened the door of the master suite. Sienna followed him into the room, and Nico found that he disliked the wary expression in her eyes. 'This is your room,' she said guardedly.

'*Our* room, from now on.' He drew her into his arms and kissed away her frown. 'You said that sex doesn't solve anything, but I disagree. Our physical compatibility has never been in doubt.'

'The fact that we are good together in bed is hardly a stable base on which to build the kind of trusting relationship we will need when we become parents.'

'Are you suggesting that love is stable? A flimsy and in many cases transient emotional response is far more likely to fail. And when it does, the fallout can be much more damaging to a child caught between two parents whose love has turned to hatred and bitter acrimony.'

Nico swung away from Sienna and strode across the room to stare out of the window. It was completely dark now and the lake was outlined by the twinkling lights of the houses and villages that hugged the shore. 'I love how peaceful it is here,' he said abruptly. 'But my mother was bored at the villa and rarely visited—which is probably why I found it so peaceful.' After a moment he said, 'I was twelve when my mother tried to take her own life the first time.'

He heard Sienna gasp and saw her reflection in the window pane when she sat down on the edge of the bed. 'I had no idea. You didn't say much about your childhood while we were married.'

Nico remembered she had said that they had been strangers on their wedding day. 'It wasn't something I found easy to talk about.' His jaw clenched. 'I still don't. As a boy, knowing that I couldn't make my mother happy so that she would want to live was hard. I felt I had let her down even though the cause of her unhappiness was my father. I blamed myself for not being around to comfort her. I was away at boarding school for most of the time and, to be honest…' he grimaced '…it was a relief to go back to school or spend part of the holidays at Villa Lionard with my Italian grandparents, away from my parents' rows and my mother's tears.'

'Jacqueline wasn't your responsibility,' Sienna said gently. 'What actually happened?'

'Danny and I were staying at Sethbury Hall for the summer. My parents had separated by then, and my father had gone to live in Paris with his latest mistress.'

He raked a hand through his hair, not certain why he felt a need to open up to Sienna about events in his childhood that he'd never told anyone else. 'My mother had promised to take me and my brother out for the day, but when she hadn't got up by lunchtime, I went to her room and found her unconscious in bed. Her skin was grey and cold and I thought she was dead.' Twenty years later, Nico remembered as if it had happened yesterday the icy shock that had slithered down his spine when he'd touched his mother's limp hand. 'She had taken an overdose of sleeping pills and left a note in which she blamed my father's infidelity for her unhappiness.'

'I'm so sorry.' Sienna's voice sounded closer and when he turned his head he found she was standing beside him. 'It would have been a terrible experience for an adult, let alone a twelve-year-old boy.' She slipped her hand into his and squeezed his fingers, compassion darkening her eyes as she asked, 'Did Jacqueline make other suicide attempts?'

'One other, and she was very nearly successful.' Nico gripped Sienna's small hand that fitted so perfectly into his much larger one. 'My father was a serial adulterer but my mother was besotted with him.'

'I only met Franco a few times but I remember that he was very handsome. He reminded me of one of those matinee idols like Clark Gable or Cary Grant.'

'He had something—charisma, charm—that made women throw themselves at him.'

'Like father, like son,' Sienna said drily.

Nico shook his head. 'No, I am not like him in one crucial respect. I enjoy sex and I enjoy women but I always make it clear at the start of an affair that I won't fall in love. My father got an ego boost from making women fall in love with him. He played with their hearts before he trampled on them. In many ways my mother was just as bad. She said she loved Franco but what she really wanted was to own him. Her possessiveness bordered on maniacal and she drove my father away with her jealousy.'

'My parents' marriage was no better than yours.' Sienna grimaced. 'The only difference is that mine didn't row, they rarely spoke to each other at all. Surely we have just given two very good examples of why we shouldn't get married.'

'On the contrary. Our parents' marriages failed because of the expectation that falling in love is a guarantee of happy ever after. But love is a fantasy, and the reality is that marriage between two people who share the same values and aspirations—in our case to be good parents to our child—stands a much better chance of lasting.'

'We lasted two years,' she reminded him.

'It went wrong between us before because emotions were involved.'

'Not your emotions, Nico.' Sienna's tone was as dry as a desert. 'Don't worry,' she said when he frowned. 'I grew out of my infatuation with you. But do you really believe that a marriage without emotions can succeed? Is a loveless marriage what you want?'

Nico could not comprehend why Sienna's question made his heart clench. Of course he wanted a partnership without the dramas and histrionics that had littered his parents' relationship, he assured himself.

'More important to me than anything else is that my son is born legitimate,' he admitted. 'After my father died, I learned that he had a number of illegitimate children. As far as I am aware Franco never had any contact with his offspring. I don't know their identities, or even how many other children he fathered. His lawyers dealt with the paternity claims and the women were paid off.'

He met Sienna's startled gaze. 'I will not abandon my child. And I know how much you want to be a mother. Our son deserves for us to be the best parents we can possibly be and although it might be considered old-fashioned to marry for the sake of our baby, I believe it is the right thing to do.' He looked down at their linked hands and lifted her fingers up to press his lips against her knuckles. 'What do you say, *cara*? Will you be my wife?'

CHAPTER ELEVEN

'I NEED SOME time to think about it.' Sienna ignored the leap her heart gave at Nico's proposal. He had made it clear that he was suggesting a marriage of convenience and it was crucial she did not involve her heart in her decision.

'What is there to think about?' he demanded, his blue eyes glittering with impatience. He pulled her into his arms and held her hard up against his whipcord body. 'We can make it work, *cara*. We are both passionate people and you will never find another man who can satisfy you like I can.'

She stiffened, angered by his arrogance. But she was strong enough to match his self-assurance, and she would not allow him to dominate her because she knew that he was as much a slave to their mutual desire as she was. Her weakness for him was also her strength, Sienna realised, and the proof was in the low groan he gave when she pressed her pelvis against his rock-hard arousal.

'Witch,' he muttered against her mouth before he claimed her lips in a fierce kiss that left her breathless and trembling when he finally lifted his head and stared into her eyes. 'Marry me and I swear you will not regret it.'

She fought the temptation to give into his strong will. 'Ask me again in a month. I'll be over twenty-two weeks then. Hopefully.' He looked puzzled and she said quietly, 'I miscarried at twenty-two weeks and I don't want to tempt fate.'

'You're superstitious?'

'I'm scared,' she admitted, looking away from him. 'I want this baby so much and I don't know how I will bear it if something goes wrong.' She expected Nico to casually dismiss her fears but he slid his hand beneath her chin and tilted her face up to his. The tenderness in his expression stole around her heart.

'The scan and other checks you had in England showed no problems,' he reminded her softly. 'Next week you have an appointment with one of the highest-regarded obstetricians in Italy who will care for you for the remainder of your pregnancy. And I intend to make sure that you eat well and get plenty of rest,' he said, lifting her into his arms and carrying her over to the bed. 'Starting now.'

Sienna lay back on the pillows and gave him a quizzical look when he stretched his tall frame out beside her on the bed. He was so gorgeous, and when he smiled at her the way he was doing now she was ready to believe that they could make marriage work a second time around. 'Do you need to rest too?' she murmured, trailing her fingers down his shirt and slipping them beneath the waistband of his trousers. 'Because I'm not tired.'

His eyes flashed with wicked intent as he flipped her dress up to her waist and stroked the bare strip of skin above the lacy band of her stocking top. 'In that case we had better find something else to occupy us before dinner, hadn't we, *mia bellezza*?'

* * *

A week went by, and then another. Sienna was so busy hiring staff and getting the new workshop up and running that she forgot her initial doubts about agreeing to move to Villa Lionard. As autumn slipped into winter, Nico seemed determined to build the foundations of a strong relationship with her. He took an interest in her business and advised her on marketing strategies to promote the Fresh Faced ethos of using sustainable and natural ingredients. Sienna had been relieved when the coup in Tutjo ended with the King returned to power, and the women's cooperatives were safe and able to harvest Marula oil once more.

The first heavy snowfall of the winter had draped the mountains in a white cloak that sparkled in the afternoon sunshine. From the workshop Sienna could see through the tall windows a couple of sailing boats skimming over the lake. The water was as blue as the cloudless sky and when she'd walked across to the workshop from the villa, the air was cold and crisp.

The sound of a car pulling up in the courtyard caused her heart to skip a beat. Nico had been away on a business trip for two days, and, although he had phoned her numerous times, she couldn't wait to see him again. She heard his footsteps on the cobbles and then his tall frame filled the doorway. He looked impossibly handsome in a grey wool coat. His black hair gleamed in the sunshine and his blue eyes were the colour of the sky.

'Nico.' Sienna flew across the workshop and into his open arms, tilting her face up as he bent his head and claimed her mouth in a deeply sensual kiss.

'Mmm, that was some welcome,' he murmured. 'I

think you must have missed me while I was away, *cara.*'

The satisfaction she heard in his voice reminded her to curb her enthusiastic greeting. 'I've been so busy that I barely noticed you weren't here,' she said airily.

An odd expression flickered on his face, but then it was gone, and Sienna told herself she must have imagined that he'd looked hurt. She felt a fluttering movement inside her and caught hold of his hand, pressing it against the firm swell of her stomach. She had been living at the villa for over a month, and maybe it was superstitious but she'd felt so relieved when she'd safely passed twenty-two weeks in her pregnancy. An ultrasound scan a few days ago had shown that her baby son was a good size and had a strong heartbeat, and she'd dared to start planning the colour scheme for the nursery.

'There, did you feel him move?' she asked Nico. They shared a smile when, right on cue, the baby kicked.

'Come back to the house. I have something to show you.' He looped his arm around her shoulders as they walked across the courtyard. Sienna loved the companionship between them that had emerged gradually over the last weeks. Their relationship might have got off to a rocky start but they were both trying to move on from the past.

'I thought you were going to stay away for one more night,' she said when they were in the sitting room and Nico stoked the fire that was burning in the hearth.

'I raced through my business meetings today so that I could fly home to be with you.' His voice was very deep, his accent more pronounced than usual, and Sienna's heart leapt at the realisation that he had meant it. He took a small package out of his briefcase and handed it to her. She tore off the wrapping paper and gave a soft cry of delight as she studied the photograph of a 4D scan image of their baby that Nico had had framed.

'Thank you. The picture is so clear, isn't it? It's so sweet that the baby is sucking his thumb.'

'Close your eyes,' he told her, 'and open your mouth.'

'Are you going to tell me why?'

'You have to trust me, *cara*.'

As Sienna obediently closed her eyes it occurred to her that she did trust him implicitly. She opened her mouth and then gave a sigh of pleasure when she tasted chocolate on her tongue. Her lashes swept upwards and she watched Nico take another chocolate out of a box of the finest Swiss confectionery and pop it between her lips. 'I *love* chocolate,' she murmured.

'I know. And you love kittens, and orphaned orangutans,' he said drily.

She grinned. 'The head of the orangutan sanctuary in Borneo was very grateful for the donation you made after we watched a documentary on TV about how orangutans are losing their natural habitat.'

Sienna glanced over at the two kittens asleep on the rug in front of the fire. Nico had brought them back to the villa a couple of weeks ago after she'd told him that she had always wanted a cat, but couldn't keep one at her flat on a busy London street. Charlie and Tiggs were adorable bundles of mischief. It was becoming increasingly hard to imagine leaving Villa Lionard and Nico, she thought ruefully. The villa felt like her home, and as the days passed—not to mention the incredible nights when Nico made love to her with passion coupled with an inherent tenderness that wrapped around her heart—she knew that she was falling ever deeper in love with him.

'I have one more surprise for you, but you will have to wait until tomorrow. Don't pout or I will have to kiss you, and you know where that always leads,' he said, kissing her anyway.

'Are you sure I can't persuade you to divulge your secret?' she murmured, trailing her fingers over the bulge evident beneath his trousers.

Nico drew her down onto the sofa. 'My lips are sealed, but I have no objection to you trying, *cara mia.*'

'I know you offered to teach me to ski, but I didn't think you meant now, when I'm five months pregnant,' Sienna said the next day when they were in the car and Nico drove past a road sign pointing to Malcesine Monte Baldo.

He laughed. 'Don't worry, we won't be skiing. But we are going to the top of the mountain in a cable car.'

'For any particular reason?'

He turned his head and gave her a look that she couldn't decipher. It was ridiculous to think he seemed nervous, she told herself. 'You'll find out soon,' was all he would say.

They took the cable car from the base station in the picturesque little town of Malcesine. Even in winter the area was a magnet for tourists and Sienna was surprised that she and Nico had a cabin to themselves, until he explained that he had booked a private trip for them. 'The cabin rotates as the cable car ascends, giving a three-hundred-and-sixty-degree view of the lake and mountains,' he said. 'On a clear day like today it's quite something.'

'The view is breathtaking.' Sienna was blown away by the sheer scale of the huge blue lake beneath them and the mountains soaring towards the sky, their snow-covered peaks glistening in the bright sunshine. 'I've never seen anything so beautiful.'

'Neither have I,' Nico said softly. But he wasn't looking at the view. He was staring at her, and her breath caught in her throat when he reached into his coat pocket and withdrew a small velvet box. He opened it and took out an exquisite oval-shaped sapphire ring surrounded by glittering diamonds. 'Will you marry me, Sienna?'

Her heart collided with her ribs. He had not mentioned marriage since he'd asked her the day he had brought her to Villa Lionard more than a month ago. Then, she had been uncertain about accepting what was still in essence a marriage of convenience. But Sienna had decided that she could not deny her son his birthright. Although Nico had not spoken of love, they had formed a close bond, and she believed that he cared for her a little. Her heart yearned for more, but she had learned that you couldn't always have what you wanted. And perhaps in time he would grow to love her in the way that she loved him, wholeheartedly and unreservedly, she told herself.

'Yes.' Her hand trembled when he slid the ring onto her finger. It fitted perfectly, as if it belonged there, just as her heart belonged to Nico.

Swept up on a wave of optimism, she felt sure that it would only be a matter of time before he fell in love with her. But for now she must suppress the joy that exploded in her heart and quell the choir of angels singing inside her. Time and patience were on her side. His beautifully romantic proposal had revealed a softer side to him, and when they were married she would have a lifetime to try to breach his defences and reach his heart that he guarded so well.

She lifted her hand up and watched the diamonds catch fire in the bright sunlight. Smiling at Nico, she said calmly, 'I agree that in the circumstances marriage is the most sensible thing to do.'

Of course marriage was a sensible option; the only option he would accept, Nico brooded. Obviously he was glad Sienna understood that his proposal had been a practical solution. So why did the word *sensible* stick in his throat during lunch at a restaurant on the summit of the mountain? He had eaten here before and knew the food was good, but his appetite had disappeared.

'Have you any thoughts on when you would like the wedding to take place?' she asked when she finished her plate of *tagliatelle* and gave a sigh of satisfaction.

'In a month. We have to give notice of our intention to marry.'

She nodded. 'It makes sense to get the wedding out of the way well before the baby is due.'

'Indeed, *cara*,' he said through gritted teeth.

'Are you all right? You haven't eaten much of your lunch.' Sienna stared at him across the table. 'Are you having second thoughts about us getting married? It was your idea. It doesn't matter to me, and it won't matter to the baby if we are married or we live together as we have done for the past month.'

'It matters that our son is legitimate when he is born,' he growled, instantly regretting his curt tone when Sienna bit her lip. What the hell was the matter with him? Nico wondered. Why did he feel a strong desire to walk around the table and kiss her until she was flushed and breathless and desperate for him to make love to her? He had no idea why he wanted to shatter her calm composure but if she uttered the word *sensible* one more time he would not be responsible for his actions.

'We'll go to Sethbury Hall to tell Iris and Rose that you are pregnant and announce our engagement. I'm surprised you haven't told your grandmother about the baby. Why did you keep your pregnancy a secret?'

'I felt embarrassed.'

'Embarrassed. Why?' He was shocked by her reply and wondered if she was ashamed to be expecting his child.

'It is the second time that I accidentally conceived your baby.' There was a defensive note in Sienna's voice. 'Rose was bound to ask me who the father is, but the situation between us was complicated, and it was easier to say nothing while my pregnancy wasn't showing. Unlike now.' She stood up and gave a rueful glance down at her swollen belly.

Throughout lunch, Nico had been unable to take his eyes off Sienna. He'd watched the sunlight bring out the myriad shades of red in her hair: burgundy, auburn and copper tones that complemented her peaches-and-cream complexion. Her smoky grey eyes were fringed by long lashes a shade darker than her hair. And as for her mouth… He swallowed hard. Her mouth was to die for. He knew how soft it felt beneath his when he kissed her, and memories of how she used her tongue with such devastating effect on his body sent a hot rush of desire down to his groin.

He pulled his mind to the present. 'You look beautiful,' he told her gruffly. 'I love seeing the evidence that my child is inside you and growing bigger and stronger every day.'

They walked out of the restaurant and she turned her head and gave him a speculative look. '*Love*, Nico? I didn't know the word was in your vocabulary. Does it mean that you will love our son?'

'Of course I will.' He was taken aback by her question. 'I am not devoid of feelings.' He'd have no problem loving his baby, who would look to him for care and protection—and who would not leave him. The thought slid into Nico's consciousness. A baby wouldn't be able to take a handful of sleeping pills or walk away from him without a backward glance. He exhaled slowly, wishing he knew what Sienna was thinking behind her cool grey gaze.

'Good,' she said gravely. 'Our baby deserves to have our unconditional love.' Something moved in her eyes: a question that Nico could not answer. But perhaps he imagined he saw a flicker of hurt on her face when his silence stretched for too long. 'We had better get on with organising a wedding,' she said, stepping away from him. 'I think it will be sensible to keep it a low-key event, don't you?'

Rain streamed down the window panes of Sethbury Hall but in the drawing room the flames leaping in the hearth were reflected in the oak-panelled walls and lent the room a rosy glow.

'Your engagement ring is stunning,' Iris said as she inspected the sapphire and diamond cluster on Sienna's finger. 'I understand that the wedding will be in Verona. A simple register office ceremony with a couple of close friends as witnesses, Nico told me.'

'Yes, we decided that a low-key wedding would be best,' Sienna said, patting her stomach, which seemed to expand daily. 'I would look like a ship in full sail if I wore a traditional white wedding gown.'

'That's not true.' Nico was leaning against the mantelpiece. He looked over at her and gave her a sexy smile that heated her blood. 'You look gorgeous whatever you wear, and you are even more beautiful wearing nothing at all.'

'Nico!' Fiery colour stained Sienna's cheeks and she could not look at his grandmother or her Grandma Rose.

Iris laughed. 'Pregnancy is often a very passionate time for a couple,' she said cheerfully. 'You are looking well, Sienna. That jade-green of your dress is lovely with your colouring. Being pregnant suits you.' She turned to Sienna's grandmother. 'Don't you think so, Rose?'

'I think that being in love is what makes Sienna and Nico both look so content,' Rose said softly.

Sienna jerked her gaze from Nico and looked down at her hand, pretending to study her ring. She sensed the tension that gripped him. She wanted to say something to fill the awkward silence, but she could hardly blurt out the truth to their grandmothers that their marriage was a practical arrangement.

She was relieved when Iris changed the subject. 'Domenico, while I remember, will you come and look at some documents my lawyer wants me to sign? I left them in the study.'

'I'll read them now, before lunch,' Nico said abruptly. Sienna looked up at the same time that he glanced over at her and she wondered why he was frowning. He'd been in a strange mood ever since they had arrived at Sethbury Hall. She suspected that he missed his brother, whom he had not spoken to since he'd learned of Danny's lies.

'It's time to forget what happened in the past,' she had told Nico. 'You need to forgive Danny.'

'How can you say that after what he did? My brother's lies drove us apart.'

'No. Our mistrust of each other was what drove us apart,' she'd said flatly. 'We can't blame other people for the mistakes we made in our first marriage.'

After Nico pushed his grandmother in her wheelchair out of the room, Grandma Rose reached over and patted Sienna's hand. 'I am so glad that you and Nico are marrying for love. I see it in the way you look at him. And his eyes are full of love for you.'

Sienna bit her lip. 'Nanna…' she whispered, but her grandmother did not hear her.

'It was very different when I married your grandfather,' Rose said. 'I was pregnant with your father, and in those days being an unmarried mother was not accepted like it is now. My parents expected Peter to marry me, and he did his duty and proposed to me.' She sighed. 'I was madly in love with him. I knew he didn't share my feelings but I hoped he would fall in love with me once we were married.'

'Did he?' Sienna's grandfather had died when she

was a child and she had vague memories of a dour, short-tempered man.

'No. He resented the marriage and felt trapped. For a long time—too long—I thought things would change and we would grow closer, but Peter started to drink heavily and my feelings for him faded.'

'Why did you stay in a marriage that made you both unhappy?'

'We both loved our son—your father—and we stayed together for his sake. But our sour relationship affected Clive. When he grew up he spoke to me disrespectfully just as his father did, and when he married your mother I'm sorry to say that he treated her badly and drank heavily like his father.'

Rose wiped away a tear. 'I spent much of my life waiting for love that never happened. I thought I was doing the right thing for my son by staying in a loveless marriage, but the truth is that your father would have had a happier childhood if Peter and I had separated.'

The conversation moved on to other things, but Sienna could not concentrate as a dawning terrible realisation turned her blood to ice in her veins. There were glaring similarities between her grandmother's relationship with her husband, and her own relationship with Nico. Like Sienna, Grandma Rose had been in love, but her husband had only married her out of duty because she had been pregnant. Sienna's father had been damaged by growing up with parents trapped in an unhappy marriage, and it had affected Clive's relationship with Rose and with Sienna's mother.

She looked over at her grandmother and saw that she had nodded off to sleep. Iris returned to the drawing room and said that Nico had gone for a workout in the gym before lunch. Sienna's heart was thumping when she walked out of the house and along the path to the old stable block, which had been converted into a gym. She had to talk to Nico and find out if she had been deluding herself to hope that the attention he'd paid her while they had lived together at Villa Lionard meant he felt something for her.

She opened the door of the gym and stepped inside. Nico had his back to her and was pummelling a punchbag with his fists. He was stripped to the waist and a pair of sweatpants sat low on his hips. For several moments she simply stood there in the shadows and watched the ripple of his hard muscles and the gleam of his satiny skin beaded with sweat. He was so beautiful. That lean, hard body was a work of art, and the power in every blow he landed on the punchbag was an indication of his physical strength.

There was something untamed about him. Untameable, Sienna acknowledged. Nico would never be owned. Even more powerful than his muscular physique was his mental strength. There was not a hint of vulnerability about this man, and the truth hit her then that Nico viewed love as a weakness.

She made a muffled sound, trying to contain her emotions, but he must have heard her, and he spun round, a concerned expression on his face when he saw her. '*Cara*, what's wrong?' he demanded, pulling off his boxing gloves as he strode over to her. 'You are so pale. Are you unwell?' His voice sharpened. 'The baby…?'

She bit her lip. Of course he was concerned for the baby. The child they had created together in the heat of passion was the only reason he had put an engagement ring on her finger, and why he was so determined to put a wedding band beside it. 'I feel fine,' she assured him, the lie battering her bruised heart.

Nico's look of relief shattered her control over the storm of feelings swirling inside her. His relief was for the baby. Everything he felt was for the baby but he felt nothing for her, and it *hurt*.

'I can't do it, Nico,' she said, her voice cracking. 'I can't go through with a loveless marriage.'

He stiffened, and she sensed his barriers go up, shutting her out. 'We agreed—' he began, but she cut him off.

'I only agreed to marry you because I thought… I hoped that you would love me eventually. But I saw your face when Rose commented that we have the look of love. I saw rejection in your eyes when you glanced at me.' His expression had pierced her heart like an arrow.

Nico put his hands on her shoulders and ignored her attempts to pull free. 'Why are you so hung up on love?' he said harshly. 'What we had in Italy—friendship, trust, affection—why aren't those things enough?'

'Because I need more.' The pain in Sienna's chest was so intense that she could barely breathe. Her lungs felt constricted as the scales fell from her eyes and she saw the truth that she had been hiding from because it was so agonising. 'I want to love and be loved and I realised today that I can't accept anything less.'

'Love is a fool's game,' he gritted. 'I saw how loving my father almost destroyed my mother, and I promised myself that I would never make the mistakes my parents made.'

'But you haven't shut love out of your life completely. You said you will love your son. And I have seen the love you have for your grandmother and your brother.' Sienna twisted out of his grip and stared at his face, searching for some small sign of softening, but she saw none. He was granite down to his core.

'It's just me that you don't love,' she choked. 'If I refuse to marry you I will deny our son his birthright, but it is better that, than for him to grow up afraid of love like his father is.'

CHAPTER TWELVE

HE WAS NOT AFRAID. Nico slammed his fists into the punchbag. *Dio*, what was it with women and their need for a fairy tale that only existed in fiction? He had witnessed the dark side of love; the jealousy and power play, the empty bottle of pills on his mother's bedside table, the wail of an ambulance's siren.

Who wanted to live on an emotional roller coaster? He had been a boy when he'd decided to jump off that particular ride and stick to something safer...

Because he was afraid to fall in love.

The truth hit Nico harder than the blows he landed on the punchbag. He had locked his heart away and thrown away the key when his mother had tried to end her life that she'd decided was not worth living without the love of Nico's father, who had been a serial adulterer incapable of loving anyone other than himself. His mother hadn't appreciated the impact of her suicide attempts on her young sons.

Love *hurt*. It was why he had avoided that pernicious emotion, but despite his determination to live his life on his terms, Sienna had swept back into his life like a tornado and made him want the one thing he had told himself he had no need of. The one thing he could not control.

Damn her for forcing him to face the issue he was desperate to ignore, he thought savagely as he tore off his boxing gloves and strode out of the gym. He had been tempted to go straight after Sienna when she'd left five minutes ago, but he'd held back, not prepared to acknowledge that the sight of her tears had ripped his heart out.

Give her time to calm down, he'd told himself. Let the storm pass and when she was in a more reasonable frame of mind he would convince her that they were fine without the gut-wrenching, terrifying emotion that he knew love was.

He walked back to the house through the rain that had started to fall again from the leaden sky. After quickly checking the rooms on the ground floor and not finding Sienna there, he ran upstairs and along the corridor to the master suite. It was empty, but he immediately noticed her engagement ring on the coffee table.

Hell. Clenching his fists by his sides, he glanced across to the window and something outside caught his attention. A figure in a vivid green dress was hurrying along the path and through the gate that led from the garden of Sethbury Hall directly onto the moors.

Sienna was leaving him *again*!

Nico heard his blood thunder in his ears. Emotions he had kept at bay since he had run out of his mother's bedroom crying, 'Mama is dead,' surged through him like a tsunami, obliterating his self-control and leaving pain and fury in its wake. How could Sienna walk away from him? If she loved him she would stay with him. If his mother had loved him she would not have swallowed the pills.

He watched the green-clad figure become smaller as Sienna ran across the moors and disappeared in the mist. *'Don't leave me!'* he roared. The silence that answered him in the empty room was a mocking reminder that she had gone.

This was why he hated love. This burning sensation beneath his breastbone, this feeling as if he had swallowed shards of glass, this stinging sensation behind his eyelids. The woman he loved was walking away, but he wouldn't let her go. He *couldn't* let her go because losing her would destroy him.

Sienna stumbled through the bracken on her way to the ruins, blinded by her tears and the rain that stung her face and soaked her hair and clothes. She needed to get away. To run away from the agony of loving a man who would never love her. Loving hurt. Nico was right to treat love as if it were a terrible, infectious disease. Once you were exposed to it you were doomed. Better then to keep well away from it.

She heard the sound of her panting breaths and slowed her pace, afraid that her frantic escape from Sethbury Hall, from Nico, might harm the baby. Her heart was beating too fast but even when she walked more slowly, the rasp of heavy breathing grew louder.

'Sienna, wait.'

The commanding voice could only belong to one person. Glancing over her shoulder, she saw Nico through the mist and rain. He must have come straight from the gym and was still wearing a pair of sweatpants. As he came closer, she saw that the rain had slicked his chest hairs against his naked torso, but it was the expression on his face that made her heart turn over. Anger and something else that she dared not define sharpened his features so that he looked predatory—and it occurred to her as he ran towards her that she was the prey.

It was crazy to even try to outrun him, but she tried anyway. 'Leave me alone,' she yelled at him over her shoulder as she tore along a path that led into the ruins of an old manor house that had long since burnt down in a fire. It was here that she had made love with Nico for the first time ten years ago. Only the outer stone walls of the house remained standing, but the outhouse was still intact and partially roofed.

She gave a cry when he caught up with her. His hand landed on her shoulder and he turned her round to face him. '*I'm* not the one leaving.' He flung the words at her. 'It's you, always you who walks away. But you are not leaving me this time. I won't allow it.'

'You can't stop me.' She gasped when he scooped her up in his arms and pushed his way through the tangled weeds at the entrance to the ruined outhouse. Purple heather covered the floor and he lay them both down onto the springy carpet.

'You don't think, *cara*?' he growled, catching her wrists and holding them in one hand.

The fight drained out of her. 'Why would you want to stop me leaving?' she whispered. The hopelessness of it was unbearable.

'Because I love you.'

'Don't.' She closed her eyes to block out his handsome face so close to hers. Too close. Even now, when she was hurting so badly, she longed to press her lips to the firm line of his jaw and kiss his mouth, lose herself in the passion that would swiftly build between them. But sex without his love would destroy her because she deserved more. 'Don't say it when I know you don't meant it. I deserve your honesty at least, Nico.'

'Sienna, look at me.' Nico's voice was low, raw, *hurting* as she hurt.

Her lashes flew open and she trembled at the wealth of emotion in his eyes. His mouth twisted. 'Why don't you believe me?'

'How *can* I believe you when you told me that you don't believe in love? You only want your baby.'

'I want you. I *love* you.' He stared into her eyes, as if by force of his strong will he could convince her. 'Danny recognised what I didn't ten years ago,' he said thickly. 'He knew I was in love with you. He was jealous of me and realised he could exploit my feelings for you, so he lied and told me that you and he had been lovers.'

He smoothed her hair back from her face with an unsteady hand, and the betraying gesture made Sienna realise with a sense of shock that the emotional turmoil in his eyes was real. 'When I confronted Danny, he admitted the part he had played in breaking us up, and I don't know if I can ever forgive him,' Nico said, his voice raw.

'When our marriage broke up, I told myself I was glad.' His eyes darkened when she flinched. 'I didn't want to care too deeply, and for eight years I believed that I was invulnerable. Love was for fools.' His mouth crooked in a wry smile. 'And then I looked around the church at my brother's wedding and saw the most beautiful woman I'd ever seen, and everything I thought I knew about myself imploded. I had to have you and for a while I convinced myself that I could have an affair with you on my terms.'

'But then I fell pregnant,' Sienna said flatly, 'and it changed everything.'

He shook his head. 'No, *tesoro*. I fell in love with you and it scared the hell out of me.'

'Nico…' The glitter of moisture in his eyes shattered the last of her defences. She pulled her wrists out of his grip and laid her hand against his cheek. A tremor ran through her when he turned his head and pressed his lips against her palm. 'I love you,' she said softly. 'I always have and I always will.'

'Then why did you leave me?' It was a cry from his heart, from the twelve-year-old boy inside the man.

'I was scared too. I had been hurt before.' She struggled to speak past the lump in her throat. 'I thought that if we married and then I lost this baby too, you would regret that I was your wife.'

'Sweetheart, don't cry.' His voice shook. 'When I proposed to you and put my ring on your finger, it was because I love you with all my heart and soul. I want to spend the rest of my life with you and face whatever the future holds together.'

The truth was in his eyes when he looked deeply into hers, and it was in his kiss when he claimed her lips. He kissed her with reverence and passion and such sweet sensuality that Sienna thought she would die from the beauty of it. She curved her arms around his neck and ran her fingers through the dark silk of his hair while he deepened the kiss and passion flared like wildfire between them, setting them both ablaze.

It was wild and elemental as their need became a

clamouring hunger. Desire, hot and fierce, made them both shake with anticipation as their wet clothes were hastily discarded. And then there was the delight of skin against skin, the rough hairs on his chest scraping against her soft breasts. He traced his hands over her body that was ripe now with his child. The hunger in his eyes reassured her. His need was there for her to see, thick and hard in her hands.

'I love you.' It was a vow; a plea for forgiveness and an everlasting promise. 'I don't think I can wait, *cara mia.*'

But he was patient as he made her body sing with his hands and mouth, and with his wicked tongue that drove her out of her mind when he curled it around each of her nipples before he moved lower and pushed her legs apart to bestow an intimate caress that made her cry out his name, her need. 'Now, Nico, please…'

And then he lifted himself over her and entered her slowly, waiting while she caught her breath and her internal muscles relaxed as he filled her. He made love to her with tenderness and passion, thrusting deep and taking her higher until she hovered on the edge with him and they tumbled together into the magical place that was uniquely theirs.

A long time later they walked back to the house hand in hand and apologised to Iris for missing lunch. 'A walk in the rain, half undressed.' Her brows lifted. 'I may not be as young as I was, but I recognise love when I see it. And besides, Sienna has a sprig of heather in her hair.'

'Do you think your grandmother guessed what we were doing on the moors?' Sienna muttered when she followed Nico into the bedroom.

'I'm sure she did,' he said as he drew her into his arms and slid her engagement ring back onto her finger. 'My grandmother is very astute, and I expect she'll guess what I am about to do right now.'

Sienna smiled at him, her heart in her eyes and her love for him blazing so fiercely that Nico caught his breath. 'What are you going to do?' she asked him.

'I'm going to love you for ever, *mio amore*.'

EPILOGUE

SIENNA BECAME NICO'S wife for the second time in a simple but deeply moving ceremony in the town hall a few miles from Villa Lionard. And on a cold, crisp winter's day their son took everyone by surprise when he arrived earlier than expected. The baby was four weeks early, but he was strong and healthy, and Sienna wept tears of relief and joy. Alessandro De Conti had his parents wrapped around one of his tiny fingers within seconds of his birth.

'Never be afraid,' Nico whispered when he cradled his son in his arms in the delivery room. 'Your *mamma* and *papà* will protect you and care for you, and most of all they will show you that love is a wonderful gift to treasure for ever.'

He looked at Sienna, his brave and beautiful wife who had given him his son and given him so much more besides. 'I love you and I love Alessandro,' he said huskily, shaken by the depth of emotion he felt. 'My heart is full, *cara mia.*'

Eighteen months later...

Cotton-wool clouds dotted the forget-me-not-blue sky above St Augustine's church in Much Matcham on a perfect summer's day. Inside the church, the sun streamed through the stained-glass windows, creating colourful rainbows on the stone floor of the nave. Huge arrangements of pink roses and white lilies had been placed at the ends of each aisle and their exquisite scent pervaded the air.

Nico was standing in the front porch of the church, from where he could see the congregation who filled the pews and were waiting for the wedding blessing ceremony to begin. The two grandmothers, Iris and Rose, were at the front of the church, and sitting with them was Alessandro, being supervised by his nanny. He was a toddler now, full of mischief and adored by his parents.

Also sitting in the front pew was Danny and his heavily pregnant wife. 'You need to end the rift with your brother,' Sienna had told Nico a few weeks after Alessandro's birth. 'Family is important, and I know you miss him.'

It had taken time, but gradually Nico had forgiven Danny, and a new understanding had developed between the brothers. Danny revealed how he had felt second-best to Nico, and Nico had been more than happy to hand over the running of the Sethbury estate to his brother. Now Danny and Victoria—who he plainly adored—lived in a wing of Sethbury Hall and were awaiting the imminent birth of a daughter, a cousin for Alessandro and a third great-grandchild for Iris. Luigi of course would always be remembered as the first child of the next generation and would be for ever loved and missed by his parents, Nico acknowledged with a soft sigh. Sienna's mother and her partner had flown over from their home in Spain, and Sienna's best friend, Carley, was there. The enormous blue silk hat decorated with peacock feathers could only belong to his mother, Nico thought wryly. But there was not a chance that Jacqueline would outshine the bride.

He heard a car pull up, and when he walked out onto the front step his breath caught in his throat as he watched Sienna get out of the car. She was wearing an ivory silk and lace gown and held a bouquet of pink rosebuds. Her rich burgundy hair was swept up into an elegant chignon and she wore a sparkling tiara.

'You wait,' she'd told him when they had decided to have their wedding blessed in a church ceremony so they could share their happiness with all their friends and family. 'This is absolutely the last time that I'll be a bride and I'm going for the full works.'

Nico forced himself to wait while the woman he loved more than life itself walked gracefully up the steps and took his arm. 'You look so beautiful, you take my breath away,' he whispered as they walked together towards the altar.

And there in front of family and friends, in front of two misty-eyed grandmothers and a lively little boy who had his father's dark hair and his mother's grey eyes, Nico held his wife's hand and pressed his lips to her finger where her wedding band now sat next to the diamond eternity ring he had placed there when they had woken in each other's arms that morning.

Sienna smiled and the unguarded expression in her eyes made Nico's heart explode in his chest. 'I love you,' she said softly.

'And I love you, *tesoro*. For eternity.'

* * * * *

THE
BILLIONAIRE'S
VIRGIN
TEMPTATION

MICHELLE CONDER

To Hilary and Marnie, writing partners in crime.

Thanks for the late nights out talking shop,
eating divine food, and drinking great wine.

Chin Chin is calling again!

Love always, M.C.

PROLOGUE

SAM FELT UNACCOUNTABLY agitated as he boarded his jet bound for Sydney. It was later than he would have liked and he was impatient to get underway.

'Will you be requiring dinner service during the flight, Mr Ventura?'

Sam folded his powerful frame into one of the leather tub chairs and tossed his mobile phone onto the table beside him before addressing his co-pilot. 'No, thanks, Daniel. Just a Scotch.'

'Certainly, sir.'

The flight from LA to Sydney would take about fourteen hours, give or take, during which Sam planned to catch up on work and sleep before he had to hit the ground running the following day. Not an uncommon occurrence for him.

Delivering his Scotch, the co-pilot headed back to the cockpit to prepare for take-off, leaving Sam to nurse his crystal tumbler and uncharacteristic edginess. As a general rule he wasn't the kind of person to second-guess himself once a decision had been made, but the question had crossed his mind more than once as to whether relocating to Sydney was the best thing to do right now.

He had a good life in LA. He surfed regularly, had a thriving legal practice that spanned two continents, lived on a great property on Malibu Beach and had any number of beautiful women he could call upon when he was in the mood for company—all drawn to the combination of power, money and good looks he'd been told he had in abundance.

Not that any of that mattered to his family, who were over the moon that he was returning home. After two years living in the City of Angels they were of the belief that he should settle back in his hometown and were more than happy with his decision to merge his highly successful legal practice with a large Australian enterprise.

The idea had been presented to him by his old university pal, Drew Kent, during a late-night dinner. Drew's father was retiring and Drew didn't want to take on the running of their law firm by himself. He was all about work-life balance ever since he'd married, and Sam, who had been in the market for a new challenge, had readily agreed to the idea.

He stared out at the night-dark sky as the plane banked hard to the right. Marriage had a way of changing a man's perspective on life. He'd seen it happen with colleagues at work and even his own brother, who had fallen in love and then, twelve months ago, got married. Valentino had gone from confirmed bachelor to happily married man with a baby faster than Sam's Maserati could hit a hundred clicks. Since then Tino had been unfailingly devoted to his lovely wife and son.

Was that what had set off the restlessness inside of him? The fact that Valentino was married and happy about it? Not that Sam begrudged Tino his happiness; quite the contrary. He loved seeing his older brother so fulfilled, and maybe one day he'd even take the plunge into matrimony himself. One day in the distant future

when he met a woman who wasn't either completely obsessed with her own career, or the potential lifestyle his
could provide for her.

Of its own accord his mind travelled back to the night,
two years ago, when Valentino had met Miller, his now
wife. Sam and Tino had been catching up in a Sydney bar
when a stunning blonde in come-take-me stilettos had
approached them. Ruby Clarkson had introduced herself
and explained how Miller needed a date for an up-and-
coming business event. Tino had jumped at the chance to
help her best friend, leaving Sam and the blonde woman
at a loose end. Since they both worked for the same law
firm, but had never met, they'd spent the night talking
shop and trading war stories until the bar had closed
and kicked them out. Not wanting the night to end, Sam
had offered to walk Ruby home and that was when the
trouble had started.

His blood heated predictably at the memory of what
had happened outside her apartment building. Or what
had *nearly* happened outside her apartment building. Despite being incredibly attracted to her, he'd meant only
to bid her goodnight, tell her it had been nice to meet
her and good luck with her current case, but somehow
she'd ended up in his arms and as soon as his lips had
touched hers he'd been lost. She'd lit a flame in him that
had only been doused when a neighbour had come out
on to her balcony calling for her errant cat.

Later his brother would tell him that he had looked
as if he'd been hit over the head with a golf club when
he'd first caught sight of Ruby at the bar, and Tino had
been right. From the moment Sam's dark eyes had collided with her wide-spaced intelligent green ones he'd
completely lost his train of thought.

It had been the same at Miller and Tino's wedding

just last year. He'd taken one look at Ruby in her dusky pink bridesmaid gown with the tantalising thigh-high split and decided to hell with it, he'd finish what they'd started the night they'd met and be done with it. That was until her date, some urbane banker-type, had stepped up beside her and ruined that particular fantasy.

Sam had downed a glass of champagne he hadn't wanted and told himself to forget it. Told himself that it was for the best. Ruby was his new sister-in-law's best friend and nothing good would come of them having a brief affair and things becoming potentially awkward later on down the track. Instead he'd forced himself to become interested in a gorgeous Sydney socialite and he'd been about to leave with her when Ruby had come rushing back into the reception room.

A small smile played at the edges of his lips. She'd been in such a flap she hadn't seen him at first and Sam hadn't stepped out of her path, choosing instead to let her run headlong into the circle of his arms as if he were just as startled by the contact as she was.

She'd stared up at him, a beguiling combination of sophistication and innocence, her gorgeous body pressed against his like Velcro on felt, her breathing laboured, and the memory of the night he'd nearly devoured her shining brightly in her lovely green eyes. For a split second his overly active imagination had caused him to believe that she'd come rushing back to find him. To tell him that she'd ditched her date and wanted to leave with him. Wanted to take him back to her place for the 'coffee' he'd stupidly passed up on the night they'd first met.

Then his oldest brother, Dante, had walked into the empty room and completely obliterated the moment.

'Sam, we're leav— Uh…sorry, junior, am I interrupting something?' he'd said smoothly.

Considering Sam had been a breath away from finding out if Ruby still tasted as delicious as he remembered, of course his brother had been interrupting, and the big idiot had known it!

Ruby's eyes had gone from glazed to mortified in the space of a heartbeat and she'd pushed out of his arms just as her date had arrived to find out what had delayed her.

Extreme sexual attraction, Sam had wanted to tell the other man.

Ruby had mumbled something about her jacket, quickly grabbed it from the back of her chair and hadn't looked back as she'd walked away. She'd been cool to him the whole day, he remembered now, and he often wondered why that was.

He also wondered what it was about her that made his libido override his iron-clad self-control where she was concerned, but he knew he'd work it out one day. And, given their shared profession, and personal connections, it would probably be soon.

His heart pounded slow and heavy inside his chest just at the thought of seeing her again. He'd deliberately not asked Valentino about her over the past couple of years. Why give his loved-up brother any indication that he had a thing for the beautiful lawyer? He'd only make more out of it than there was and the last thing Sam wanted was to raise Miller's awareness of how attractive he found her best friend.

But their paths would surely cross and he was curious as to how he would feel about her when it happened. Who knew, perhaps the incendiary attraction that sent his system into overdrive whenever she was in the room would have finally worn off? He'd lost interest in plenty of other women before. Surely Ruby wouldn't be any different in the end.

He swirled the Scotch in his glass. Did Ruby still remember the night they'd met? Did she still think about it? And did she still work for Clayton Smythe or had she moved on to new pastures? He'd left the firm himself shortly after that night to start his own practice in LA and had ruthlessly suppressed all interest in her, so he had no idea what she was up to now. Some sixth sense warned him that, for all her bold confidence, Ruby was a soft touch deep down and therefore not to be trifled with. Not that he planned to trifle with her on any level. It would be pointless in the end and Sam had stopped chasing pointless passions after watching his world-famous father chase his motor-racing dreams to the exclusion of all else.

Theirs had never been a close relationship, his father dying in a tragic racing accident before Sam had been able to gain his attention or his approval—though God knew he'd wasted enough time trying to win both. He still remembered the time he'd trailed his father around the racetrack on his ninth birthday. It had been a disaster waiting to happen. He'd sat there all day, waiting to spend time with his father, only to have his old man drive off at the end of the day without him. As usual his father had been so preoccupied with work he'd completely forgotten Sam was even there. Fortunately one of the office girls had eventually noticed him sitting on a sofa, swinging his legs, and called his father on the phone. Sam had then been stuck in a taxi and delivered home alone.

His mother had been furious with his father but Sam had brushed it off. That had been the last time his father had kicked his pride to the kerb, Sam had made sure of it. Not that it mattered now. He'd learned a valuable lesson that day and he'd never hung himself out to dry like that again. Never made anything so important that he couldn't walk away from it at the end of the day.

'A good thing,' he muttered into the ensuing silence, pulling out his phone and switching his mind from the past, where it didn't belong, to the present, where it did.

He was due to arrive in Sydney around noon and head straight into meetings with his new business partner before changing into some fancy-dress costume for a party he'd promised to attend.

A few months back he'd won a huge copyright case for Gregor Herzog and his wife—Australia's darling couple of the theatre world—when someone had tried to pass the couple's costume designs off as their own. Over the course of the case the Herzogs had become firm friends and they had invited him to their annual masquerade ball—a huge charity extravaganza that just happened to coincide with Gregor's fiftieth birthday celebration this year.

'Please come, Sam, my good friend. It would be an honour to raise a toast to you on my birthday.'

Sam already regretted his somewhat rash agreement to attend but a promise was a promise and Sam's word was his law.

Fortunately, he rarely suffered jet lag, but still, he hoped that Gregor and Marion wouldn't mind if he only made a fly-in and fly-out appearance. What with family obligations to fulfil the rest of the weekend, and a new company to take control of on Monday morning, he didn't have a lot of time for frivolities like masquerade balls. Or thinking about gorgeous blondes with long legs, he mused, that strange, restless feeling returning as Ruby Clarkson once again jumped into his head.

He shook her image loose, unfolded his large frame from the chair and fetched his laptop from where his co-pilot had stowed it prior to take-off. The fact that the woman could turn him on from twelve thousand miles away should be mildly disconcerting—and it was! It made him realise that at some point he was going to have to figure out how to get the troublesome blonde out of his head. Something he hoped to put off for as long as possible.

CHAPTER ONE

THE THEME ON the gold-leaf invitation for Sydney's most
renowned masquerade ball this year had been 'daring,
romantic, seductive…'

Tick, tick and *tick*, Ruby thought, stifling a yawn
and giving a smile she hoped conveyed *Having a great
time* and not *I wish I was sipping this glass of Riesling
at home on my sofa in front of the latest instalment of*
Law & Order.

And wearing comfy pyjamas, Ruby mused longingly
as she took in the packed ornate ballroom.

A lavish ball was the last place she wanted to be after
a gruelling eighty-hour working week that had gone from
bad to worse and still required more hours to be put
in, but she was here in support of her sister, so leaving
wasn't an option just yet.

And she supposed it was an interesting interlude from
her everyday life sitting in her poky little law office,
fighting the good fight. When else would she get the
chance to join the who's who of the theatre world in a
multimillion-dollar Point Piper mansion with unrivalled
harbour views beyond the infinity pool?

Everywhere Ruby looked there was a dazzling display
of elaborately costumed guests milling about and talking in a profusion of excitement and colour. It was like

stepping back in time with women in wigs and masks and men with feather-plumed hats drinking impossibly elegant flutes of champagne that sparkled like liquid gold beneath the light of a thousand chandeliers. Frescoes of cherubs and deer stared down from the ceiling and the iconic gunmetal-grey Sydney Harbour Bridge glowed through the open French doors, reminding everyone that they were in fact in Sydney and not visiting some Venetian mansion on the banks of the Grand Canal during *Carnevale.*

Ruby surreptitiously adjusted the neckline of her fitted gown, which kept slipping to reveal a little too much cleavage for her liking. She was supposed to be Marie Antoinette but her mirror had deemed that she looked more like Little Bo Peep on steroids, making her thankful she was well-hidden behind an elaborate black lace mask.

'You know I really appreciate you coming along with me tonight, don't you?' Molly murmured.

Thanks to live music from the twenty-piece band where a well-known pop star was belting out her latest hit, Ruby had to lean in close to catch her sister's words.

'I'm enjoying myself,' she fibbed, not wanting Molly to feel guilty about roping her into accompanying her. Molly was on a personal quest to waylay some in-demand director and convince him that she really needed to star in his next award-winning Hollywood epic. Molly had paid her dues at drama school and appeared in small-to-medium theatre productions and TV shows, and Ruby would do anything to help make her sister's dreams come true.

'No, you're not,' Molly said, shrugging good-naturedly. 'But I appreciate the lie. I'm also under strict instructions to make sure you have fun and relax for once.'

'Let me guess.' Ruby gave her sister *that* look, knowing full well where her instructions had come from. 'Mum told you to find me a nice man I can fall in love with so I can produce lots of grandbabies.' Nothing new there. 'Which is so not going to happen, and, for the record, I take serious umbrage at the insinuation that I don't normally relax and have fun because I do. All the time!'

'Oh, did I only insinuate that last bit?' Molly feigned a shocked expression. 'I meant to say it outright.'

'Ha-ha.' Ruby narrowed her eyes menacingly. 'I know how to relax.' She had a yoga class booked the following morning, didn't she? '*And* how to have fun.'

'You work,' Molly corrected. 'But that's okay. Tonight I will ply you with drinks and ensure that you meet some tall, dark and handsome man to while the evening away with.'

Ruby grimaced. As any self-respecting lawyer knew, weekend work was par for the course. Particularly with the big cases, and Ruby had just embarked on one of the biggest of her career, so men were not a priority for her right now. If they ever had been.

'You can't tell if a man is handsome or not while he's wearing a mask,' Ruby pointed out, 'and you already know that I don't hold to Mum's mantra that a woman isn't complete without a man on her arm.'

'Mum is old-school,' Molly agreed. 'You can't hold that against her.'

'I don't hold it against her. I'm just not intending to follow in her footsteps.'

'By not dating at all?'

'I date,' Ruby defended, tucking a recalcitrant strand of her blonde hair back under her poufy white wig. 'When I have the time.'

Molly gave her a good-natured eye-roll. 'The last time you went on a date, dinosaurs roamed the earth.'

Ruby laughed at the visual. 'I'm not a romantic like you and Mum. I don't see "the one" in every man who looks my way.'

'That's because you never give any guy a decent chance. You find something wrong with all of them and quickly move on. But seriously, Rubes, just because Dad left Mum for another woman it doesn't mean every man will do the same to us.'

Ruby couldn't deny that their father's desertion had left her somewhat jaded when it came to romance, but that wasn't the only reason. In her experience men wanted more from a woman than they were prepared to give and she had yet to meet a man who challenged that theory.

Even Sam Ventura.

Especially Sam Ventura—even if he now was her best friend's brother-in-law.

And why did his name leap into her head every time the conversation turned to men and marriage? He was the very last man she should be thinking about in that way. Two years ago he'd charmed her and kissed her senseless before making a trite promise to call and then failing to follow through on it.

Not that she should have been surprised. She'd been taken in by his good looks and intelligent conversation, but neither of those things was a precursor to nice manners and true decency. At least not where he was concerned!

Lord, but it still made her blush to recall how she had invited him up to her apartment for coffee.

Coffee!

She might as well have just said *bed* and been done with it.

His failure to call and the subsequent photo she'd seen of him with his arm around another woman the following day at a polo match had solidified for her that men weren't worth the effort. The worst thing for Ruby was that she had let Sam *in* that night. She'd let down her guard with him in a way she never had before, and worse, she'd thought they'd shared a connection. A connection that had transcended the physical.

Fool that she was.

She'd found out via a visiting LA attorney that Sam had a reputation for being a charming rogue who made Casanova look like a good bet. Something she wholeheartedly believed after how easily he had nearly seduced her that night. He'd made her feel like a besotted thirteen-year-old in the throes of her first crush, carrying her phone around for a whole week, waiting for a phone call he'd never intended to make.

Her extreme reaction to him was something that had scared her witless because she had always imagined herself immune to the romantic vagaries that governed her mother's life. She supposed she had Sam to thank for showing her otherwise. Showing her that if she wasn't careful she could be just as susceptible to a pretty face and buff body as the next woman.

Not that she *would* thank him. She didn't want to have anything to do with him again. He was too big and too male and definitely too full of himself to be of interest to her. Something she hoped she'd made crystal clear by ignoring him at Tino and Miller's wedding last year.

'I don't think every man is an EC,' she denied to Molly now, using their shorthand for Emotional Coward. 'But I do wonder how we're even sisters. You're like Snow White, talking to all the animals and skipping through the flowery fields, and I'm—'

'The Wicked Queen,' Molly filled in. 'Only you're not afraid of ageing, you're afraid of commitment.'

'I am not afraid of commitment.'

Molly's eyebrow rose above her white mask as if to say *I'm not getting into that argument again*. But it wasn't true.

'I'm cautious,' Ruby countered. 'I don't feel the need to leap into something before I've had a chance to study it from all angles.'

'You're not supposed to study love,' Molly laughed. 'You feel it. You experience it. You *live* it.'

Ruby shuddered. 'You might. I don't.' And what would Molly say, she wondered, if she knew Ruby hadn't even gone all the way with a man yet? That she was still a virgin like an old maid from the Victorian era!

Suddenly a loud honking sound drew her attention. Molly giggled as an irate swan cut a swathe through the glittering crowd and started pecking at the golden tassels hanging from an unsuspecting woman's gown. The woman reeled back and would have slipped if the man standing beside her hadn't put his hands out and swiftly caught her.

Ruby felt the breath back up in her lungs as she took in the man's height and the breadth of his shoulders, the angle of his leonine head and dark hair styled in loose layers that could only have come from an upmarket salon.

'Oh, my,' Molly murmured. 'Would you get a load of that?'

Ruby watched as the man wearing a masculine bronze mask competently corralled the indignant bird outside and returned to check if the woman was okay.

'He's gorgeous,' her sister added on a sigh.

'You can't possibly know that,' Ruby scoffed. 'He's wearing a mask that covers half his face.'

'He carries himself like a man who doesn't need to be handsome but is. Look at those shoulders—'

'Padding.'

'And the way his thighs fill out his dark suit trousers. No padding there, I'm guessing.'

Despite Ruby's protestations, Molly was right—the man exuded power and confidence and his square-cut jaw, smooth olive complexion and sensual mouth conveyed that he was likely very good-looking behind the bronzed mask. He was also very familiar...

It's not him, she assured herself, her eyes taking in the way his lips twisted into a half-cynical, half-sexy grin as the grateful woman gripped his arm and whispered something into his ear.

It couldn't be him. Sam Ventura lived in LA and, even if he was visiting Sydney, what would he be doing at a fancy-dress ball thrown by theatre people?

Well, he wouldn't be here, she reasoned. It was her imagination running overtime. Again. 'Men like that only want one thing from a woman,' she told Molly with lofty finality.

'I know.' Molly sighed. 'Do you think he would want it from me?'

'Molly!'

Ruby was saved from reminding her sister that she'd just ended a relationship with one feckless boyfriend and hardly needed another when one of Molly's friends approached her. Perturbed by how very much the dark-haired man reminded her of Sam Ventura, Ruby offered to go to the bar, where they were serving on-demand cocktails.

'Cosmopolitan,' Molly requested.

'Same,' her friend added.

Leaving them to their excited chatter, Ruby headed for the gilt-edged bar that looked as if it was a permanent fixture but was most likely shipped in from Italy especially for the night.

She sighed as she joined the queue at the bar. Molly truly believed that love awaited her around every corner, while Ruby was of the view that danger awaited her. She wasn't looking for romance and happy-ever-after. Her independence had been too hard-won to hand over to some man who would want her to compromise everything she had and then most likely walk away without a backward glance anyway. A man like her father. And like Sam Ventura.

No, that wasn't fair. She might not like Sam very much but she didn't know him well enough to tar him with her father's particular brush. Still, why give a man who had *heartbreaker* written all over his too handsome face the chance to prove that he was? And why was he still on her mind? she wondered grouchily.

Love turned thinking women into veritable psych-ward patients, she knew that. Just look at how she had been after only kissing the man that one foolhardy night. He'd pulled her into his arms and she'd nearly lost her dignity and her panties in one fell swoop! Not that she'd been in love with him, but she'd certainly been in lust with him and that had been more than enough to keep her up late some nights.

'Sorry, darling,' a male voice crooned too close to her ear as she was jostled from behind. Ruby glanced over her shoulder and caught a glimpse of four colourful characters wearing Zorro-style masks with their eyes on her cleavage.

Very original, she thought, turning away and steadfastly ignoring them as she waited for the woman in front of her to collect her drinks order. If there was one valuable lesson Ruby had learned from watching her mother all these years, it was not to let her emotions do the thinking for her. Only fools rushed in and when they did they were often sorry with the results.

'So I said, listen, doll-face.' The guy who had jostled her spoke behind her with an over-the-top drawl. 'You want it, you know where to find it. On your knees.'

His companions guffawed as if they were smug private school boys at a secret frat party instead of a posh event. Ruby rolled her eyes. Boys masquerading as men, she thought, half listening as they traded stories about their sexual exploits that were clearly too far-fetched to be believed.

'Wait till you hear this one,' one of them said in a low voice. 'The other night Michael picked up this girl and get this—' the wag paused for effect '—he says he kissed her and didn't even realise it was his ex until she slapped his face and told him they'd broken up six months earlier. Apparently she'd changed her hairstyle and got implants.'

'God, I wish I had his life,' a nasally voice whined. 'He's an animal.'

Before she could give them a snarky look another voice interceded, a deep, velvet-coated voice she'd listened to all evening one long-ago night.

'He's an idiot,' he said. 'No man forgets a woman he's kissed. At least he doesn't if he has any integrity.'

Ruby's heartbeat doubled and her skin turned pasty beneath her heavy make-up. *It couldn't be him. It just couldn't!*

'What can I get you, ma'am?'

Startled by the question, Ruby stared blankly at the bartender.

'To drink,' he offered, gesturing to the vast array of colourful bottles on the marble shelf behind him.

'Sorry.' Ruby cleared her throat and forced herself to relax. 'I'll have…' She frowned, trying to remember what Molly and her friend had asked for. 'I'll have two Cosmopolitans and a white wine.'

'Riesling? Chardonnay? Chab—?'

'Whatever's strongest,' Ruby cut in. *And make it fast, please.* Her palms were sweaty and she clasped them together, willing herself not to turn around to check who owned that all too sexy voice.

Fortunately she didn't hear it again and when the bartender finally returned with her order she threw him a relieved smile and grabbed her drinks.

Keeping her head down, she turned and would have run smack into the side of one of the men if a masculine hand hadn't shot out in front of her. Liquid sloshed over the side of one of the glasses and her eyes flew upwards to meet concerned brown ones.

Bedroom brown eyes with thick, dark lashes.

Her pulse raced erratically. It was the man in the bronzed mask. The tall one with the impossibly wide shoulders and long legs. The one who had saved the woman from being eaten by the swan. The one with the chocolate-brown hair brushed back in mussed waves just like Sam's, and the impossibly kissable mouth perfectly positioned in a smoothly chiselled jaw. Also, just like Sam's.

A shaft of liquid heat detonated low in her pelvis, sending plumes of sensation outwards just as it had done in that trendy pub two years ago. Just as it had done at Miller's wedding one year ago.

It's not him, she assured herself. *It's not him. It's not—*

'Sorry about that.' A hint of a lazy smile played at the edges of his mouth. 'My fool acquaintance wasn't watching where he was going.'

Ruby froze, her IQ falling by a hundred points. The man who—*please, God*—couldn't be Sam Ventura cocked his head with bemused candour at her stultifying silence, his gaze falling to her lips before drifting lower and stopping on the drinks she was gripping precariously in front of her. 'You need a hand carrying those?' His dark gaze returned to hers. 'I'd be more than happy to assist.'

Mentally berating her stunned-mullet act, Ruby kicked her brain into gear and clamped her lips together. This was *not* Sam Ventura. He was just a very good-looking, powerfully built replica who *seemed* very much like Sam Ventura.

'Thanks, but no, thanks,' she bit out in a low tone. 'Believe it or not, I don't need a man to make my life perfect.'

And why on earth had she said that?

Grimly aware that she had silenced them all, she turned her back on the little group and willed her jelly legs to hold her upright as she hurried back to Molly.

Well, well, well, if he hadn't just been put in his place by the very beautiful, and very cool Ruby Clarkson, Sam mused, watching as she disappeared into the crowd as if the hounds of hell were after her. Because, as surprising as it was to run into her so soon, it *was* her; there wasn't a shred of doubt in his mind.

A fiery spark of heat ignited inside him as he noted the graceful, swan-like neck and hourglass figure in the lavender gown. Obviously she hadn't recognised him and that was a little…*disappointing*?

Two years ago he'd kissed her and felt as if he were standing on a tight wire being swung from side to side without a safety net to catch him. One year ago he'd wanted to repeat the experience and could have sworn she did too, and now she passed him by as if he was what? Nobody special? An irritant, even?

Ignoring the four bozos he hadn't liked in high school and liked even less now, Sam grabbed his beer and headed into the party as the men behind him laughed uproariously at another lewd story that was as likely to be true as Sam suggesting that his father had put him first as a boy. Pure fantasy.

Shoving that thought back where it belonged, he took a pull of his beer.

Had Ruby really not recognised him?

The thought was like a burr in his side as he caught sight of lavender silk from across the room.

Not her, he realised as the woman lowered her hand-held mask to speak to her companion. His heartbeat steadied and he frowned as he realised that it had sped up in the first place. He wasn't here to hit on anyone. He certainly wasn't here to hit on Miller's off-limits friend. Yet he couldn't deny that his senses were instantly charged at having seen Ruby again so unexpectedly. Which had answered one of his earlier questions—no, the attraction he felt for her hadn't lessened. Not even a little.

But what about for her?

He stood and watched the lively partygoers for a moment, wondering if he should prop up the bar for a bit, or head to a quieter corner until enough time had passed that he could leave. Or maybe he should hunt Ruby Clarkson down and wait for her to recognise him.

And what then? a little voice taunted. *Surely you're not thinking of finishing that thing you started two years ago?*

Sam tilted the bottle of beer to his lips and took another long, fortifying pull.

Was he thinking that?

He couldn't deny that the idea still held some appeal. More than some appeal, if he was being honest. Ruby Clarkson was a beautiful woman. What man wouldn't want a long-legged, curvaceous honey-blonde woman spread out beneath him, naked and wanting in his bed, those glorious green eyes glazed over with desire, her lips plump and wet from his kisses, her creamy thighs parted for his possession?

Sam's body hardened at the images rampaging through his head and softly cursed his wayward libido. No doubt she'd be great in bed. Great in *his* bed.

And there was that niggly note of ownership that had given him such pause two years ago. The caveman element that only she drew out of him. He didn't like it. He didn't like how effortlessly she drew him to her, or how often he thought about her. He certainly didn't like how possessive he felt about her. Would one night with her in his bed solve that? Would one night rid him of the powerful pull she seemed to have over him or would it only make it worse?

Sam's brooding gaze noticed a hint of lavender drift through the crowd towards the dance floor. Well, there was really only one way to test that theory, wasn't there? Not that he intended to take her to his bed tonight. He wasn't that desperate. But he could have a little fun with her, couldn't he? A little innocent fun just until she recognised him. A smile curved the edges of his lips as he set off towards the dance floor. How long would it take her? One minute? Two?

Suddenly the evening looked a whole lot more interesting than it had half an hour ago.

CHAPTER TWO

'I DON'T SEE anyone who looks like a pirate,' Ruby said as she stood on tiptoe to see over the packed dance floor. 'Are you sure that director is even here?'

'Katy said he was.' Molly's lips tightened determinedly. 'I have to find him. I'm psyched up to approach him, and who knows when I'll get another chance like this? It's not as if I can get a ticket to these kinds of events just by clicking my fingers.'

Ruby gave her sister a faint smile and tried not to look over her shoulder again for the man in the bronzed mask. She'd felt his eyes on her as she'd all but run from the bar, and she'd been so sure he'd follow her she'd been on tenterhooks ever since.

'I think that's him,' Molly whispered, low-level excitement running through her voice.

Ruby's stomach lurched. Then she realised that Molly hadn't meant Sam Ventura's doppelganger and told herself to stop fretting and breathe. It wasn't Sam. Sam was in LA.

She glanced at the man Molly was so set on meeting and did a double take. The director-slash-pirate was big, blonde and fierce-looking. 'Are you sure that's him?'

'Almost certain. Let's dance so I can get closer.'

'You dance, I'll hold the drinks,' Ruby said, taking

Molly's half empty cocktail glass and nodding towards the dance floor. The sooner Molly introduced herself to the famous director and begged for an audition for a part in his next movie, the sooner they could leave. 'Time to walk the gangplank, my lovely.'

Molly surreptitiously smoothed a palm down the side of her gown. 'I thought you said this was a hare-brained idea?'

It was a hare-brained idea but seeing her confident, madcap sister suddenly nervous, Ruby softened. 'It's a great idea. He's going to love you. Just remember: no public sex.'

Molly smiled at that. 'Of course not. Sex can come after I've won an Oscar for starring in his film and if we fall madly in love with each other.' She straightened her shoulders and set her jaw determinedly. 'You sure you won't dance with me?'

'In this dress?' Ruby glanced down at her enhanced cleavage. 'Not a chance.'

Molly scowled. 'You're no fun.'

'I know. I work really hard at it.'

Laughing, Molly blew out a nervous breath and headed into the fray. Ruby sometimes envied her little sister her ability to put herself 'out there' like that. Ruby could do it for her clients but when it came to pursuing something for herself…well, she wasn't that brave, and knowing that was one of her greatest strengths.

Sipping her drink while she held Molly's, she savoured the crisp lightness of the wine, almost forgetting about the man in the bronzed mask until she glanced up and found him prowling towards her, a sexy grin on his face.

Instantly her breath backed up in her lungs and her pulse took off like a rocket. As if he sensed her response, a heated gleam entered his eyes, darkening them from chocolate to mink. 'When you ordered those drinks I didn't realise you intended to drink them all by yourself,' he said, his intimate tone and soft laugh inviting her to play along with his charming joke.

A shiver snaked down Ruby's spine at the sound of that deep, velvety chuckle. Oh, this guy was smooth. Dangerously smooth. He was also most definitely Sam Ventura. What was the point in trying to deny it any longer?

'Another lame pick-up line,' she said with cool derision. 'How very original of you.'

Instead of taking her comment as the put-down it was meant to be, Sam seemed highly amused by it. 'I didn't realise I'd delivered a first one.' His eyes glowed from behind his mask as he grinned down at her. 'Now, if I told you that you had the kind of smile that could stop a man at fifty paces…that would be a lame pick-up line.' His smile widened. 'It would also be true.'

Ruby blinked up at him, feeling a distinct height disadvantage without her usual four-inch heels on her feet, her gown not long enough to accommodate them. His tone implied that he thought she was a stranger, but how was that possible? She had recognised him straight away—would recognise him blindfolded in a dark room just by the prickling awareness he set off inside her.

She didn't know whether to be insulted or glad that he hadn't recognised her in turn. Maybe both. It only seemed to confirm that the mutual connection she had believed was special between them the night they met hadn't been special or mutual at all.

Something inside her chest plummeted just a little more. Her pride, no doubt, because what woman's pride wouldn't be dented when a man who had kissed her as if he couldn't get enough of her now had no clue as to who she was just because of a silly costume?

Dismayed to have her worst fears confirmed, Ruby deliberately disguised her voice with a smoky edge. Let him try and pick her up, she thought with rising irritation. Let him try and use all his sophisticated charm on her and have her turn him down this time. She'd like nothing better than to see him dig a hole for himself and then reveal her identity at the last minute. It was no less than he deserved for not calling her when he'd promised that he would. And, yes, she knew she needed to get over that but she really hated when a man said one thing and did another. She'd experienced the disappointment of being let down by her father too often as a young girl to put up with it in her adult life.

'Great outfit by the way. I'm thinking you're—'

'Don't say Little Bo Peep,' she warned menacingly.

Sam laughed softly. 'If you were Little Bo Peep you'd have a staff. And sheep. Which might not work with those ducks earlier.'

'Swans.'

'Ducks, swans…feathered fowl who belong in a pond, not at a masquerade party.' His dark eyes glittered with lazy male appreciation as he gazed at her. 'Not without a mask at least.'

Ruby's lips twitched and she quickly sipped the last of her wine. She was not going to find him charming this time around. She was not going to feel breathless with awareness, or tingly with anticipation. She was not going to remember the gentle way he had tucked a strand of her hair behind her ear before he'd said goodnight to her two years ago. Or the way he had looked at her as if she amazed him. It had made him impossible to forget.

Impossible to get over. And thinking like that was just asking for trouble.

'So no nursery-rhyme jokes and no lame pick-up lines,' he agreed. 'Want to dance instead?'

'I don't dance with strangers,' she mumbled, glancing furtively towards the dance floor in the hope that Molly was ready to go home. Of course, Molly was nowhere to be seen.

'Stranger?' He cocked his head. 'That's easy enough to remedy—'

'No!' Her eyes widened on his. She wasn't ready to reveal who she was to him. She didn't want to have an awkward conversation about the past. It wasn't as if they were friends. They weren't, and they never would be. Better if he just left her alone and was none the wiser as to who he was trying to hit on. 'No names.'

'No names?' He gave her a curious look.

'Half the fun of wearing a mask is being anonymous. Don't you agree?'

'This is my first masked ball. I'm new to the etiquette.'

'Then allow me to educate you.' Her voice dropped further to a husky purr. 'Names aren't necessary.'

'Is that right?' The lights dimmed around them as the music turned soft and sensual. Ruby's heart thumped against her ribcage. She really needed to get away from him and the way he made her feel.

'So if you don't want to dance and you don't want to trade names—' his gaze drifted to her lips like a feather-light caress '—what do you want to do?'

Kiss you, she thought, her body already responding to his lingering look. *I want to kiss you and never stop.*

'One dance.' He gave her a slow smile as if he knew the appalling direction in which her mind had just taken her. 'I'm harmless, I promise.'

'I'll call you tomorrow, I promise.'

The last thing Ruby wanted was to find herself in Sam's arms again but he was so smooth he'd divested her of the two glasses she'd been clutching like a lifeline and had her there before she had time to blink.

Which only made her angry. What was it about this man that eroded her natural born caution? She didn't want this and she certainly didn't want him. Only, she knew she was lying to herself. There was something about Sam Ventura that got to her every single time and try as she might she couldn't seem to do anything about it.

She risked a glance up into his eyes to find him watching her closely. Did she feel familiar in his arms? She was shorter without her heels on but...

Oh, get over yourself, Ruby Jane. He doesn't know who you are so forget it. Have a laugh.

But she couldn't have a laugh, not with his heat surrounding her and setting her pulse racing, not with his face so close to hers she could see the beginnings of his beard coming in, and not with his scent, spicy and masculine with a hint of sandalwood, short-circuiting her brain.

All she could do was remember the feel of his skin beneath her fingertips, slightly rough, his lips warm and firm against her own. It was like being sent back in time. She wanted to feel those lips again. She wanted to feel the power of his need again, his hunger for her. She'd never felt like that in a man's arms before and it was nothing short of addictive.

No man forgets a woman he's kissed before. At least he doesn't if he has any integrity.

Did he remember kissing her? Would it come back to him if she was to reach up and kiss him now?

Inwardly shocked to realise where her thoughts were leading her, Ruby jerked back. Kissing Sam Ventura was the last thing she should be thinking of doing. This man was dangerous to her equilibrium. She knew it as surely as she knew her own name.

'You okay, angel?' He drew her closer as she stumbled, bending to murmur in her ear. Ruby's breath caught as his warm breath skittered across the sensitive skin of her neck. That name—he'd called her angel two years ago as well...

Shaking off the unwanted memory, she firmed her resolve against his effect on her.

'No, I'm not okay,' she said, making her first sane decision of the night and stepping out of his arms to push blindly through the throng of oblivious partygoers as she rushed from the room.

A stone terrace loomed in front of her, showcasing a captivating view of the harbour beyond, and Ruby headed for it, swiftly moving some distance down a narrow terraced walkway lined with fairy lights that wound around the side of the house.

'Wait.'

Unaware that Sam had followed her, but not surprised, she stopped, the throb of the music just a low beat now they were outside.

'What happened back there?' His concerned gaze caught hers, his eyes scanning her face. He was so close to her she could feel the heat and energy from his body permeating her own.

Panic was what had happened back there. Jumbled senses and racing pulses was what had happened. Need and want...

'Listen,' he began, reaching for his mask. 'I think it's time we—'

'No!' Ruby startled him into silence when she grabbed for his arm and prevented him from unhooking his mask. She couldn't think of anything worse than him unmasking himself now because he'd expect her to do the same. Which would put her in the position of explaining why she had acted the way she had. It would mean she would have to explain how she'd felt so overwhelmed by the heat of his body, his touch on her waist, his breath against her skin, that she'd run. Explain how in that moment she had wanted more of it. More of him.

'Hey…' he murmured softly, accurately reading her inner distress, his fingers gentle as he touched her chin. 'Look at me.'

She did, the low light of the garden casting shadows across his strong jaw and carved lips, his dark hair falling forward over his mask.

He was so beautiful. So masculine. The bronze of the mask giving him an otherworldly appearance that only added to his appeal.

Ruby's breathing altered, becoming choppy as they stared at each other. She tried to shake her head to clear her senses but his fingers prevented her from breaking eye contact with him. She irrationally felt light-headed, drunk on the clean, intoxicating scent of musk and man. Then his other hand sought the nape of her neck and she didn't know if he leaned down further or she stretched upwards but suddenly his lips were on hers, warm and firm and utterly compelling.

Wide-eyed, she met his stunned gaze and then she couldn't help herself: she lowered her eyelids and opened her mouth. She heard a deep groan rumble out of his chest as he felt her submit to the inevitable and he slanted his lips more fully across hers to deepen the kiss. It burned through her like liquid fire, drugging her, consuming her, triggering an avalanche of need deep inside she was powerless to resist.

A faint voice in her head warned her that this was a mistake, that if she played with fire she'd get burned. She heard it and accepted it, but stronger than that was this fierce, unbidden need for this moment to continue, for this pleasure never to end. She didn't know if it was the intimacy of the night, the mask hiding her identity from him or the fact that she'd denied herself any form of sensual pleasure for so long, but she knew she was as lost to his touch as she had been two years ago. Maybe more so.

His lips moved over hers, sure and confident, her senses so attuned to the feel of him that she felt when he would have pulled back from her.

'Don't,' she murmured softly, her arms around his neck. 'Please, don't stop.'

Sam groaned and complied with Ruby's request even though logic and instinct told him to—*for God's sake, man*—rein it in. It had been like this with her two years ago. Intensely intimate, sinfully erotic. Just the touch of her mouth against his was enough to have him losing his head. Now, holding her like this, feeling her unguarded response to him was sheer, unadulterated torture.

His arms banded around her, urging her closer, the soft, desperate whimpers coming from the back of her throat driving him to move them both further into the shadows cast by a small, cut-away corner of the building.

Her arms tightened around his neck and Sam ran his hands down over the boning of her gown. She arched against him, her breasts rising and falling above the low-cut neckline, threatening to spill out. Breasts he'd longed to see, longed to taste.

Telling himself that he'd stop this lunacy in one more moment, he slid his hand along the slender curve of her arm and shoulder and down to cup her rounded flesh in the palm of his hand.

Her breath caught inside her chest and she arched higher against him. Sam sensed the need in her, felt it in his own blood, and seared an urgent path of heated kisses down the long line of her neck. Her head fell back as a shiver went through her, her body leaning more heavily against his. He braced his arm across her lower back, his feverish eyes taking in the creamy skin of her décolletage, pearl-white in the ribbons of moonlight that breached the overhanging trees.

Heat and fire coursed a dangerous path inside him, burning up all rational thought as sensation overwhelmed him. A vessel blew its horn somewhere out on the harbour, someone laughed gaily as they jumped into the pool. Sam barely heard a thing, the sounds receding beneath the heaviness of his own thundering heartbeat.

Ruby's lips were soft and yielding beneath his, feeding off his with the same violent hunger that turned him harder than stone. He shifted closer, bringing their bodies into perfect alignment, taking her soft moan deep into his mouth.

'Damn, you taste good,' he murmured, his lips moving to the sensitive skin beneath her ear. She writhed in his arms, her greedy hands growing more restless and bold as they ran over his shoulders and into his hair.

His mask was in the way and he was about to wrench it off when she pushed his jacket back and he had to shuck out of it. Then her sharp little nails raked his skin as she tugged his shirt out of the waistband of his trousers. Hunger bit deep and he hauled her upwards, his mouth returning to hers with a primal need.

Sam had been with many women in his thirty-one years, pleasured more than he could remember, and he knew he was a good, giving lover, but this…touching Ruby, hearing her soft cries of pleasure as he discovered what pleased her, was a sensual delight he hadn't reckoned on. He was completely at the mercy of his senses and he not only wanted to take everything she had to offer but he was also prepared to give her everything in return.

'More,' she begged, leaning into him and kneading his back muscles like a hungry kitten might a downy quilt. Sam swore under his breath and gave her what she wanted, urging her back against the vine-clad wall of the house and putting his hands all over her. Moulding her hips and her ribs, the soft swell of her round breasts. Breasts he had to see. Had to touch.

Somewhere in the back of his head an alarm bell was ringing but it was competing with the soft sounds of their mutual need, and really, what was one more minute of madness?

Lifting her so they were at eye level, Sam leaned forward and kissed the rounded swells of her breasts and then forced the top of her gown to give so that one pert nipple popped free.

'I want to taste you.' His voice sounded guttural with urgency and he didn't wait for her response, lowering his head and taking the tight pink bud deep into his mouth. He flicked her aroused flesh with his tongue, relishing the soft keening sounds that told him she was as lost to this madness as he was.

'Oh, God.' She arched into his hold, her fingers threaded through his hair. 'I need you,' she said on a rushed breath, her fingers fumbling as they moved to his belt buckle.

Knowing he should stop, but unable to, Sam gathered the yards of fabric between them and skimmed his hands along her thighs. A tiny, flimsy scrap of silk was all that separated him from paradise and with one tug it gave, falling to the ground between them.

A low growl radiated up from his chest as his fingers found her soft and wet. He wanted to drop to his knees and taste the sweet honey coating his fingers but she was already rising against him.

'More, please, I want more.'

He caught her mouth and propped her against the wall. Part of his brain tried to kick in, tried to remind him that he was a civilised man who did not have sex with women outside at important parties, but the hot throb of her body shredded his sanity and made a mockery of his self-control.

All he could think about was replacing his fingers with his throbbing shaft and making her his. Something she obviously wanted just as badly because she was tearing at the zip on his trousers and then he was free and she was open and ready, her thighs cradling his hips intimately against his body.

That first contact of his flesh against hers gave him pause because he didn't have a condom on him. Cursing himself for his lack of preparation he was about to tell her when her lips cruised down the line of his neck and she bit the tendon between his neck and shoulder.

A shiver went through him, a groan dragged from deep inside as he forgot all about reason and responsibility and gave into a need that was stronger than he was, entering her on one hard, perfect thrust.

She was so tight. So snug… His body tensed as he fought to control his most basic urge to possess her.

'Relax for me, angel, and this will go easier.'

Sweat beaded his forehead but before he could fully process that there was something untutored to her movements Ruby angled her body upwards and took him deeper, scattering his thoughts.

'Slowly,' he urged, holding her hips steady between his hands. 'That's it, let me all the way in.' He groaned as her silken muscles rippled around him, holding him tight. Careful not to crush her, Sam placed a hand against the wall to support them both, his legs shaking as he strove to hold off his own release until he felt hers first.

'Oh, God.' She clutched at him, her little nails scoring the nape of his neck. 'I… I…' Her body squeezed his, small lake-like ripples pulling him in deeper and harder as her body sought, and found, the ultimate release.

As soon as he felt her peak Sam let go, moving inside her with controlled power as his own climax raced through him like never before.

He didn't know how long they stayed like that, their bodies joined in the most fundamental way, their lungs heaving. Gradually he became aware of their surroundings: the way his shirt stuck to the damp skin on his back, a cicada making a racket in a nearby bush, the low throb of the music coming from far inside the house.

He lifted his head from where it was buried against Ruby's sweetly curved neck, his legs so weak he had to fight to hold them both upright. He felt her shift against him and the enormity of what they had just done, of how out of control he had been, hit him hard.

He cursed softly and lowered her to the ground. He didn't regret many things in his life but taking Ruby with all the finesse of an untried schoolboy just might turn out to be one of them. He wanted nothing more than to wrap her up and take her home so that he could do that all over again. In a bed this time. 'Are you okay?' he prompted softly, knowing that he felt as dazed as she looked.

'Water.' She blinked up at him, her mask slightly askew from his fingers. He wanted to rip it off, yank off the wig and let all her long, golden hair tumble free. 'I'm so thirsty,' she croaked. 'Do you mind?'

Sam raked his hair back from his forehead. No, of course he didn't mind getting her a glass of water, but first he wanted to apologise, tell her he hadn't meant for things to go that far. At least not outdoors, at a party of all places! He cursed inwardly again. 'Sure, water.' The apology could wait. 'Just…stay put until I get back.' Hesitating, he glanced down at her, his brows pulling together as he took in her trembling mouth. 'You're sure you're okay?'

She nodded, fussing with her voluminous skirts so that she wouldn't have to look at him.

Leaving his jacket on the ground Sam strode back the way they had come, blinking as he rounded a corner and his eyes met the brighter lights of the terrace, small clusters of partygoers thankfully ignoring him as he stalked inside.

Quickly fetching a glass of water, he rehearsed a short speech in his head on his way back, trying to come up with some plausible explanation for what had just happened between them, only to find the place he had left her empty.

Worried, he spun around, searching out the shadowy garden for any sign of lavender silk. It took him a full minute to realise that she wasn't there. Then another to realise that she'd done a runner. Worry gave way to guilt that he'd taken things so far with her, and finally to fury that she wasn't still waiting where he'd left her.

Did she do this kind of thing all the time? Pick up a

man, have unforgettable sex with him and then ditch him when his back was turned? Was that why she had insisted that they keep things anonymous?

Jaw clenched, Sam yanked off his mask and tossed it to the ground. He couldn't quite bring himself to believe that she had used him in such a way, but if she thought he wouldn't pursue it she couldn't be more wrong.

CHAPTER THREE

'RUBES, IF YOU don't hurry up you'll miss yoga,' Molly called from outside her bedroom door.

Still in bed, Ruby rolled over and wondered if she could pretend to be asleep. Considering that she hadn't slept all night, she felt heavy enough to pass it off as real.

'Ruby?' Molly opened her door and poked her head inside. 'Are you ill?'

Yes, she was. She had just told a man she didn't even like that she *needed* him the night before. While they'd been having sex. Outside. At a party. The very thing she had warned her younger sister not to do!

Sex?

Was that really all it had been? It felt more like a cataclysmic event that had changed everything for ever from this point on. Certainly it had been the most erotically charged event of her life. In fact, before last night she had never understood how anyone could get so carried away with a man that they didn't stop when their common sense asserted itself. Unfortunately if her common sense had asserted itself she hadn't heard it.

It was the way he had looked at her and touched her that was the problem. He made her feel so special and so hot she literally lost her mind in his presence. Not that she *was* special. How could she be when he hadn't even known her name?

'Ruby?'

Or that she'd been a virgin? Although there was a moment of hesitation where she'd wondered if he had guessed at her inexperience. It had been cowardly, but the fear that he would question her about that, coupled with his soft curse of regret afterwards, had been the reason she had run when he'd gone to get her water. Not her finest moment, for sure, but when faced with the alternative of unmasking herself and saying 'Hi, it's me, Ruby. Great sex, by the way, thanks for the initiation' she'd chosen the easier, less confronting option. And didn't regret it for a second!

The fact that Sam Ventura would never know she had been the one he'd had hot vertical sex with was the one saving grace that made her confident she could face the day.

'Ruby, you're scaring me.'

Ruby glanced up to find Molly's worried brows knitted together. 'What? Sorry.' She forced her mind back to the present.

'You don't look well. What happened last night?'

'Nothing. I'm fine.' Ruby pinned a smile on her face, hoping that one day it would be true. 'Give me five minutes and I'll join you for yoga.'

'You sure you're up to it?'

No. But it was better than lying around in bed thinking about how stunningly erotic sex with Sam had been and how she was unlikely ever to experience anything like that again.

'I'm sure.'

Her sister looked unconvinced. 'I've made coffee, so hurry.'

As soon as Molly closed the door Ruby dashed out of bed. She knew from texting her sister last night that she'd met with the director and after some convincing he'd agreed to give her a call to set up an audition. Thankfully, Molly hadn't cared that Ruby had left the party without her, happy to continue on with the thespian crowd after successfully completing her quest.

And yoga was the best thing that she could do. It helped re-centre her enough to keep her mind off her excruciatingly bad decision on Friday night and stopped her from conjuring up future disasters as a result of her uncharacteristic indiscretion. Future disasters like the fact that she'd had sex for the first time in her life with a man who didn't even know her name. Like the fact that if Sam had still worked for the same firm as her, and ever found out it was her and told someone, the gossip would be all over chambers before she'd finished swiping her key card in the office lift.

Fortunately he lived in LA, so he was as likely to find out it was her he'd had sex with as she was of flying to the moon.

Small mercies, she conceded as she ducked out of the Monday morning summer rain and into the coffee shop she regularly haunted before work. She'd almost convinced herself that she'd pushed the whole Friday night affair from her mind when a tall, broad-shouldered man entered the coffee shop behind her, shaking the morning drizzle out of his dark hair.

With her heart in her mouth Ruby waited for him to turn towards her and as he did she felt a sense of unreality come over her when she realised it wasn't Sam.

The man gave her a small smile as she continued to stare, and Ruby made an apologetic face and swung back to the barista fixing her coffee. She felt jumpy all of a sudden and that just wouldn't do. She wasn't going to run into Sam in the middle of George Street. If anything she'd call Miller later in the day, find out how long Sam was in town and then avoid him for the duration.

If only the sex hadn't been quite so good.

Not good. More like amazing, mind-blowing, *incredible*. Other phrases that came to mind were: over, never to be repeated, and *stop thinking about it!*

Determined to listen to her saner side, she nodded at the dark-haired man whose attention she still inadvertently had as she strode out of the coffee shop and crossed the road to her office. The sooner she started work and felt normal again, the better.

'Hey, Ruby.' Veronica, her upbeat secretary, called out as she held the lift door open. 'How was the Herzog gig Friday night? Did you meet anyone nice?'

Why was everyone so interested in her love life all of a sudden? 'The Herzog party was fabulous.' She knew if she didn't show the right amount of enthusiasm that Veronica would prod her for more information. 'How was your weekend?'

'Took the kids to the zoo and saw the baby panda. So cute. So was there anyone interesting at the party? A celebrity or two?'

'Not that I noticed. We were in masks, don't forget, so that made it harder to recognise anyone.' Thank God. 'Why are you getting off at the third floor?' Their office was on the fourth.

'There's a meeting in the big conference room. Didn't you get the memo? Mr Kent Senior is making an announcement. We all received emails about it on Friday night.'

Ruby had come straight from court on Friday night and even though she remembered seeing the internal memo in her inbox she had forgotten to read it as she was rushing to get ready for the party. 'When is it?'

'Now,' Veronica said. 'Aren't you coming?'

'Of course.' Ruby stepped out of the lift, mentally re-organising her morning while juggling the file she'd been reading, her leather briefcase, hot coffee and her phone.

'Want me to hold something for you?'

Ruby shook her head. 'I'm good. Any idea what the meeting's about?'

'Rumour has it that our firm is about to merge with a big-shot outfit from the States.'

Ruby paused with her coffee halfway to her lips. 'Sorry?'

'But Bridget from IT said it was about Mr Kent Senior finally retiring and Drew taking over as managing partner.'

Ruby released a relieved breath. That sounded more like it but she wished Mr Kent could have just sent the information in the memo. She had a full day already mapped out and fitting in a Monday morning conference would be like trying to thread yachting rope through a sewing needle.

Seeing her expression, Veronica gave her an encouraging smile. 'It's supposed to be brief.'

'It's always supposed to be brief,' Ruby grouched before letting her bad mood wash away. So she'd be inconvenienced for half an hour. She loved her job and if Mr Kent wanted to go out with a bang then she wouldn't begrudge him his moment. He'd built a wonderful firm and deserved to have everyone acknowledge the work he'd done.

Manoeuvring herself into the overcrowded conference room, she greeted various co-workers with a smile as she moved towards the back. There was a real buzz in the air and Ruby craned her neck to get a glimpse over the sea of heads as to who was seated at the front of the room, only catching a glimpse of her boss, Drew Kent. Drew was a great boss: level-headed and fair-minded even when he didn't completely agree with some of the cases she took on, like her current one. It made her try that much harder to prove her worth, which she supposed was one of the reasons she'd done so well in the firm since she'd started working here twenty months ago.

'Everyone, if I could have your attention, please.'

Ruby sipped her coffee as Drew took the floor.

'It is with great pleasure, and much relief, that I announce the retirement of my father, who we all thought was not going to leave the building unless it was feet first. Fortunately my mother has convinced him that there is more to life than the law, even though we all know that isn't true.' A cluster of moans interspersed with chuckles filled the cramped space, making Ruby smile.

He said a few more words about his father's being an inspiration and introduced him to rousing applause. Mr Kent Senior then good-naturedly harangued his son in return and suggested that the only reason he'd finally agreed to leave the firm in Drew's capable hands was that someone highly regarded had agreed to merge his firm with theirs and help Drew run the show. Surprised murmurs filtered around her like a colony of bats preparing to take to the skies at dusk.

Ruby's ears pricked as she waited to hear who the newcomer was, and when she heard the name Ventura International her stomach plummeted to the ground faster than a lead ball dropped from the Sydney Tower.

'I'm sure you'll all join me in showing your appreciation for the fact that we've lured one of the most esteemed names in law back from the United States and doubled our legal reach by merging two great firms together.'

Although the crowd clapped heartily, Ruby stayed stock-still. This couldn't be happening. It just couldn't. She forced herself to oxygenate her lungs but it felt as if she'd never done it before and it was a skill she had yet to master. The coffee she'd consumed churned in her stomach and she had to swallow hard to keep it down. How was this possible? It was a nightmare. It was a disaster. It was…there were no words to describe how she felt other than numb. Totally and completely numb.

She heard Sam say a few words about how much he was looking forward to working with everyone and what it meant for him to be there but all Ruby heard was *'I want to taste you.'*

Oh, God, she was going to be sick.

Suddenly everyone around her was forming a line in order to congratulate the new managing partner and Ruby's stomach did another weird flip. She had to calm down. She had to pull herself together. She had to find a bathroom before she lost her breakfast all over the carpet.

'Can you believe we're going to be working out of Wellington Towers from tomorrow onwards?' Veronica said with barely concealed excitement. 'The foyer alone is as big as an aircraft hanger and apparently it has one-hundred-and-eighty-degree views of the harbour. No more cramped offices and narrow hallways. We're going to be working in the lap of luxury. I can catch the ferry to work now rather than taking the smelly old bus!'

Right now Ruby would believe that the sky was falling in if Veronica told her. 'Wellington Towers?' Her brows lowered in confusion. She'd clearly missed that part of Sam's speech.

'Apparently Sam owns it. Five floors of office space were cleared out over the weekend to make way for the merger. A lot of the hardware and case-sensitive info has already been moved out too, so it's just our personal stuff that has to be—Ruby, are you okay? You look white as a sheet!'

Ruby glanced at Veronica and gripped her forearm. 'Actually, I feel terrible. Just…' She looked around wildly as she felt herself being inched forward in the line to greet their new boss. 'I'll see you in my office.'

Veronica frowned. 'Sure, sure. Want me to give Mr Ventura your apologies?'

'No.' Ruby squeezed her arm. *Lord, no.* 'Just don't mention me *at all*.' Because she was going to have to resign, so why bother mentioning her name?

Five minutes of deep yoga breathing later she felt no better, but at least she was no longer thinking about resigning. She loved her job and there was no way she was going to have her career sidelined by a man. She'd made that vow a long time ago.

And why would he sideline her career anyway? He didn't know she was the woman he'd had sex with at the party on Friday night. As far as Sam was concerned, she was Miller's best friend he had shared a few kisses with a couple of years ago and that was it. No big deal. Nothing to get bent out of shape about. And perhaps he'd been too drunk to remember kissing her that night two years ago…she certainly hoped he was too drunk to remember having sex with her at a party three nights ago.

Nearly knocking over one of the paralegals as she exited the bathroom, she apologised profusely over her shoulder and stepped straight into the path of the long, self-assured strides of her current boss and…*her new boss*.

Heart hammering, Ruby first met blue eyes and then

molten brown, her breath backing up in her lungs, her brain automatically registering how big and devastatingly good-looking Sam Ventura was *sans* mask. He was a couple of inches taller than Drew, his white shirt with the blue stripe perfectly complementing his olive skin tone, his navy-blue suit jacket stretched perfectly across his broad shoulders.

Her gaze lingered on his clean-shaven jaw and sensual mouth. He had pleasured her so thoroughly on Friday night her body immediately felt hot all over. Hot and weak. Especially when she remembered the way his mouth had felt on her breast, the way he had used his teeth and his tongue to torture her with mindless pleasure.

Coffee surged out of the spout of her to-go cup and dribbled over her fingers. Squeaking in dismay, she brought her hand to her mouth to capture the drops before they hit the carpet and nearly tipped the whole contents out instead.

Sam reached forward to pluck the cup out of her nerveless fingers while Drew handed her a handkerchief from his breast pocket.

'Ruby? *Hell*. Are you burnt?' Drew asked, concern lacing his voice.

'No,' Ruby croaked. *Just embarrassed*. 'It was cold.'

She kept her focus on Drew, knowing she would turn stop sign-red if she looked at Sam.

'Okay, well, I'm glad we caught you. I didn't see you in the conference room at the meet and greet,' Drew said.

'I was there,' she assured him. 'I uh…had to duck out.'

'So you know Sam and I are sharing the managing-partner role?'

Ruby's lips stretched into a tight smile. She'd missed that bit of the speech as well. 'Great. Congratulations.'

She cast a quick glance at Sam to include him in her felicitations, only to find him studying her far too intently.

Ordering herself to *act normal,* she gritted her teeth and broadened her smile to make it more genuine. 'Welcome to the team.' A team that would soon be less one lawyer. Her. Because her first instinct had been spot-on: she would have to resign. There was no way she could see him in the office every day and remember everything they had done in Technicolor detail and then actually work for him in any sort of professional capacity.

'Thanks.' Sam's deep voice reverberated through her whole body, tightening every nerve ending to an excruciatingly fine point. 'I'm pleased to be here.'

She nodded, wondering if he had known she worked at the firm before Friday night…which was completely irrelevant because he didn't know he'd even been with her on Friday night. *The cad!*

'It's good we ran into you,' Drew said, cutting into her increasingly irrational thoughts. 'I was just bringing Sam to your office.'

Ruby tried not to show her alarm. 'You were?'

'Yes. With Mandy about to go into labour any day now, Sam has agreed to oversee the Star Burger case and I'd like you to bring him up to speed. Once this thing hits the media it's going to be bigger than *Ben Hur*, and I'd feel much better having a senior partner on board.'

As much as Ruby wanted to ease Drew's mind right before his first child was born, she had this case well in hand. 'Really, I have everything under control,' she advised him, hoping she sounded cool instead of defensive.

'Your last update said you were planning to put a political bigwig on the stand. This thing is getting huge, Ruby.'

'I'm not just planning it,' she stated crisply. 'I intend

to do it.' She didn't mean to bristle but she knew Drew had been dubious about her taking this pro bono case in the first place, and there was no way she was going to pull her punches now or, heaven forbid, drop the case altogether. Star Burger was an immensely popular chain of restaurants throughout Australia. The owner, Carter Jones, had franchised his business but had neglected to put in ethical standards to protect his employees. As a result everything from discrimination to racism and underpayment ran rampant throughout the organisation, and Ruby aimed to prove that it started at the top down.

Winning would not only mean that her badly treated clients were paid the money owed to them, it would also give a group of young people who were typically vulnerable in the community a voice they'd never had before. 'And it already is huge.'

'Which is why Sam needs to help you out,' Drew said, 'he has experience with cases like this.' He looked from Sam to her. 'Plus he said you already know each other.'

He had? Ruby swallowed. 'Only because my best friend married his brother. We don't actually *know* know each other.' Okay, so that time she had definitely sounded defensive; she knew it and steadfastly refused to look at Sam.

'I can take it from here, Drew,' Sam assured the other man calmly. 'You still want this?' He held the cup of cold coffee up to her.

'No. But it's a reusable cup, so you can't throw it away.'

'Fine.' He held on to it for her. 'You'll have to lead the way. I have no idea where your office is.'

Unable to come up with a plausible reason to defer their meeting, she gave him a tight smile. At least he didn't know what had transpired between them on Friday night. It was a small comfort, considering she did know and it was all she could think about, but she clung on to it anyway.

Cool as a cucumber, Sam thought, watching the sway of Ruby's body as she marched ahead of him, her pencil skirt lovingly outlining the sweet curves of her bottom and long legs that ended in skyscraper heels. This was the Ruby he'd met two years ago in the bar, all sharp edges and take-charge attitude wrapped in a glossy, un-ruffled package.

Or so she would have him believe. Because she wasn't entirely unruffled if her inability to maintain eye contact with him was any indication. That could be shock, of course, at having him turn up at her workplace. He was a little in shock himself. He hadn't known where Ruby worked before today and there was no way she could have known he was about to merge his firm with Kent's.

They had deliberately kept the merger quiet so as not to tip off the markets until it was a fait accompli. But this development, having Ruby as an employee, certainly threw a spanner in the works. He'd planned to get her phone number off Miller this week and call her up. Demand an explanation as to her actions last Friday night and then tell her what he thought about them. Tell her that next time she had sex with a man, she needed to wait around so that he could make sure she was okay and see her home.

Given that she was treating him like a veritable stranger right now, she probably wouldn't have responded to his call very positively. But they weren't strangers at all. They were lovers. Well, maybe not *lovers*. A lover didn't run out on a man after she'd sent him to heaven and back, did she?

Sam frowned, his earlier fury with her returning full force. Did Ruby even know it was he who had been inside her delicious body not fifty-eight hours ago? He who had made her come so hard that she had clung to him like a baby koala about to fall out of a tree? The thought that maybe she *hadn't* known had crossed his mind more than once over the weekend, but he'd immediately dismissed the notion. She'd known it was him. He was sure of it.

But what if she hadn't? What if he'd been little more than a random hook-up she'd used to scratch an itch? Sam felt a deep growl rumble inside his chest. A part of him didn't like to think that was all it had been for her, which was slightly irrational because wasn't that all it had been for him?

Her stride slowed as she reached a secretarial desk, her face only slightly softening as she listened to the woman behind it. He studied Ruby's profile. Her thick, straight hair was bound tightly at the base of her skull and he wanted to unwind it and mess up each blonde strand until it sifted like silk through his fingers.

'If you'll give me a minute,' she said coolly, turning to look at him. 'I need to take an important call before our meeting.'

Sam planted his hands on his hips as he regarded her. Was this a power play? Make him cool his heels while he had to wait for her?

'Fine,' he finally said, attempting to give her the benefit of the doubt.

'Would you like a coffee while you wait, Mr Ventura?'

'Sam,' he automatically corrected the secretary. 'And no. I'm fully caffeinated. Thanks.'

'No worries.' She smiled widely at him and he could see she wanted to say more but he paced around the small space like a caged tiger, his mind boiling over with the possibility that Ruby had no clue as to who he was other than her best friend's brother-in-law.

'You can send Mr Ventura in now, Ronnie.' Ruby's voice sounded over the intercom, raising his hackles. Mr Ventura, was it?

Of course, idiot, you're in the office, not a bar.

Fine. He'd be calm and professional in return. Let her know he preferred first names in the office just as Drew did and then he'd ask her if she was okay. And perhaps why she'd sent him on a fool's errand on Friday night and then run away from him.

'I'd like to get something straight,' she said, seated behind her desk like a queen attempting to exert control over a particularly unruly minion. 'I know how busy you must be with the merger, and the move to new office space this afternoon, so I don't want you to feel that you have to involve yourself in the Star Burger case. I have an incredible team working with me and we really do have everything well in hand.'

The woman had spunk; he'd give her that. 'And hello to you too, Ruby. It's good to see you again,' Sam drawled, somehow managing to hold his fast-rising irritation in check.

She had, he noticed with some satisfaction, the good grace to blush. 'It's ah…nice to see you too.'

Like hell it was, he thought, refusing to sit down opposite her like the good boy she expected him to be. Instead he took his time studying her office as if he were truly interested.

'I just don't want you to think that I need your assistance right now,' she continued as the silence lengthened between them. 'I know you must be incredibly busy.'

'So you said.' He picked up a colourful paperweight

from her bookcase and tossed it into the air. 'Nice piece. Who gave it to you?'

'My mother.' She moistened her cherry-red lips, a signature look of hers if he remembered correctly. 'After I made Senior Associate.'

'That's right.' He looked across at her. 'Drew said you're very good at your job.'

'Extremely good,' she corrected, more defensive now than uncertain. 'I've worked hard to get where I am at Kent's.'

'I didn't say you hadn't.'

'I know, but some people assume it's because of Drew's affirmative action strategy and—oh, never mind.'

'Relax, Ruby,' he said, finally dropping into the club chair opposite her desk now that he had control of the conversation. And her. 'This isn't a job interview. I wasn't having a go at your position in the firm. I'm sure you've earned it.'

Her eyes narrowed. 'Yes, I have. Now, what is it you need from me exactly?' *Before you hurry up and leave*, her tone implied.

'That depends.' Sam quirked a brow. 'What are you offering? Exactly?'

She took a deep breath and he took more pleasure than he should in knowing that he'd succeeded in riling her. 'Mr Ventura—'

'Sam,' he interrupted. 'You can start by calling me Sam and then you can continue by telling me why you're so prickly.'

'I'm not prickly.'

'As a porcupine being poked with a stick.' He relaxed back in the seat. 'Unless this is your usual working demeanour, and if it is then I might start questioning how you got so far so fast after all.'

'I apologise,' she said stiffly, smart enough not to take his bait again. 'I didn't mean to sound rude. I'm still getting my head around today's announcement about the merger and the changes that will bring.'

'Understandable. Now, tell me what the phone call was about.'

'Phone call?'

'The one you had to take while you left me outside, cooling my heels.'

'I didn't do that.'

'You did, but I'm not going to quibble over it. Did the call have anything to do with the Star Burger case?'

She frowned, clearly not wanting to share any information with him. 'Yes. But, as I said, I know you must have a hundred things on your plate, so you don't need to worry about this case right now.'

Sam looked at her, taking in the smooth line of her jaw and the challenging glint in her green eyes. Of course he had to worry about the case. Star Burger Restaurants was owned by one of the wealthiest men in Australia, a known pig of a man, who habitually treated people badly. Four months ago a group of young migrant workers had formed an alliance and decided to do something about their shocking working conditions and had approached legal aid for help. Legal aid had directed them to Ruby's desk and the case had grown exponentially until they now had a class action on their hands. It would be a landmark case in Australia if they won.

But he'd get to that later. First up he wanted to find out what Ruby's deal was and whether it had anything to do with their tryst on Friday night. 'So your resistance to having me work on this case is not because you're worried that Drew thinks you can't handle it, but for my benefit—is that right?'

'I can handle the case just fine.' She frowned darkly. 'And I think it's overkill to have you stepping in at this point, especially if you're under the impression that I *need* you. I mean, that I need your *help* or…anything.'

'Pity that's not your call to make, isn't it?'

His tone was cool and challenging and Ruby had no comeback because they both knew he was right: it wasn't her call to make.

'This is a David and Goliath case, Ruby,' he continued softly. 'Once it hits the media, Carter Jones will go after your clients' reputations with a vengeance and you'll need to be ready.'

'I know all this. I know we're the underdogs.' Concern pleated her brow. 'It's an impossible case to win, everybody says so, but no matter what you say to me, I have no intention of dropping it.'

'Dropping it?' Where had that come from?

'Yes. I know Drew was concerned about Kent's taking it on in the first place, and I know he's worried about how big it's going to get, but it's too important to drop now. We've come too far.'

Sam frowned. 'Have I asked you to drop it?'

'No.' Her chin came up and she unconsciously moistened her lips again. 'Are you going to?'

'No. But I know Carter Jones and I know how ruthless he can be. If this case goes to court it could severely damage his standing in the community, not to mention Star Burger Restaurant's profit margin. He won't allow that at any cost.'

'Then he should have made sure he took better care of his employees,' she said with a spiritedness Sam couldn't help but admire. 'Because this case is going all the way, Sam. These boys need justice and I intend to see that they have it.'

'Well said, and you'll get no argument about that from me. But surely you can see how having a lead partner on the case transmits a level of gravitas to the proceedings that might not otherwise be there.'

'You mean it will intimidate the opposition to have Sam Ventura on the case?'

Sam inclined his head. 'I have a reputation for winning, but then so do you. I think Drew's idea is that together we'll make a formidable team.'

'And if I disagree?' she asked archly.

Sam regarded the jut of her chin and stiff back and decided to push her some more. 'Another decision that isn't yours to make.'

She made a low sound in the base of her throat, her eyes shooting daggers at him. 'Fine. Do whatever you like. It's not as if I can stop you from coming in and taking over, is it?'

Sam ran a frustrated hand through his hair. 'Ruby, this isn't about your ability to run the case, or us dropping it, and it's not about me coming in and taking over. But this case is a class action. You're going to need senior counsel on it whether you like it or not.'

She gave a heavy sigh, her shoulders slumping a little. 'It's not a class action any more. Another client has dropped out, leaving only six.'

'Six?' That shocked him. 'You started with nineteen.'

'I know. Carter Jones and his cronies have already started intimidating them. The boys don't understand the system and therefore they don't trust it. But the remaining six want to go ahead and I intend to stand by them.'

Sam drummed his fingers on the arm of his chair. Six wasn't going to be enough to defeat Jones. 'Set up a meeting with all nineteen,' he said decisively. 'I'll speak with them.'

'All nineteen?' Ruby looked at him dubiously. 'I'm not sure that's a good idea. I don't want the remaining six to pull out as well.'

Sam raised a brow. 'You don't trust me very much, do you, Ruby?'

'It's not a question of trust,' she said, her eyes not meeting his. 'I don't want you wasting your time if you don't have to.'

'Now it's my turn to get something straight with you,' he began quietly. 'I'm a big boy, Ruby, and believe it or not I'm fully able to decide what is, and what isn't, a waste of my time. Understand?'

'Of course.'

Sam watched her even white teeth sink into her bottom lip and felt his body react. He could see that she still wasn't happy about him stepping in and he now knew it wasn't entirely due to her ego being pricked. Which left only one other issue outstanding between them.

'Now is that it? Or is there another reason you don't want to work with me?'

Harried green eyes cut to his. 'I didn't say I didn't want to work with you.' She let out a breath and, to her credit, tried to smile. 'You're Miller's brother-in-law. Why wouldn't I want to work with you?'

'Perhaps because we have more history between us than my brother and his wife,' he said equally as coolly. 'Perhaps because I've had my mouth on yours.'

Not to mention on your neck, your hair, your breasts.

A momentary flicker of panic darkened her emerald eyes before she shut it down, reaching for her water glass, her hand trembling only slightly as she brought it to her lips. 'That was two years ago and has nothing to do with any of this.'

'Doesn't it?'

'Of course not. It was an impulsive, late-night thing on both our behalves and it meant nothing.'

Sam didn't like hearing her say it had meant nothing to her, even though he had told himself the same thing at the time. But what happened two years ago was chicken feed compared to what had happened between them on Friday night.

'Since we haven't seen each other since then,' she continued doggedly, 'we should…we should…' She shrugged one slender shoulder. 'Just forget it ever happened.'

Sam stared at her for a beat. 'But we have seen each other since then, Ruby.' His ego scratched at the surface of his skin, goading him to push her. 'At Miller and Tino's wedding nearly a year ago? Don't you remember?'

'Of course.' Relief was stamped into each breathless word. 'How could I forget? It was a beautiful night.'

'How's the banker, by the way?'

'Banker?' A small frown notched between her brows. 'Oh, you mean Chester. He's a stockbroker.'

'I didn't ask *what* he was. I asked *how* he was.'

'He's good. I think he's good. Anyway, moving on…'

Unbelievable, he thought with growing incredulity. She was not going to acknowledge Friday night at all. And that left him in a bit of a quandary because not only did he want to mention it, but he also wanted to repeat it.

Not a good idea, Samuel. You're her boss now.

'Maybe I'm not ready to move on,' he found himself saying, regardless of what he'd just told himself. 'Maybe I want to explore things some more?'

'Explore things?' He'd admire her poise more if that pulse at the base of her throat wasn't fluttering like a trapped bird trying to get away from a hungry cat. 'Why would you want to explore anything about Chester Harris?'

Sam shook his head and told himself to back off. Whether she knew he had been the one she had been urging to take her on Friday night or not didn't matter. He had to let that go. Stop obsessing over it. If he wasn't careful he'd make this whole thing more important than it needed to be and that should have been more than enough to cool his interest in her.

More than enough to stop him from wanting to slip beneath the polished, professional facade this woman wore as convincingly as she had worn the black lace mask on Friday night and find out if the fire that had burned so brightly between them was for him and him alone.

'Don't stop. Please, don't stop.'

His jaw flexed. Because, as irrational as it might be, he wanted her to admit that she had known exactly who she had welcomed into her stunning body, and he wanted to have her there again. Hot and wet just for him.

But he couldn't do that. She worked for him. Even more reason he should use his brain and let this thing between them die a natural death.

Which meant no more leading questions about what that kiss had meant to her two years ago, and no informing her that he knew she was the woman he had held against a wall and buried himself deep inside until he'd seen stars last Friday night.

Watching her now, he told himself to take a very large step backwards. His feelings—whatever they were—for Ruby Clarkson didn't belong in the office. Or in his head.

He'd been back in the country for three days, he was hardly looking for any kind of relationship, and on top of that Miller would probably deliver his balls on a plate if he started something with her best friend, only to drop her a week later.

A best friend who looks like she would rather stick

hot needles in her eyes than start something with you, Ventura.

'Sam?'

Her confused voice broke into his thoughts. 'What?'

She frowned across at him. 'I asked if you agree with me.'

No, dammit, he didn't agree with her. Especially when he'd been so lost in thought he hadn't even heard her. 'Agree with what?' he barked, coming to a stop in front of her desk, his fingers digging into his hipbones.

'That we should forget all past—' she cleared her throat, moving a document from one side of her desk to the other '—*interactions* between us if we're going to work together.'

When he didn't immediately respond she lifted her gaze to his, one eyebrow raised in query as if they were discussing the merits of cucumber sandwiches. Her cool regard was like waving a red rag at a particularly irate bull and Sam ignored all his earlier good advice to himself to back off and went straight for her jugular. 'Friday night,' he said with a savage smile. 'Did you enjoy yourself on Friday night?'

A swift tide of emotion darkened her eyes and then she blinked and it was gone. When she spoke her voice was as steady as an ocean liner, her brow puckered with just the right amount of confusion as to appear genuine. 'Why would you ask me about Friday night?'

God, she would make a formidable opponent in court, he thought with unwilling admiration, his ego slightly mollified by the overactive pulse still thrumming at the base of her neck.

'No reason.' He forced a lazy smile to his lips. 'Miller mentioned that you work long hours. Even weekends. I wouldn't want you to burn yourself out.'

'Oh.' She glanced over his shoulder at the door as if she wanted it to open magically and suck him outside. 'I'm not nearing burnout. Thank you for asking.'

She rubbed the outer edges of her left eye as if to control a twitch. Sam's smile grew. Oh, she knew all right. She knew he had been the man who had been inside her at the Herzogs' party, the man who had pleasured her so deeply, so thoroughly, so *intimately* he'd had to hold her upright immediately afterwards so she didn't fall over. He was dead sure of it now. And damn, if that didn't ease the choke hold she had on his unaccountably fragile ego.

'My pleasure,' he purred, buttoning his jacket and willing to back off now. 'Set up that meeting with every one of our Star Burger clients. And Ruby?' He stopped at her door and smiled at the wary expression on her face. 'Thank you for your time. It was very enlightening.'

CHAPTER FOUR

RUBY SAGGED IN her seat the moment Sam closed her office door behind him.

Good lord, she was never going to be able to work with him. He was too big and too dangerous to her equilibrium, sucking all the air out of the room until she could barely breathe.

The way he had looked at her, all hot and intense…it was all she could do to hold herself aloof. And when he had asked about last Friday night…her eyes narrowed as she recalled his bland expression. She'd almost been certain he'd been toying with her, but he was a master when it came to inscrutability.

Even so, there was no way he could know that he'd been with her at the Herzog party. No one had known her there, as far as she was aware. The only way he would know it was her was if she told him. Which she wasn't about to do. Ever.

'Here are some boxes,' Veronica said, carrying in two cardboard flat-packs she immediately set about constructing on Ruby's desk. 'I know you have a lot to do today so I'll take care of the packing up. Just remember tomorrow when you finish in court to head to the new office building. With the amount of manpower Sam has provided we'll definitely be in by then. And we're on the executive floor.' She waggled her brows. 'I'm going to do my best to get us a view of the harbour. How *was* your meeting with His Hotness before? He looked a lot happier when he left than when he was standing around waiting for you.'

'His Hotness?'

'That's what a few of the girls have already nick-named him. I'm married, but I wouldn't mind locking lips with him just once in this lifetime. I'm sure my husband would forgive me.'

Veronica grinned and Ruby tried to grin back. 'He's unlikely to remember you afterwards,' she said with enough bite to have Veronica looking at her strangely.

'What does that mean?'

'Nothing.' Ruby pushed back from her desk and started shoving things into the first box. 'Ignore me. I'm upset that another client has opted out from the Star Burger case. I have to set up an appointment for all of them to meet. I think Sam has some idea that he can convince them to re-commit to the case.'

'Maybe he can. He's awfully compelling.'

About to tell Veronica she didn't really want to hear how 'compelling' their new boss was, she stopped when there was a knock at her door.

'Werner meeting about to start in five, Rubes.' Grant Campbell, a rising-star associate in the firm, poked his head through the door. 'We're in conference room four.'

'On my way,' she said, grabbing her laptop and acci-dentally upending five case files in the process.

She glanced at Veronica. 'Ever get the feeling you should have stayed in bed some days?'

'All the time,' Veronica quipped.

And that was pretty much Ruby's day, chasing her tail and trying to keep up with work until she fell into bed that night so tired she didn't even think about Sam the whole night. Or mostly.

By Wednesday morning she felt marginally more in control, though she used that term loosely because she could already feel her nerves buzzing around inside as if she were high on caffeine. Which she wasn't because she hadn't even had time for a coffee so far this morning.

She stared at the view of the Opera House outside her new office window. Veronica had done well, nabbing a great space for them in the impressive tower. The Manly ferry pulled up to the wharf, unloading a small colony of workers and a few eager tourists onto the fastidiously tidy Circular Quay area far below.

She was just wondering if she had time to work out how to use the state-of-the-art coffee machine in the kitchen when her phone buzzed. She glanced down to find a text from Grant regarding the Star Burger case. Apparently some of the nineteen plaintiffs had arrived and were drinking cola and eating cake in the conference room.

Sending him a quick thank-you in reply, she rolled her chair back and scooped up her file notes on each one of her clients along with her laptop.

Even though she had emailed Sam the information yesterday morning, he had asked that she stop by his office an hour before the meeting to go over their strategy together. It was the last thing she wanted to do, given that she'd steadfastly avoided any contact with him the last two days, but it had to be done.

Today she wouldn't be able to hide in her office if she thought she heard him outside her door, or turn the other way when he was coming towards her down the hallway, her insides jittery as she waited for him to call out to her and ask her to stop. Her fixation on his whereabouts in the office was making her crazy and, what was worse, interfering with her usually fanatical concentration levels.

Channelling all things serene, she pushed her feet back into her favourite don't-mess-with-me stiletto heels and checked her immaculate red lipstick before making her way to the end of the hall, knocking sharply on Sam's office door.

Sam uncoiled from behind his glass desk as she entered his lair, an unreadable expression on his face. She noted his impressive physique in his pale blue shirt, royal blue tie and charcoal suit trousers. He looked like the uber-successful lawyer that he was and she knew her clients would be incredibly intimidated by his powerful aura. Couldn't the man tone it down just a little bit?

'Why the frown?' he asked, his voice gravelly as if he hadn't spoken for a while.

Deep breaths, she told herself. He might live up to his new 'hot' label but she was a professional. Plus, she'd been there, done that, and now she was blushing and he was looking at her in that intense, curious way of his. How he didn't know that they had been as close as two people could ever be was beyond her, and it was definitely absurd for her to be thinking like that when she was *extremely happy* that he didn't know it was her at the masquerade ball.

Not that she should be thinking about *that* night at all. This case was incredibly important for her and she genuinely cared about her clients, who she had rapidly come to think of as 'her boys'.

Boys who were only teenagers and new to the country, a couple of them barely speaking English but all of them hungry to learn and to find a place to belong where their safety wasn't at risk every other minute of the day.

Star Burger Restaurants should have provided them with a place of employment that espoused the egalitarianism that most Australians liked to be known for. It hadn't, and it was Ruby's job to prove that management had not only known how her clients had been mistreated, but also that the rot in the organisation was filtered from the highest level down.

Would Sam take the case as seriously as she did? Or would he see it as a vehicle to showcase his prowess in the courtroom? And why did that matter if he helped them win?

'Stop biting on your lip,' he rasped, 'and tell me why you're frowning.'

Ruby released her newly tortured flesh, hoping she hadn't eaten her lipstick off in the process. 'I'm frowning,' she said softly, 'because I'm concerned about our meeting today. Some of these kids went through a traumatic experience working for the Star Burger chain and it's been really hard gaining their trust. I don't think going over things yet again is going to help.'

Sam sat down on one of the white leather sofas set in an L-shape looking out over the cloudless blue sky of a summer's day. 'They'll have to repeat their stories if it goes to court.'

'Which is why most of them pulled out.'

'No. Most of them pulled out because Carter Jones started a smear campaign against them. We need to get those clients to re-engage in the case if we want to win and you know it. Come. Sit down.'

'They don't trust the system,' she told him, reluctantly doing as he'd bid and taking a seat on the spare sofa adjacent to his. 'And why should they? It hasn't done them any favours so far.'

'It will after we win their case.'

Ruby's brows drew down. 'Just don't push them too much, okay? They don't know you from Adam.'

Sam cocked his head, his gaze raking her face to the point of discomfort. 'You care about these boys almost more than you care about winning, don't you?'

'I care about doing what my client wants me to do,' she said, pushing her hair back behind her ears. She didn't want Sam to think she brought excessive emotion to her cases because it was one thing to be passionate about work, but quite another to be so involved you stopped being impartial and became ineffective.

'I have been around the block once or twice, Ruby—I do know what I'm doing.' He gave her an all-encompassing look. 'Is that the only thing making you so jittery right now?'

Ruby's head reared back. 'First you say I'm prickly, now you say I'm jittery. I'm neither,' she said hotly, her stomach doing a somersault and making a mockery of her words. Lord, if he could see through her so easily, she was toast.

'Good. Then help me work out the best strategy to get the full nineteen boys back on board. If we want to beat Jones we're going to need them to at least agree to show up in the courtroom, even if they have no intention of taking the stand. It will give our current clients a confidence boost and hopefully worry the hell out of Jones.'

Ruby unclamped her lips and found herself envying Sam his ability to remain so composed while she felt as if her insides were getting ready to audition for the lead role in one of Molly's musicals. But then he wasn't constantly distracted by flashbacks as to how it had felt to have her hands all over his body on Friday night. How it had felt to have his hands all over hers. And why couldn't she manage to put that behind her? It had been five days already.

'I know you care about these boys, Ruby,' he said softly. 'You're not as hard-nosed as you'd like me to believe.'

Ruby opened her file notes and lifted her chin. 'I'm exactly as hard-nosed as I want you to believe.'

Sam shook his head and moved from his sofa to hers, his powerful thigh brushing against hers as he settled too closely beside her. Fire shot through her at the slight touch and she surreptitiously adjusted her position further along the settee, ignoring his sidelong glance.

'Ready?' She arched a brow in question.

'Always.' He took the first file from her and Ruby exhaled as his agile brain switched from her to work, forcing her own to follow suit.

Three hours later Ruby was quietly impressed with the way Sam had approached the case. He did know his stuff and had gone out of his way to put the boys at ease, asking insightful questions and never pushing in a way that might be construed as threatening or manipulative.

Now, with the meeting about to finish up, she couldn't wait to get out of there. A whole morning of being this close—and this aware—of her new boss had her nerves strung tight. And some sixth sense told her that Sam knew exactly how she was feeling.

It seemed that she only had to take a breath and he glanced her way. It was unnerving. *He* was unnerving. Why on earth had she become so carried away on Friday night that she'd ignored every cautionary note in her head that screamed *Stop!* and instead had listened to the racy one that had moaned *More*?

'Thank you all for coming today. I know it wasn't that convenient but I truly believe if we stand together we can win this case for you,' Sam began. 'I also think that it's vital that we win this case for you. Your lives mean something here, they mean something to us, but you need to stand up and believe that too if you want to see justice done for each and every one of you, now and in the future.' A couple of the boys fist-pumped the air in agreement, while others shifted uneasily in their seats, none unmoved by Sam's passionate discourse. 'I know you have to think about everything that was said today but if you could email Ruby by the end of the week with your decision as to how you want to proceed we would greatly appreciate it.'

Relieved to have the meeting over with, Ruby stood up hastily and shook each one of the boys' hand as they headed for the door. A couple of them gave her a hug and she returned it enthusiastically. Grant stopped beside her, giving her a *that went well* look, but before she could head out with him Sam asked her to stay behind in a voice that brooked no argument.

Glancing back, Ruby found that Sam was scrawling notes in a file and not even looking at her. Grant raised a brow at her in question. Sam's directive had come across more like a command but the last thing she wanted to do was extend the meeting. Her nerves were shot.

'Actually, I have another meeting I need to prepare for,' she said politely. 'Can it wait?'

Sam frowned as he glanced up at her. 'No. It can't.'

Ruby moistened her lips. 'Perhaps an email, then?'

Grant coughed into his hand and quickly gathered up his laptop and file notes as he caught Sam's darkening expression. 'I'll leave you to it.'

Aware that she had probably overstepped the lines of professional decorum with that last suggestion, she stood tensely waiting for Sam to finish making his notes.

And waited.

And waited.

Finally he leaned back in his chair and looked at her, his long, thick lashes concealing his expression from her. 'Mind telling me what that was all about?'

'What?' she asked, stalling for time.

'Your desire to scramble out of here as quickly as possible.'

'I don't scramble,' she said indignantly.

'You also don't have a meeting to get to. I checked with your secretary earlier because I wanted you to stay back and go over a few key points with me.'

Irritated at his high-handedness, Ruby bristled. 'How dare you go over my head and ask Veronica about my movements? If you want to know my schedule you can ask me.'

'I didn't go over your head. You were busy talking and I saw no point in interrupting you for something so small.'

His raised brow told her she was overreacting—and not only that but it was also a reminder that he was her boss and could do what he damned well pleased—so she sucked in a deep breath and forced her lips to curve upwards. 'Fine. What key points?'

'Thabo and Jeremiah were particularly nervous today and their stories didn't seem to stack up with their original depositions. Why is that?'

'Jeremiah has a minor learning disability. It's one of the reasons he was ridiculed in the workplace. He's been on medication ever since to manage his anxiety and I think it messes with his memory.'

'We should strike him from the client list, then.'

'We can't. He deserves to be heard as much as anyone else.'

'I didn't say he didn't. But we have to be practical.

He'll get compensation like the others, but he shouldn't be subjected to the witness box if this goes to court. It could make his health worse.'

'If?'

'Don't get your back up again. I very much doubt Carter Jones will let it go all the way.'

'But it has to. How else will our clients receive full validation for how they were mistreated?'

'Money will go some way to appease them.'

'That's not true,' she fumed. 'You know they're not motivated by money. They want justice.'

'They'll get justice. Now tell me about Thabo.'

'I have a feeling Thabo is standing in for someone else who doesn't want to come forward.' She tucked a strand of hair behind her ear and noticed his eyes follow the movement. 'I think it might be a woman. If you haven't noticed there are no women on the case because they're too frightened to come forward. I think that's why Thabo is defensive.'

'Which also makes him a weak link.' Sam frowned. 'But the women need to be as equally compensated as the men. Can you find out if we can get any of them to come on board?'

'Of course.' She cleared her throat, suddenly aware that she'd moved closer to him during their discussion. 'Is that all?'

'You tell me?' His rough tone did nothing to placate her frazzled nerves.

'I have nothing else to tell you,' she said carefully, unnerved by the sexual tension that suddenly permeated the air between them.

'I think you do.'

The way he looked at her tangled her insides up and twisted her emotions into a tight ball. He was so attractive with his shirtsleeves rolled up and the top button of his shirt loosened, the curl of chest hair overlapping the button screaming that he was all male. Something she already knew by heart.

'And I think it's past time we addressed the elephant in the room, don't you?'

'Elephant?' She had a sick feeling she knew where this was heading. 'There is no elephant.'

'Then why are you so keen to avoid me every chance you get?'

Ruby hunted around for an explanation and went with what was uppermost in her mind. 'If you must know, I don't think we can work very well together.'

'Why not?'

Now, there was a question she had no intention of answering. 'The why, or why not, isn't important.' She hated that she felt so flustered and defensive and that only made her feel more so. 'I respect you as a fellow lawyer and as my boss, I just don't respect...' Her eyes shot to his as she realised what she'd been about to say.

'You just don't respect what, Ruby?' His voice was predator-soft. 'You don't respect me as a man. Is that what you stopped yourself from saying?'

Yes, it had been because how could she respect a man who had sex with random women whose names he didn't even know? 'I didn't say that—you did. But I don't see any point in letting this get personal between us. It will only make things harder.'

Sam gave a short, harsh laugh. 'It's a bit late for that, don't you think, *angel*?' The tone of his voice had all the hairs on the back of her neck standing on end. 'Things are about as personal as they can get between us, I'd say.'

Ruby tried not to overreact to the word 'angel', fighting to remain calm. 'If you're talking about how I wanted to leave the meeting, I—'

'I'm not talking about that.' He dismissed with a careless flick of his wrist, his gaze disturbingly direct. 'I'm talking about Friday night.'

He waited a beat but Ruby found her tongue frozen to the roof of her mouth.

'Last Friday night, to be exact.' When she remained mute he gave her a sardonic smile that only elevated his good looks. 'You know… You and me. Sizzling-hot sex outside at the Herzog party. Or are you going to tell me it wasn't you in the lavender silk dress and black lace mask?'

Oh, God, she had been wrong.

He knew. He *knew*! The words reverberated inside her head, a stinging heat singing along her cheekbones as if she were being pricked by a thousand tiny hot needles.

Their gazes clashed and held and Ruby couldn't look away from his gorgeous brown eyes to save herself.

'I can see you're still going to try and deny it,' he said, the savage note in his voice letting her know that he was far from impressed with her. 'Which is a little disappointing, to say the least.'

'I'm not going to deny it,' she said with asperity, mortification setting in as she recalled how she had begged him for more that night.

'Well, that's a start,' he grated, his gaze penetrating every one of her natural defences in a way no man ever had before.

What was it about Sam that made him so lethally attractive to her? It just wasn't fair.

'A start to what?' she asked, recognising for the first time that he was truly annoyed, but at a loss as to know why he would be. She hadn't demanded anything from him, or called his phone off the hook like a love-struck fool. Shouldn't he be rejoicing about that instead of scowling at her?

'To you being honest. I did wonder if you were going to try and blame the alcohol. Maybe claim that you'd had so much to drink that you didn't know what you were doing. That you didn't know *who* you were doing it with.'

If only I could! But what did he want her to say? That she found him so completely and utterly irresistible that she hadn't been able to stop? That she had wondered what it would be like to be intimate with him for so long that when it finally happened she hadn't *wanted* to stop? 'I knew what I was doing.' She lifted her chin, determined that he would never guess how deeply she was affected by the intimacies they had shared—or how much she had enjoyed it. 'And I'm not ashamed of what happened.'

A scowl darkened his face. 'Were you ever going to mention it?'

'No,' she answered after a brief pause, her heart pounding like a jackhammer behind her breastbone.

'You had an itch and I scratched it.' His lips twisted into a cool smile. 'Is that it?'

Taken aback by the force of that comment, Ruby scowled. 'There's no need to sound so crass.' Was that the way it had been for him? She felt a little sick at the thought, immediately reminded of the soft curse of regret he'd made before he'd set her on her feet. 'But yes, I suppose you could put it that way. What's your excuse? Or don't you need one? You're a man, I was an available woman. Isn't that the way the story goes?'

Dead silence followed her accusation and when he spoke his voice was grim. 'That would imply that I got more out of our lovemaking than you did. Which is not my recollection of events.'

Embarrassment at just how much she had begged him to keep going burned a hot trail down her throat. 'Oh, come on, Sam. Lovemaking? Let's at least call it what it was.'

'By all means.' A muscle flexed in his jaw. 'Enlighten me.'

Ruby gripped her laptop tighter. 'It was sex. Great sex, by the way. Ten out of ten to you, but it was still just sex.'

'It was nowhere near ten out of ten,' he corrected her.

Well, sorry. Hurt cut across raw nerves as if he'd just lashed her with a whip.

His dark eyes held hers as if he knew exactly where her mind had taken her. 'Ten out of ten would have meant we were in a bed, naked, and we had all night together.'

'Oh.'

Well, then.

Not sure where to look, she watched him covetously as he moved to the window and stared outside. Without his eyes on her, Ruby breathed a little more easily, but her reprieve was short-lived as he swung back to face her.

'There's something I want to know.'

Ruby held her breath at the serious note in his voice. 'What?'

'Was that your first time?'

Caught completely off guard by the question she blinked at him. Had it been so obvious?

A soft curse rent the air.

Crimson-faced, she turned to leave.

'I didn't use protection.'

His words landed between them like boulders off the side of a mountain, staying her. 'I'm on the pill.'

His eyes narrowed as he looked at her. 'Why is a virgin on the pill?'

'Because I was planning to have sex with someone that night, and you were the lucky recipient. Why do you care?'

'Because I was worried I might have made you pregnant,' he argued. 'An unwanted pregnancy is the last thing either one of us needs right now.'

The image of Sam Ventura's baby growing inside her womb did weird things to Ruby's equilibrium. Not wanting to consider that any of those things were bad, she shook her head. 'Rest assured, I'm not pregnant. No need to worry.'

An emotionally charged beat passed between them and all Ruby could think about was the way his sexy mouth had felt on hers and how much she wanted it there again.

Deep down, she rued the day she had approached Sam in that bar two years ago. It had set off a series of wants and needs inside of her that she could only ever imagine him fulfilling. She hated the romantic feelings he had once inspired in her and she was very afraid that if she gave herself to Sam—truly gave herself to him—he would take more than she would want to give, knocking down every one of the barriers she had built up specifically to keep him out.

'I apologise,' he said, a measure of self-disgust running through his voice. 'It shouldn't have happened.'

Did he mean they shouldn't have had sex? Somehow that only made her feel worse. She really didn't need more proof as to how divergent their experience of that night had been. She'd already seen the regret on his face; she didn't need to see it again.

'Please don't.' She put her hand up as if to ward him

off but he was still on the other side of the room. 'We're both adults and it was my decision as well.'

'I wasn't apologising for the sex, Ruby.' His brown eyes glittered dangerously into hers. 'I'm apologising for not protecting you. For being…rough.'

'You weren't rough,' she assured him huskily.

His eyes pierced hers. 'I should have realised that you weren't experienced.'

'Why should you?'

'Because it's a man's job to take care of a woman in that situation.'

'I disagree. This is the twenty-first century. Women are emancipated, in case you didn't realise.'

A muscle ticked in his jaw. 'Emancipation had little to do with Friday night,' he growled. 'But let's just say it's not the way I usually behave with a woman.'

At the mention of his other women Ruby expelled a rushed breath. This was information she didn't want inside her head. Ever. 'Look, can we just not discuss this any more?' Surely there was a much more important and safer topic for them to discuss. Or they could both just leave the room and pretend this conversation had never happened at all. 'Don't you have a meeting to go to or a new client to woo?'

Ignoring her question, he came around the table until he was no more than two feet from her. She nearly took a step back but caught herself just in time.

'Why did you run away afterwards?'

Startled by his question, she met his gaze. 'Sorry?'

'It's a simple question, Ruby. I want to know why you left before I returned with your water.' His bronzed throat worked as he swallowed. 'Did I scare you somehow?'

Being so close to him now, she couldn't avoid the

sensation of heat and male power emanating from him. There was also impatience, as if he wanted to close the gap between them and take her into his arms again. Or was that just her who wanted that to happen?

Jarred by the unexpected vision of how he would look naked, and desperate to close down this attraction any way she knew how, Ruby shook her head. 'I was fine. I just didn't see the point in hanging around.' Not to mention that she'd been terrified at how easily he had made her feel so much, so quickly. Terrified at how easily she had given in to the attraction between them. It had made her feel weak and powerless; two states she had often seen her mother fall into with the men in her life. 'I mean, it wasn't as if either of us was looking for a repeat performance, was it?'

Sam's jaw clenched. 'You have no idea what I wanted, but be that as it may, it would have been polite for you to have been there when I returned. I didn't know if I'd hurt you in some way.'

'You didn't hurt me, Sam,' she said on a rush, memories of the pleasure he had given her making her knees tremble. 'And you didn't scare me. I was just... I wanted to put the whole incident behind me as soon as possible.'

'Incident? It wasn't a car accident,' he bit out.

'I know that! Really, I'd rather not talk about it, if it's all the same to you.'

'I can see that.' She didn't like the derisive glint in his eyes, or the way he stepped forward. 'But I very much doubt that you've been able to put the whole *incident* behind you.'

Heat flamed through her. It was pretty hard to put something behind you that came back in full, cinematic glory every night when you tried to go to sleep. Not to mention those times it was standing right in front of you. Like now.

'God, you're arrogant.' Against her better judgment she took a step towards him. 'But *be that as it may*, we work together now. You're my boss.'

Sam frowned. 'I didn't know that on Friday night. It wasn't as if Drew sent me a list of Kent's employees to pore over.'

'So if you'd known I would be working for you on Friday night then it wouldn't have happened?' she challenged.

'Believe it or not, Ruby, I didn't mean for things to go as far as they did.'

'So you're blaming me for the fact that they did!'

'No.' He braced his hands on his hips, scowling down at her. 'Dammit, would you stop being such a little hot-head? I'm telling you that I never mix business with pleasure, and I usually take a woman out to dinner before I sleep with her.'

'We didn't sleep together, Sam.' A charged silence followed her statement and Ruby suspected Sam was remembering exactly what they had done, just as she was.

'A technicality,' he said shortly.

'And a moot point, since it's never going to happen again. And, for the record, I don't mix business with pleasure, either.'

Fortunately, she wouldn't have to think about that for much longer she decided as a conversation she had overheard between her colleagues the day before came back to her. An interoffice transfer was not something she'd ever considered in the past but it might be exactly what she needed. And sure, it might be considered a little impulsive and she'd never been the impulsive one in her family before, but, compared to having sex with a man she hardly knew outside at a party, a work transfer was minuscule. 'Nor do I want to start a relationship with any man any time soon. In case you're wondering.'

'Career first? Is that it, Ruby?'

'Always,' she responded briskly.

'Well, I don't recall saying anything about a relationship either,' he mocked.

'Sorry,' she said tightly. 'I meant to say fling, or affair, or whatever you call your little liaisons.'

The muscle in his jaw jerked once more. 'You're really trying my patience, you know that?'

Ruby was saved from having to respond when one of the new paralegals poked his head in the door. 'Oops, sorry,' he said, a little red-faced when he recognised Sam. 'I thought the last meeting was supposed to be done by now.'

'It is done,' Ruby assured him, tilting her chin in Sam's direction. When he didn't immediately agree with her she frowned. 'We are done, aren't we, Mr Ventura?'

He studied her with hard eyes that saw far too much for her liking and revealed far too little. 'We're done,' he finally granted. 'For now.'

CHAPTER FIVE

'ALLISON FROM HR has popped up to see you,' Veronica said, poking her head into Ruby's office. 'Have you got a sec?'

'Sure.' Ruby parked her thoughts on the file notes she was making about a new case and ushered Allison into her office. Not that she'd been all that productive. It was five o'clock on Friday night and her concentration had been shot as of about an hour ago. Maybe more. At least *this* Friday night she was going straight home to the safety of her apartment, where there would be wine, her beloved *Law & Order*, and both Ben *and* Jerry waiting for her.

'Hey,' Allison said, taking a seat opposite her. 'So I got your email and I thought I'd come up in person to check if you're serious about this interoffice transfer before I start working on it.'

Ruby tucked a wing of hair behind her ear. After her disastrous meeting with Sam she'd sent Allison an email about transferring out of the Sydney office, but now she wasn't so sure about it. She knew Kent's looked highly on those who expanded their knowledge by working in other offices, but was that really what she wanted to do? Certainly she'd feel less jumpy if she knew Sam wasn't able to pop his head into her office when she least expected it, or if she didn't have to worry about running into him in the hallway, but wasn't moving to another country a little drastic?

'Ten out of ten would have meant we were in a bed, naked, and we had all night together.'

Okay. Possibly not.

'Yes, I'm serious. I wouldn't mind expanding my horizons and challenging myself a bit more.'

'In another country?'

No, another planet might be better, but apparently Mars was still uninhabitable. 'They say a change is as good as a holiday,' Ruby offered with a shrug. 'And it won't be for ever. I just think I need something a bit different right now.'

Allison gave her a sympathetic smile. 'Man trouble?'

Ruby felt herself flush. 'Sort of.' Hadn't she vowed when she was younger that she'd never let a man interfere with her career as her father had done to her mother?

But that wasn't what was happening here, was it?

'I feel for you,' Allison said. 'And you're in luck. We have a couple of placements coming up. One in the US and the other in London. Do you have a preference or would you like me to put you down for both?'

The US was a little close to where Sam had previously worked. If she moved there and then he returned for work that would defeat the entire purpose of the exercise.

'London,' she said on a decisive note. She'd never been to London. It was cold, yes, but there was the West End, Covent Garden, double-decker buses and, best of all, no distracting boss.

'Okay.' Allison stood up. 'I'll make sure your name goes to the head of the queue. I owe you a favour.'

Ruby knew Allison was referring to the previous year when she'd helped her nephew out of a spot of shoplifting trouble. 'You don't owe me at all,' she said with a mock frown. 'But I appreciate the sentiment.'

'No worries… Oh, hi, Sam.' Allison stepped to the side to allow the man Ruby was dead keen on avoiding into her office. 'Hope you had a nice time interstate yesterday.'

'Very productive, Allison, thank you.'

Of course he already knew Allison's name. She was bright, bubbly and *single*. *And none of your business*, Ruby told herself.

'Great, well, I hope you both enjoy the long weekend.' She waved at Ruby as she left, fanning herself as she passed Sam, a cheeky grin on her face.

Ignoring the butterflies milling around in her stomach at finding herself alone with him, Ruby gave Sam a level look.

'What can I do for you?' she asked, hoping her tone hit somewhere between professional and unaffected.

Sam glanced back at Allison's departing figure. 'You got problems with HR?'

'No.' As Managing Partner, he probably had a right to know her long-term plans at the firm but she had no intention of sharing them at this point. Not when she wasn't completely certain of them herself. 'Allison just stopped by.' Which was true enough.

'Good.' He moved further into her office, closing the door behind him. 'I received your update that we now have fifteen of the original nineteen plaintiffs back on board, as well as five women. That's great news.'

'It is.' Ruby had been ecstatic when the boys had responded so favourably to Sam's pep talk, encouraging their female counterparts to come forward. 'We have a class-action suit again. Thank you. If you hadn't insisted on meeting with them we'd have had more of an uphill battle ahead of us.'

'Don't thank me. We still have an uphill battle ahead of us, but we're a team now. If you need something I'd like to think that you'll call on me to help you get it.'

Ruby nodded, swallowing the weird lump that had formed in her throat. She wondered what it would feel like if they really were a team, with none of this awkward tension between them. 'I appreciate the offer,' she began tentatively. 'But I'm good. Next week we'll file proceedings, and then there will be a mountain of documents to review before—' she stopped as she realised she was rambling. 'You already know the legal procedure.'

'I do,' he agreed wryly. 'And the Star Burger case isn't the only reason I'm here.'

'Sorry.' Feeling as gauche as a first-day trial lawyer, Ruby tried for a smile. 'Why else did you stop by?'

'Lawson Publishing House have their national conference on this weekend and Drew is supposed to attend the keynote address tonight as a thank-you for the work the firm did for them last year. Since Mandy isn't feeling too well right now, he asked me to fill in.' He rubbed the faint stubble on his jaw and Ruby noted the tired lines on the outer edges of his eyes. Maybe he wasn't sleeping any better than she was. 'Since the chairman and I haven't met and you've worked closely with him on one or two issues, Drew thought it would be a good idea for you to attend with me. He apologised for the late notice, but the whole thing shouldn't last for more than an hour. Two at the most.'

In the past Ruby would have had no problem representing the firm at such an event. She'd done so on more than one occasion. But tonight, with Sam? She controlled her breathing as she held his gaze, her mind immediately conjuring up images of him and her, the wall behind her, his body in front. Heat surged low in her pelvis, sparking little tremors of need inside her.

'Apparently we're free to leave after the keynote is finished,' he continued. 'Before that, though, there is a bit of mingling to be done.'

It wasn't the mingling she was worried about. 'I... I...'

Have an appointment with a tub of ice cream? Have to wash my hair? Do my nails?

'You what?' he asked, nonchalantly leaning against the side of her desk and piercing her with a dark look. 'Can't think of anything worse than spending an evening alone with me?'

'I hardly call attending a business function an evening alone with you.'

'I wouldn't either. So why the look of dismay?' His eyes raked over her face. 'Disappointed that it's *not* an evening alone, perhaps?'

The memory of what had happened between them a week ago, of how she had responded to him, lay hot and heavy between them.

'Of course not.' Her chin rose as she fought to slow her heartbeat. 'But what if I already have a date for tonight?'

'"Then you'll have to cancel it,' he said so softly she knew it wasn't a suggestion.

She wanted to tell him that if she really did have a date she'd do no such thing, but the look in his eyes stayed her. 'Fine.' She huffed out a breath. 'Fortunately for you, I believe that work is more important than anything else anyway.'

'Work is never more important than anything else,' he said with such conviction she felt a little taken aback. 'But regardless, this *is* a work function and your commitment to the firm is duly noted.'

'Lucky me.' She closed the law-review tome she'd

been consulting earlier with a thud. 'Which hotel is the conference being held at? I can meet you there.'

'No need.' He straightened away from her desk, his eyes cool. 'I've ordered a car.'

Stuck in the back of a car with Sam Ventura during rush-hour traffic...

'Terrific,' she said with a wide smile.

Sam tuned out the keynote speaker's lengthy address and tuned into the blonde sitting beside him. Not hard when his body was already so aware of her it ached.

While he'd been interstate the previous day he'd decided to ignore the searing attraction between the two of them. He'd already witnessed her turning the other way in the corridor when she saw him coming more than once and it annoyed the hell out of him. What did she think he was going to do? Throw her over his shoulder and drag her into the nearest office to ravish her? He'd already told her that he never mixed business with pleasure and it was a code he'd never broken.

Before.

A moody scowl twisted his lips. The truth was, he still wanted her badly and he didn't care about the fact that she worked for him. He didn't care about anything other than taking her and watching her shatter in his arms again until the only name she could form on her well-sated lips was his. It wasn't a desire that made sense, given the strength of it, but it wasn't one he seemed able to fight either.

Much to his consternation.

The whole idea of being led around by his passions was anathema to him. Yes, he went after things he desired, and yes, he was usually successful in achieving them, but he wasn't a risk-taker like Tino, or a win-at-all-costs guy like Dante. He was the easy-going brother. The one least likely to feel deeply about anything or anyone.

Except when it came to Ruby Clarkson.

He took a healthy swallow of the cabernet sauvignon in his glass, easing out a slow breath. The woman was turning out to be a conundrum, and ignoring the stunning attraction between them only seemed to drive his need for her even higher. Would one more night together resolve that? One more night on his terms to work this crazy attraction out of his system. He didn't know, but his body liked that idea a whole lot more than it did avoidance.

He noticed Missy Lawson, the chairman's newly divorced daughter, bearing down on him and glanced at Ruby. She had her hair loose, the shiny golden strands like twin curtains framing her perfect face, her black dress, long enough to be demure in the office, short enough that it showed off her sensational legs. It made a man think about setting his fingers to the zipper at the back and sliding it slowly downward.

'Time for us to leave,' he growled softly, noticing a fine tremor go through her as his hand settled against her lower back. He inhaled through his nose, drawing her rose-tinted scent into his lungs before he thought better of it.

'The keynote's not finished yet,' she whispered back.

'I know.' He glanced over his shoulder to see Missy getting closer. 'I won't tell Drew if you don't.'

Ruby glanced behind him and then tipped her face up to his, her eyes dancing with an impish light that reminded him of the Ruby he had met in that bar two years ago. 'Missy looks like she wants another word with you.'

Sam took Ruby's arm in a light hold. 'Exactly why we have to leave.'

As he was about to surreptitiously tug her towards the exit doors the keynote chose that moment to wrap it up. Polite clapping ensued and before Sam could take control once more he found their way blocked by someone else. A man this time.

'Ruby.' Chester Harris, the stockbroker from Tino and Miller's wedding, zeroed in on Ruby like a heat-seeking missile.

'Sam.' Missy Lawson did the same to him as she barrelled to a halt beside him.

'Chester,' Ruby said with surprise.

'Missy,' Sam said through gritted teeth. 'We were just leaving.'

'My father wants to run a small legal matter past you,' Missy purred. 'It shouldn't take long.'

Sam unclenched his jaw long enough to let Ruby know he'd be no more than five minutes.

'That's fine,' she said, 'I can find my own way home.'

Sam stopped her with a look. 'Do not leave without me this time, Clarkson.' His tone promised all sorts of trouble if she did.

Ruby's eyes flashed like polished emeralds in the bright light of the hotel ballroom, her jaw tight. He didn't know if her curt nod at his blatant order meant that she would wait or not, and he was further irritated when she allowed Chester Harris to take her arm as they walked away. Had he been the date she'd needed to cancel in order to be here with him?

Realising that the knot behind his rib cage was jealousy only made Sam's mood blacker. He really needed to get a handle on Ruby Clarkson and how she made him feel.

Thirty long minutes later he assured John Lawson that his latest author was unlikely to be in breach of any copyright laws, gave Missy what he hoped was a polite smile and went in search of Ruby.

His blood pressure, already raised by Harris's proprietary manner with her earlier, shot a little higher when he found him hemming Ruby in against one of the large supporting pillars in the cavernous room.

'Harris,' he said in a low, dangerous voice. *I believe you have something of mine.* 'I didn't expect to see you here tonight.'

'Sam Ventura.' He gave Sam a smile that displayed every one of his freshly capped teeth. 'The last time we met was at your brother's wedding if I'm not mistaken.'

'Was it?' Sam considered the merits of bruising his knuckles on the other man's jaw and taking a few of those shiny teeth out in the process. If nothing else it would distract him from the unexpectedly possessive thought he'd just had about Ruby being his. It made him feel raw. Exposed.

Ignoring Harris, he stared down at Ruby. 'Ready to go?'

'You're leaving already?' Harris's eyes widened with interest. 'Together?'

'We came together,' Ruby supplied hastily. 'We shared a car.'

They'd shared a lot more than a car and right now Sam didn't give a damn if Harris knew it. 'And now we're leaving. Together,' he finished, setting his hand to the small of Ruby's back as he steered her towards the exit.

Sidestepping his touch, Ruby smiled at various delegates as they worked their way out of the room.

'Why did you have to say that?' she hissed, frowning at him as their limousine driver opened the rear door.

'Get in.' Ignoring her question, Sam ushered her into the plush interior and followed close behind. Her gaze glittered with feminine outrage as he settled on the leather seat opposite her, which only irritated him more.

'Are you going to answer me?' she demanded hotly.

'No.'

'No?' Ruby all but vibrated against the soft leather seat. 'You just told Sydney's biggest blabbermouth that we were leaving together in a voice that implied we were *leaving together.*'

'How you could ever go out with someone like that I'll never know.'

'I didn't go out with him.'

'Glad to hear it. So why did you take him to Tino and Miller's wedding?'

'None of your business.'

Sam noted her stony profile and stiff shoulders, the colour high along her cheekbones. Could it be that Harris had just been a beard at the wedding? A way of keeping Sam at bay? Irritatingly, if it had been, it had worked.

'Don't worry, I think I know.'

Ruby gave up glaring at the window and glared at him instead. 'Know what?'

'Why you took Harris to the wedding. You wanted me but you didn't want to admit it.'

'You are so full of yourself I'm surprised your enormous ego can fit inside the car with us.'

'And you're snippy.' He leaned forward, his knees brushing the outside of hers. 'Snippy, prickly and jittery. Now, why is that, do you suppose?'

'I don't know, Sam. You're the one who knows everything, so you tell me.'

'I think you can't forget what happened between us last week any more than I can.' A flush rose up along her cheekbones and he wanted to reach out and tug her onto his lap. 'I think you're not sleeping properly because you can't forget how it felt to have my hands on you.' His voice dropped to a rumbling purr. 'My mouth.'

Her eyelids fluttered shut for a brief second.

'Tell me when you knew it was me,' he pressed softly, not realising how important her answer was until he'd voiced the question.

She frowned across at him, not following where his mind had gone before a cynical smile twisted her lips. 'I don't see what that has to do with anything.'

'Humour me.'

'Why?' she parried. 'If anyone should be asking that question it's me.' She looked down her nose at him. 'After all, you were the one who claimed that a man with any integrity should know if he's ever kissed a woman before.'

It took Sam a moment to place that comment and when he did he laughed. 'You knew it was me that early on, huh? Well, that does stroke my enormous ego. So why the anonymity?'

She shifted restlessly in her seat. 'Maybe I didn't feel like making small talk.'

'And maybe there's more to it than that,' he said, knowing he was right when she narrowed her eyes.

'As I said, I should be the one asking you that question.' She gave him a cool look. 'When *did* you figure out it was me?'

He leaned back against the soft leather upholstery and tried to remember the last time he'd enjoyed talking to a woman as much as he did Ruby. 'I knew the exact moment you turned those frosty green eyes on me,' he said quietly.

She glanced back at him, her eyes suddenly wary. 'If that's true then why didn't *you* say anything at the time?'

'I did. I offered to carry your drinks.'

She bit into her bottom lip, her brows drawn together. 'I thought you were trying to pick me up.'

A grin spread slowly across his face. 'I was.'

'Oh—'

Before she could blast him with yet another fiery put-down a car horn honked and almost immediately their driver swerved, muttering curses as he slammed on the brakes. The car lurched to a sudden halt and Ruby slid from her seat straight into Sam's arms.

Startled, she braced her hands against his shoulders, her breath caught somewhere between her lungs and her throat. He knew because his hands were on either side of her ribcage, right beneath the swell of her soft breasts.

The car started forward, the driver muttering an apology over his shoulder as he manoeuvred around a stalled taxi in the centre lane.

'What happened?' Ruby asked breathlessly.

'Fate,' he answered roughly, one hand lifting to slide beneath the thick fall of her hair as he brought her mouth to his.

As soon as his lips covered hers she opened for him, her eager tongue tangling with his with a hungry abandon that matched his own.

She moaned softly as he deepened the kiss, her fingernails digging into his shoulders.

'Sam.' His name was a sensual plea on her lips as she met him kiss for kiss, her hands forking into his hair to drag him closer. The pleasure of having her body plastered up against his was exquisite, the taste of her explosive. He wanted to put his mouth all over her, sucking and licking her, particularly between her soft, golden thighs. He told her as much and the sexy little noise she made nearly undid him.

'Yes, angel, kiss me like that.' Ravenous for more,

Sam urged her legs to part, pulling her astride his lap, his hands moving lower to slide along her outer thighs, pushing her dress up over the curve of her bottom. A low groan was ripped from his throat as she moved against him in wanton abandon.

'Christ, Ruby.' His lips attacked her neck, his hands fisted in her hair to lock her in place, his blood pumping thickly through his veins. This was exactly how it had been last Friday night. Wild. Uninhibited. *Insatiable.*

'A man could get addicted to this mouth,' he said, taking her bottom lip between his teeth and urging her closer.

She moaned, her lips tracking over his jaw and his chin, her little teeth nipping at his skin.

It felt as if they were both cocooned in a warm, dark room. Just the two of them. Man and woman at their most elemental. No past or future to come between them. No masks and no running.

Just total surrender and a sexual chemistry that blew his mind. His fingers stroked along the edge of her lace panties, his sex-induced brain trying to warn him that he was going too far again. That he needed to stop this madness because—

'Mr Ventura, sir, we have arrived at our destination.'

Because they were in the back of a limousine.

Sam knew Ruby hadn't heard the driver because her fingers were still fumbling with the buttons on his shirt. For a second he nearly closed the partition between them and the driver and let her continue. Then sanity asserted itself. 'Ruby, sweetheart.' He took her hands in his. 'We have to stop.'

'Stop?'

She blinked up at him, her slumberous gaze turning from glazed to glaring in a heartbeat.

'Oh, God.' She pushed off his lap and fell awkwardly onto the opposite seat, smoothing her skirt down her legs, regret written all over her beautiful face. 'Of course we have to stop.'

'Like we should have stopped last Friday night?'

'Absolutely.'

'And I suppose you want to forget about this *incident* just like you've *forgotten* the last one.'

'Absolutely.'

For some reason her ready agreement only fuelled his irritation. So did that regal, untouchable air she cloaked herself in. Something that might have been a little more effective if her lips weren't still swollen and moist from his kisses. 'Only you haven't forgotten last Friday night any more than I have. Isn't that the truth, Ruby?'

'The truth is we work together, and Chester is probably spreading salacious stories about us right now.'

'In this case he'd be right.'

He knew it wasn't fair to goad her like that but, dammit, she was making him feel as if he was fully responsible for that kiss and she'd been as into it as he had been.

'He would not be right,' she snapped, scowling at him.

'He would. But it's late. If you want to argue some more about it you'll have to invite me up for coffee.'

Clearly embarrassed to find that they were parked outside her apartment building, Ruby threw open the car door, nearly catching their circumspect chauffeur in the chest. 'That,' she said loftily, 'will never happen again. I learn from my mistakes. I don't repeat them.'

'Pity.' Sam's eyes narrowed, his fingers manacling her wrist before she could toss her hair over her shoulder and exit the car. 'Because this time I would have said yes. But fair warning, sweetheart—the next time my mouth is on yours we'll be horizontal and I'll be taking my time. That is,' he paused, his thumb stroking lightly over the pulse pounding in her wrist 'after you've asked me nicely.'

Ruby pulled her wrist out from under his hold and shot him a fulminating glare. 'You cannot possibly imagine how much I dislike you right now.'

Sam couldn't help himself: he laughed. 'Oh, I think I can.'

He watched the long, lean lines of her body as she stalked straight-backed away from the car. When she was safely inside her glass security door he leaned his head back against the seat, gave the driver his address and asked himself what it was about this woman that drove every civilised thought from his head. Even now, when he told himself to go and find a nice, even-tempered woman who knew how to appreciate him, he wanted this one with a fierceness that defied logic.

Ruby Clarkson, it turned out, was more than a simple conundrum; she was a colossal pain in his rear end.

CHAPTER SIX

RUBY WOKE THE following morning with a start, sitting bolt upright in her bed, a particularly carnal dream of her and Sam naked and sweaty and *horizontal* front and centre in her mind.

Groaning, she collapsed back against her fluffy pillows and stared at the ceiling. If last night had proved anything at all it was that her willpower to keep away from the man who haunted her days and her nights was practically zero once he put his hands on her, making that potential job in London look better and better.

Determined that next Friday night she was going to keep well away from him, she rolled over and checked the time.

Molly had stayed at a friend's the night before so she wouldn't be bursting in any second to push her to do yoga.

Maybe she'd skip it today. She had a ton of work to do anyway, along with another embarrassing escapade with her boss to try to forget about.

God, when would she learn?

Not any time soon, it seemed. Thankful it was Saturday, the first day of the long weekend and she'd have no reason to see Sam for three whole days, she flipped onto her stomach and thought about going back to sleep.

Then her phone pinged, sending her senses onto high alert.

Miller's name flashed on the screen and Ruby groaned out loud. Oh, no! Long weekend. Beach house. A month ago Miller had suggested that they have a girly weekend together. How had she forgotten that?

'Would you believe I'm nearly ready?' Ruby hedged, answering the phone as she stumbled out of bed and staggered into the bathroom.

'How could you forget?' Miller complained. 'I left a reminder message on your phone last night.'

She had? 'Sorry, I didn't get it. I'm a really bad friend.'

'Were you working late again? Is that the problem?'

'Yeah… I had a function and…never mind.' She peered at her wan reflection in the mirror, pressing on the dark circles beneath her eyes. 'Am I too late to still make it?'

'Of course not. But there's been a slight change of plan. Red is a bit under the weather, so he and Tino are joining us. I hope that's okay.'

Red was Redmond Ventura, Miller and Tino's adorable toddler and, as the first baby in their circle of friends, a pseudo-nephew to both her and Molly. 'Of course it's okay,' Ruby said. 'I'll even take Red tomorrow morning so you and Valentino can have a sleep in together.'

'I knew I loved you.' Miller laughed. 'By the way, Tino has— Oh, drat, Red's crying.'

'Go and get him,' Ruby urged, grabbing her toothbrush and turning the shower on. 'I'll be there in… twenty minutes?'

Miller snorted. 'Sure. See you in an hour, then.'

Ringing off, Ruby ducked into the shower. She had a special bottle of champagne in the fridge to help celebrate the long weekend with her best friend. The fact that she'd forgotten that as well was a testament to how much Sam Ventura was messing with her head.

But not any more. As of now, Ruby would banish the man from her mind and her life and pull herself together. And a weekend away with Miller and her family was just the ticket. She wouldn't have time to moon over Sam, or wonder what he was doing and with whom he was doing it. She certainly wouldn't have time to think about kissing him.

Fair warning, sweetheart, the next time my mouth is on yours we'll be horizontal and I'll be taking my time.

Good grief! She blew out an unsteady breath, a rush of desire turning her insides hot and shivery at just the memory of how he had kissed her in the back of their limousine.

Just behind the driver.

She groaned, shaking her head. A week ago her life had been ticking along perfectly. She had work, yoga, good friends and Netflix. Now she had angst, indecision, erotic dreams and *longing*.

The longing was the worst. It was like a secret weakness she didn't want to admit to having. Instinctively she knew that if she ever slept with Sam again she'd be changing her life for him before she knew it, followed by crying with her friends when it all went wrong. Because it would go wrong. It was inevitable. Sam was a heartbreaker. And he was too demanding, too arrogant. He would want more from her than she was prepared to give and she was very afraid she'd give it anyway.

A sense of foreboding flashed across her skin like a cold draught. Her father walking out on them all those years ago had left her with a natural sense of caution when it came to men that had always held her in good stead. So no, she was not going to let Sam any closer than he already had been *ever again*. That would be like carrying a metal pole onto a football field in the middle of an electric storm and hoping not to get struck by lightning.

'Good pep talk.' She smiled at her reflection and skipped out of the bathroom. Miller's beach house beckoned, where she could swim, chat, play with Red and relax to her heart's content.

Quickly pulling on white shorts and a striped top, she pushed her feet into her favourite beaten-up espadrilles, packed her bag and raced down the stairs, thankful that she only had to wait a few minutes before her cab driver arrived.

'Double Bay Wharf,' she said, settling back against the seat and closing her eyes. Too late she remembered that her e-reader, with the newly downloaded crime novel on it, was on her bedside table. She hoped Miller had some trashy novel she could lose herself in just in case the champagne didn't do the job of getting Sam out of her head at night.

Arriving at the wharf, she skipped down the wooden gangplank towards Valentino's latest motorised toy, *Miller's Way,* and felt lighthearted as she smiled at a one-legged seagull that was completely unconcerned about her presence.

Rows of pristine white yachts bobbed side by side in the bright sunshine, and the deep blue of the harbour sparkled as if tiny diamonds had been dropped from the sky and floated across the surface as mystical as rainbows. It was a good day to be alive and she had three whole days of bliss stretched out in front of her. Three whole days of rest and relaxation and not wondering about whether she was going to accidentally run into a certain somebody when she least expected it.

* * *

Sam brooded as Valentino bent over the boat engine, absently stroking the black and tan puppy in his arms.

'Wrench,' Valentino said, his head stuck inside the engine bay.

Sam handed him the tool. The restless fluff-ball wriggled in his arms, eager to explore his new surroundings. He'd had the thing for two hours. A rash decision that was as unlike him as his actions with Ruby since returning to Sydney. And he couldn't exactly blame jet lag for his loss of control last night, or for picking up the puppy at the rescue centre. Perhaps he had some superbug eating away at his brain bit by bit.

'I said wrench.' Valentino frowned at him. 'This is a ratchet.'

Sam glanced into the toolbox. He pulled out the wrench.

'You sure you're okay?' Tino glanced up at him.

'Fine.'

Tino grunted. 'About as fine as this engine.'

Ignoring his brother's pointed comment, he focused on the engine trouble. 'Will you get it running?'

Valentino threw him a look as if to say *Will the sun set in the west?* He stuck his head back in the hull. 'I'd better. Miller's been looking forward to this weekend all month. And Ruby's bringing champagne. Hopefully on ice.'

Sam's whole body went rigid at Tino's throwaway comment. The puppy whimpered and he eased his grip from around its soft belly. 'Ruby?' Part of the reason he had made the early-morning decision to take his brother up on his offer to spend the long weekend at the beach house was to put some space between Ruby and his sudden obsession to dial her number every five seconds. Why hadn't he asked Tino if she would be coming along?

Because he hadn't wanted Tino to question his sudden interest in Ruby's whereabouts until he had some plausible answers that made sense. And look how spectacularly that had backfired on him now. He frowned at the puppy that stared back at him with huge, guileless brown eyes. He didn't know what had possessed him to get the mutt either. He'd been walking past the animal rescue centre and the next thing he knew he was signing papers and being instructed on brands of puppy food.

'You know, I have a mind to call back that fancy-arsed mechanic...' Tino muttered, issuing a string of curse words under his breath. 'Guy wouldn't know a carburettor from a custard tart.'

Sam ignored his brother's mumblings. He was still reeling from the fact that Ruby would soon be joining them.

Ruby for a whole three days with his brother and fiercely protective sister-in-law in tow...

'God, I'm good!' Tino smirked as the boat's engine rumbled to life beneath his feet, wiping his hands on an old rag.

'So about the weekend...' Sam began, thinking that he didn't care if Tino thought his behaviour was strange or not.

'Yeah?' Tino looked at him curiously. 'What about it?'

The puppy squirmed like a bag of worms in his arms, yapping at something over his shoulder. Sam turned in time to see Ruby coming aboard and his heart did a weird flip inside his chest. She looked confident and radiant, her long hair pulled into a haphazard ponytail, a dazzling smile curving her soft pink lips. He'd rarely seen her without make-up and right now she looked golden and youthful and more beautiful than ever, like a sun goddess come down to earth to shine just for him.

Catching the uncharacteristically poetic sentiment, he shook his head. It didn't seem to matter to his brain that she was completely off-limits to him. She excited him as no other woman ever had and, while he might not like that on an elemental level, if he was completely honest with himself he didn't want it to stop either.

Ruby didn't notice Sam until she had both feet planted on the boat. If she had when she'd only had one foot on board she might have turned and run. As it was she could only stop and stare at him.

He wore aviator sunglasses, his long, lean body encased in a T-shirt that emphasised his flat belly and wide shoulders, and fitted board shorts that hugged his muscular thighs. His feet were jammed into boat shoes, his arms full of an exuberant black and brown puppy with one adorable ear folded forward. Both their gazes were trained on her. It struck her almost immediately that she had never seen Sam in casual wear before and he was ten times more dangerous to her this way than in a custom-made suit. Heat seared her insides, her body uncaring that last night he had been so arrogant she'd wanted to throttle him.

As she watched Sam lowered the squirming bundle of fluff onto the deck and it raced towards her. She instinctively went down on her haunches and the puppy jumped into her arms, licking her face.

'Some guard dog he is,' Sam grumbled, coming to a stop in front of her.

Finding it hard to hold herself aloof with the puppy all over her, Ruby laughed joyously. 'He knows I'm a friend. Don't you, boy? Girl?'

'Boy,' Sam replied, just as Miller came up from below deck carrying Redmond in her arms.

'Hey, Ruby.' Miller hugged her as she stood up. 'Forty-five minutes. I'm impressed. By the way, Tino invited Sam, so our girls' weekend has definitely been gatecrashed.'

'So I see,' Ruby murmured.

'Let me take your bag.'

'I've got it.' Sam reached for it first and hoisted it onto his shoulder before Ruby could object.

'Thanks, Sam.' Miller grinned widely, shifting Red to her other arm so that he could reach out and play with Ruby's hair. 'I'm so glad you're here. Tino, Ruby's—'

'Here, I know.' Valentino pushed out of the engine bay one-handed and came up behind his wife, taking an excited Redmond from her arms. 'Glad you could make it, Ruby. And right on time.'

The puppy jumped up at her again, his nails scoring the skin on her knee. Ruby winced and grabbed his paws, petting his head. 'You're going to be a giant, aren't you?'

'Sorry.' Sam moved forward. 'He hasn't learnt any manners yet.'

'He's yours?' She was surprised. She hadn't expected Sam to be a pet person. Pets seemed so permanent for a man who wasn't the relationship type.

He picked up the puppy and wiped slobber off his face as it licked him. 'Yes, he's mine,' Sam answered her. 'I just got him this morning from the rescue centre.'

'Someone disowned him?'

'They did more than that.' His voice deepened with disgust. 'He was thrown into a wheelie bin with his brothers and sisters.'

'Oh, you poor thing.' Instinctively Ruby reached out

her hand to stroke between his ears, the move bringing her closer to Sam than she would have liked. 'What's his name?'

'Mutt.'

'Mutt?' She scowled at him. 'You can't call him that.'

'I haven't named him yet. Maybe Shep.'

'Too passé,' she said. 'What about Caesar?'

'And give him unnecessary illusions of grandeur? There's only room for one alpha in this pack.'

Ruby rolled her eyes, unable to prevent a smile from forming on her lips. 'I hope he gives you a run for your money.'

Miller laughed. 'He's already got Sam wrapped around his over-large paw, from what I can see.'

'Looks can be deceiving, Millsy,' Sam countered. 'What would you call him?' he asked Ruby.

Ruby studied the puppy, tapping a finger against her bottom lip. 'Kong.'

'Kong?'

The scepticism in his voice made her laugh. 'He's going to be enormous,' she said; 'you can tell by the ears and the feet.'

Sam turned the dog to face him, holding him at arm's length. 'Are you a Kong?'

The puppy barked enthusiastically and Miller laughed. 'He likes it.'

'And it's a hell of a lot better than Mutt,' Tino drawled. 'Come on, Red,' he said, 'time to get underway.'

'Ah, wait…' Ruby trailed off as three pairs of eyes turned towards her. Unbidden, her gaze sought Sam's. She wanted to say that she had changed her mind about the weekend. That something had come up. Something urgent and completely unavoidable. Only her fuzzy brain couldn't produce a single excuse that sounded urgent or unavoidable. Especially with Sam looking at her with that half-cocked grin as if he knew exactly what she was thinking.

Her pregnant pause lengthened into uncomfortable territory, the sun beating down hot and inviting on her head, the waves gently lapping at the side of the hull.

'Did you forget something?' Miller asked. 'We probably have it at the house if you have.'

Ruby had that same embarrassing feeling she'd had two years ago. The one where she made a mountain out of a molehill, thinking that Sam had felt more for her than he really had. The one that had made her sit by the phone all weekend, not even questioning if he'd call, but actually believing that he would.

'No,' she said, forcing a smile to her lips. 'I didn't forget a thing.'

If Sam wasn't bothered by having her around this weekend then she wasn't going to be bothered having him around either. Or at least she wouldn't *show* that she was bothered.

After docking at Tino and Miller's private jetty, Ruby made a beeline for the state-of-the-art kitchen, fetching two mugs from the kitchen cupboard and reaching for the old-fashioned kettle on the stovetop. 'Tea?'

'Tea?' Miller crinkled her nose in disgust, placing a box of fresh produce on the granite countertop. 'Is it too early for champagne?'

'Where do you want these?' Sam stepped inside with another box of supplies under one arm.

'Over there,' Miller said, indicating an empty place on the bench behind Ruby.

Quickly skirting sideways, Ruby sucked in her breath as Sam's elbow brushed her stomach on his way past.

'Sorry.'

'No, I should have…' Ruby pressed closer against the sink and ducked around him to move to the other side of the bench, ignoring his delicious scent as it wafted into her nose.

'Great house,' Sam said easily, and Ruby envied him his composure. Her pulse was beating dangerously fast yet again. 'I can see why you bought it.'

'I know. We loved it as soon as we saw it.' Miller smiled, looking between her and Sam. 'You know, the place two houses along is up for sale.'

'That so?' Sam said.

'Yep.' Miller rinsed Redmond's sipper cup under the tap and stowed it on a shelf. 'Maybe you should look at buying it. Then, when you find a woman to settle down with, our kids can spend summers together, running back and forth between each other's houses.'

'You got it all planned out, Millsy,' Sam said with an easy smile.

'It's the organiser in her,' Ruby interjected. For some reason Miller's words had conjured up a picture so sweet it made Ruby's chest ache. 'But Sam isn't interested in relationships. Isn't that right, Sam?'

Sam took a bottle of water from the fridge, unscrewed the cap and raised it to his lips, his eyes seeing more than she wanted him to see. 'Depends how good the house is.'

Miller laughed.

Ruby didn't.

'And the type of relationship we're talking about,' he added softly.

Ruby's heartbeat picked up at the way he was looking at her, the lid of the kettle she'd been unknowingly fiddling with clattering to the counter as it slipped out of her grasp. Snatching it up, she jammed it back into place. 'The permanent type, of course.'

He shifted closer to her, subtly hemming her in against the hob. 'Perhaps I just haven't met the right woman yet.'

'Really?' She gave him a withering look. 'You're going to play that hand?'

'What's wrong, angel? You looking for love and happily-ever-after?'

'No.'

She absolutely was not looking for that.

'Ah, well, there goes my plan to ask you to marry me and put me out of my misery.'

Knowing that she only had herself to blame for this conversation, Ruby told herself not to bite. She did anyway. 'Marry you?' She nearly choked on the word. 'I wouldn't marry you if you were the last man on earth and civilisation relied on us to…to…' She felt her face flush with heat.

'Procreate?'

She heard the laughter in his voice and her lips clamped together. 'Exactly!'

'Oh, well. You can't blame a man for trying. A word of advice, though…' He nodded over her shoulder at the kettle. 'You might want to put some water in that before you boil it. It works better that way.'

Exasperated at how easily he riled her, Ruby glared at his broad back, refusing to admire the width of his shoulders or the narrowness of his hips as he strolled out of the back door.

'You going to explain all that or do I have to work for it?' Miller said into the ensuing silence.

Ruby glanced over at her, appalled to realise that she'd forgotten her friend was even in the room with them.

'What's to explain?' she hedged. 'He likes to provoke me and, fool that I am, I fall for it every time.'

'I was talking more about the wicked sexual tension between the two of you,' Miller said, fanning her face. 'It was a little hot in here for a while.'

Ruby let out a sigh. 'You're not going to let up on this, are you?'

'Of course I will.' Miller gave her a too-innocent look. 'If you don't want to tell me what's going on between the two of you then I completely respect that.'

'Fine. We slept together—or, rather, we had sex.' She winced as Miller's jaw hit the floor. 'Yes, you heard me right. And it was against a wall. At the Herzog party.'

There it was, out in the open. No big deal. She was only glad Miller wouldn't realise it had been her first time. If she knew that then it would totally be a big deal. She'd want to know, why Sam? Why then? And how did Ruby answer that without telling her best friend that no other man had ever affected her as Sam did?

'The Herzog party? As in *the* Herzog party? The one anybody who is anybody tries to get an invitation to every year?'

'Is there any other?'

'Well, then.' Miller set her shoulders as if she were about to mine iron ore from a deep quarry. 'We're going to need something stronger than tea. Or champagne.'

Ruby groaned into her hands. 'Please don't make it out to be more than it is. It's never happening again.'

Miller placed a crystal tumbler on the bench in front of her. 'Uh-huh…'

'It's not! I swear.'

'You know I want details.' Miller poured a measure of Johnny Walker into both their glasses. 'How? Why? Which wall?' She grinned as Ruby made a face. 'How good was it? That kind of thing. I mean, the Ventura boys have a bit of a reputation, so I'd be surprised if it wasn't good, but…'

'It wasn't good.' Ruby sipped the amber liquid and let the warmth of it settle in the pit of her stomach. 'It was fantastic. But it was a one-off thing.'

'Uh-huh.'

'Would you stop saying that?' she griped. 'It was.'

'Why?' Miller sat down on a bar stool and eyed her speculatively.

'Because, well…why would it happen again?'

'Because he looks at you like you're a tinderbox he wants to set a match to and you're so on edge you look like you need that match.'

'Miller, be serious!' Ruby implored. 'I'm not into sex for the sake of it, you know that. And he's my boss. There's only one way that can end. And it's not well.'

'Hmm, his being your boss is a bit of an issue, but it's not the end of the world. Lots of bosses and employees get married.'

'Are you listening to yourself?' Ruby asked, her brows nearly hitting her hairline at the hopeful tone in Miller's voice. 'You've gone from sex against a wall to a white dress and church bells in a matter of seconds. Being married has clearly fried your brain.'

'Can you imagine how much fun it would be if you married Sam, though?' Miller's blue eyes lit up with glee. 'We could—'

'Do nothing!' Ruby used her courtroom voice to cut off her friend's romantic diatribe before it got started. The last thing she needed was her loved-up friend playing matchmaker or, heaven forbid, putting unwanted ideas into her own head.

'Okay, maybe that was a step too far, but I am grappling with the concept that you, Ms Proper Lady Lawyer Extraordinaire, had hot, crazy sex at a party!'

'I know. But can we not talk about it any more? I'm trying to forget it even happened.'

'Not that you have, have you?' Miller asked softly.

'Can I plead the Fifth on that?'

'No.' Miller laughed. 'Australia doesn't have amendments. And I'm not trying to embarrass you. I just want you to relax a little, Rubes, be happy. You deserve it. Not all men are bad, you know. Sam's not.'

'So says the woman who got the last good one.'

'The last good what?'

'Apple,' Ruby filled in quickly as Valentino strolled into the room and slipped his arm around his wife's waist.

Picking up on her cue not to mention any of this to her husband, Miller gave him a searing kiss to distract him. It worked and Ruby slipped out of the back door unnoticed.

Feeling slightly niggled, she kicked off her espadrilles and stepped onto sun-warmed paving stones, sighing at the blissful invitation of the blue-tiled infinity pool that looked as if it continued into the even bluer waters of Elvina Bay.

Crouching down on her haunches, she trailed her fingers across the surface of the pool, enjoying the cool deliciousness of the water as it trickled between her fingers.

Redmond's delightful baby laugh caught her attention and she glanced up to see Sam lying on the lawn, pretending to struggle beneath the combined weight of the toddler and the puppy.

'Okay, okay, you got me.' He groaned, taking care to keep the puppy from launching himself on Redmond and knocking the baby over. 'Ouch, Kong, that's my finger.' He ruffled the dog's fur and gave him a playful push. The puppy loved it, launching himself even harder at his new master.

A strange sensation rushed into Ruby's chest as she watched them play. So he was good with kids and animals. And he was smart. Attractive. Of course he was. All the Ventura men were. It was some freak gene that made them tall, god-like and irresistible to unsuspecting women.

You want to get married and put me out of my misery?

God, he was an ass!

A *too tempting* ass as he leaned up on one hand, his powerful biceps bunching as he moved, his wide chest the perfect foil for the toddler snuggled up against him. He bent his dark head to Redmond's, nuzzling his fine baby hair and making him giggle with helpless delight.

That was just unfair, she thought, forcing her gaze back to the pool. He was unfair. Why did he have to come back to Sydney and turn her life upside down? Why did he have to kiss her? Touch her? Make love to her?

Miller's gentle prodding that she wanted Ruby to be happy played back inside her head. She *was* happy. *Very* happy. Or she had been until Sam had blown back into her life! And, while Miller saw Sam as one of the 'good' ones, that was only because she was married to his brother. She was blinkered. Ruby had already experienced Sam walking away from her once without a backward glance. She didn't want that to happen again. Something inside her warned her that she wouldn't cope as well as she had the first time.

Suddenly realising that Sam was watching her, she let out a slow breath and attempted to marshal her chaotic emotions. Seeing her still crouched by the pool, the puppy cocked his head, his floppy ear bouncing as he scampered towards her.

'Watch the pool,' she cautioned as he bounded along the edge on unstable baby legs. He lapped at her face and she wiped her cheek with the back of her hand. 'You have to stop doing that,' she laughed.

Having followed, Sam offered her a hand up, his other wrapped around Redmond's chubby legs, balancing the toddler high on his hip like a natural.

Ignoring his hand as politely as possible, Ruby stumbled to her feet. 'I didn't know you were going to be here this weekend,' she said on a breathless note, somehow needing him to know that she hadn't planned this. That she wasn't *chasing* him.

'And wished that I wasn't,' he concluded. 'Am I right?'

Ruby shot him a quick glance, unsure how to respond to that in a way that wouldn't ratchet the tension between them even higher.

'Jesus, Ruby,' he growled under his breath. 'I'm not going to jump you. Not without an invitation anyway.'

'All evidence to the contrary,' she retorted, miffed at his arrogance and the fact that if he was to touch her right now she'd probably dissolve into a puddle of lustful cravings. She hadn't slept properly since he'd crashed back into her life, and her defences were clearly suffering as a result.

'That's a low blow.' His bedroom brown eyes locked with hers. 'You wanted that kiss in the cab last night as much as I did.'

'I'm not going to argue with you, Sam. It's pointless.'

'So is pretending that we don't want each other,' he said softly.

'No, it's not,' she denied. 'It makes everything a lot less complicated.'

He threw her a shrewd look. 'Less complicated or more?'

'Less,' she said vigorously. 'Definitely less.'

'I don't know, angel. It's not less complicated for me. In fact, it's downright difficult.'

Sam's hooded gaze travelled down over her throat and breasts that felt heavy and achy, and farther to her bare legs and feet before slowly making its way back to her eyes, heating her up in the process and leaving her in no doubt as to exactly how he found it difficult.

'That's just sex, Sam,' she said, glad Red was too young to understand a word they were saying. 'You can get that from anyone.'

'You're wrong, it wasn't just sex.' He let the squirming toddler down beside a beach ball he was trying to reach. 'It was incredible and I want it again.' His voice grew rough. 'I want *you* again.'

Ruby's heart thundered inside her chest, her whole body leaning towards his even though she hadn't moved. 'What happened to your credo of not mixing business with pleasure?' she asked huskily.

A sparkle entered his eyes. 'For you I'm willing to make an exception.'

Red made a sound of frustration and Sam bent to scoop the toddler into his arms once more before sauntering back towards the house, the puppy on his heels.

'I'm not, Sam,' she called after him with belligerent finality.

Sam turned back slowly, a wry smile curving his lips. 'And that's your choice.'

Ruby gnashed her teeth together at his easy capitulation. If it was her choice, why did it feel more like a battle? A battle she was waging with herself?

Frustrated, she stared out at the tranquil view but

quite unable to take it in. If it was her choice, how was it that every day she saw him, every minute she spent with him, she wanted him more? And what would happen if she did the unthinkable and gave in to the chemistry between them again? Who would be there to catch her if she fell?

CHAPTER SEVEN

THE FOLLOWING MORNING when Ruby stepped into the kitchen she felt bright and eager to start the day.

Sam was wrong. It was a *lot* less complicated to ignore the attraction between them, not more so. She'd done it all night at dinner the night before and she'd had a great time.

She'd been civil to Sam, talking with him and laughing at his jokes, listening to him and Tino recount stories of their childhood and not even noticing the way his black shirt had turned his eyes the same colour and hugged his muscular chest to perfection. Nor had she trembled when he'd accidently brushed up against her while they'd done the cleaning up together, and her heart definitely hadn't beat faster when she'd bid everyone goodnight and felt Sam's dark gaze trained on her the length of the hallway that led to the bedrooms, staring at the ceiling for an hour afterwards until she'd heard his heavy tread take him to his own room.

And if she could truly convince herself of all that she'd consider dropping law to follow Molly into the theatre.

The problem was that she had no idea how to switch off her emotions around Sam. Nothing in her past experiences had equipped her to deal with how she felt when she was in his arms, and it was nothing short of terrifying.

Not expecting to find anyone up, she came to an abrupt halt in the doorway when she noticed Sam sprawled out asleep on the wide modular sofa.

She must have disturbed him because he stirred, groaning as he rolled onto his side, blinking inky black lashes as he looked across at her. Yawning, he rubbed his belly, his T-shirt riding up in the process, making her breath hitch.

As if he caught the sound, his gaze gave her a thorough sweep, making her aware that she was wearing nothing but a silky nightshirt over cotton panties.

Should have dressed first, idiot, she berated herself.

'You can come in, Ruby,' he rumbled sleepily. 'I won't bite.'

Unfortunately Ruby remembered that he did. Right on that sensitive spot where her neck joined her shoulder. 'I thought maybe Redmond would be up. I was going to take him so Miller and Valentino could sleep in together.'

'They're not here.'

About to head back to her room to put more clothes on, Ruby stopped and swung around to find Sam sitting up, his long legs wide apart, his broad shoulders hunched slightly forward as he stroked Kong's ears. 'What do you mean, they're not here?'

'Miller received a phone call early this morning saying that her mother is in hospital. Since Red was already up, they decided to head back to be with her.'

'In hospital? Is she okay?'

'She fell on her way to the bathroom. Suspected broken wrist and ankle.'

'Oh, that's terrible.' Ruby stared, stunned. 'I should call her. Check how she is.' Halfway across the room to retrieve her phone, she stopped. 'Wait. They took the yacht?'

'They did.'

'So how are we going to get back?'

'I told Tino I'd take care of it.'

Ruby's eyes narrowed. 'You'd take care of it. What does that mean?'

Sam passed a hand through his hair, stifling another yawn. 'It means I'll take care of it. I didn't want to worry Miller with the logistics. She was frazzled enough.'

Ruby rubbed her forehead. He might not have wanted to worry Miller, but she really didn't like the idea that she was now stranded at the beach house with Sam. Alone. 'What time was this? Why didn't anyone wake me?'

'It was about five-thirty. No one wanted to wake you.'

'They woke you,' Ruby countered. 'Why not me?'

Sam glanced at the ball of fur at his feet and scowled. 'Tino and Miller didn't wake me. He did. Apparently mutts don't keep normal sleeping hours.'

Any other time his disgruntled scowl might have been endearing, but Ruby wasn't in an affable mood. 'So we're stranded here?'

'I hardly think you can call us stranded. I can phone any time and charter a boat to come and pick us up.'

'So why haven't you done it already?'

Sam gave her a narrow-eyed look, clearly not liking her tone. 'I don't know, Ruby,' he drawled dangerously. 'Maybe because it's only seven in the morning and even charter companies have operating hours. And I fell back asleep. Is that a good enough reason for you?'

Ignoring his rhetorical question, she scowled as he pushed to his feet and ambled into the kitchen. Ruby unconsciously tracked his movements, mortifyingly aware of everything about him from his broad shoulders all the way down to his muscular thighs and well-shaped feet. A curl of heat smouldered deep inside her.

'Want a coffee?'

Aware that she'd been caught staring, she blinked, irritation at her own lack of self-control overriding her embarrassment. The man knew how good-looking he was. It wasn't as if he wasn't used to women staring at him.

'No.' She raised her chin. 'What I want is to go home.'

Ignoring her statement, Sam started fiddling with the dials on the coffee machine.

'Did you hear me?' she asked briskly. Now that Miller and Valentino weren't here to act as buffers she saw no reason to continue to hang around and pretend that she and Sam were going to be able to get along.

'I think the charter company in Circular Quay heard you,' he said, not bothering to turn around.

'Good.' Ruby tapped her foot to keep a lid on her escalating emotions. 'I hope they send someone over quickly.' She crossed her arms over her chest, glaring at his broad back. 'Did you plan this?'

Sam turned slowly towards her, his expression inscrutable. 'Did I plan what?' His tone was low and silky and clearly annoyed. 'Miller's mother's accident?' He placed the flats of his palms down on the granite bench between them, a dangerous glint darkening his eyes. 'Yeah. I took my private jet over to her house early this morning, knocked her down in her hallway and made it back in time to let Kong out for a toilet break. Not bad, eh?'

Ruby pressed her lips together at his sarcastic tone, determined to keep a lid on her temper. 'That wasn't what I meant and you know it. I was talking about Miller and Valentino leaving. If someone had woken me I could have gone with them.'

'My apologies,' Sam said in a voice cold enough to

freeze liquid nitrogen. 'It wasn't that you thought I'd injured an old lady in my quest to have you, just that you think I'm so desperate to get you into my bed that I'd orchestrate Miller and Tino leaving without you. Is that it?'

Okay, put like that, it did seem a tad...*hysterical*. Not that she'd admit as much to him.

'Such a high opinion of me, Miss Clarkson,' he continued with ruthless precision. 'What will you accuse me of next? Kidnapping? Unlawful imprisonment? A man could get at least twenty years for any one of those crimes with the right lawyer.'

'Don't be ridiculous,' she snapped, rubbing her brow.

'I'm not the one being ridiculous, angel. You are.'

She knew that. She was just too strung-out to care. 'And stop calling me angel.' When he did it reminded her of how it had felt to be pressed up against his hard, hot body. And how it would feel to be there again.

'You know, I'm not sure if I should live down to your clearly heinous opinion of me and drag you into the bedroom to have my way with you, or walk out of here and let you find your own way home.' He glared at her so hard Ruby felt like a bug under a microscope. 'Now, do you want a damned coffee or not?'

'Yes, I want a damned coffee.' She needed something to get through the debacle of being stranded in this beautiful house, in this beautiful beach setting, with a man who drove her crazy.

'And just so we're clear,' Sam said with deadly emphasis, 'I don't need to resort to underhand tactics to seduce a woman.' He slapped a mug down on the bench in front of her but didn't let go when she reached for the handle.

'I'm very upfront and honest about my needs.'

'And I'm not?'

'Not even close.'

Ruby gripped the handle of the mug, unconsciously registering the warmth of where he had held it. 'Well, at least you can't accuse me of breaking a promise,' she said, turning her back on him.

'Excuse me?'

'Forget it.' She wished she hadn't said anything because she could hear that she'd piqued his interest.

'That was a pointed comment. Explain it.'

'No.'

She put the mug to her lips, her eyes going wide when he rounded the bench to stand in front of her.

Run, an inner voice whispered, *fast*.

'Let me put it another way,' he warned softly. 'You're not leaving this kitchen until you explain yourself.'

'Really?' She lifted her chin belligerently. 'And what if I don't?'

'Then you might well be able to charge me with kidnapping *and* unlawful imprisonment.'

Ruby thought about her options, deciding by the determined jut of his jaw that they were most likely limited. 'Fine.' She huffed out a breath. 'You want to know what I meant, I'll tell you.' She took a quick, fortifying sip of coffee, which was irritatingly delicious. 'Two years ago you walked me home, kissed me breathless and then made some banal promise to call me and never did. Not only that, but the next day I also find out that you escorted another woman to the polo.' Her lips pursed in a moue of distaste. 'I always wondered if you told her that you'd been locking lips with me the night before or if you just moved on without a thought?'

Sam frowned. 'I didn't take anyone to the polo. I went alone.'

'You either think I'm completely daft, Sam, or you have an appalling memory.' She rolled her eyes at his deepening frown. 'Skinny? Beautiful? Redhead? Ring any bells?'

'Ruth Simons?' He stared at her. 'She wasn't my date. She approached me to say hello, we talked about old times and then we went our separate ways. And no, I didn't mention that I spent the night before kissing you *breathless* because it would have been none of her damned business.'

Was he telling the truth?

A litany of her father's broken promises spiralled through her head:

'See you at your softball game this weekend, Rube-licious!'

'Let's go out for your birthday this year, somewhere special for once...'

'I'll call you tomorrow, pumpkin. I promise.'

And her mother's time-honoured advice: *'If you let men walk all over you, Ruby Jane, they'll treat you like a doormat for ever.'*

'It doesn't matter,' Ruby said, confusion and uncertainty replacing the flush of anger that had driven her emotions higher. 'None of it matters.'

Refusing to let her retreat, Sam stepped into her personal space, looming over her. 'I think it does.' His astute gaze held hers. 'I was wrong to say that I'd call you and then not follow through. I hurt you, I think. I'm sorry.'

Shocked by the sincerity of his apology, all Ruby could do was stare up at him.

'It's okay,' Ruby whispered, hating the thready quality in her voice that clearly depicted the hurt she hadn't wanted him to see. 'It's not as if it has any bearing on the here and now.'

'It clearly does or you wouldn't have mentioned it.' His hands came up to curve around her shoulders. 'And you need to know that I *was* intending to call you. I just…' He grimaced. 'I got cold feet at the last minute. I can't explain it other than to say that I wasn't ready for you back then.' His gaze held hers, his voice low. 'I'm not sure I'm ready for you now. But I know I want you. More than I've ever wanted any other woman before. And you want me too. I can see it in your eyes.' His hands slid to her neck, the roughened pads of his thumbs tilting her chin up. 'Feel it in your touch, in the way you tremble against me, like now. Why is it so hard for you to admit it?'

Ruby grabbed his wrists, unsure if she meant to dislodge his hold or press it closer. 'Because it doesn't make sense… Because nothing good can come from it… I don't know.' She shook her head. 'I can't think straight when you're this close to me. All my good sense seems to fly straight out the window.'

'Mine too.'

His lips came down over hers in a hard, hungry kiss that whispered of hot nights and silk sheets. A kiss that seduced and mastered at the same time as it tempted. Ruby sank into it, a low moan vibrating up from deep inside her. His tongue swept into her mouth, bold and confident, sending sensual sparks to every available nerve ending in her body. Her fingers forked into his thick hair, her body arching into his. This was what she wanted. What she craved.

'Yes,' he murmured, his hand rising to cup her breast, his thumb tracking over her aching nipple. 'Yes, Ruby, kiss me like that…just like that.'

Ruby quivered against him, her fingers slipping beneath the hem of his T-shirt to flatten against his taut abdomen. Her body hit sensual overload as the memory of how good it felt to have him inside her collided with the reality of dense, rock-hard muscle in the flesh.

At her quicksilver response the kiss grew even hotter, becoming more like a duel between two highly strung adversaries. A duel of competing desires. Punishing and claiming. Demanding and giving. Fierce, and yet sweetly tender at the same time.

Sam's hands on her body were sure and strong as they shaped her, his mouth sucking at her neck and making her skin pebble with greedy anticipation. Her own hands were busy learning his shape, working over his chest and revelling in the feel of all that taut, hot muscle.

'Sam—' Her voice broke as he bent and gently bit down on her nipple through her silk nightshirt, her body aching with a primal need that threatened to overtake her.

Sam muttered something under his breath, an oath, and then suddenly he was pushing her away.

'Dammit it, Ruby.' He held her at arm's length, his breathing as uneven as hers as he fought to get himself under control. 'I want you badly but I distinctly told you that the next time this happened it would be because you asked for it.'

Ruby blinked up at him, her passion-drugged senses taking longer to come online than his.

'Is that what you're doing?' he said gruffly. 'Are you asking me to kiss you? To make love to you?' He stabbed a hand through his hair. 'Because there's only one place this is headed, and if that's not what you want then you'd better let me know now while I still have self-control enough to stop.'

Ruby's lips felt swollen and tender, her nerves strung so tight they vibrated beneath the surface of her skin. She did want this. But she didn't. The conflicting desires made her feel as if she had a split personality. One telling her to go for it. The other telling her she was heading for a fall.

Sam shook his head, clearly reading her indecision for what it was. 'Don't bother answering that. It's written all over your face.'

'Where are you going?' she asked as he stalked away from her.

'To call a charter company to come and take you back to Sydney.' He looked at her over his shoulder. 'That is what you want, isn't it?'

He didn't wait for her answer and Ruby paced the large kitchen space, her bare feet slapping against the cool, hard tiles. What she wanted was about ten hours to pull herself together. And then another ten to give herself a stern talking-to. Her body still throbbed from where he had touched her, her legs as wobbly as an uncooked pudding.

She knew she was doing the right thing in not giving in to her desire for Sam, but that feeling was difficult to maintain when her heart went into overdrive every time he walked into a room. He was everything she shouldn't want and did. And when she was in his arms she simply forgot that she worked for him and that he would walk away from her when he was done. She forgot that he got under her skin like no man before him and threatened everything she thought she knew about herself.

'When?' His harsh bark sounded loudly in the silent room. Ruby turned to see him stalking towards her, his phone to his ear. He stopped well short of her, his cool gaze holding hers as he listened to whoever was on the other end of the line, his strong thighs braced apart, muscles taut, a brooding scowl drawing his brows together.

He looked like a walking advertisement for a gloriously pumped-up demigod in his prime.

Ruby's heart leapt inside her chest. The same giddy rush she had felt in his presence two years ago welled up inside her. 'When what?' she asked, her voice husky.

'When can you be ready to leave? Is thirty minutes too soon?'

Staring at his gorgeous, stony face, Ruby felt a surge of emotion and need swell inside her. The right thing to do, the *safe* thing to do, was to lock away all these feelings and tell him that she could be ready to go in five minutes, not thirty. But deep down she also knew that for the first time in her life she wanted something with an intensity that transcended the need for a safety net. She wanted him.

'Yes,' she answered, her lips dry as dust.

If possible his scowl deepened. 'How long, then?'

Before she could change her mind Ruby walked up to him and took the phone from his hand, putting it to her ear. 'Sorry,' she murmured, her eyes never leaving his. 'Prank call.' Then she depressed the End Call button and handed the device back to him, her breathing slightly ragged.

Sam stared at her, tension rolling off his big body and crashing into hers, making her insides quake.

Silence surrounded them, broken only by the soft sounds of Kong dreaming from his basket, and the rhythmic ticking of the wall clock.

'Be very sure, Ruby,' Sam said quietly, his voice rough and deep. 'My self-control isn't that good right now.'

Ruby moistened her lips, excited by the way Sam's dark gaze tracked the movement. It gave her a rush of feminine power to know that she turned on this highly charged male to such a degree. 'Neither is mine.'

Sam took a step that brought him right up against her and slowly drew her into his arms, his fingers tilting her chin up so that her eyes stayed locked on his. Heat poured off him, pressing against her body like sun-drenched stone. He was so tall and powerfully built she couldn't prevent the thrill of excitement that raced through her.

'No more denials?' he said fiercely.

'No.'

'And no more masks.'

'No.'

His hands shifted to her waist, rough and insistent as he lifted her so that her legs came up to wind around his waist.

'And no more pretending that this is about an itch any man can scratch.'

'Did it annoy you when I agreed with that?'

'Extremely,' he growled.

A thrill shot through her at the possessive note in his voice. 'Sam?'

'What?'

Ruby leaned forward and kissed the side of his neck the way he liked, breathing in his heady scent and revelling in the delirious taste of salt and man that was quintessentially Sam. 'Are you ever going to kiss me again?'

His smile was slow and lazy and promised passionate retribution for her impudence. 'Just waiting for you to ask me, Clarkson,' he murmured against her lips. 'Just waiting for you to ask.'

CHAPTER EIGHT

NOW THAT HE had her exactly where he wanted her, Sam felt his fingers tremble as he was gripped by a powerful emotion he couldn't name. It was deeper than anything he'd ever felt with a woman before and it nearly gave him pause. He knew this thing with Ruby was all-consuming but he was fairly certain he had a handle on it. Or was he only fooling himself?

Carrying her toward the bedroom, he bit down gently on the silky flesh of her earlobe, rewarded by her deep shudder and the quick, feminine hitch in her voice. She arched her neck to give him free licence to roam.

Of course he wasn't fooling himself. This thing, this incendiary chemistry between them, was just that. Chemistry and heat and—

'Dammit, Kong!' Sam cursed as he pushed open the door to the bedroom he'd used the night before and nearly tripped over the puppy that rushed in ahead of him. 'Sit!' he commanded, not caring if the pup obeyed him or not.

'Did he sit?' Ruby asked, nibbling his lower lip.

'Don't care,' he muttered. Her teasing ministrations had stripped away every vestige of sophistication he possessed and left a Cro-Magnon Man in his place. Still, he forced himself to slow down and lowered her to the centre of the bed. A row of tiny buttons split her nightshirt and Sam's gaze fastened on them, taking in the twin points of her hard nipples, which poked through the thin fabric. Unable to help himself, he lowered his head and captured one tight bud between his lips, bathing the cloth with his tongue.

A low moan escaped Ruby's lips and he glanced upward to find her lower lip caught between her teeth. 'You have beautiful breasts,' he murmured. 'So responsive.'

She shifted restlessly on the mattress, her fingers going to the top button of her shirt. Sam shook his head, straddling her and taking both her wrists in his hands and placing them on either side of her head. 'Let me,' he ordered roughly. 'I told you in the limo that I'd be taking my time when I finally got you horizontal. If you use those clever fingers on either one of us you'll destroy what little control I have left.'

She moistened her lips, heaving a sigh. 'There's no need to take your time. I'm so ready, Sam.'

Enjoying having her at his mercy, he bent over and licked the seam of her lips, moving back before she could tangle her tongue with his.

'Stop teasing,' she moaned.

'Oh, Clarkson,' he chuckled. 'I haven't even started yet.' But he was very afraid he wouldn't get to do everything he wanted to do because with every expanse of creamy skin he exposed he lost a little bit more of himself in the process. Knowing he should probably be a bit more worried about that, he couldn't bring himself to care. Especially when she was now naked save for a pair of panties emblazoned with the slogan Right Here, Right Now.

He quirked a brow in question.

Ruby gave a husky chuckle. 'Christmas gift from Molly. I wasn't expecting anyone else to see them.'

'Just make sure no one else does,' Sam growled, taking her mouth in a searing kiss that set them both to panting.

Working down the slender column of her throat, he shifted lower so that he could cup her breasts and admire the dusky-rose peaks. She arched up from the bed, her fingers kneading his waist and bunching his T-shirt high. Raising his head, he reefed it off over his head one-handed and groaned as her nails raked down over his torso and belly, covering his rigid length with the flat of her hand, his erection surging against the laces of his board shorts.

With growing urgency he trailed hot kisses over her collarbone, rubbing his stubbled jaw across one taut nipple and then the other before covering them in turn with his mouth, torturing her responsive flesh with his tongue and teeth before taking her deep into his mouth.

She moaned, arching higher off the bed, and Sam's hands went to her hips as he kissed lower. 'Much as I like these,' he murmured, shifting to the side and pulling her panties down her long legs, 'they have to come off.'

Smoothing a hand down her body he hooked one of her legs over his outer thigh and slid a hand down between their bodies to cup her silken curls. They were damp, the scent of her arousal turning him even harder as he parted her and stroked his fingers inside her silken heat.

She sobbed his name and need surged inside him. 'God, Ruby, you're beautiful.' Shifting lower, he urged her onto her back and held her thighs apart, kissing the backs of her knees before moving higher.

'Sam—' she gripped his hair, her fingernails digging into his scalp and sending goose pimples along his nape '—I need—'

'I know what you need.' He eased her thighs wider to fit his shoulders between them and touched his tongue to her tender flesh. She writhed beneath him and he had to anchor her hips to the bed with his forearm as he feasted on her honeyed centre, lapping at her and teasing her until she was keening and thrashing, and calling his name over and over.

He could tell she was close, her body shuddering and moving against him, and he quickened his movements, driving her higher, needing to hear her come for him, needing to feel it against his tongue. It had never been like this for him before. This deep-seated need to please a woman, to hear her soft cries of surrender as he pleasured her. And when finally she peaked it was the sweetest moment he could ever remember having.

Not giving her any time to recover, he crawled over her supine body and took her mouth in another drugging kiss. Despite his highly aroused body, it was almost enough: pleasuring her and having her come apart in his arms. But then her nimble fingers reached for the laces on his shorts and he knew she was as hungry to have him inside her as he was to be there.

Taking over the task, he reefed his shorts open and groaned in aching relief when her fingers circled him, gripping him in her tight fist. His eyes closed as she wriggled down the bed and replaced her fist with her mouth. He groaned again, forking his hand into her tumbling mass of hair as she used her lips and tongue to drive him as wild as he'd just driven her.

'Ruby, angel...' He lifted her upwards and rolled her beneath him. 'I need to be inside you,' he ground out, positioning himself between her thighs, widening them with his knees.

'Yes.' She gripped his face in her hands and brought his mouth down to hers as his body surged deep.

Then he swore. 'Condom,' he growled against her lips.

'I'm protected. Remember?' Her body rose to his and Sam bit back a groan as he sank further inside her tight sheath. Barely giving her time to adjust, he moved in her, filling her over and over with sure, deep strokes. It was as if his body belonged to some primitive part of himself he hadn't accessed before because he felt possessed. Possessed by some need to claim her and make her his.

'Relax, angel—you're so tight. Yes, God, yes, like that.'

He shuddered as her velvet heat clenched and released around his girth, her body milking his and emptying his brain of everything but her. Gripping her bottom in his hands, he angled her against him and drove even harder into her, urged on by her pleading little cries for more until in one fiery liquid moment they both hurled over the edge of reason and space and into the most satisfying release he had ever felt in his life.

He must have slept because at some point Ruby had snuggled into his arms. Or had he moved her there? Right now he didn't care because her feminine weight pressed up against him was all he could think about. Sensing that she was awake, Sam gently smoothed her hair back from her forehead. 'We finally made it to a bed,' he murmured, wondering if he had ever felt this sated before.

'Are you gloating?' she murmured sleepily.

'Not at all,' he said, knowing that was exactly what he was doing. 'I'm just relaying that I'm happy. Soft mattress. Soft sheets. Softer woman. What more can a man want?'

His stomach grumbled and Ruby blinked up at him, her gorgeous green eyes still slightly glazed from sleep.

'Food?' she suggested.

'Are you offering to fix me breakfast, angel?'

'Hmm, let me think about that.' Her eyes narrowed into threatening slits as she mock glowered at him. 'No.'

Sam laughed, reaching out to trace a finger down her cute, haughty nose. 'Well, if you're not going to fix me breakfast, what are you going to do for me?'

'Kick you out of bed,' she suggested sweetly. 'So you can fix me breakfast.'

Sam collapsed onto his back, taking her with him. 'After I've just serviced you like that?'

'Serviced me?' She lifted her head and her blonde hair cascaded like a waterfall of silk over one shoulder. Sam didn't bother resisting the temptation to thread his fingers through it. It was the most untidy he'd ever seen it and he loved the fact that he was responsible for mussing it. 'Serviced me?' she repeated. 'Like a horse?'

'Stallion.' He chuckled softly. 'Want me to do it again?'

Pink bloomed in her cheeks. 'Does it involve that thing you did with your tongue?'

'It might,' he promised, rolling over on top of her and covering her body with his. 'Did I hit the spot with that one?'

'Maybe…' she groaned as he smoothed her hair back and anchored her head for a hard, hungry kiss.

'You're insatiable,' she breathed, her hands roaming over the powerful slab of muscles that bisected his spine.

His lips tracked a path to her breast. 'With you I am,' he murmured, teasing the tip with his tongue.

'Sam…' Her voice trailed away as his lips fastened over hers once more, her hips angling upwards. Taking the invitation, Sam rolled her onto her stomach and stretched her hands high above her head.

'You okay with this?' he murmured against her ear.

'That depends on what this— Oh, yes. Yes. Definitely yes.' That last word was said on a long sigh as his thighs moved between hers and he entered her from behind. The contact was electrifying, wickedly good, and he had to grit his teeth to hold his orgasm at bay so she could reach hers first.

Coming back from that explosion of sensation wasn't easy, not even when Kong scratched at the door and barked urgently.

Ruby gave a half-moan, half-laugh. 'That's Kong.'

'No, it's the neighbour's dog,' Sam said, enjoying the sensation of having her beneath him, wrung out from the pleasure he'd just given her.

'In the bedroom?' She laughed, wriggling out from under him. 'I hope not. Sam—let me up—he must need to go out.'

Sam groaned and rolled onto his back. 'That dog has the worst timing in the world.'

'You're hungry, anyway,' she reminded him, scooting out of bed and grabbing his T-shirt off the floor.

He let his eyes travel over the long length of her before his T-shirt swallowed up the view. 'I know.'

'For food.' She gave him a stern look and reached for the door. 'Ah, I take back what I said.' She glanced at him over one shoulder. 'Kong doesn't need to go out. He's already left you a surprise.' Laughter lit her voice. 'Lucky for you, Miller and Valentino have floorboards.'

'Yeah, lucky for me,' Sam grumbled, not that he was truly upset. How could a man be upset on such a great day?

Somehow Sunday morning turned into Sunday evening, then Monday morning and now Monday afternoon. Neither she nor Sam had mentioned hiring a boat to return to Sydney, and when she'd called to ask after Miller's mother, she had blithely said that she and Sam had decided to stay at the beach house to discuss the big case they were working on.

She doubted Miller believed her, but she didn't push it. Maybe she could sense Ruby's emotional fragility down the end of the phone. Which, if she was honest, came and went depending on what they were doing.

If they were in bed together it was somehow nonexistent. Her mind, body and very essence were wholly taken up with Sam and everything they did to each other. There was no room for doubts when he laid his masterful hands on her body, expanding her sexual repertoire in ways that were utterly exhilarating.

If they were doing something casual like cooking together, or out walking Kong, taking in the bush setting and listening to the kookaburras herald that night was fast coming, then she felt a little more out of her depth.

Coming across the grand old beach house near Miller and Tino's, as they had done earlier that morning, had completely thrown her for a loop.

Having remembered Miller's comment that it was for sale, Sam had immediately wanted to investigate.

'I don't think we should,' she'd told him, trailing after him. 'It's private property.'

Sam had looked at her like a kid spying a Christmas tree. 'Where's your sense of adventure, Clarkson?'

'I lost it at law school,' she deadpanned, making him laugh.

'So what do you think?' he asked after peering into the downstairs windows.

'I love it.' She glanced at the peeling paint, and the

overgrown vines spiralling out of control around the ve-
randa posts. 'It's got so much character.'

'Want to buy it?'

'Me?' She laughed lightly, a sudden vision of her and
Sam poring over paint samples and soft furnishings filling her head. 'Miller suggested you buy it so your future kids could all grow up together. I wasn't a part of
that deal.'

She'd wandered away from him then, a bittersweet
ache welling up in her chest. 'It looks like hard work,'
she'd added, refusing to get caught up in the romance of
the images that had taken hold and wouldn't let go. 'To
make it beautiful again, I mean.'

Sam had come up behind her and slipped his arms
around her waist. 'You should know by now that I don't
mind hard work. Especially when it comes to beautiful things.'

Ruby had a strange feeling that he'd been talking
about her and she'd blindly reached up to kiss him, replacing her intense emotional reaction with heat and
need. He'd swiftly taken over the kiss and they'd barely
made it back to Miller and Tino's house before he'd rav-
ished her again.

Now, as they lay together under an ancient gum tree,
the mid-afternoon sun dappling the lawn with interesting shapes while a few brave insects buzzed lazily in the
heat, Ruby was trying not to go into full-on panic mode.
Kong lay beside them, his fur slightly damp from where
Sam had playfully hosed him down to help him cool off.
They'd gone for a short run together along the beach, and
the pup was exhausted from the effort.

Ruby turned her face up to the sun as she remembered
fixing lunch together and making sweet, tender love afterwards. She barely recognised herself in Sam's pres-

ence. She couldn't remember the last time she'd felt this relaxed, and there wasn't a yoga pose in sight. Instead there was just him. Sam and his magic hands that knew just how to touch her, Sam with his gentle manner and infinite patience when he discovered Kong had treated his new shoe as a chew toy, and Sam with his intelligent conversation and broad, broad shoulders it would be so easy to lean on for a while.

Right from the beginning Sam had been able to strip away the guardedness she'd carried with her for ever, and sleeping with him, being like this with him, only seemed to make it harder to keep things in perspective. How much harder would it be if she actually fell in love with him?

In love with him?

This wasn't about love. Sam wouldn't want that from her and neither one of them had mentioned anything about emotions, or indeed, any of this going beyond the long weekend. In fact, Ruby knew that it couldn't go beyond the weekend because, regardless of what Sam thought, continuing to sleep together would definitely complicate their working life.

Ruby's heart thumped hard as her phone beeped a text message and, desperate for the distraction, she fished it out of her pocket as if it were a hundred-pound gold nugget she was trying to scratch out of the dirt.

'It's a text from my mother,' she said, sitting up so abruptly that Sam's fingers tangled in her hair.

Gently disentangling the strands, he scanned her face, which had grown pale as she read the long message.

'Something wrong?'

Ruby blinked, her brain trying to make sense of her mother's text. 'No. Yes. My mother is getting married!'

Sam looked at her, one arm behind his head, his brows

knitted together as he watched her. 'You don't seem very happy about that.'

'I'm not. I mean, I am, but...' She shook her head. 'Honestly, I don't know what I feel.' Apart from agitated and unsettled. She jumped to her feet, instinctively needing to put space between her and Sam. 'My mother has this eternal optimism when it comes to relationships and it's so alien to me I find it hard to relate to.'

She paced over to the edge of the property and stared out at the bay beyond the trees. She felt Sam come up behind her, stiffening in case he tried to touch her.

'I don't follow.'

'My mother doesn't make very good decisions when she's in a relationship.' She turned towards him, hugging her arms over her stomach. 'She gets very needy and then it all goes wrong.'

'Is that what happened between her and your father?'

'In some ways.' She gave a hollow laugh. 'They used to fight all the time and sometimes it got so bad I would find Molly hiding under her bed and I'd read to her to help block it all out.' She glanced towards the bay again. 'I never understood it. My father never seemed happy and yet my mother had given up her career for him, which she later regretted when he left her for a work colleague.'

'That's tough.'

'It was. It took my mother a long time to recover and nothing I could ever say made her feel better about it.'

Sam frowned, his hands in his pockets as he watched her. 'Why was it your job to make her feel better about it? You were only a child.'

'I don't know. I think she became depressed and I was the only one available to help. Honestly, I would have done anything to make her happy back then.'

Sam gave her an astute look. 'So you were the res-cuer of the family.'

'Rescuer?' Her short laugh was more an embarrassed cough. She couldn't believe that she'd just blurted out her family secrets like that. This weekend was about sex, not some lame therapy session. 'Hardly.' She made to move away from him but he stopped her, clasping her arms gently and drawing her resistant body closer.

'How old were you when your father left?'

'I was fourteen and—' She swallowed heavily, un-sure how to switch topics without being obvious. 'It was the best thing really.' Apart from her mother going into a deep depression for a couple of years. 'Well, not the best, but it was certainly more peaceful after he left. Calmer. Only...'

'Only you missed him,' he finished for her, accurately interpreting the forlorn note in her voice.

'Yes.' She blinked back tears she hadn't realised had collected behind her eyes. 'Which is stupid because it probably wouldn't have worked out anyway.' She tried to smile to lighten the moment but her mouth wobbled and she ducked her head against Sam's shoulder. 'Why is love so difficult?'

'Because the human need for connection is so power-ful, and sometimes you want that any way you can get it. Even if the other person doesn't want the same thing.'

Sensing that Sam was speaking from personal experi-ence and more than ready to talk about something else, Ruby tilted her head back. 'Has that happened to you?'

'In a fashion.' His mouth twisted into a slight gri-mace. 'My old man was hardly ever around when I was growing up but that didn't change the way I felt about him.'

Ruby already knew from when Miller and Tino had

got together that Sam's father had died in a fiery racing accident when Sam was young. 'Because he died, you mean?'

'No. He was unavailable long before that. He had his career and he didn't need much else.' *Certainly not him*, his tone implied. 'He was a larger-than-life figure who lived a life far removed from the real world.'

'Did you ever consider following him into racing like Valentino did?'

Sam laughed. 'Once. But I was told that I didn't have the reflexes for it so instead I concentrated on my studies. I decided if I couldn't impress him with my physical prowess, I'd do it academically. I should have known from watching my siblings that it wouldn't work. Not even Tino got our father's full attention and it was clear from early on that he had racing talent. I think it's fair to say that my father wasn't very family-oriented.'

Ruby had had no idea that they shared the similar experience of having emotionally distant fathers and her arms instinctively went around his waist to offer comfort. 'I'm sorry, Sam. I didn't know.'

'Why would you?' He smoothed her hair back from her forehead. 'But the past is the past. You can't change it. You just deal with it and get over it.'

'Do you?' she asked, thinking about herself as much as Sam. 'Do you get over it or does it change you in ways you can't reverse?' Because love wasn't something she'd ever trusted and she didn't know how to get around that. Or even if she wanted to.

'Who knows?' he said, scooping her into his arms so suddenly she squealed.

Kong barked, dancing around Sam's feet as he sensed the rising excitement between them.

'What are you doing?' Ruby clung to Sam's neck.

'You'll find out.'

'Sam?' She spied the sparkling swimming pool with dubious delight. 'I'm not wearing a swimsuit.'

Sam grinned down at her, his gaze hot. 'Neither am I.'

Kong scratched at the bedroom door later that afternoon and Sam buried his head beneath the pillows. 'That dog is going back to the rescue centre as soon as we get back to Sydney,' he grumbled.

Ruby stirred beside him and planted a kiss on his shoulder. 'No, he's not. You love him too much to give him back. But stay here. I'll let him out this time.'

Sam rolled over and snatched her close against him before she got very far. 'Can you bring back my phone? I should check when Tino is picking us up later on this evening. Not that I want the weekend to end.'

'All good things come to an end,' she murmured, wriggling out of his arms and throwing on his T-shirt.

Closing his eyes, Sam wondered about her last comment. Was Ruby right? Did all good things have to come to an end or could they go on endlessly? Before he could conjure up an answer Ruby flew back into the room.

'Oh, my God, you have to get up. Valentino is here.'

'Already?'

'Yes, it's five o'clock in the afternoon, and I think he saw me.'

Sam's gaze drifted down over her figure, clad in another one of his T-shirts and nothing else. They hit her mid-thigh and had become her weekend wear because they were so easy to remove. 'That could be a problem.' His eyes turned heavy-lidded. 'I'll have to kill him if he saw anything.'

'Stop joking around. You have to get up. Get dressed.'

Sam yawned, not seeing the problem. After mak-

ing love and talking for most of the day he was completely sated.

Not that they'd talked about anything important. Like
what would happen once they returned to Sydney. He'd
thought about it after Ruby had fallen asleep earlier on
and he knew he wanted things to continue between them
once they got back. No doubt she would see it as a com-
plication but it didn't have to be. The truth was he liked
her. He liked spending time with her in bed and out,
he liked her sass and her fire, he liked her professional
confidence and the way she pushed herself and others
to help those in need.

His gaze softened as he watched her searching for
something under the bed. He especially liked seeing
her laugh when his dog slobbered all over her face, and
he loved her skyscraper-shoe collection. Why would he
want to give that up and move on before he was ready?

'Sam! You're still in bed!'

Seeing her panic, Sam wondered if he shouldn't be
doing the same thing. Certainly he hadn't been overly
comfortable disclosing his feelings about his father as
he'd done earlier, but then he hadn't been nearly as uncomfortable as she had been talking about hers. He wondered if he shouldn't be more alarmed about how much
he had shared with her, and then became distracted by
her sweet curves.

'Calm down,' he said in a reassuring tone. 'Tino already knows you're here.'

Kong barked at the door and Ruby nearly jumped out
of her skin. 'Yes, but he doesn't know I'm here like this—
with you! He thinks we're working on a case.'

'So what? He'll figure it out in time.'

'I don't want him to figure it out. If someone at the
office should find out…' She left the rest of the sentence

hanging but Sam got the general gist and didn't like it. He rolled out of bed and yanked on his board shorts, trying not to become irritated. 'My brother isn't indiscreet and last time I checked he didn't work for me.'

'I still don't want him or Miller to know about...' Her hand waved between them as if she was at a loss for words, and that infuriated him even more. 'I mean, one night at a party is explainable—sort of. But this...'

'This?' Sam wondered how his voice remained so calm when his head felt as if it might explode.

'This weekend.' She angled her stubborn chin higher. 'It's between us and no one else.'

'Let me get this straight.' Sam stalked towards her, a dangerous smile on his face. 'You want me to be your dirty little secret going forward, is that it?'

She frowned. 'No, that's not—'

'Good.' He tunnelled his fingers into her hair and tilted her face up for a hard, brief kiss. 'Because I don't operate that way.'

But in the end he had operated that way. He'd closed Valentino's curious glance down with just a look and carried their bags onto the yacht. Fortunately his brother wasn't a stupid man and had taken the hint, making small talk to fill the lengthening silence.

Apparently he'd sent Sam a text that morning informing him that he'd collect both him and Ruby a little earlier than planned, which Sam would have known if he'd bothered to check his phone. As it was a public holiday, he hadn't seen the need. And he'd been too busy. Too busy making love with Ruby and catching up on sleep he hadn't got the night before.

A tight sensation settled in his chest as the yacht skimmed over the increasingly choppy waves. He could only ever remember wanting one other thing as much as he wanted this woman. Back then his father had been out of reach. Ruby wasn't. *Was she?*

And what exactly did he want from her?

He brooded over the question as he watched her. He might not know exactly what he did want, but he knew what he didn't—and that was for her to continue to treat him like a leper after the weekend they'd just indulged in.

He scowled as the yacht finally steered a course into the brilliantly bejewelled Sydney Harbour. The wind whipped Ruby's hair back as her face lifted to the bright sunshine and the tight sensation worsened. They'd barely exchanged two words since Valentino had picked them up. Instead Ruby had questioned his brother about how Miller's mother was, and whether or not she needed anything; basically acting as if she hadn't spent the last two days coming apart in his arms.

What she hadn't done was follow the normal trajectory he was used to, where a woman expected more from him than he was prepared to give, and subtly tried to question him about what happened next.

Irritated because the one woman he *did* want to expect more from him actually *didn't*, Sam strode from the yacht after Tino docked, growling at Ruby as she accepted Tino's offer of a lift home, firmly directing her to his own jeep and driving her home himself.

She didn't say anything on the way, petting Kong and staring at the Sydney landscape she'd seen a million times before. Needing to work out his own agenda, Sam had left her to her thoughts, but now, as he pulled up outside her apartment block, he knew he had to say something.

Moving Kong to the back seat, he went around to open

Ruby's door, barely restraining his irritation when he found her already waiting for him on the kerb.

'I'll walk you up,' he clipped out, reaching for her bag.

'No need,' she said clasping the handle as if it were full of jewels and she was staring at a newly released prison inmate. 'I had a lovely time this weekend. Thank you.'

Sam ground his teeth together. 'This isn't exactly the way I planned for it to end, Ruby.'

'It was a little awkward with Valentino turning up like that but—'

'I'm not talking about my brother. I'm talking about you and me.' His voice was deep, rough. 'Spend the night with me.' He placed his hands on her shoulders. 'Come back to my place and let me fix you dinner.'

'I can't.' She wouldn't meet his eyes. 'I have to look over work stuff and—'

'Do it at mine.'

'Molly expects me home. We agreed to talk about Mum's situation.'

'Her wedding, you mean.'

'Yes.' He could feel the tension emanating from the tight muscles in her shoulders and wanted to ease the burden she felt. 'Your mother is a big girl, Ruby. She can take care of herself.'

'I know that.' She pulled back from him and he knew he'd offended her. 'I'm not an idiot.'

'I didn't say you were.'

Frustrated, Sam dragged a hand through his hair. The more Ruby tried to put walls up between them, the more he wanted to tear them down. 'I'm only trying to offer you support.'

'I don't need your support, Sam. I'm a big girl as well.'

'Dammit, would you stop being so prickly?' His hands slid down to her hips and he tugged her closer. 'I don't want to argue with you. I want to see you again.'

Her head went back as she frowned. 'Sorry?'

'Did you seriously think one weekend is all I would want?'

'Yes. No! I don't know.'

'Well, it's not,' he said gruffly. 'I want more.'

'How much more?' she asked huskily.

'I don't know,' he answered honestly. 'But I do know I don't want this to end yet.'

Ruby bit into her lower lip, her fingers turning the front of his T-shirt into a piano accordion.

'What about you?' His voice sounded rough. 'What do you want?'

'I don't know either,' she said hesitantly. 'We work together and—'

'That's a real sticking point for you, I know.' He stared down at her. 'So, okay, lay it on me.'

'What?' she asked warily.

'Some scenarios.'

'Scenarios?'

'Imagined situations you think are going to go wrong in the future.' He flashed her a grin. 'You can start with your biggest fear.'

Her eyes flew wide as if to say that there was no way she would be starting with her biggest fear. 'So you can shoot it down?'

'Of course.' His grin widened. 'Come on, Clarkson—I'm good at this, trust me.'

'Fine.' She drew in a deep breath. 'If we continue this and someone at the office finds out the gossip would be hideous.'

'The only way anyone at work can find out is if one

of us is indiscreet and talks. I'm not going to do that, and I doubt you are either.'

'You could become uncomfortable seeing me in the office every day and change your mind about mixing business with pleasure.'

'And fire you presumably?'

Ruby raised a brow at his cavalier tone. 'It's been done before. And you are my boss.'

'True. But I'm not that small-minded.'

'What happens if one of us decides to end things?'

'We behave like mature adults and go on as normal.' He gave her a slow grin and tugged her closer. 'Anything else?'

'I'm sure there is but I can't think of it right now.'

'Because you're creating mountains where there are none.' He leant in and kissed her. 'Say yes.'

'Sam.' She groaned against his lips, her arms tight around his neck. 'I think you could wear down a Sherman tank just by looking at it.'

Sam frowned. 'I don't want to wear you down.' Was she saying that she didn't want this? That she didn't want *him*? It felt like a sharp blade had just been rammed through his midsection. 'If this isn't what you want then just say the word and I'll walk away right now.' Even if it seemed impossible to do so. 'Is that what you want, Ruby—do you want me to walk away?'

'No.' The word was barely a whisper but it kick-started his heart again. 'I don't want you to walk away, Sam, but I'm not very good at this. I don't know how to make it work.'

The words rushed out of her as if she was taking an enormous risk just saying them. The echoes of that feeling resonated somewhere deep inside Sam as well. 'You make it work one step at a time,' he said gently. 'At the office we keep things to business as usual, and on the weekends...' He gave her a slow smile and slipped his hands into her hair. 'On the weekends we burn up the sheets together until we can't move. How does that sound?'

'Like trouble,' she said, pressing closer. 'But okay, if we do this we have to keep it simple.'

'Very simple.'

Ruby nodded so seriously Sam had to pull back from kissing her again. 'No unnecessary promises and no re-percussions,' she pressed.

'None.'

'And no emotional entanglements. From either one of us.'

The light breeze swept a few strands of hair across her face. Sam pushed them back. 'Ever do anything without a caveat, Clarkson?'

'Not usually,' she grumbled reluctantly. 'Is that a prob-lem?'

'No, my crazy little control freak, it's not.'

'I am not a—'

'You are and I love it.' He crushed her lips beneath his in a greedy kiss, only coming up for air when they were both breathless and wanting.

'Feel what you do to me, Ruby. What we do to each other.' He ran the pad of his thumb across her lower lip, soothing her swollen flesh. 'What have you got to lose by saying yes?'

Her eyes were heavy-lidded with a desire he knew was reflected in his own. 'Nothing,' she whispered.

But what Sam heard in her voice, what he *felt* when she tightened her arms around his neck, was *everything*. And he didn't know if he was the one thinking that, or she was.

CHAPTER NINE

ON THEIR NEXT weekend together they flew to Melbourne, hired a car and drove along the rugged cliffs of the Great Ocean Road.

Victoria wasn't as warm as New South Wales, so Sam had stopped at a local market and bought her a shawl to wrap herself in. They'd stayed in a gorgeous house overlooking the sea in Apollo Bay, lit an open fire in the hearth and toasted marshmallows, talking about everything from horror exam days at university to the merits of the government's new environmental-law package, and favourite Broadway musicals—none in Sam's case, loads in hers.

Ruby found out that Sam had gone into law because his father was usually scathing about it, and she'd told him how she had an over-developed sense of fairness that drove her to want to set things right.

The following weekend Sam had flown them to Far North Queensland, where they'd stayed in an eco-resort and snorkelled with dolphins, and slept out under the stars. Kong had gone with them on both trips, proving to be an excellent travelling companion apart from the sofa leg he had chewed at the house in Apollo Bay, and which Sam had already replaced with a more expensive version.

When both Molly and Miller had asked where she was going she had made up some new, top-secret case that she had to oversee, and, although they had looked suspicious, they were used to her working over weekends, so it wasn't that much of a stretch for them to believe her.

That had been two weeks ago and since then Ruby had hardly seen, or heard from, Sam. Mainly that was due to Drew and Mandy having had their baby, a beautiful little girl, which had caused Sam's responsibilities to double. Then last week he'd had to fly to LA when an old case he'd been working on had blown up. He'd been sorry to cancel yet another weekend together but he'd had no choice.

He'd even thanked her for taking it so well, but what had he expected? That she would get clingy? Ruby didn't do clingy. Ever.

And really, Sam's being away had been a good thing. Her own caseload had significantly increased since the merger and she'd needed a lot of uninterrupted time to get on top of it.

She'd also used her free weekend to catch up with her mother and Phil, the fiancé.

They'd lunched at a chic French bistro on the previous Sunday, and her mother had been delighted to fill her in on the story of their romance.

Apparently theirs had been a whirlwind affair—her mother's favourite kind—and Ruby only hoped this one would last longer than the many others over the years. Though, to be fair, none of the others had made it to the engagement stage. It still surprised Ruby that after her father had walked out, leaving her mother shocked and devastated, she was optimistic enough to date as often as she had and to even try marriage again. But she had to admit that her mother did seem happy with Phil, and that was all Ruby had ever wished for her.

With Sam's sage words in her ear—words she hadn't wanted to hear at the time—about her mother being a big girl and able to take care of herself, Ruby found herself biting her tongue rather than warning her mother to be careful. Of course, she didn't think that her behaviour was *that* different from the norm, but Molly had frowned at her after the lunch and asked if she was okay.

'Fine,' she'd said blithely. 'I've just decided to stop trying to save Mum when it's obvious she doesn't want, or need, that from me any more.'

Molly gaped at her. 'Okay, where's my sister and how much do you want for her return?'

At the time Ruby had given her *that* look, but deep down she wondered the same thing. She did feel different at times—looser and less worried about everything, and always wondering what Sam was doing. Like now, for instance, when she should be preparing for a major meeting with Carter Jones she was actually working out the time difference in LA.

And every time she wondered if she was being a bit naive in agreeing to see Sam past that long weekend at the beach house, every time she wondered if she wasn't getting in a little over her head, her body would pulse with remembered longing and she couldn't bring herself to end it.

Yet.

But what was he doing now? Working, as he had said, or was he catching up with friends? Had he run into an old flame? Was his lack of contact a signal that he was already tiring of their relationship? Ruby's stomach bottomed out. Had the time they had spent together been enough for him, while for her the more time she spent with him, the more she *wanted* to spend with him?

It took everything in her not to get uptight or paranoid, and she felt as if she'd succeeded right up until she heard his voice outside her office coming down the hallway.

'That's great news. Have their CFO call me. Those contract negotiations can get tricky when you least expect it, so she needs to be fully briefed ahead of time.'

Ruby only had a moment to collect herself before Sam was standing, larger than life, in her doorway, so handsome it hurt her heart to look at him.

Grant muttered a greeting, barely looking up from his computer, his fingers working furiously on the contract they were planning to put to Carter Jones in less than two hours' time.

Leaving Grant to it, she smiled at Sam, only to find his expression so serious a lump formed in her throat. He *had* met someone in LA. Someone at a party, he was sorry, but what could he do? It was back to business as usual for them.

'I've just heard that Jones has called a mediation meeting for this afternoon,' he said, his dark eyes holding hers. 'Are we ready for it?'

Quickly shifting gear from the personal to the professional, and hating the sick, insecure feeling clawing at her stomach, Ruby exhaled slowly. 'Yes. He's panicking because of the media leak last week, and also because we've refiled a motion with the court for a class action suit. He's also no doubt wanting to capitalise on the fact that the mobile phone videos we have showing his managers browbeating their employees will likely be inadmissible in court.'

'Move in for the kill while he assumes we're hurting more than he is,' Sam suggested.

'Yes.'

Nodding, Sam glanced at his mobile phone. 'I've cleared my diary for the next few hours. What time are you both leaving for his office?'

He'd cleared his diary? Ruby hadn't even known he was back in the country. He hadn't sent her a single text since asking how her afternoon went with her mother on Sunday. God, she hoped he didn't sense how off-balance she felt right now.

'An hour.'

Holding her gaze, Sam spoke to Grant. 'Give us a minute, would you, Grant?'

It wasn't a request and Grant didn't take it as one, balancing his open laptop in his arms as he left them alone.

Sam closed the door behind him and Ruby's throat bobbed as she swallowed. 'Was there something else?'

Sam came towards her, rounding her desk in three easy strides. 'Yes.' He pulled her to her feet, his eyes searching hers. 'I've missed you.'

Stunned, Ruby could only stare up at him. She'd slipped her shoes off under her desk, so she felt tiny as he towered over her, his dark, hot eyes pinning her to the spot. Her heart was beating so hard inside her chest she'd be surprised if he couldn't hear it as clearly as she could.

'You've got exactly two seconds to tell me no before I kiss you,' he murmured gruffly.

'I…' She moistened her lips, utterly intoxicated by the heady rush at having all that power and strength completely focused on her.

'One.' He stepped forward.

'We shouldn't.'

He took another step, his gaze on her mouth. 'That's not a no. Two.'

Not realising that he'd backed her against the wall until she felt its solid presence behind her, she flattened her hands against his hard chest. She knew if she told him to back off that he would. In a second. She didn't want him to. Instead she slid her hands to his shoulders and moaned his name as his mouth crashed down over hers.

The kiss was delicious. Deep and drugging. Sam's rough growl and powerful body letting her know just how much he wanted her. Ruby went liquid.

At that point she wouldn't have cared if Drew and his father, and the whole executive team, were crowded into the room taking notes. She'd missed Sam more than she wanted to admit and it was heaven to be in his arms again. To be touching him again.

Fortunately Sam did care, easing back to rest his forehead against hers. When he felt her legs take her weight once more he released her and took a step back. 'Sorry. I know that crossed your line, but the last two weeks have been interminable. Have dinner with me tonight.'

'Okay.' It wasn't the weekend but she couldn't have cared. 'Oh, no! I can't. I promised Molly I'd run through lines with her tonight. She has a big audition coming up.'

'How long will that take?'

'Not all night.'

His smile was slow and full of sensual promise just as Veronica hurried in carrying a packing box. 'I just found this in— Oh, sorry, I didn't realise you had someone with you.'

'I was just leaving,' Sam said smoothly. 'Tonight,' he added before leaving them.

Veronica set the box on Ruby's desk. 'I finally located

your missing books.' She started unpacking them. 'So what's on tonight?'

'Nothing...' Ruby surreptitiously smoothed the corners of her mouth, thankful that she hadn't reapplied her lipstick after lunch. 'Just a...a work thing.'

'Oh, okay.' Veronica gave her an enigmatic smile as she retreated to answer the ringing phone on her desk. 'Well, enjoy your *work thing* and don't forget your shoes this time.'

Ruby groaned. She hadn't fooled Veronica one bit. She closed her laptop and slipped on her heels, a small smile tilting her lips. Probably she should feel a bit more worried about that. And maybe she would if her body wasn't still buzzing from that kiss.

By the time they reconnected in the car that whisked them to the Star Burger building, Ruby was glad to have Grant along for the ride. She was a bag of nerves and she knew that was only because Sam was with them. Usually, she felt completely in charge by this stage of the proceedings, knowing that her preparation was rock-solid in the cases she worked on. Now, though, there was so much at stake and part of that was impressing Sam, which should not have been uppermost in her mind.

Pulling herself together, she flipped the switch on her emotions and focused on what she had to accomplish as the three of them strode into Carter Jones's palatial suite of offices. After they were left cooling their heels for ten minutes Sam quietly informed the snooty receptionist that he would walk out and terminate all future negotiations with the restaurant giant if they were left to wait a second longer.

Miraculously, Carter's personal assistant arrived—a woman who looked as if she'd stepped from the pages of *Glamour* magazine—and escorted them to a richly designed conference room.

Two minutes later Carter Jones, a large, balding man with bulging eyes strode in, flanked by Tom Roberts, his head lawyer, and six minions. Ruby knew of Tom's reputation as a corporate shark and had little time for the man, who was as unscrupulous as he was smart. She didn't bother to return his superior smile and nor did Sam or Grant.

Carter didn't smile at all, glaring across the table at her and saying nothing, while Tom shuffled papers and started his opening pitch. Which was basically 'we won't pay and you don't have a case'.

'Please tell me you didn't call us all the way down here just to go over old ground, Tom,' Ruby said pleasantly. Having had him blustering on the phone to her on more than one occasion last week, she really wanted to close this case, not drag it out.

Tom's mouth turned down at the corners. 'We know you're wanting to get local MP Tessa Miles involved to support your evidence—or lack thereof—but she won't go on the stand, Ruby. You're following a dead dodo with that one.'

Ruby gave him a cool look. 'I'd recheck my information if I were you, Tom. Not only will Ms Miles go on the stand, but she's already provided us with her written testimony. And yes, it is signed.'

That got Tom's attention, and while he conversed with one of his minions Carter Jones stared down his nose at her, dismissing her out of hand before eyeballing Sam. 'Who's running this dud outfit, Ventura? You or your subordinate?'

'Don't mind me,' Sam said, 'I'm just window-dressing on this one.'

Carter tossed a mint into his mouth and chewed noisily. 'You can't win this case, Ms Clarkson. Those little videos you're so proud of will be deemed inadmissible in court.'

'Quite possibly,' Ruby agreed, 'but, with Ms Miles's testimony and more potential clients contacting our office because of the recent media storm, we don't need them.'

'What other potential clients?' Tom asked, choking on his water.

'Didn't you get my memo, Tom? You might want to check with your staff. We should be up to fifty by the time we get back to the office.'

Unsure whether to believe her or not, Tom stood up, sprouting reams of legal precedents and inadequate documentation until Carter snarled at him. 'Sit the hell down and shut the hell up. You've been completely useless on this case from day one, Roberts.'

Tom turned crimson under the weight of Carter's frog-like glare, his fellow lawyers shifting uneasily in their seats. Ruby almost felt sorry for the man. Almost.

'All right, how much do those hungry little bloodsuckers want from me?' Carter all but spat at her.

'Carter, I think we should take a moment to consider our options,' Tom suggested quietly.

'Take all day,' Sam drawled. 'It won't change anything.'

'I don't need a moment,' Carter barked. 'Give me a figure.'

Ruby named a fairly meagre sum that their clients had agreed upon, even though she had informed them that they were due a lot more.

'Is that all?' Carter Jones laughed incredulously. 'You mean to tell me that I've been fighting this dog of a case for a pittance? I'll accept your resignation forthwith, Roberts.'

'That's not all we want,' Ruby added softly.

Carter's bull neck swivelled to meet her direct gaze. 'We also want you to make a yearly donation to refugee centres around the country.' She named a figure and this time it was much more substantial.

Carter gave a hacking cough. 'You're pushing your luck, lady.' He passed his gaze to Sam. 'You going to just sit there and let her get away with this, Ventura?'

'And a public apology,' Ruby continued as if he hadn't spoken. 'In writing to each and every plaintiff.'

Carter's thin lips were pressed so tightly together they looked like a jagged surgical scar. 'No deal.'

'I was hoping you'd say that.' Ruby smiled. 'I can't wait to meet you in court, Mr Jones.'

'Fine. I'll do what you want.' A thick white line of spittle collected at the corner of Carter's mouth as he called her a derogatory name under his breath.

'You call my associate that again—' Sam said with such lethal softness it was scarier than waiting for a bomb to go off '—you and I will have a talk in a closed room.'

Carter's beetle-like gaze sharpened as it moved between her and Sam, and Ruby felt her face turn pink as his upper lip curled unpleasantly. 'Like that, is it?'

'It's not like anything,' she interjected forcefully, knowing immediately that she should have kept her big mouth closed.

Carter started to laugh and Sam cut him off with a look.

'We'll have the contract on your desk within the hour,' he said, taking over while Ruby could do nothing but inwardly curse her own ineptitude.

'It's in his inbox as we speak,' Grant murmured, typing on his computer.

'Dipping the wick a bit close to home, aren't you, Ventura?' Carter said snidely.

Having finally pulled herself together, Ruby gave Carter a quelling look. 'You keep going, Mr Jones, and you'll have a defamation suit launched against you as well as a class action. If that's all, gentlemen—' she cast a glance around the room '—we'll be on our way. Sorry you lost your job, Tom.'

Physically vibrating with tension, Ruby thought she might snap in half as the three of them entered the lift and pressed the button for the ground floor.

'I think we just won,' Grant ventured softly into the heavy silence.

They had, but Ruby was still so fired up on humiliation at Carter Jones's slur that she couldn't even bring herself to enjoy it. There was no way she could bring a defamation case against him because what he had said was true.

'Ruby—'

'I'm fine, Sam,' she said, wanting to shut him down so that she could deal with her emotions alone.

Unaware of the tension radiating between the two of them, Grant shook his head as if he was coming out of a long daze.

'I can't believe Jones caved in like that. Well, I can, but...' He cut Ruby a curious look. 'What was with the fifty extra potential clients? I thought we'd only picked up one more.'

'I might have embellished a bit with that,' Ruby admitted with a half smile.

'Genius,' Grant murmured as they stepped out into the solid wall of the oppressive Sydney humidity. 'You are officially my new hero, Ms Clarkson. So?' He gave them both a broad grin. 'Drinks at Mickey Dee's? I'd say we've earned it after that.'

Going to their local haunt was the last thing Ruby felt like doing. So much harder to hide and lick her wounds in a public space. 'Not for me,' she said. 'I'm going back to the office to call our clients and let them know the outcome.'

'Sorry. I also need to return to the office,' Sam said, opening the back door to the limousine and waiting for Grant to move inside before subtly blocking Ruby's way with his body.

'I can tell you're going to be irrational about this,' he murmured so that only she could hear. 'But I would have defended any one of my colleagues in exactly the same way.'

Ruby kept her gaze level with the top of the car. It wasn't so much Sam's defence of her that had upset her; it was her own reaction in giving herself away that bothered her. 'I said I was fine.'

When he didn't immediately move out of her way she glanced up to find him frowning. 'Forget Carter Jones and concentrate on the fact that you did a brilliant job in there. You do a brilliant job full stop.'

'Thanks.' She felt emotion well up in her throat, clogging it.

Oh, God, she couldn't do this. She couldn't be with Sam and not because of work, or her reputation, and not because Veronica had guessed there was something going on between them or because Carter Jones had been crude, but because she had fallen in love with him.

Completely and irrevocably.

An incontrovertible mistake, given that they were

only having an affair. An affair she knew would end at some point. Leaving her crushed.

The knowledge slid into place inside her with the ease of a softball player sliding into home plate—followed swiftly by a tide of rising panic.

Finally Sam inclined his head and moved out of her way. 'You're not okay, but we'll discuss it tonight.'

Would they? Ruby was already wondering how she would be able to get out of seeing him. She was so far out of her comfort zone right now she'd need the Hubble space telescope to find it.

And what she needed more than seeing Sam was distance. Distance to work out how she had gone from great, casual sex to love when she'd been so careful to avoid it.

Back in his office Sam ran a frustrated hand through his hair.

He knew Ruby was upset with the not so subtle threat he'd made to Jones in their meeting but, dammit, she was being unreasonable about that. Sam was used to defending people; it was what he did. No hesitation. No sign of weakness. His father had hated weakness. 'If you hesitate, you lose—it's that simple,' he'd used to say.

Sam had taken the mantra to heart—at first to try and please his father, but after that he'd seen that it worked. But Ruby saw his methods as—what had she said?— being like a Sherman tank. Was that the problem? Was that what she'd reacted to so strongly? Well, he couldn't say he wouldn't do it again. That would be a lie. No one insulted his woman and got away with it. Ever.

His woman…

He knew that was what she was even if she didn't yet. The realisation had hit him hard the night before when he'd been at a work dinner in LA. As usual he'd been thinking about her, wondering what she was up to, and whether or not he should call her, when the woman beside him had placed her hand on his knee beneath the table. Sam had been so surprised he hadn't reacted immediately. When he had it was to lean in close and tell her that he was taken. She'd pouted up at him, looking at him from beneath her lashes, and asked if he'd been sure, and he'd said, 'Unequivocally.' And he was.

Meeting Ruby had knocked him on his backside two years ago and he'd been slowly sliding into love ever since. That night at the Herzog party had sealed his fate, if he had only known it then, but now that he did he couldn't imagine being with anyone else.

And he was pretty sure she felt the same way about him.

He glanced up as Wilma, the secretary he'd inherited from Mr Kent Senior, knocked and entered his office. 'I thought you'd left for the night,' he said.

'Nearly, Mr Ventura. I just have a few things to tidy up before I go.'

He smiled at her, absently wondering how Tino had first told Miller how he felt. Had he come straight out and said that he loved her, or had he done it with flowers? Serenaded her over a candlelit dinner? Should he organise flowers to fill the grand old beach house he'd just purchased beside Miller and Tino's? Get someone to deliver a meal there, set up a few candles and maybe attach a note to Kong's collar? Hadn't a woman he once dated told him she'd seen it on the internet and it was the cutest move ever?

'Mr Ventura? Sir?'

Realising he'd completely zoned out, Sam gave Wilma a quick smile. 'Sorry, Wilma. What have you got for me?'

'A couple of letters to go into tonight's post.'

No, he wouldn't use his dog, but he would do it at the new beach house. He'd organise dinner and candles. Maybe some soft music… Or was that overkill?

A frown formed on his face. Why was the idea of telling a woman he loved her and wanted to marry her so difficult? Because that was the other part of this: he wanted to marry Ruby and spend the rest of his life with her.

'Is there something wrong with the letter, sir?'

Letter?

Sam stared at the pieces of paper he hadn't even realised he was holding. He blew out a controlled breath. 'No, Wilma, nothing.'

Scanning the contents, he quickly scrawled his signature across the bottom of both letters and handed them back. 'Anything else?'

'The Cutter brief you wanted me to change, and some interoffice transfer documents. Congratulations, by the way, on winning the Star Burger case. The office is buzzing with the news. We're going to miss Ruby when she's gone.'

'Thanks.' Sam took the Cutter brief, planning to review it at a later— 'Gone?' He glanced up at Wilma. 'Gone where?'

'The London office, sir.'

'Ruby. As in *my* Ruby?'

'Well, that's a very nice way to put it, sir. Yes, your Ruby.' She beamed him a smile. 'I have her and Stephen Price's transfer documents for you to sign off on. I know it's all done on computer nowadays but Mr Kent Senior liked to keep a paper copy of staff changes so that he was always aware of who went where. It harks back to the days when the firm was the size of a corner shop.' She gave him a small laugh. 'I wasn't sure of your preference, so I erred on the side of caution.'

A terrible coldness settled over Sam. He took the remaining papers Wilma offered and stared down at Ruby's transfer document without really seeing it. 'Did Ruby apply for this or did London request the transfer?'

'I'm sorry, sir, I couldn't say, but if you like I can— Mr Ventura? Sir? Is something wrong?'

Yes, there was something wrong, Sam thought grimly as he strode out of his office. *There was something very wrong.*

Ruby's secretary gave him a startled glance as he approached her desk.

'She in?'

'Yes, she is. She's—'

Sam didn't wait to hear the rest, pushing the door to Ruby's office wide open even as he told himself to calm down.

Not that it did any good. He'd never felt more blindsided by anything in his life.

Ruby stopped pacing as soon as Sam burst into her office, her heart doing that little quickstep it always did when she saw him.

'We need to talk.'

Her eyes raked his face. He was looking at her as if she'd committed a crime, every well-honed muscle in his body drawn tight. Was he here to discuss her response to his threat to Carter Jones? She had already decided that she might have overreacted a little in the meeting, but she was nowhere near ready to discuss the reason behind it.

Equally he could be looking all dark and foreboding because something had gone wrong with the deal. It wouldn't surprise her at all if Carter had tried to renege on the agreement he had made after the fact, and she inwardly cringed again at how easily she assumed Sam would be in her office for personal reasons rather than professional ones.

'What's wrong?' she asked, deciding that he must be here because of Carter Jones. 'Has something changed in the Star Burger decision?'

'Not to my knowledge.' His tone was clipped, cold. It made her shiver. 'Wilma just gave me this to sign.'

He handed her a document and it took Ruby a moment to realise it was her interoffice transfer request. She hadn't realised that HR had approved it.

'When were you going to tell me about it?'

Startled by his harsh tone, Ruby frowned. 'I don't know. I hadn't given it much thought.' In fact, she hadn't given it any thought. She'd been so busy and so preoccupied lately she'd completely forgotten she'd even applied for it. God, she really was a mess.

'You hadn't given it much thought?' He shook his head, his frown deepening. 'You applied for it, didn't you?'

'Well, yes, but…' She had only applied because she didn't think they'd be able to work together and since then she'd had other things on her mind. Things like what they would do together on the weekends, and whom he was with when he wasn't with her. Things that were all embarrassing indications that yet again she had regressed to the emotional maturity of an insecure schoolgirl where Sam was concerned. 'Is that a problem?'

If possible his expression turned even darker. 'What kind of a question is that? Of course it's a damn problem.'

Ruby moistened her lips. 'I'm usually pretty good at remembering things. I'm sorry—I guess I've been busy.'

'Too busy to let me know that you're moving to London?'

'Well, I wasn't sure if it would even be approved and—'

'And you thought you'd wait, is that it? Spring it on me at the last minute?'

'No.' She frowned as she tried to make sense of his mocking tone. 'That's not how it was at all.'

'Then how was it, Ruby, because I'm a little confused about what's going on here?'

He wasn't the only one. Her mind was such a jumble of emotions and feelings she felt dizzy. And worst of all she knew that she couldn't share any of that with him. 'Perhaps we could talk about it later,' she volunteered, wanting time to sort out some sort of strategy where Sam was concerned. 'After work.'

'Oh, yes, of course. Work. Your favourite crutch.' His lips twisted into a hard slant. 'Well, not this time, Ruby. We've played by your rules long enough. Now we play by mine.'

'My rules?' Ruby said incredulously. 'How can you say that? I've done everything you asked of me.' She'd set every weekend aside for him, not making any plans that didn't include him, or that couldn't be changed at the last minute. She'd kept her phone close and waited for him to call—longed for him to call. She'd dreamed of him, missed him, given her heart to him… 'I've given you everything you wanted.'

'Hardly, angel,' he dismissed scathingly. 'But none of that matters now. All that does is this.' He stabbed a finger at the transfer notice that lay on her desk between them. 'And whether you want me to sign off on it or not.'

Tell me you don't want to sign it, she pleaded silently. *Tell me you want me to stay here. With you.*

The unexpected thought caught her unawares, tightening her throat. Should she tell him what she was thinking? Should she open up and admit how she felt about him?

An ancient argument between her parents came rushing back to her. She'd been about to ask her father to help with her maths homework while her parents were sitting at the kitchen table. Then her father had stood up, shaking his head, accusing her mother of being too needy, too clingy. Ruby had witnessed her mother's devastation, her utter helplessness, as she'd begged her father not to leave her. He'd done so anyway and Ruby had made a silent vow that no man would ever be able to accuse her of the same thing. That she would never want a man more than he wanted her. And yet that was exactly how she felt right now. History repeating itself one generation on.

Swallowing hard, she shoved back the tears that threatened to clog her throat and lifted her chin. 'Why wouldn't I want you to sign off on it?' she asked crisply.

A muscle flicked in Sam's jaw. 'Well, that's the million-dollar question, isn't it, angel? And frankly I can't think of a single good reason why you wouldn't.'

CHAPTER TEN

'LET ME SEE if I've got this straight,' Dante drawled, sitting on the barstool beside him. 'You asked her if she wanted you to sign the transfer papers and then you signed them without waiting for her answer? How does that work exactly?'

'I didn't need to wait for her answer. Her silence was telling.' Sam looked between Dante and Tino and wondered which one of them was more stupid. 'She wouldn't have applied for it if she didn't want to go.'

'But you signed it and you don't want her to go.'

'I didn't say that.' Sam took another sip of his beer. He'd known it would be a mistake to come out with his brothers straight after his altercation with Ruby, but they hadn't exactly given him a choice. After he'd stormed out of Ruby's office he'd found both brothers at the bank of lifts, waiting for him. Having just flown down from Brisbane, Dante had met with Tino and they'd descended on Sam with the express purpose of taking him for a drink. He'd told them that he wasn't fit company for anyone right now and that had sealed his fate. Of course they had wanted to know why.

Now he was in the same pub that he'd met Ruby in two years ago, propping up the bar and forced to fill his brothers in on what had happened, and so far they weren't happy with the abridged version.

'Didn't have to say it,' Dante said, lobbing a peanut into his mouth. 'You wouldn't be upset at signing it if you'd wanted to.'

'Thanks for the analysis, Dr Freud. Can we move on now?' Sam could feel himself getting more and more riled by his thickheaded older brothers, and if they weren't careful he'd bite.

'Dante's right,' Tino put in. 'If you wanted to sign it, you'd be fine with it.'

'Do either of you idiots realise how close I am to taking this conversation outside? With the both of you?'

'Could be fun,' Dante said. 'Like old times.'

'We could mess up his pretty face,' Tino agreed.

'Look who's talking, Boy Racer,' Sam muttered, calling Tino by Miller's pet name for him.

'Trying to get personal, junior?' Tino laughed.

'Trying to get you to shut up,' Sam griped.

'Oh, man,' Tino said softly. 'You're in trouble, aren't you?'

'I have no idea what you're talking about,' Sam said testily.

'Neither do I,' Dante drawled.

'He's in love.'

'In love?' Dante looked aghast. 'Not possible.'

'He's also still here,' Sam grumbled. 'And I'm not in love.' Why give his brothers more ammunition than they already had? 'I'm annoyed that I'm losing a good lawyer. One of the best in the firm to a place…to a place that's about as exciting as having your nails done.'

'Most women enjoy having their nails done,' Dante pointed out.

'Shut up, D.' Sam growled darkly. 'You don't know what you're talking about. The fact is why would she want to go anywhere else when everything she needs is right here?'

'Hell.' Dante gave Tino a look. 'I think you're right.'

'Dammit, you two. I already feel enough of a fool without either of you rubbing my face in it.'

Tino and Dante stared at him without speaking and he knew that both of them had the patience to wait him out. Well, Dante did; Tino's patience depended on his mood.

Finally Sam sighed. 'Okay, I'm in love with her. There. Happy? Can we move on now?'

'Sure,' Dante said, offering him a sympathetic grimace. 'I'd want to move on too if it were me.'

Only Sam realised that he wasn't ready to move on after all. 'You know, the stupid thing is that before this happened I was going to call you,' he told Tino. 'Ask you for advice.'

'You were going to call Tino for advice?' Dante's expression was almost comical. 'I know more about women than he ever will.'

'*Knowing* more women than I do doesn't mean that you know more *about* them,' Tino corrected. 'What did you want to know?'

'Doesn't matter now.' Sam raised his glass to his lips, only to find it empty. 'The moment's passed. For good.'

Dante signalled the bartender. 'Another round. Or two. I have a feeling we're going to need a lot more alcohol to get through this.'

'Of course it matters,' Tino said. 'You need a plan to win her back.'

'Or another beer.' Dante pushed a fresh glass in front of him. 'Here, have this one.'

'I didn't *win* her in the first place and it would be

pointless to try again. I told you, it's finished. *Finito. Terminado.* How many languages do you need me to say it in?'

The truth was, Ruby didn't need him. Not the way he needed her, and he wasn't going to grovel. Nor was he going to talk about it endlessly. 'How's the hotel business, D? Bought any new skyscrapers lately?'

'Forget Dante,' Tino instructed. 'We're not finished with you yet.'

'Maybe we should talk about me,' Dante noted. 'Because I don't know what the hell has happened to the both of you. You meet a pretty face, she plays hard to get and next thing you're—'

'Careful, Dante,' Tino warned. 'Your time will come.'

'If it ever does, promise me you'll nail me inside a coffin and plant an oak tree over my body.'

'With pleasure,' Sam growled. 'And Ruby's not like that. She didn't play hard to get. Well, actually she did.' He gave a rough laugh. 'If you knew how hard I had to work to… The trouble is, she's so damned prickly and defensive and argumentative. She overthinks everything and she's an absolute control freak.'

'She sounds like a real peach,' Dante drawled.

Sam shook his head. 'You have no idea. The woman is impossible.'

'Glad you worked it out.' Dante downed his beer. 'Women are trouble and we lone bachelors need to stick together.'

'Right,' Sam agreed, taking another pull of his beer and thinking that it tasted like dirt. Why couldn't anyone make a decent beer any more?

'You are so screwed, Samuel,' Tino noted.

Sam glared at his brother. 'Just because you're married doesn't mean it works out for everyone. I'll be fine.'

'I get it, bro—it's hard to talk about your feelings. I know. I nearly made the same mistake with Miller.'

'You're wrong, Tino. I'm fine with expressing my feelings. I was very expressive when I turned up in her office. I nearly...' He'd nearly dragged her across her wide desk and kissed her until she told him she wanted no one else but him. Told him that she'd never leave him. 'Anyway... It's not me who can't express myself, it's Ruby. She's as closed as a clam and as soon as you get close to her she throws up an unscaleable wall.'

'So what did she say when you told her how you felt? When you told her that you loved her, and wanted to be with her?'

Sam shook his head. 'What are you talking about? I didn't tell her...' He glanced from one brother to the other, realisation dawning slowly. 'Hell. I'm an idiot.'

'The thing is,' Tino began quietly, 'our father didn't leave us with a great legacy. All those times he shut us out he made it pretty hard for any of us to talk about our feelings, let alone embrace them.' A muscle in Tino's jaw worked overtime. 'I remember how hard you worked to get him to notice you, brandishing your athletics trophies and academic awards whenever he came through the door, and then—it was just after your tenth birthday, I think—you stopped. It was like you just gave up. Closed yourself off.'

'Ninth,' Sam corrected, his gut knotted as he remembered being left at the track on his birthday. 'I realised that giving up was easier.'

'We all gave up. In our own way. But it didn't make any of us happy.'

'I don't know—it felt pretty good to me,' Dante said.

'That's because you're thickheaded.'

'Thickheaded?' Dante spluttered indignantly. 'No one's

thicker than Samuel here. And anyway, don't make this about me! I'm not the one foolish enough to fall in love.'

Sam shook his head. He wanted to bop his brothers on the nose but he knew they were only trying to help. It was the way it had always been between them, and Sam had often wondered what he'd have done without them growing up.

'Tell her how you feel,' Tino urged quietly. 'It will probably be the biggest risk you'll ever take, but it's worth it.'

'Whatever you're going to do, you might want to decide sooner rather than later,' Dante murmured under his breath. 'A gorgeous blonde just walked into the pub and if I'm not mistaken she has your name written all over her. More's the pity.'

Sam swivelled around to face the main entrance, where three women stood, their eyes adjusting to the dim lighting, and one of them was his Ruby, looking like a vision.

'Miller!' Ruby growled, her eyes alighting on Sam sitting at the bar beside his two brothers as soon as she entered the pub. 'Please tell me you didn't know Sam would be here.'

When she'd called Miller and broken down over the phone her best friend had immediately called Molly and they had agreed to meet at their favourite bar. On the car trip over they'd pretty much heard the whole story. How she and Sam had agreed to a weekend-only affair, how she'd stupidly fallen in love with him and how she planned to move to London. Because what else could she do? Working in the same office as Sam was absolutely untenable under the circumstances. At least, it was for her.

Now she felt a sense of déjà vu tightening her insides

because this was the exact same bar she'd met Sam in two years ago.

'Don't hate me,' Miller began sheepishly. 'But I might have known.'

'I don't hate you. But I might kill you,' Ruby promised. 'I already told you that he signed the transfer papers and told me that work was my favourite crutch. What did you think was going to happen by bringing us together like this?'

'I don't know. Something?'

'He might have a point about the whole work-as-a-crutch thing,' Molly offered.

'Molly?' Ruby gave her sister a furious look. 'Whose side are you on?'

'We're on yours, sweetie,' Miller soothed. 'That's why we're here.'

'You could tell him how you feel,' Molly offered.

'Tell him how I feel?' Ruby looked at her sister, aghast. 'Not everything turns out like a Disney movie, Molly. You should know that.'

'I'm taking back what I said about you being scared of commitment,' Molly muttered. 'I'm inserting the word *petrified* instead.'

'I wouldn't say anything else if I were you.' She jabbed a finger at her sister in exasperation. 'Since you were no doubt in on this plan to sabotage me like this, I'm going to replace you with a cat. At least pets are loyal.'

Before Ruby could think about turning around and walking back outside, Sam rose from his bar stool and prowled towards her, the merry after-work crowd seeming to automatically part to make way for him.

Her heart very nearly stopped as he came to a halt in

front of her, his tie askew and his hair rumpled as if he'd run his hand through it a thousand times.

'I didn't know you were here,' she said, not wanting him to think that she had anything to do with this unwanted set up.

'I have no doubt about that,' he murmured in his black-velvet voice. 'But now that you are I'd like to talk to you.'

Forget his sexy voice, Ruby told herself, *and instead concentrate on how you're going to get over him. Properly this time.*

'I don't think that's a good idea.'

'Ruby!' Molly exclaimed, elbowing her in the ribs.

'Will you give us a few minutes?' Sam asked, smiling at the two traitors beside her.

'Of course,' they readily agreed, rushing over to join Tino and Dante at the bar and leaving them alone together.

Sam frowned as he took in the boisterous crowd. 'Let's take this into the beer garden. It's most likely quieter than in here.'

Wanting to ask him what 'this' was, but not sure she could speak without getting emotional, Ruby reluctantly let him take her hand and lead her outside. Whatever he had to tell her, she vowed to listen and say nothing. Then she'd walk away and never see him again. It would be better that way. There was really no need for him to know how badly she felt about how things had ended between them.

'You look pale,' he said, stopping beside a large potted fern that softened the brickwork on the building. 'Do you need to sit down?'

No. What she needed was him. She just couldn't tell him that. 'I'm fine, just...just say what you want to say. I'm ready.'

Or not.

'Hell, Ruby, you don't make anything easy for a man, do you?'

She didn't know what he meant by that because she was trying to make this as painless as possible for both of them.

'Look, Sam, we complicated things by having an affair and now we have to uncomplicate it. I get it.'

'Affair?' he said with quiet menace. 'Is that what you call it?'

'I don't know. Affair…fling…'

'Don't you dare say hook-up,' he warned. 'I hate that term.'

'I wasn't going to but I think I understand why you want to talk to me, and you don't have to worry. I'm not going to harass you, or cry all over you, or tell anyone what happened. Well, other than Miller and Molly but they won't say anything to anyone. I promise.'

'I'm not worried about office gossip, Ruby.' Frustration etched his tone. 'That was always your issue.'

'Well, if you're worried I'll make a nuisance of myself and want more from you, I won't. I would never do that. I would never behave like that.'

'Why not?'

Ruby frowned. 'Why not? Because who would want someone like that? Someone clingy and needy?'

'Sweetheart, I feel clingy and needy every time you get within two feet of me.'

'What?' She blinked up at him as if she hadn't heard him right. 'How…? You can't be serious.'

'I am.' And as if to prove it he leant down and kissed her, taking her mouth with a savage hunger that incited her own.

Ruby's hands fisted in his shirt as she melted against

him, the chemistry between them immediately hitting combustion levels, as it always did when they were this close. Sam groaned as he thoroughly explored her mouth, reluctantly drawing back and grimacing as he glanced at the small round tables filled with people pretending not to notice them.

'I don't know what it is about you and public places, but you're hell on my self-control,' he complained. 'You always have been.'

Ruby didn't know whether to be insulted or thrilled by the admission, the after-effects of that kiss still messing with her brain. 'It's only Wednesday night,' she said. 'Friday night is the one we usually muck up.'

'Actually I'd say Friday night is our best night so far. Along with a couple of Saturdays and Sundays thrown in for good measure.'

'Sam,' she implored huskily. She wasn't in the mood for him to tease her, or try to get her to relax. Her emotions were too fragile to cope. Too raw. 'Please hurry up and tell me what you want.'

'Well, that's easy,' he said simply. 'I want you.'

Ruby felt slightly dizzy at his words. She knew he meant in bed and her heart broke a little because she wanted that too but she also wanted the rest. She wanted the fairy tale Molly was always spouting on about. The one that didn't exist. 'I'm sorry but I can't go there again,' she said on a rush, unconsciously wrapping her arms around her stomach. 'Please don't ask me to.'

Sam took a step back, his eyes dark. 'Is that because of the way I responded to your transfer to London? Because if it is I know I didn't handle it well.'

'It's not that.' She swallowed hard. 'I don't blame you for being upset about the transfer. You're my boss and I should have told you earlier.'

'I didn't get upset because I'm your boss, Ruby. I was upset because, while I had been sitting in my office trying to work out how to tell you that I love you, I imagined you were sitting in yours picturing how you were going to escape to London.'

Sam's words sent a shockwave through Ruby, turning her eyes wide. 'What did you say?'

'I love you. But I don't blame you for doubting me,' he said softly. 'I feel like I've been dancing around my feelings for you ever since we met. But I do love you, Ruby. With all my heart.' He took her trembling hands in his. 'It took me a while to recognise how I felt because I learned at a young age that it was easier to turn away from these kinds of feelings than it was to face them.'

'Because of your father.'

'Yes, and every time I thought you were putting work ahead of me it was like facing his rejection all over again. It made me want to protect myself. But I don't care about any of that now. I've had time to think about what it would mean to let you go and I don't want to. Ever. If you want to go to London then I'll go with you.'

Not expecting him to do anything like that for her, Ruby stared up at him. 'You'd really do that for me?'

'Ruby, don't you know by now that I'd do anything for you?' His eyes were full of love and heat as he looked at her. 'I love you more than I thought it was possible to love anyone. That day at the beach house when I asked you to marry me—'

'You were trying to get a rise out of me.'

'I was.' A wry smile tugged at his lips. 'A little, but as soon as I said it part of me knew I was also serious. I want you, Ruby. I want to be the man who makes you smile first thing in the morning and last thing at night, I want to be the one who makes you happier than you ever have been before and I want you beside me. Day and night. I want to know that when I get home from work you'll be there, and I have to believe that you want that too or I'll go mad.'

Ruby bit her lip, hardly daring to trust that any of this was real. 'Oh, Sam, I do. I do want that too, but—'

'You're scared.' He gently smoothed her hair back from her face. 'I get that, angel. I get that you have little faith in men and that I'm partly responsible for that, but let me make it up to you. Let me spend my days proving to you that men do keep their promises. That I keep mine.'

'That wasn't just your fault, Sam. You were right when you said I use work as a crutch. Work has always been my safety net. It was my vehicle to independence and self-sufficiency and it could never surprise me by wanting to move on when I least expected it.'

'You don't need a safety net with me, Ruby, because I'll never want to move on from you.'

'Oh, Sam, I love you so much.' Unable to contain her joy a moment longer, Ruby threw her arms around his neck. 'I think I fell in love with you right here two years ago because I could never forget you no matter how hard I tried.'

Sam shuddered against her. 'And thank God for that because I couldn't forget you either. Now, about London—'

'I don't really want to move to London,' she interrupted.

'You don't?'

'No. I put in for a transfer when you joined the firm because I didn't think I could see you in the office every day and not want you. I didn't think I could cope if you turned up one day with another woman on your arm.'

'Little fool,' he admonished softly, kissing her so tenderly Ruby's heart felt as if it might burst out of her chest. 'Once I saw you again there's been no one but you. I love you, Ruby. Only you. I even bought the beach house near Miller and Tino because you loved it. It's in your name. I wanted to give it to you tonight.'

'What? That's crazy.'

'That's how you make me feel most of the time. Crazy and happy and… Why are you crying?'

'Am I crying?' Ruby swiped her fingers across the tears she hadn't realised were rolling down her face. 'Oh, Sam, I'm so happy. I had no idea I could ever feel like this!'

'As long as you only feel like this with me. For ever.'

'I do. I will.'

'Hold that thought.' He gathered her closer and pulled a small box out of his pocket. 'I saw this in LA and I can tell by the look on your face that you want to say no, but I want to marry you, Ruby. I want to marry you and prove to you that relationships are worth banking on. I want to show you how good we are together, and I want everyone to know that you're mine.'

'You're wrong, Sam—I don't want to say no, I want to say yes so badly I know that I shouldn't.'

'You definitely should.' He flipped open the box to reveal an enormous diamond ring sparkling inside.

'Oh, my…'

Sam cupped the nape of her neck and tilted her head back, his eyes full of a possessive heat that made her giddy. 'Oh, my, yes? Or oh, my, no?'

'Oh, my, yes,' Ruby whispered on a laugh. 'Oh, my, a thousand times yes.'

'Thank God.' Sam kissed her soundly and slid the ring onto her finger to a rousing applause from everyone around them. 'Because we belong together. We always have.'

Embarrassed to realise that she'd been so lost in the moment nothing else had existed except Sam, Ruby buried her face against his neck.

'I think I'd better get you home before I ravish you against an outdoor wall again,' Sam murmured, tucking her in against his side.

'Promise?'

He turned her in the circle of his arms and looked down at her. 'Sweetheart, I hereby promise to ravish you and love you for the rest of your life, no matter where we are.'

Ruby grinned and wrapped her arms around his neck. 'Then I promise to love you and ravish you right back.'

'God, I hope so.'

Ruby laughed at the hungry desperation in his voice. 'Do you think we should go inside and tell the others what's going on?'

Sam glanced over her shoulder and Ruby turned to see their small party raising a toast to them through the pub window. 'I think they've probably already guessed, love, and if I know Miller she's already been on the phone booking us a wedding venue.'

'I don't mind,' Ruby said. 'Do you?'

'Not a bit. You're mine now.' He drew her up onto her toes, his mouth hovering over hers. 'And not just for weekends or clandestine meetings outside at posh parties.'

'Okay.'

'You're mine for ever.'

'Okay.' Ruby entwined her arms around his neck and pulled his mouth down to hers. 'Whatever you say, Sam.'

Sam groaned. 'It feels like I've waited a long time to hear you say that and you're not even naked.'

Ruby laughed, happiness bubbling over inside her. 'Then what are you waiting for?' she whispered.

'Privacy,' Sam growled, swinging her up into his arms and carrying her out of the pub.

Ruby clung to his shoulders. 'I can't wait,' she said happily, knowing that she wasn't just talking about the night ahead, but also the rest of their lives together.

* * * * *

MILLS & BOON

Coming next month

A CINDERELLA TO SECURE HIS HEIR
Michelle Smart

'Do not misunderstand me. Getting custody of Domenico is my primary motivation. He is a Palvetti and he deserves to take his place with us, his family. In my care he can have everything but if custody were all I wanted, he would already be with me.'

She took another sip of her drink. Normally she hated whisky in any of its forms but right then the burn it made in her throat was welcome. It was the fire she needed to cut through her despair. 'Then what *do* you want? I think of all the work we've done, all the hours spent, all the money spent–'

'I wanted to get to know you.'

She finally allowed herself to look at him. '*Why*?'

The emerald eyes that had turned her veins to treacle lasered into hers. He leaned forward and spoke quietly. 'I wanted to learn about you through more than the reports and photographs my investigators provided me with.'

'You had me investigated?'

'I thought it prudent to look into the character of the person caring for my nephew.'

Her head span so violently she felt dizzy with the motion.

He'd been spying on her.

She should have known Alessio's silence since she'd refused his offer of money in exchange for Dom had been ominous. She'd lulled herself into a false sense of security and underestimated him and underestimated the lengths he would be prepared to go to.

Everything Domenico had said about his brother was true, and more.

Through the ringing in her ears, he continued. 'Do not worry. Any childhood indiscretions are your own concern. I only wanted to know about the last five years of your life and what I learned about you intrigued me. It was clear to me from the investigators' reports and your refusal of my financial offer that you had an affection for my nephew…'

'Affection does not cover a fraction of the love I feel for him,' she told him fiercely.

'I am beginning to understand that for myself.'

'Good, because I will never let him go without a fight.'

'I understand that too but you must know that if it came to a fight, you would never win. I could have gone through the British courts and made my case for custody—I think we are both aware that my wealth and power would have outmatched your efforts—but Domenico is familiar with you and it is better for him if you remain in his life than be cut off.'

She held his gaze and lifted her chin. 'I'm all he knows.'

He raised a nonchalant shoulder. 'But he is very young. If it comes to it, he will adapt without you quickly. For the avoidance of doubt, I do not want that outcome.'

'What outcome *do* you want?'

'Marriage.'

Drum beats joined the chorus of sound in her head. 'What on *earth* are you talking about?'

He rose from his seat and headed back to the bar. 'Once I have Domenico in Milan it will be a simple matter for me to take legal guardianship of him.' He poured himself another large measure and swirled it in his glass. 'I recognise your genuine affection for each other and have no wish to separate you. In all our best interests, I am prepared to marry you.'

Dumbfounded, Beth shook her head, desperately trying to rid herself of all the noise in her ears so she could think properly. 'I wouldn't marry you if you paid me.'

Continue reading
A CINDERELLA TO SECURE HIS HEIR
Michelle Smart

Available next month
www.millsandboon.co.uk

COMING SOON!

We really hope you enjoyed reading this book. If you're looking for more romance, be sure to head to the shops when new books are available on

Thursday 2nd May

To see which titles are coming soon, please visit

millsandboon.co.uk/nextmonth

MILLS & BOON

LET'S TALK Romance

For exclusive extracts, competitions
and special offers, find us online: